Praise for *If I Were You*

"Lynn Austin is a master at exploring the depths of human relationships. Set against the backdrop of war and its aftermath, *If I Were You* is a beautifully woven page-turner."

SUSAN MEISSNER, bestselling author of *Secrets of a Charmed Life* and *The Last Year of the War*

"I have long enjoyed Lynn Austin's novels, but *If I Were You* resonates above all others. Austin weaves the plot and characters together with sheer perfection, and the ending—oh, pure delight to a reader's heart!"

TAMERA ALEXANDER, bestselling author of *With This Pledge* and *A Note Yet Unsung*

"*If I Were You* is a page-turning, nail-biting, heart-stopping gem of a story. Once again, Lynn Austin has done her homework. Each detail rings true, pulling us into Audrey and Eve's differing worlds of privilege and poverty, while we watch their friendship and their faith in God struggle to survive. I loved traveling along on their journey, with all its unexpected twists and turns, and sighed with satisfaction when I reached the final page. *So* good."

LIZ CURTIS HIGGS, *New York Times* bestselling author of *Mine Is the Night*

"Lynn Austin has long been one of my favorite authors. With an intriguing premise and excellent writing, *If I Were You* is sure to garner accolades and appeal to fans of novels like *The Alice Network* and *The Nightingale*."

JULIE KLASSEN, author of *The Bridge to Belle Island*

"*If I Were You* is an immersive experience, not only into the dangers and deprivations of wartime England, but into the psychological complexities of characters desperate to survive. . . . With her signature attention to detail and unvarnished portrayal of the human heart,

Lynn Austin weaves a tale of redemption that bears witness to Christ's power to make all things new."

SHARON GARLOUGH BROWN, author of the Sensible Shoes series and *Shades of Light*

"Lynn Austin's *If I Were You* is a powerful story of heart-wrenching loss, our desperate need to be understood, to forgive and be forgiven, and the loving sacrifice found in true friendship. A compelling read, beautifully written, celebrating the strength of faith and the power of sisterhood."

CATHY GOHLKE, Christy Award–winning author of *The Medallion*

"A master at inviting readers onto a journey and sweeping them away with her elegant prose, Lynn Austin once again transports readers back in time to England. *If I Were You* is a beautiful story about courage, relentless love, and the transforming power of forgiveness."

MELANIE DOBSON, award-winning author of *Memories of Glass*

"Lynn Austin's tradition of masterful historical fiction continues in *If I Were You*, an impeccably researched look into the lives of two remarkable women. Her unparalleled skill at evoking the past . . . will appeal to fans of Ariel Lawhon and Lisa Wingate. While longtime fans will appreciate this introspective tale from a writer who deeply feels the nuances of human nature, those uninitiated will immediately recognize why her talented pen has led her to near-legendary status in the realm of inspirational fiction. An unforgettable read."

RACHEL McMILLAN, author of *The London Restoration*

"Lynn Austin knows how to create conflict with her characters. *Par excellence.* Her latest novel is no exception. *If I Were You* tells the story of a *Downton Abbey*–like friendship between Audrey, from the nobility, and Eve, a servant at Audrey's manor house. . . . Bold and brilliant and clever, *If I Were You* will delight Lynn's multitude of fans and garner many new ones."

ELIZABETH MUSSER, author of *When I Close My Eyes*

Also by Lynn Austin

IF I WERE YOU

LYNN AUSTIN

Tyndale House Publishers
Carol Stream, Illinois

Visit Tyndale online at tyndale.com.

Visit Lynn Austin's website at lynnaustin.org.

TYNDALE and Tyndale's quill logo are registered trademarks of Tyndale House Publishers.

If I Were You

Copyright © 2020 by Lynn Austin. All rights reserved.

Cover photograph of women walking copyright © Lee Avison/Arcangel. All rights reserved. All other cover illustrations and photographs are from Shutterstock and are the property of their respective copyright holders, and all rights are reserved. Frame © Digiselector; war planes © Debbie Firkins; countryside © Kevin Eaves; clouds © Matt Gibson; old paper © Lotus Studio; flourish © Roberto Castillo.

Author photograph taken by Laura Veldhof, copyright © 2016. All rights reserved.

Designed by Faceout Studio, Jeff Miller

Edited by Kathryn S. Olson

Published in association with the literary agency of Natasha Kern Literary Agency, Inc., P.O. Box 1069, White Salmon, WA 98672.

Unless otherwise indicated, all Scripture quotations are taken from the *Holy Bible*, King James Version.

Ephesians 2:10 in the author note is taken from the Holy Bible, *New International Version*,® *NIV*.® Copyright © 1973, 1978, 1984 by Biblica, Inc.® Used by permission. All rights reserved worldwide.

If I Were You is a work of fiction. Where real people, events, establishments, organizations, or locales appear, they are used fictitiously. All other elements of the novel are drawn from the author's imagination.

For information about special discounts for bulk purchases, please contact Tyndale House Publishers at csresponse@tyndale.com, or call 1-800-323-9400.

Library of Congress Cataloging-in-Publication Data
Names: Austin, Lynn N., author.
Title: If I were you / Lynn Austin.
Description: Carol Stream, Illinois : Tyndale House Publishers, [2020]
Identifiers: LCCN 2019052041 (print) | LCCN 2019052042 (ebook) | ISBN 9781496437297 (hardcover) | ISBN 9781496437303 (trade paperback) | ISBN 9781496437310 (kindle edition) | ISBN 9781496437327 (epub) | ISBN 9781496437334 (epub)
Classification: LCC PS3551.U839 I3 2020 (print) | LCC PS3551.U839 (ebook) | DDC 813/.54--dc23
LC record available at https://lccn.loc.gov/2019052041
LC ebook record available at https://lccn.loc.gov/2019052042

Printed in the United States of America

26   25   24   23   22   21   20
11   10   9   8   7   6   5

For Ken, always

And for our family:
Joshua, Benjamin, Maya, and Snir

And our two newest blessings:
Lyla Rose and Ayla Rain

With love and gratitude

Prologue

LONDON, NOVEMBER 1945

Eve Dawson bolted upright in bed. Someone was pounding on her door. Sirens wailed outside, growing louder. Approaching. She leaped up, her instincts screaming for her to run to the air-raid shelter. But no. The war was over.

The pounding grew frantic. She shoved her arms into her dressing gown, her limbs clumsy after being jolted awake. Her flatmate, Audrey, sat up in the narrow bed beside hers. "What's going on?"

"I don't know." Eve wove through the jumble of mismatched furniture in their tiny flat and opened the door.

A police constable. Breathless, as if he'd just run a race. "You need to get out. Straightaway! They found an unexploded bomb in the rubble across the street. Come on, come on!" He waved his hand in frenzied circles, gesturing for them to follow him into the hallway and down the stairs.

"I'm not dressed," Audrey said from behind Eve. She would say that. Always the proper lady.

"There isn't time!" the constable said. "If that thing explodes, it will take out the entire block. You girls need to get out! Now!" He left them standing in the doorway in their pajamas and pounded on their neighbors' door with the same urgent message.

1

Eve grabbed her coat, shoved her feet into the first pair of shoes she could find. Audrey moved in her slow, deliberate way, picking through the pile of shoes by the door as if deciding which pair matched her pajamas. "Come *on!*" Eve said. She pushed Audrey's coat into her arms. "I don't want to die today, do you?" She towed her down the hall toward the stairs.

They were almost to the bottom floor when Audrey halted. "Wait! My purse! It has my ID badge and ration coupons." She turned back.

Eve yanked her forward. "Forget it. Not worth dying for. I, for one, would like to live!" She remembered the tiny baby, growing in secret inside her, and for the first time she wanted her child to live, too.

A blast of cold air struck Eve when she opened the front door, blowing through her unbuttoned coat and thin pajama pants, making her shiver. The dawning sun peeked below the clouds, offering no warmth. Across the street, a team of soldiers moved through the rubble of stones and bricks as if walking on egg-shells. Workers had been clearing it for the past week, starting early every morning. Eve shivered again. The UXB could have exploded anytime.

"This way . . . this way," the constables urged. "Quickly, now. Keep moving." They herded everyone down the street, away from the bomb site. Bewildered people poured from neighboring buildings to flee alongside them. Eve recalled those terrible months of the Blitz. The panicked sprints to air-raid shelters while sirens wailed. Stumbling along in the dark of the blackout. But the war had ended three months ago.

"I thought we'd never have to run from bombs again," Audrey said. "I thought we didn't have to fear for our lives anymore." She was winded, slowing down.

Eve slowed her pace to match, even though she longed to sprint. She had always run faster than Audrey. "Well, it seems we were wrong."

"The Nazis destroyed this block a year ago. I can't believe that bomb has been lying there all this time, just waiting to explode."

"Shows how fragile life can be." It was one of the many lessons Eve had learned during the war. Loved ones could be alive one moment and gone the next. And didn't this fragile child inside her deserve a chance to live, too? As soon as they allowed her to go home, she would throw away the address for the back-lane doctor willing to do the procedure. Or maybe the UXB would incinerate his name along with everything else. Maybe this was a sign from God—or whoever directed things—that this was what she should do.

They reached the end of their block. Another constable pointed across the street to a church that had served as a shelter during the Blitz. They scrambled down the stone stairs, huddling inside the crypt with hundreds of other people in pajamas and dressing gowns, waiting for experts to defuse the bomb. Eve had plenty of time to think of all the things she wished she'd rescued. Audrey was right about needing her purse. It was going to be a huge bother replacing all her ID cards and ration books.

"What time is it?" Audrey asked. "We'll be late for work. Do you think the church will let us use the telephone so we can call and explain?"

Eve looked at her watch, a present from Alfie. "It's too early to call. Not even seven yet. Honestly, Audrey, you worry about the dumbest things." Eve wore the watch all the time, even to bed at night. If the UXB did go off, at least she had one thing to remember him by.

Audrey inched closer, leaning in, lowering her voice. "Eve, listen. I need to tell you a secret."

Eve hid a smile. It was so like Audrey to be so serious, so dramatic.

"Should I cross my heart and swear on my life not to tell?" Eve asked.

Audrey didn't smile. "I think I'm pregnant."

Eve barely stopped herself from saying, *I'm pregnant, too.* They had done everything else together these past six years, so of course, why not have babies together? Except that Audrey had a husband and Eve didn't. "Congratulations," she managed to say, hugging her.

"I haven't written to tell Robert yet. I'm afraid to. It was an accident. We took precautions . . ."

"He'll be happy, just the same," she said, squeezing Audrey's hands. "Especially if it's a boy. Doesn't every man want a son?" She remembered, too late, how Audrey's father doted on his son, ignoring his daughter all these years. She wished she had bitten her tongue.

Audrey didn't seem to hear her as she continued on. "This morning, with this bomb—I realized how badly I want to stay safe from now on. We risked our lives so many times during the war, and it didn't seem to matter because nobody knew what tomorrow would bring, whether we would live or die, or if the Nazis would pour across the channel and murder us. But the war is over and Robert is safe, and I want to stay safe, too, until it's time to move to America to be with him. I want our baby to be safe."

"So what are you saying?"

"I'm leaving London. I'm going home to Wellingford Hall."

Eve took a moment to respond. "What about your job? And our flat?"

"I'll give them my notice. Today, even. You won't have any problem finding a new flatmate."

It would happen, eventually. Eve knew that once the mountains of paperwork were sorted, Audrey would leave England and follow her GI husband to his home in America. This bomb that had dropped into their lives was an omen of change. For both of them.

"I'm going to miss you, Eve," Audrey said.

"Me, too." Eve would be alone again. Alone to cope with all the decisions and changes that a fatherless baby would bring. Why had she dared to believe that Audrey would always be by her side? That Audrey would always need her?

Three long hours later, they climbed the stairs from the crypt, the UXB safely defused, the area searched for more hidden dangers. "I feel like a fool wearing only pajamas," Audrey said as they emerged onto the street.

"We aren't the only ones." Eve gestured to the other shivering people scurrying home beneath gray November skies.

Audrey hurried inside their building as soon as they reached the front door, but Eve paused for a moment to stare across the street at the familiar pile of rubble. The police and soldiers were leaving, and workmen climbed among the bricks again with their shovels and barrows. It chilled her to think that something so deadly lay hidden while she went about her everyday life. The UXB might have exploded any second, obliterating her and everything she owned. How many more hidden dangers lay ahead in her path?

Audrey would go home to Wellingford Hall and then make a new home in America with her husband and child. But where was home for Eve? If she kept her child, where would they live? How would they survive? Eve knew what it was like to grow up without a father.

One day at a time, she told herself. She had survived the war that way. One day at a time.

1

She lay in a lounge chair beside her mother-in-law's swimming pool, reveling in the warmth of the summer sun. The clear water reflected blue sky and cottony clouds—until four-year-old Robbie leaped into it with a shout, shattering the tranquil surface and splashing her with icy droplets. "Come in, Mommy. The water is warm!"

"Not right now, love. Maybe later." She wiped her sunglasses and opened her *Life* magazine, content to lounge in the sun's drowsy heat.

Someone called her name. "Miss Audrey?" She swiveled to see her mother-in-law's maid hurrying from the house. "Miss Audrey? Sorry to bother you, ma'am, but you better come on inside."

"What's wrong, Nell?"

Robbie leaped into the pool again with another resounding splash, showering them both. The maid didn't seem to feel the cold spray.

"There's a woman at the door, says she's you. Even talks like you. Has a little boy and a whole pile of suitcases with her."

"What?" She scrambled up from the lounge chair, wrapping a towel around herself as if it could shield her.

"Yes, ma'am. She says she's Audrey Barrett and the little boy is the missus's grandson. Says we're expecting her."

Oh no! No, no, no! Fear tingled down her spine and raised the hair on her arms. The same stunned feeling that came seconds after a bomb detonated. She opened her mouth but nothing came out.

"Didn't know what to do," Nell said, "so I say for her and the boy to come inside and wait."

Her heart hammered against her ribs. She swallowed and finally found her voice. "I'll talk to her, Nell. Will you get Robbie out of the pool and bring him inside?"

"Yes, ma'am."

She hurried into the house barefoot, a fist of dread punching her stomach. *It can't be. Please, God . . . this can't be happening.* She halted in the hallway and peered into the foyer—and there she stood. Her best friend. Her worst fear. She held a small, dark-haired boy by the hand. She had been peeking into the home's formal living room, where Nell had been vacuuming, but turned and saw her. Her friend's eyes widened with shock. "Eve! What in the world are you doing in America?" She took a step forward as if they might embrace, then halted.

It shook Eve to hear her real name spoken again. Her heart thudded. How she wished she could shove this intruder out the door and return to a quiet afternoon beside the pool, to the life she had lived for nearly four years. Instead, she planted her hands on her hips, pretending to be brave as she had so many times before. "What are you doing here?"

"I brought my son to America to meet his father's family. . . . They live here, don't they?" She looked at the envelope in her hand as if to be sure. "This . . . this is their address . . ."

The back door slammed. A moment later, the maid came in with Robbie, still wearing his plastic floating ring, dripping water on the parquet floor. "Everything all right, ma'am?" Nell asked, looking from one to the other.

"Everything's fine." She led Nell toward the living room, speaking quietly. "We were flatmates during the war."

"Why she saying she's you?"

"I think you may have misunderstood. I'll fix my friend a glass of iced tea and then she'll be leaving."

"What about all them suitcases? You want Ollie to fetch them inside for her?"

"Never mind about the luggage. Please, continue with your vacuuming, Nell." She waited for her to go, then turned to her son. "Robbie, please take this little boy to your playroom for a few minutes."

"But I wasn't done swimming."

"We'll go back in the pool after these people leave." And they had to leave. She watched him trudge off to the first-floor playroom, battling to control her panic, then gestured for her former friend to follow her into the kitchen. The boy clung to his mother as if they were glued together. Eve fetched two glasses from the cupboard, pulled an aluminum ice cube tray from the freezer, and yanked on the lever to release the cubes. Her damp fingers stuck to the cold metal. She remembered the day the workmen found an unexploded bomb across the street from their London flat, how it had lain there in secret for months, waiting. That was the power of secrets. Even the most carefully hidden one could explode when you least expected, demolishing the wall of lies you'd constructed around it. But she would find a way to defuse this bombshell. She wouldn't let it destroy the life she'd rebuilt, the home she had found for her son.

She poured tea into the glasses and sat down at the kitchen table, studying her friend for a moment. She was still pretty at age thirty-one with porcelain skin and amber hair, still trim and shapely. Her friend had been born with a silver spoon in her mouth, as they said, but the war had tarnished all those spoons. What mattered now was how to get rid of her. She had barely taken a sip of her iced tea or calmed her fears enough to devise a plan when Robbie slouched into the kitchen again, his baggy, wet swimsuit still dripping.

"I'm hot, Mommy. Can we go back in the pool now?"

"I'd like you to play with your new friend for a few minutes."

"He won't come with me." Eve took a good look at the boy's thick, dark hair, his coal-black eyes, and the tiny cleft in his little chin, and her heart raced faster. Anyone with two eyes would be able to see how much he resembled his father. She needed to get him and his mother out of this house before Mrs. Barrett returned. Eve pushed back her chair and stood.

"I have ice cream in my freezer at home. Would you boys like some?"

"No, I want to swim in Nana's pool!" Robbie stomped his bare foot for emphasis.

"Later. We'll swim later. After we have ice cream. Come on, let's all go to our house." Maybe if Audrey saw how happy and settled they were here in America, she would go back to England and leave them alone. "Put on your shirt, Robbie. And your shoes. Give me a minute to get dressed, too." She ducked into the powder room where her clothes hung and struggled into them, hampered by her sweaty skin.

Once dressed, she opened the front door to lead the way outside and nearly tripped over the mound of suitcases piled on the front step. "Are all of these yours?" she asked. How long was Audrey planning to stay? It looked like forever, judging by the amount of luggage. Eve hefted two suitcases and hauled them to her car. "Let's hope everything fits in the boot. Get in the car, Robbie."

"Wait . . . why . . . ? What are you doing?" Audrey sputtered. "I'm here to visit Mr. and Mrs. Barrett."

Eve didn't reply as she shoved in the rest of the suitcases. They had to leave before Mrs. Barrett returned from her tennis match at the country club and the world Eve had created began to implode. "Just get in the car, Audrey. I'll explain later."

"But they're expecting me."

Eve squared her shoulders and willed the fear from her voice. "No. They're not expecting you. Get in the car." She held the passenger door open.

"But . . . I still don't understand what you're doing here in America. When you left Wellingford Hall, you vanished into thin air. I had no idea where you went or what became of you. And now you're here in my mother-in-law's home? You owe me an explanation, Eve."

"I saved your life, remember? You would be dead right now if it weren't for me, so please, just get in. I'll explain on the way."

Eve could see that her words had shaken Audrey.

Audrey climbed into the front seat and settled her son on her lap. Tears slipped down her face. "We used to be friends, remember? We looked out for each other. What happened?"

"The war happened, Audrey. It changed us. And we're never going to be the same again."

Eve backed her car into the street, then sped away. They drove in silence for several minutes before Audrey spoke again. "What's going on, Eve? I want to know what you're doing here with Robert's family."

Eve's heart thudded faster. "You decided not to come to America, remember? You made up your mind to stay in England. You said Wellingford Hall was your home and you didn't want to leave it. Ever."

"Well . . . things changed. . . . But that doesn't explain why—"

"How did you get here? Boat, airplane?" Eve floored the accelerator, driving as if racing through London in her ambulance again, delivering casualties to the hospital. She barely paid attention to traffic as panic fueled her, and nearly drove past a stop sign. She slammed on the brakes so hard that Robbie tumbled onto the backseat floor. Audrey, still holding Bobby on her lap, had to brace against the dashboard. "Sorry . . . ," Eve mumbled. "You were saying . . . ?"

"We came by ship to New York City, then by train, then taxi—the same way you did, I presume. What does it matter how we—?"

"How is Wellingford Hall? I want to hear all about Mrs. Smith and Tildy and Robbins and George . . ."

"They're gone. All the servants are gone. Father sold Wellingford Hall. It's no longer our home."

Wellingford Hall—sold? Eve slowed the car. She needed a moment to absorb that bombshell. She had always imagined that she and Robbie would return for a visit one day, and it would be exactly as she remembered it. She would gather around the table in the basement with her fellow servants and talk about the past. And Mum.

Sold.

The London town house was also gone, so where would Audrey live? *Not here. Please, not here!* Eve downshifted, glancing around at the traffic, barely aware of what she was doing.

"So you decided to come to America? But surely you . . . I mean, it's very different here. Not at all like home . . ."

"The Barretts are the only family I have left. I'm moving here with Bobby."

This can't be happening.

"I wrote and told them I was coming. I don't understand why they weren't expecting me."

The letter. Eve had intercepted a letter from Audrey a month ago. She often fetched the mail for Mrs. Barrett whenever she visited because Robbie liked to chat with the postman. When she'd seen the return address, Eve had slipped the letter into her purse. She hadn't bothered to read it before tossing it into her rubbish bin at home. Now she wished she had. She could have told Audrey not to come, that the Barretts were getting on with their lives and didn't want a war bride they'd never met barging in.

Eve's panic subsided a bit as she steered her car into her neighborhood, passing rows and rows of identical bungalows. She'd thought the community looked very American when she'd first seen it, with its tidy green lawns and white picket fences. Now the neighborhood seemed stark and boring. The land had been a cow pasture before the war and the streets still looked naked with only a few spindly trees, struggling to grow. She had a fleeting image of the lush, formal gardens at Wellingford Hall, remembering the rainbow of colors, the gravel walkways, the comforting *clip-snip* of George's pruning shears.

Before the war. Before everything changed.

Audrey leaned forward to stare through the windshield as they turned in to her driveway. "This house . . . it looks like the one Robert was going to build for me."

Eve couldn't reply. She remembered the brochures and floor

plans Robert had sent, remembered Audrey's anxiety and uncertainty. *"The house seems so small . . . only two bedrooms!"*

"Fewer rooms for you to clean," Eve had told her. Eve parked beneath the carport and was just opening her kitchen door for everyone when a familiar pickup truck pulled up and tooted the horn. *Tom.* He called to Eve from his open window. "Hey, Audrey!"

Eve and Audrey both turned and answered at the same time. "Yes?" Could this get any more complicated? Eve hurried to the truck, where Tom sat with his arm on the windowsill. "Hi, Tom. What brings you here?"

"I stopped by to see if you and Robbie wanted to come out to the farm with me. We're bottle-feeding a new baby lamb."

"Thanks, but we have company," she said, gesturing to them. "Maybe another time—"

"Uncle Tom! Uncle Tom!" Robbie called as he scampered down the driveway. "Can I go out to the farm with you?"

"Not today," Eve said, catching him before he reached the truck. "We're going to have ice cream, remember?" She lifted Robbie into her arms and turned to say goodbye to Tom, but Tom wasn't looking at her. He was staring at Audrey and her son, studying them. "An old friend of mine from London stopped by for a visit," Eve said, backing away from him, inching toward the house. "We have a lot of catching up to do. Cheers, Tom! Toodle-oo!"

"Yeah, bye." He didn't move his truck. He was still staring at Bobby and Audrey.

Eve hurried back to the carport and herded everyone into the house. She pulled Popsicles from the freezer and tried to send the boys into the back garden to eat them, but Audrey's son refused to leave his mum's side. "Would you like one?" she asked Audrey. "Everyone in America eats these when it's hot outside. There's a month's worth of sugar rations in each one."

Audrey didn't seem to hear her. "Wait! Was that Tom?" she suddenly blurted. "Robert's friend, Tom? One of the Famous Four?"

Eve could have lied and said no, but the pieces of her life were quickly slipping from her grasp like a fistful of marbles and she couldn't seem to catch them fast enough. She nodded.

"I would have loved to meet him." Audrey peered through the window in the kitchen door as if she might run down the driveway to stop him. Thankfully, Tom had driven away. "The last we heard he'd been wounded . . . somewhere in Italy, wasn't it?" Audrey asked.

"Yes. He survived, though."

"The four friends . . . ," Audrey mused. "Robert, Louis, Tom, and . . . who was the fourth?"

"Arnie."

"That's right. Robert was so distraught when he learned that Arnie had a nervous breakdown. He used to tell me stories about how the four of them grew up together and played on the same sports teams."

"Mostly basketball. It's very popular over here. Do you want one of these Popsicles?"

"How did Tom know who I was? Or . . . was he talking to you? Was he calling *you* by my name?"

"Well, I . . . He . . ."

"What's going on, Eve?" She looked puzzled, but Eve could tell the pieces were starting to fall into place. "He called you Audrey— and you answered him!"

Eve couldn't draw enough air to speak.

"You stole my place, didn't you? That's why you were at the Barretts' house!"

"Listen, Audrey—"

"You're posing as me and saying that Harry is Robert's son. You keep calling him Robbie, but his name is Harry."

"I can explain—"

"You're even living in my house—Robert's house!"

Eve stared at the floor. She didn't reply.

"How could you deceive all these people, Eve? Why would you do such a terrible thing?" Audrey looked as shell-shocked as she did after the V-1 rocket attack.

At last, Eve's fear exploded in a burst of anger. "You didn't want this life, Audrey! You were too scared and too stupid to take it after Robert died. You tossed it into the rubbish bin, so I grabbed it! This is the only home my son has ever known. I won't let you waltz in here now and steal it away from him."

"Steal it away from him? *You're* the one who has stolen *my* son's family! Bobby has a right to his grandparents' support. He has a right to know his father's family."

"It's too late to change your mind. They're my family now. This is my home, my son's home—not yours. You can't take it back." Eve didn't care how shocked or angry Audrey was. It was too late to change things now.

"But we have no other place to go!" Audrey cried.

"Neither do we!" Eve struggled to breathe as they stared at each other in silence. Their sons gazed in wide-eyed confusion at the drama taking place, the Popsicles forgotten. "Listen, Audrey. For as long as we've known each other, you've had all the advantages and I've had none. You're Audrey Clarkson—the spoiled rich girl, the aristocrat! You went to a fancy school to learn how to marry a wealthy husband, so surely you can find a man in London who'd be willing to marry Alfred Clarkson's rich little daughter. A man who could buy you a house twice as big as this one—twice as big as Wellingford Hall!"

Audrey closed her eyes as if trying to shut out Eve's words. Then she bent forward and covered her face as she began to weep. Great, heartbreaking sobs shook her slender body. Eve remembered how those cries had moved her to pity when they were children. She had crept upstairs to the forbidden part of Wellingford Hall to offer Audrey strawberries and sympathy. And friendship. But not this time. No, not this time.

2

WELLINGFORD HALL, ENGLAND, 1931

"You can't send Alfie away!" Audrey's voice sounded tiny in the enormous lounge. Father glanced at her, then continued as if she hadn't spoken.

"It's the finest boys' school in England," he said. "I know you'll make me proud, Son." He stood with his hand on her brother's shoulder as if in blessing, his expression stern yet proud. Father's dark hair had become sparse, with gray hairs at his temples. He ignored Audrey's outburst. She was invisible to him. She always had been.

Alfie lifted his chin, his shoulders straight. "Yes, sir." He had grown nearly as tall as Father. If the news that he was being packed off to boarding school alarmed him, he didn't reveal it. But then her brother always had been more courageous than Audrey. He was her best friend. Her only friend. The only person who made her life bearable.

"You'll make friends with young men from the finest families, Son. It's an opportunity I wish I'd had."

A sob escaped Audrey's throat. Mother rolled her eyes and leaned forward to tap the ash from her cigarette. Her ruby lipstick stained one end of the long holder. "Kindly take Audrey away until she can compose herself, Miss Blake," she said, addressing their governess.

Audrey swallowed and swiped at her tears. "I'm . . . I would like to stay, please."

"No more outbursts?"

Audrey shook her head, then caught herself. Mother hated empty-headed nodding and shaking of heads. "No, ma'am."

Father was still talking to Alfie as if the rest of them didn't exist. "We'll head up there a few days before the fall term starts so you can get settled. Williams can drive us. It's a fine school, a very fine school."

"May I come, too?" Audrey asked.

Mother huffed. "It's a boys' school, Audrey."

"I mean when Father takes Alfie there."

Mother drew on her cigarette, then spoke through the cloud of smoke as she exhaled. "You'll be getting ready to leave for your own school by then. That's the other news we were about to share before you started fussing."

"What school?" Audrey looked at Miss Blake, who had tutored her and Alfie until now. The governess averted her eyes, studying the contents of her teacup.

"I've arranged for you to board this fall at the same girls' school I attended," Mother said. "You'll like it there."

Neither Mother nor Father would look at Audrey. Alfie offered her a weak smile. Hysteria bubbled up inside Audrey like a fizzy drink that had been shaken. Knowing the reaction her tears would receive, she asked to be excused and fled to her room to weep alone.

She didn't know how long she'd wept when she heard a soft

knock on her door. Her pillow was damp, her eyes swollen and sore. "Who is it?" It wouldn't be Mother or Father. She prayed it wasn't Miss Blake.

The door opened and Alfie stuck his head inside. "May I come in?"

She scrambled off her bed and ran to hug him. "Isn't it awful how they're sending us away?" she asked.

He gave her a quick squeeze, then wriggled free. "Don't take it so hard, Sis. We knew this day was coming."

"I didn't!"

"I'm nearly fourteen, Audrey. That's a bit old to take lessons in the nursery with a governess, don't you think?"

"But you're my best friend!"

"Listen, you'll make plenty of new friends in no time."

The thought of making friends frightened her. She didn't know how to do it. Father had recently turned sixty, and none of the men who came to Wellingford Hall for his shooting parties had children her age. Mother's friends, all in their early forties, never brought their children when they visited from London. "I don't want to leave and go away to school," Audrey said. "I refuse to go."

"I really don't want to, either," Alfie said. "But Father is quite set on it. He wants me to have all the advantages he never had. All the upper-crust boys go to this school. And he donated a lot of money to get me admitted."

Audrey sat on the edge of her bed, exhausted after crying so hard. "I'll miss you, Alfie. It'll be so quiet around here without you."

"I'll be home on holidays. And we'll still vacation by the sea every summer and sail on Father's boat. I'm old enough to captain it myself now. I'll take you out, just you and me. I'll even teach you how to sail it. Would you like that?"

"I would!" The idea terrified her, but she wanted him to think she was brave.

"Good," he said with a grin. "That's something to look forward to, isn't it?"

Alfie left for boarding school a month later. It was the worst day of Audrey's life. She watched him climb into Father's automobile, piled high with trunks and suitcases, then couldn't bear to watch him drive away. She fled up the curving stairs to her room without looking back.

The school she was to attend didn't start for another week. She'd had a month to adjust to the idea but Audrey still didn't want to go. And yet Wellingford would be unbearable with only dreary Miss Blake to talk to all day. She stared out her bedroom window at the settling dust cloud from the auto. The distant woods at the far edge of the lawn beckoned to her. She would run away.

Audrey tiptoed down the stairs and into the lounge, careful to listen and look in all directions. The French doors stood open to let in the late-summer breezes, and she hurried outside, avoiding the crunching gravel walkways in the formal gardens and crossing the lawn to the woods as if chasing a ball that had gotten away. They would find her too easily if she took the road into town, so she would simply vanish into the woods. Anger and sorrow propelled her steps at first, but the deeper into the woods she walked, the harder she struggled to make her way through the tangled underbrush. The trees grew closer together, their branches snagging her clothing and scratching her bare arms and legs. Her flight halted when she came to a brook, the water gurgling like a fountain as it rushed over rocks and dead limbs. She had no idea how to cross it. Tears of frustration welled and overflowed.

"Hello down there!"

Audrey cried out, startled. She clutched her heart as if to keep it inside her chest as she looked up. A girl in a faded cotton skirt and blouse sat on a tree branch above her, bare legs swinging.

"You frightened me!" Audrey said.

"I know!" the girl said, laughing. "You should have seen your face. You jumped straight up in the air like a scared rabbit." Audrey watched her climb down, as strong and nimble as a boy. She landed in front of her, grinning as she brushed moss and bark from the front of her clothes. Her gray eyes danced with amusement. Freckles covered her nose and cheeks like gold dust. "You're Audrey Clarkson, aren't you?"

"How did you know?"

"I know everything about you."

"You do not."

"You're twelve years old, like me, and you live in Wellingford Hall with your father, Alfred, your mother, Rosamunde, and your older brother, Alfie." She ticked off each item on her fingers as she spoke. "Your father didn't have to fight in the Great War like everyone else's father because he was rich and—"

"No, his job was too important. He owns coal mines and railroads and things. That's why he didn't fight."

"Oh, right." Her mocking tone told Audrey she didn't believe her. "Your 'important' father stayed home while mine fought and died in the Battle of Amiens. I never even got to meet him." Her golden-brown hair was coming loose from her braids and had bits of leaves and pine needles stuck in it. It had a reddish glow when the sun shone on it.

"I'm sorry about your father," Audrey said. She couldn't imagine such a terrible thing. "I hardly see my father—" she began, by way of apology.

"But at least you have one." The girl crossed her ankles and sank to the ground, as graceful as a wood sprite. She took off her shoes and socks. Audrey had never seen such worn footwear before, or socks that had been patched and darned so many times. "Your mother is the daughter of a duke or an earl or some such title," the girl continued, "but she married your father for his money, even though he's ages older than she is. And now she's a socialite who stays in London most of the time and loves parties and dancing."

Audrey's cheeks grew warm at such an unkind summary, yet she couldn't deny that the gist of it was true. "Who told you all this?"

"My mum. She works for your family in Wellingford Hall. She wanted to stay home and take care of me after I was born, but she had to go to work because my daddy was dead. Granny Maud looks after me. The only time I ever see my mum is on her day off."

"Where do you live?"

"In a cottage in town. Your father owns it—along with everything else in town. His man comes to collect our rent, rain or shine. I saw your family in church last Christmas. I go every Sunday with Granny Maud. I'll bet you never even noticed me, did you?"

Audrey shook her head, embarrassed. She wanted to change the subject. "What are you doing way out here in the woods?"

"I'm about to have a picnic." She stood again, leaving her shoes and socks beneath the tree. "It's a beautiful day for one, don't you think? But it's not going to be like one of your picnics."

"What do you mean?"

"Your servants lug tables and chairs and fancy white cloths and china out to your lawn so your maids can serve tea." She gave a mocking curtsy, then shook her head. "That's not a real picnic!"

"What's a real one like?"

"Come on, I'll show you. Take your shoes off so you can wade out to that little island in the middle of the brook. It's the perfect place for a picnic."

Audrey hesitated, then dusted dirt off a rock before sitting on it to remove her shoes and socks. "I suppose I may as well accept your invitation. I'm leaving home, you see."

"Really?" The girl smirked. "Where are you going?"

"I'm not sure yet. But they sent my brother away to boarding school, and now they want to send me away, too. I won't go! I just know I'll be dreadfully homesick."

"Won't you be homesick if you run away?"

Audrey hadn't thought of that. She felt tears brimming again. "I just don't know what else to do to make them listen to me."

"Well, while you're deciding, let's have our picnic. Come on." She skipped across the stream, hopping from one stone to another as if she had wings on her feet, then turned and beckoned to Audrey from the tiny island, midway across. "Come on!"

Audrey couldn't do what the girl had done. The stones looked slippery, and besides, some of them teetered when the girl stepped on them. The water didn't look very deep, so she decided to wade across. The shock of the ice-cold water made her suck in her breath. The girl laughed. "Cold, isn't it?"

After two steps, Audrey wanted to retreat. The current tugged at her ankles and the tiny stones on the streambed bit into her feet. But she kept going. She wanted to impress this girl for some reason. She took a few more steps, shivering in the chilly water, and then she was there.

"You made it! Sit down." The girl gestured to a patch of weeds and dirt and sat down on the ground, cross-legged. She unfastened a napkin that was pinned to her waistband and opened it to reveal a plump sausage roll and a scone. She carefully broke each treasure into two pieces with her filthy hands and laid them on the napkin. "Help yourself," she said. Dirt rimmed her bitten fingernails.

Audrey didn't want to seem rude. And the food did look good, the sausage roll golden and crispy, the scone studded with plump currants.

"This was supposed to be my lunch but I skipped school today."

"Skipped? Why?"

"Because the sun is shining for the first time in days, and I needed to be outside."

Audrey bit into the roll. She couldn't identify the spices but it tasted delicious. "Won't you get into trouble for skipping?"

"I don't care," she said, lifting her shoulder in a shrug. "I already know as much as the teacher does."

"You don't really."

"It's true!" She laughed and leaned closer. "If I tell you a secret, will you give me your solemn promise not to tell anybody?" Audrey hesitated before nodding. "No, no, no," the girl said, laughing again. "You can't make a solemn promise like that! Don't you know anything about sharing secrets?" Audrey shook her head. "You have to put your right hand over your heart, like this, and say, 'Cross my heart and hope to die. I swear by my very life not to tell.'" She scooped up a handful of leaves and crushed them in her fist, letting the bits drift to the ground.

Audrey swallowed. Her heart drummed very fast. A thrill of fear shivered up her spine as she covered her heart. "Cross my heart and hope to die," she said. "I swear by my very life not to tell."

The girl inched closer. "My mum borrows books from your father's library. She brings different ones home for me each time she comes and then returns them. I'm very careful with them. But that's how I know as much as my teacher."

"Don't you have books at your house?"

"Ha! We don't even have books at my school!"

"I can't imagine a school without books." Audrey swallowed

the last bite of sausage and wished she had a serviette to wipe her hands. It had been delicious but a bit greasy. The girl wiped her fingers on her skirt.

"Well, I'm sure the fancy school you're going to will have plenty of books."

The reminder dimmed Audrey's delight with the picnic, as if the sun had crept behind a cloud. "I don't want to go away and leave Wellingford Hall. I miss being home even when Alfie and I are on holiday at the seashore."

"Then why are you running away?"

Audrey didn't reply. She didn't know.

"They'll come searching for you, you know."

"I know."

"Here, eat your scone." The girl handed it to her. Audrey took a bite. It was as good as Cook's scones. Maybe better. She wished she had a cup of tea to go with it.

"Why don't you go to day school, like I do," the girl asked, "and then go home at night? I walk to my school, but you could ride in your father's automobile."

Audrey stopped eating. "That's a very good idea."

"Don't look so surprised. I'm just as smart as you are. I'm just not as rich." She shook the crumbs off the napkin and repinned it to the waistband of her skirt.

"I feel bad for eating half your lunch."

"Well, the next time you decide to run away, you can bring your lunch along to share with me."

"The next time?"

The girl rolled sideways on the ground, laughing. "You're so thickheaded! It's a joke, Audrey Clarkson. You aren't really going to run away this time, and so there won't really be a next time. And they aren't going to invite me to a picnic on your lawn, are they?"

"I'm sorry. I would like very much to invite you."

The girl stood in one smooth movement and brushed off her skirt. "Come on, let's wade to the other side and I'll walk you as far as your lawn. You can tell them what you decided about school."

Audrey waded through the icy water again, the stream tugging at her steps. The back of her dress was damp from where she'd sat on the ground. She would be in trouble with Miss Blake but she didn't care. They put on their shoes and the girl led the way down a path that Audrey hadn't noticed. She halted at the very edge of the woods as if hesitant to step onto the thick, manicured grass. "Bye, Audrey Clarkson. Good luck!"

"Thank you. And thank you very much for the picnic." She turned toward home. The sun lit up the windows on the west wing of Wellingford Hall as if setting them ablaze. Audrey took a dozen steps, then turned back. "Wait! You never told me your name." But the girl had vanished into the woods.

⁂

Eve followed the narrow path through the woods, her excitement building. Wait until Granny Maud heard about her picnic with the girl from Wellingford Hall! The ninny had been running away from home. Imagine! Who would ever run away from a fairy-tale place like Wellingford Hall with dozens of servants to grant her every wish?

Granny would be waiting with a pot of tea brewing beneath the tea cozy and a bite of pastry, warm from the oven. She would fold Eve into her soft arms as if it had been ages since she'd last seen her instead of just this morning. She would tut-tut over Eve's rumpled dress as she picked bits of leaves from her hair with her knotted fingers and then ask about her day. Granny wouldn't care that she'd skipped school, but she would be very surprised to hear that she'd met the rich girl from Wellingford Hall. Granny read the Bible aloud to Eve every night before bed, and it seemed like Jesus had a lot of grim things to say about rich people who didn't share what they had with the poor.

A blue jay scolded Eve from the treetops as she emerged from the woods to cut through the cemetery. Granny was teaching Eve the names of all the birds and the songs they sang. Granny talked to the little wrens who nested in the back garden as if they were her children.

Eve ran the last few yards to their cottage and burst through the door calling, "Granny Maud! I made a new friend today, and you'll never guess who it was. Never in a million years!" Her granny was asleep in her chair by the range, her knitting limp in her lap. She didn't stir, even when the wind slammed the door shut behind Eve. Granny's hearing, like her eyesight, was becoming worse and worse. Eve crossed to the range to put the kettle on for their tea, but the fire was barely warm.

"Granny!" she said, speaking loudly enough to wake her. "You let the fire go out." She still didn't move. Eve knelt beside her chair and shook her shoulder, gently at first, then harder and harder, shouting her name. "Granny Maud! Wake up!" Her knitting needles and half-finished sock fell from her fingers. Something was very wrong.

Eve scrambled to her feet and raced to their neighbors' cottage, her legs like clumsy logs. She didn't knock. "Mrs. Ramsay! Come quick! Something's wrong with Granny. She won't wake up."

Mrs. Ramsay wiped her hands on her apron as she hurried after Eve. "Wait out here, child," she said when they reached the cottage door. Eve shook her head and followed her inside. Mrs. Ramsay crouched beside the chair and covered Granny Maud's wrinkled hands with her own. Tears filled her eyes as she gently stroked Granny's face. "She's gone, Eve. I'm so sorry."

"No! She . . . she can't be! She wasn't even sick!" Eve's heart tried to squeeze out of her throat, choking her.

"She passed on peacefully, dear."

"But she was fine when I left this morning!" Eve's thoughts whirled like windblown leaves. She longed to start the day over again and do everything differently so it would have a different ending. This was her fault. "I—I should have come home sooner! I shouldn't have left her all alone!"

"I don't think it would have mattered. It was her time, Eve." Mrs. Ramsay reached to take her hand but Eve pulled away. She dropped to her knees in front of the chair, resting her head on Granny's lap as she loved to do. It no longer felt soft and warm. Eve buried her face in Granny's skirt and sobbed.

Mrs. Ramsay stroked Eve's hair. "I'll send Charlie up to Wellingford to fetch your mum. Come to my house and I'll fix some tea."

Eve shook her head. "I need to stay here with Granny Maud. The fire went out. I need to take care of it."

Mrs. Ramsay opened her mouth as if she might argue, then closed it again. "I'll be back as soon as I can."

Everything seemed unreal. Mum arrived home and it wasn't even a Sunday afternoon. She cried with Eve and rocked her in her arms. For as long as Eve could remember, Granny Maud had taken care of her while Mum worked up at Wellingford Hall. Granny kept house, cooked Eve's meals, darned her socks, mended her clothes, took Eve to church, and made sure the cottage was warm all winter long. Granny told Eve how much she loved her every day of her life. How could Eve live without her?

Everyone came to Granny Maud's funeral in the village church. They loved her as much as Eve did, and they talked about how quick she'd been to help anyone in need, even if it meant going without herself. The sun shone as they buried her in the graveyard, and it seemed unfair that the sky didn't rain down tears. She was laid to rest beside her husband, the grandfather Eve had never met. Mum picked up a fistful of dirt and dropped it onto her coffin but Eve couldn't do it.

The villagers gathered in Granny's cottage afterwards, sharing food and stories. "You'll always have us as your family," the vicar said. But nobody's hug was as wonderful as Granny Maud's. When the last person left and Eve and Mum were alone, the cottage felt dark and empty, as if Granny had been the source of light and warmth.

"Do you think she's in heaven, Mum?" Eve asked.

"Of course she's in heaven. She loved Jesus—you know that."

"So she's with my daddy now?"

Mum nodded. "Yes. And they must be so happy to be . . ." Tears choked her voice before she could finish. She sank down in Granny Maud's chair as if she lacked the strength to stand. Eve lifted the framed photograph of her mum and dad from the dresser and sat on the floor with it beside Mum's chair. Mum looked young and pretty, Daddy handsome in his uniform. "You get your love of the outdoors from your father," Mum said. "You're so much like him. You have the same color hair and freckles just like his." Mum brushed her fingers across Eve's face as if she could feel them. Granny Maud said each freckle marked a spot where an angel had kissed her. Pain twisted through Eve's stomach. Granny was gone. Gone! Just like her daddy.

Eve often dreamed of what her life would be like if he hadn't died. She would live on the farm with him and Mum and Granny Maud. Daddy would tend his sheep and cows and Mum would stay home with Eve instead of working at Wellingford Hall. She would sing as she worked in the kitchen the way Granny used to do.

"We need to decide what to do next," Mum said. "You can't live here all by yourself while I'm working at Wellingford or staying up in London with Lady Rosamunde."

Eve knew her childhood in this little cottage had ended. And even though she couldn't imagine leaving the only home she'd ever known, Eve didn't want to live here all alone where every sight and scent reminded her of Granny. "I want to work at the manor house with you."

"Oh, Eve. No." Mum pulled her into her arms and held her tightly. "I never wanted you to go into service. Never. So many things changed after the war, and now there are much better jobs for smart young girls like you besides being maidservants. I had dreams of you taking a typing course someday or maybe working in a shop. But you're only twelve—still too young for either of those." She released Eve again and stroked her hair. "I hoped to leave Wellingford Hall myself someday, but there was never enough money left over after paying the rent."

"We'll have more money now that we aren't living here. We can save up."

"That's true, but—"

"Besides, I don't mind going into service. You've done it all these years, so I can, too."

"Maybe for just a few years. And we'll save all our money for your future." Eve saw the sadness in Mum's eyes despite her attempt to smile.

"I'll get to see you more often," Eve said. "And I won't have to wrestle with this cranky old stove anymore." She gave the range a kick.

"They'll make you work very hard up at Wellingford until you prove yourself. And you'll have to take orders from Mrs. Smith, the housekeeper."

"I know. Just until I'm sixteen, right? Just until we save enough money."

Tears filled Mum's eyes again. "All those years that I spent downstairs in that dark servants' hall, I was able to imagine you running outside, climbing trees, and playing in the woods. You're so free-spirited, Eve, and I never wanted you to work in that cold, dark manor house. Now you won't even be able to go to school . . ." She couldn't finish.

"I don't mind, Mum. Really, I don't. Granny Maud used to say, 'Rain or shine, just take the day the Lord gives you.' Remember?"

Mum nodded. She wiped her tears. "I suppose we'd better start packing. We don't have very much, do we?"

"Our job will be easy." Eve swallowed the tears that were trying to escape and lifted the framed picture of Jesus from the nail in the wall. He carried a lamb on His shoulders, and *"The Lord is my shepherd"* was printed across the bottom in gold letters. Granny loved telling stories about how Eve's daddy used to tend his flock of sheep on the farm. Sometimes, one of them would squeeze under the fence and wander away. And Daddy would go looking for it, bringing it home just like the shepherd in the story Jesus told.

"You remember these words, Eve," Grandma would say, pointing to the picture. "You may not have a father here on earth, but you have a heavenly Father. And the Lord will always be your faithful shepherd." Eve wrapped the framed picture in one of Granny's afghans to take with her to Wellingford Hall.

She awoke in her bed in the cottage the next morning for the very last time. Outside, the gray clouds hung so low Eve could almost touch them, as if they offered misty tears in sympathy. She closed the cottage door with a silent goodbye, and she and Mum started up the long road to Wellingford Hall carrying everything they owned.

Just as the great manor house came into sight, they were halted by a flock of sheep, blocking the way as they straggled across the road and through the pasture gate. The shepherd greeted them with a tip of his hat.

Eve knew then that the Good Shepherd would watch over her in her new home.

3

WELLINGFORD HALL, 1932

Eve knew how to disappear. In the nine months that she'd been a scullery maid at Wellingford Hall, she'd become an expert at climbing through a window or slipping outdoors unnoticed to escape for a few minutes, then reappearing where she was supposed to be as if she'd never left. As long as she worked hard and got everything done, no one took much notice of her disappearances. Today she peered through the grimy scullery window at the green world beyond, and the warm spring sunshine and blue sky beckoned to her through the wavy glass. She hurried to finish scrubbing Cook's best copper pot with washing sand and dried it to a gleaming shine, then climbed up on the scrub table so she could squeeze through the tiny window and escape. It was a tight fit. Eve had grown taller during the past few months and her shoulders were broader. She wouldn't be able to squeeze through the opening much longer, but for now, she was free.

Her eyes watered in the bright sunshine after working in the dismal cellar. She waited for them to adjust, listening for the sound of George's trimmers snapping and clipping. Eve found him pruning a row of boxwood in the formal gardens. She loved the beautiful world of bright flowers and green bushes that George had created, divided into neat geometric shapes by gravel walkways. Water burbled from the fountain. Marble statues and benches lay tucked behind bushes, waiting to be found. Eve could no longer roam through the woods, but exploring Wellingford's formal gardens was the next best thing.

George stopped snipping and pulled a rag from his back pocket to wipe sweat from his brow. "How's my favorite lass?" he asked. "The world treating you okay today?"

"It's treating me just fine, George." Gravel crunched beneath her shoes as she bounded over to hug him. With his slender, compact frame and round, bristly face, brown from the sun, George reminded her of a whiskery otter she'd once seen in one of Mr. Clarkson's nature books. George walked to church on Sunday with Eve and Mum and sat in one of the pews with them. Eve didn't have a grandfather, but she imagined that if she did, he would be just like George. "I wish I could work outside with you all day instead of inside," she said.

"I wish you could, too, lass. You're a sight prettier than those oafish lads from the village who work for me." He stuffed the rag into his pocket and leaned toward her, lowering his voice as if telling a secret. "Can you spare a minute, Eve? I've got something special for you." He took her hand as they wove through the manicured flower beds toward the kitchen garden near the stables, now converted into garages for Mr. Clarkson's automobiles. George halted beside a sunny garden patch. "The first strawberries are ripe—see them in there? Go ahead and pick yourself a few."

"Strawberries!" Eve dropped to her knees and plucked a

deep-red one from the vine, then popped it into her mouth. She closed her eyes as she savored the juicy sweetness.

"Take as many as you want, lass. Just don't tell anybody, especially Tildy." He gave her a wink. Mum said George and Tildy, the cook, were sweet on each other, but Eve couldn't imagine two people as old as them falling in love.

She ate a few more berries, then filled her apron pockets with them. George helped her up. "Thanks, George. I'll eat the rest by the kitchen window in case Mrs. Smith yells for me."

"You're very welcome, darling."

George had known her daddy before the war, and Eve loved to ask about him. "He was a fine young man, your father," he'd told her. "Pity you never knew him. That war was . . ." He shook his head as if unable to find the words. "Such a waste. . . . Such a hellish waste of life. You never saw a young man more smitten than your father. Flirted shamelessly with Ellen. I think he used to let his sheep out of the pen on purpose so they would wander down here, and he'd have an excuse to see her. Of course, your mum was a beauty. Still is. You take after her, lass."

Eve walked back to the formal gardens with George, then squeezed out between the bushes again. As she stood beside the scullery window, she heard someone weeping in the manor house above her. The sound came through an open window on the second floor. Was Miss Audrey home from her fancy boarding school? She'd been away for most of the time Eve had worked at Wellingford, returning home only a handful of times. Now she was crying her heart out over something.

Eve slipped through the kitchen door, then tiptoed up the servants' staircase. Her own bedroom was on the third floor with the other servants' rooms, but she stopped on the second floor beside the forbidden door that led to the Clarksons' bedrooms. Mum worked in there as Lady Rosamunde's personal maid, but Eve had never been in the Clarksons' part of the house before. She wasn't allowed. She heard the pitiful cries from the stairwell and made up her mind to open the door. Once in the hallway, it was easy to follow the sound. A soft carpet muffled her footsteps. She trailed her fingers along the walls, which were covered with pretty striped paper. Sparkly electric lights lit the way. Eve hesitated outside Miss Audrey's door before knocking on it.

"Who's there?" a voice called from inside.

Eve opened the door a crack and peered inside. "It's me."

"I didn't summon a maid," Miss Audrey said, sitting up on her grand bed. "What do you want?"

Eve glanced around to make sure Audrey was alone, then ducked into the room and closed the door behind her. For a long moment, Eve couldn't say why she'd come, struck dumb by the fairy-tale room. It was as large as her entire cottage in the village, and every wall was covered with pale-blue paper with tiny white flowers. Miss Audrey's enormous bed had a tentlike roof of soft-blue cloth with tied-back curtains around the sides. A thick, patterned rug covered the floor, and one entire wall of the room had shelves filled with books and dolls and even a little toy house. Eve wasn't finished looking at everything when Audrey said, "You're the girl from the woods! What are you doing here?"

"I brought you something," she said, carefully scooping the strawberries from her pocket. They were still warm from the sun. "I just picked them." Eve stepped closer and poured them into Audrey's lap. "Try one."

Audrey brushed a speck of dirt off one and put it into her mouth.

"Good, aren't they?" Eve asked.

"Yes. Thank you." Audrey gave a little shudder as if trying to dislodge one final sob.

"I was going to eat all of them, but you sounded so sad that I thought you needed them more than me."

"We could share them." Audrey returned two of the berries. Eve closed her eyes as she chewed, letting the juice fill her mouth. "How did you get into my house?" Audrey asked.

"I live here now. I work down in the scullery. Your window was open and I heard you crying, so I wanted to cheer you up. Why don't you come outside with me? Whenever I feel sad, it always helps me to go outside."

"Mother is angry with me. I'm meant to stay in my room."

"Well, I'm meant to be scrubbing pots but I don't always do what I'm meant to do. The rain finally stopped and the sun is shining for once. Come on."

Audrey hesitated, then climbed off the enormous bed and followed Eve to the door.

"You still owe me a picnic lunch, remember?" Eve said, turning to her. "But I won't claim it today." She led Audrey down the hall, to the servants' door.

"Wait. Where are you going?"

"I can't go down the main staircase. I would get lost, for one thing, since I've never been in your part of the house before. And for another thing, Robbins would shoot me on sight if he caught me. Follow me."

She led Audrey down the back stairs, pausing to listen when they reached the bottom. Silence. Most of the servants rested in the afternoon before the rush of preparations for the evening meal. "Can you run?" Eve asked. "We have to make a dash through the kitchen to the back door before Tildy sees us. Ready?" She didn't give Audrey time to reply before sprinting across the room and through the door. Miss Audrey followed at a dainty jog. Eve led her through an opening in the hedge and into the formal gardens, then collapsed on a patch of grass beside the fountain. "It's beautiful in here, isn't it?"

"I can't run as fast as you," Audrey said, panting.

"Nobody can. I was always the fastest runner in school at the end-of-term races. I won all the prizes."

"I dare not be gone for very long," Audrey said after she'd caught her breath again. "And I mustn't get my school uniform dirty."

"Let's just sit here for a few minutes, then. I love all the different kinds of flowers, don't you? So many colors! I would spend all my time in this garden if I were you."

"You never told me your name the last time we met."

"You never asked. It's Eve. Eve Dawson." Tears flooded her eyes as she remembered what else had happened the day they'd met.

"What's wrong?" Audrey asked.

"When I got home from our picnic that day, I found Granny Maud . . . I thought she was asleep but she was already in heaven." Eve paused, waiting for the tremor in her voice to go away. Her grief was still a raw wound, even after all these months. "I couldn't live all alone, so Mum got me a job here as a scullery maid."

"That's sad. I'm sorry about your grandmother."

"Me, too." Eve scrubbed her eyes to rub away her tears. "Why were you crying just now?"

Audrey heaved an enormous sigh. "Mother is furious with me. I was so miserable and homesick at my boarding school that I became ill. The headmistress had to ring up Mother and tell her to send Williams to bring me home. I did what you said, at first. I told Mother I didn't want to board there and I begged her to let

Williams drive me every day. She refused." Audrey sounded as if she might start crying again. "All the other girls board there, and Mother said I would never make friends unless I did, too. But the school term is nearly over and I still don't have a single friend! They all have their own little groups and they either ignore me or play mean tricks on me. Last night they put dead beetles in my bed."

Eve looked away to hide a smile as Audrey gave another sob. Beetles and mice skittered around the scullery all the time. Eve wasn't afraid of them.

"Mother says I'm being stubborn and childish," Audrey continued, "but she doesn't realize how lonely I am. I want to sleep in my own bed in Wellingford Hall, not in a room with all those horrid girls!" She started crying again.

Eve wanted to be patient. But it wasn't as if someone in Audrey's family had died. She was merely feeling sorry for herself. If Granny Maud were here, she would say there were plenty of people in this world who were worse off than Audrey was. She would add that, rich or poor, God had a reason for putting everyone in the place where He wanted them to be.

When Eve had enough of her sniveling, she said, "Miss Audrey? Hold out your hand. Palm down, this time." Audrey gave a little frown and wiped a tear but she did what Eve said. Her skin was smooth and as white as milk, as delicate as a lily petal. Eve stretched out her own hand and held it next to Audrey's. "Look how different our hands are."

"Why is your skin all red and cracked like that?"

"From cleaning pots and washing floors and scrubbing your front steps every morning." She stood and helped Audrey to her feet. "Come on, I want to show you something else." She led her out of the garden, back into the kitchen, and through the arched doorway that led into the scullery. Flaking plaster covered the low ceiling and stone walls. Large flagstones paved the uneven floor. It had only one tiny window—the one Eve had crawled through. Tin washtubs teetered in piles along with stacks of dented buckets for carrying hot water from the kitchen range. At night, only a single oil lamp lit the space. Mice hid in the corners and sometimes darted past Eve's feet. "Have you ever been down in this part of your house before?" she asked.

Audrey took a step back. "No. It's like a cave!"

"This is where I work every day," Eve said. "I wake up before the sun and finish scrubbing the last pot after dark. But you don't hear me sobbing and crying and feeling sorry for myself, do you? Things are the way they are. Granny Maud used to say, 'It doesn't do any good to sit in the mud and mope. Either get up and wash yourself off or get used to the puddle.'" Eve heard the jingle of keys, a warning that the housekeeper was coming. She wanted to pull Audrey into the scullery and hide but it was too late. Mrs. Smith had spotted them.

"Miss Audrey! What in the world are you doing down here?"

Audrey looked like a startled fawn, even though she wasn't the one who would be in trouble. "I would love to have your terrible life, Miss Audrey," Eve said, hurrying to finish what she wanted to say. "I would be glad to go to your school—or *any* school— but I have to work down here. And I would love to have your nice clothes and your shelves full of books and your grand, big house, but I'll never have any of those things, even if I live to be a hundred."

Audrey seemed frozen in shock. Eve wondered if she'd even heard what she said. Mrs. Smith gave Eve a withering glare before resting her hand on Audrey's shoulder and gently steering her away from the scullery. "Come. You belong upstairs, Miss Audrey."

"I try not to think about all the things I don't have," Eve continued, speaking louder now as she followed behind. "My daddy is dead, Granny Maud is gone, and I can't live in our little cottage anymore. But it's not so bad here. Mum and I have a lot of friends. We're saving our money so I can take a typing course and get a job in the village or maybe even London."

Mrs. Smith paused when they reached the steps leading up to Miss Audrey's part of the house and gave Eve a stern look. "That's enough, Eve. Go back to work." Instead, Eve followed them up the stairs to the baize-covered door.

"Know why that door is padded and covered with cloth on our side?" Eve asked as Mrs. Smith opened it for Audrey. "So you and your family won't hear us or smell us. Your side of the door is all carved and pretty and ours is plain. That's how different your life is from mine."

"Be quiet, Eve."

"I'll be your friend, Miss Audrey, if you want me to be," Eve called after her. The door swung shut. Eve hurried back down to the scullery, knowing she was in trouble. She sank down on a wooden stool, determined not to cry, and waited for the telltale jingle of the housekeeper's keys. It came soon enough.

"What am I going to do with you, Eve?" Mrs. Smith asked, folding her arms across her chest. She didn't look as angry as Eve expected her to be.

"You'll tell me to pack my things, I suppose."

"You're right—I should do that. But your mother is Lady Rosamunde's personal maid. If I fire you, she'll leave as well, and the missus would be frantic without her." She studied Eve for a long moment, and Eve thought she detected sympathy in her eyes. "Imagine, telling Miss Audrey off the way you did! What were you thinking?"

How could Eve explain that she was only doing what Granny Maud used to do whenever Eve fell into a well of self-pity?

"I guess we'll just have to wait and see what trouble comes down from above," Mrs. Smith finally said. "I'm sure we'll be hearing from Miss Blake or even Lady Rosamunde herself before too long."

Eve returned to her chores, waiting for the sky to fall. If she had any regrets for what she'd said, they were for Mum's sake, not her own. Mum might lose her job because of her.

Shortly before dinner one of the chambermaids brought Eve an envelope with her name printed on it. She dried her hands on her apron and tore it open, eager to get the bad news over with as quickly as possible.

Dear Eve,

I hope you didn't get into trouble because of me. You were right. I was feeling sorry for myself. Thank you for the strawberries and for cheering me up. You are a very brave person.

Your friend,
Audrey Clarkson

Audrey heard Miss Blake's familiar knock on her door—three soft, swift taps—before she bustled into the room. "It's time to go down, Audrey. Are you ready?" She straightened the bow on Audrey's dress and smoothed a loose curl that had fallen into her eyes. Mother would scold both Miss Blake and Audrey if her manners and appearance weren't perfect. Miss Blake was in her late thirties, plump and pale and plain, a distant second cousin of Mother's who had never managed to find a husband before falling on hard times. Even though her services as a governess were no longer needed, she remained a part of the household.

"No more tears, Audrey," she said sternly. "Your mother won't be pleased if you continue to cry and mope."

"Yes, ma'am."

"Let's go. And mind your posture."

Each evening when Audrey was home, she was required to go down to the drawing room with Miss Blake to speak with her parents for a few minutes before Mother and Father went through to dinner. Audrey had been planning what she would say ever since Eve showed her the scullery. She needed to be courageous. If Eve could work in that terrible cave all day, Audrey could face her parents in the drawing room. She would speak her mind without any tears, just as Eve had.

"I trust you've finished being dramatic and are ready to behave like a proper young lady again?" Mother asked when Audrey halted in front of her. Mother looked beautiful as she lounged on the sofa, her sequined gown sparkling like sunshine on water. A trail of smoke drifted from her long cigarette holder and floated toward the ceiling.

"Yes, Mother. I'm very sorry for the way I behaved."

"I should hope so. You were an embarrassment to yourself, not to mention your father and me. A young woman your age shouldn't cry and carry on in public the way you did or demand to be driven home." She tapped a ribbon of ash into a nearby dish.

"I know. I'm sorry, Mother." Audrey straightened her shoulders and pretended she was Eve as she prepared to speak her mind. "I have a request to make of you and Father." He wore a dark tuxedo and crisp white shirt and stood with his back to them, looking through the window as he waited for his guests to arrive. He paid no attention to Audrey.

"A *request*?" Mother emphasized the word as if it were unusual. She seemed amused.

"Yes. Please consider how humiliating it would be for me to return to school after the other girls treated me so cruelly, and please allow me to remain home. I'm desperately unhappy there and would like to continue my education here with Miss Blake."

"*Desperately* unhappy?" Mother echoed. She was mocking her, but Audrey kept her chin lifted, her tears at bay.

"Yes. My stomach aches all the time when I'm there. The pain gets worse every day."

"Oh, for pity's sake, Audrey." Mother looked away.

"Please don't make me go back there." Her voice wobbled but she didn't cry.

"You're being childish and ridiculous."

Father turned from the window to face them. "Don't make her go if she doesn't want to, Rosamunde." His voice was gruff, but he was frowning at Mother, not at Audrey. "Do you want her to grow up to be as sickly as her aunt?"

"She can't hide away here like a recluse. Audrey needs the company of other girls."

"Not if they're going to torment her. You may stay home, Audrey."

"Thank you, Father." She had been trying so hard not to cry but her father's kindness threatened to undo her. She wished she could hug him. "I promise to study very hard with Miss Blake and do everything she asks."

"Fine!" Mother stubbed out her cigarette as if she had a grudge against it. "But you will attend finishing school when you turn sixteen and I won't tolerate any arguments."

Audrey floated up the stairs, elated by her victory and her reprieve from boarding school. She wished she could tell Eve how brave she'd been. Audrey thought about Eve as she climbed into bed that night and was still thinking about her the next day as Miss Blake explained Lord Byron's poetry to her. When it was time for afternoon tea, Audrey decided to take action. "Kindly ask Mrs. Smith to send up tea for three today," she told her governess. "I would like to invite Eve Dawson to join us."

"I don't know any Miss Dawson. Is she from your school?"

"She's one of the servants. Eve works in the scullery."

"You cannot take tea with the scullery maid," Miss Blake huffed. "It's unheard of. Your mother will never allow it."

"Mother doesn't need to know. Eve was very kind to me yesterday when I was upset, and I would like to have tea with her to thank her."

"I'll need to speak with the housekeeper first."

"I'll go with you." Audrey followed Miss Blake downstairs to the grand foyer to send for the housekeeper. The faint jingle of Mrs. Smith's keys signaled her approach.

"Miss Audrey has asked to take tea with Eve Dawson. Do you know who she is?" Miss Blake asked.

If the request surprised the housekeeper, she hid it well. According to the household hierarchy, she and the governess functioned independently and were nearly equals—although Audrey thought that Miss Blake, who had her own private room on the second floor, was just a notch higher than Mrs. Smith. "Eve is the daughter of Lady Rosamunde's lady's maid. Ellen's girl," Mrs. Smith replied.

"I didn't know Ellen was married, let alone had a daughter," Miss Blake said. "I thought all of Wellingford's servants had to be single."

"Eve's father died in the Great War."

"Do you think she would be a suitable . . . guest . . . for Miss Audrey?"

"Eve is very hardworking and cheerful. Everyone downstairs

likes her. I don't believe it will do Miss Audrey any harm to take tea with her."

It made Audrey's stomach ache to hear them talking about her as if she weren't there. She was tired of being treated like a child. "Wellingford Hall is my home," she said. "I shall invite whomever I want for tea." She felt very brave but the two women still ignored her.

"Are this scullery girl's manners acceptable?" Miss Blake asked.

"I believe so. Her biggest fault is that she speaks her mind when she should remain silent."

"Mrs. Smith!" Audrey said, gaining her attention. "Eve was right yesterday. I was feeling sorry for myself. I'm glad she spoke up. She isn't mean like the girls at school. I insist on inviting her to tea." The two women looked surprised, as if wondering how she suddenly had become so outspoken.

"Very well," Miss Blake said. "Miss Dawson may take tea with us in the schoolroom this afternoon."

Audrey squirmed with excitement later as she waited for Eve.

Eve arrived carrying their tea tray, while the maid who usually brought it coached her. "Take small steps, Eve. . . . Don't walk too quickly. . . . Keep the tray level."

Eve looked relieved when she finally set it down without spilling anything. "I did it," she said with a grin. She wore the same baggy dress and stained apron as yesterday.

"Now, ask Miss Audrey if she would like anything else," the maid prompted.

"Will there be anything else?" Eve asked with laughter in her voice. Her grin made Audrey smile.

"Yes. I would like you to sit and have tea with me. I owe you a picnic, remember?"

Eve's surprise was only momentary. After a quick glance at the maid and then at Miss Blake, who was already seated, Eve pulled out a chair and sat. Audrey sat across from her and waited for the maid to arrange the plates and cups and napkins and cutlery. After pouring tea into each of their cups and setting a plate of tiny sandwiches on the table, and another with biscuits and fairy cakes, she took a step back.

"You may be excused," Audrey told her. She could hardly wait to tell Eve how fearless she'd been. "I decided to do what you said, Eve. I decided to wash off the mud and change the way things are rather than sit in the puddle. I convinced Mother and Father to let me study here with Miss Blake from now on. Thank you for giving me the courage to speak up."

"You're welcome." Eve looked pleased.

"Help yourself to a sandwich." Audrey put two of them on her own plate, but Eve hadn't touched any of the food or sampled her tea. She looked nervous.

"Are you sure this is for me?"

"Yes. The ones with cheese are my favorites." She saw Eve look up at the governess before reaching for one of the sandwiches. Next time, Audrey would ask Miss Blake to let them take tea by themselves. "Did you mean it when you said you would be my friend?" Audrey asked.

"If they'll let us." She stared down at her plate as she ate.

"They will. It has already been decided. By me." For some reason, Eve wasn't her usual, cheerful self, and teatime quickly became awkward. No one seemed to know what to say. When the sandwiches were gone, Audrey turned to Miss Blake. "Would you mind terribly if Eve and I shared the fairy cakes in private?"

The governess didn't reply. Audrey tried to read her expression and couldn't tell if she was insulted or simply surprised. Miss Blake folded her napkin and placed it beside her plate before standing. "As you wish, Miss Audrey."

"Who is she?" Eve asked after Miss Blake left.

"My governess. And she's my teacher now that I'm not going to boarding school."

"I've never seen her down in the servants' dining room. Does she live here?"

"Her room is up here, with us." Audrey didn't want to talk about Miss Blake or any of the other servants. She leaned across the table. "Since you're my best friend now, we need to tell each other secrets and share all the things we'd like to do someday."

Eve's grin returned. "Okay. But can I have another fairy cake first? I know I only gave you half a scone when I shared my lunch with you, but—"

"You may eat the whole plateful!" Audrey said, smiling. She pushed the plate toward Eve, then poured more tea into her cup. "If you had one wish, what would it be?"

"You already granted it with these cakes!" Eve said with a mouthful. "Tildy sometimes sneaks one of these to me if you leave leftovers from your tea, but I've never had two!"

And Audrey took these daily treats for granted. "What else would you wish for?"

"Are those all your lesson books?" she asked, pointing to the pile on Audrey's desk. She nodded. "I wish I could learn interesting things instead of scrubbing all day."

"I'll be happy to share my books with you. Maybe you can come upstairs for a few minutes every day and let Miss Blake tutor you, too."

Eve stared at her lap, twisting her napkin.

"What's wrong?" Audrey asked.

When Eve looked up, her smile seemed forced. "Nothing. Now it's your turn to tell me what you'd wish for."

Audrey didn't hesitate. "I wish I were as brave as you. You have so much courage."

Her answer seemed to amuse Eve. "What would you do with your courage once you had it?"

"Well . . . my brother wants to teach me to sail Father's boat this summer." A shudder rippled up Audrey's spine at the very thought of it. "I don't want to let him down, but I'm afraid to go out on the open water, and it would be even more frightening without Father. I could never take the wheel myself."

Eve rested her elbow on the table and propped her chin on her hand as if giving the matter some thought. Mother would be appalled. As for Audrey's fears, Mother would roll her eyes and say, *"Oh, for pity's sake, Audrey."*

"Hmm . . . Sailing a boat would take a lot of courage," Eve finally said. "Why don't you start by doing things that are only a little bit scary and get braver gradually? Maybe you could make a list of things and check them off one by one."

"I'm afraid of so many things, I wouldn't know where to start."

Eve laughed the same joyous way she had laughed in the woods the first time Audrey met her. "I think I know one! Remember those beetles the girls put in your bed? I can bring you some dead ones from the scullery so you can get used to them."

Audrey shuddered as she forced a smile. "That would be very kind of you."

"It will be our secret. Now, I'll tell you a secret if you promise not to tell anyone."

Audrey tried to recall the ritual Eve had taught her. She placed her hand over her heart and said, "Cross my heart and hope to die. I swear by my very life not to tell."

Eve leaned close and said, "I'm learning to drive an automobile! Williams, your driver, is teaching me."

"Why do you want to do that?"

"Because I don't have people to drive me everywhere like you do, and there's someplace I want to go."

"Where?"

"To London. I want to put flowers on the tomb of the Unknown Warrior. He might be my father, you know."

Audrey couldn't imagine such a thing. But Eve was her best friend and she could see this was important to her. "I have an idea," Audrey said. "We always close up Wellingford Hall and go to our London town house for the Season from April until June, and—"

"I know. My mum has to go with yours and I don't see her for three whole months. Mrs. Smith says the rest of us have to scrub Wellingford Hall from top to bottom while you're away."

Audrey waved her hand to erase Eve's words. "No, listen. I'll ask Mrs. Smith if you can work at the town house. Then we could visit the tomb together."

"Do you think they'll let me?"

"Maybe . . . if I ask . . ." Audrey didn't know where she would get the courage—but the longing on her friend's face made her determined to try.

After that first tea date, Audrey made sure Eve was invited upstairs for tea at least once a week. Little by little, Audrey's courage grew, especially after Eve delivered two dead beetles for Audrey to hold. Eve paged through the schoolbooks after they'd taken tea and Audrey explained Miss Blake's lessons. Sometimes Eve took a book downstairs to read. Spending time with Eve made Audrey happier than she'd felt in her life. At last, she knew the joy of having a best friend.

"I'm not the scullery maid anymore," Eve announced one afternoon, her voice high-pitched with excitement. "They hired a new one and made me the kitchen maid instead."

"That sounds nice. What does a kitchen maid do?"

"I help Tildy all day, washing and chopping vegetables, peeling potatoes, and running to the storeroom whenever she needs something. I also get to stir things on the stove when she's doing something else. It gets very busy down there, especially when your mother invites guests for dinner. Tildy yells at me and everyone else!"

"But no more cold, dark scullery?"

Eve laughed. "No. Now I get to work in a boiling-hot kitchen. I don't know which is worse!"

Audrey didn't understand how Eve could laugh at such terrible conditions. It made her ashamed to complain about anything.

"I have more good news," Eve continued. "Tildy says she'll need me to help her in London during the Season. Maybe I really will get to visit the Unknown Warrior's tomb."

"You will. I'll take you there myself. I promise I will!"

Eve leaped up from her chair and surprised Audrey with a fervent hug.

4

Audrey had barely arrived in London from Wellingford Hall when Mother summoned her to the town house's morning room. The windows were closed against the drumming rain, and smoke from Mother's cigarette hung heavy in the cramped room, stinging Audrey's eyes and making them water. Mother lounged on her chaise near the window, as beautiful as a movie idol with her hair bobbed in the latest style. She was gorgeous, no doubt. Yet Audrey often wished for an ordinary mum with a worn dress and warm, welcoming arms. Like Eve's mum.

"I trust Miss Blake has coached you on how to conduct yourself in social situations while we're here in London?" Mother asked.

"Yes, Mother. I'm prepared."

"You've outgrown your childish hysterics?"

"Yes, Mother." Audrey's heart thumped faster with each question, aware of the new situations she would soon face and her own awkward shyness. Yet her well of courage felt full, thanks to

Eve. Her friend would arrive by train with the other servants later today. Audrey couldn't wait to hear how Eve had enjoyed her first train trip.

"You will be attending several teas and socials while we're here in London," Mother continued. "You'll need to make a good first impression at these events and do what's expected of young ladies from your station in life."

"I believe I'm ready, Mother. Miss Blake says I am." But she couldn't deny the slippery-sick feeling that washed through her stomach at the prospect of meeting strangers and being examined, judged.

A flash of lightning lit the room, but the grumbling thunder sounded far away. Clouds made the morning room dark and dismal. Their London town house was a narrow building five stories tall and attached to town houses on either side. With windows only in front and back, the rooms always seemed dreary to Audrey—especially today, when rain erased the small park across the street. The rooms were tastefully decorated, opulent even, but Audrey never understood why Mother preferred living here instead of stately Wellingford Hall with its spacious rooms, plentiful windows, and views of trees and rolling hills.

Mother drew a breath through her ever-present cigarette holder, a green one to match her emerald silk dress and jacket. "You're still too young to think about finding a husband, but I expect you to watch the older girls and learn from them for the future. The Season is all about making the right connections. You'll be joining a sorority of sorts, and I want you to be received into the very best coterie, right from the start. Then all the proper doors will open for you." Mother seemed talkative for once, not in a hurry to run off somewhere, as she chatted on about the purpose of the Season and the social interactions that would eventually lead to marriages among London's prominent people. Mother wouldn't venture out until after the rain let up, so Audrey sat down in a wing chair across from her to listen, aware that their moments together were as rare as rubies.

"Did you meet Father here in London during the Season?" she found the courage to ask.

Mother gave a mirthless laugh as she crushed out her cigarette. "Certainly not! Your father didn't become part of the London scene until after we married."

"How did you meet him?"

Mother narrowed her eyes as if considering how much to reveal. "He pursued me with the help of a mutual friend."

"And you fell in love with him?"

Mother's brow puckered in a frown. "Why all these questions, Audrey?"

"I've been reading Elizabeth Barrett Browning's poetry, and she makes falling in love sound wonderful." Even now the poet's words echoed through Audrey's mind and warmed her heart: *I love thee to the depth and breadth and height my soul can reach.*

"What else would one expect from a poet?" Mother sounded irritated. "You'll soon learn that love isn't the only reason people marry."

"Why did you marry Father?"

She gave a thin smile. "I liked the life he could offer me. And he liked my father's title." The coldness of her reply alarmed Audrey. She was about to ask what it felt like to fall in love when Miss Blake entered, interrupting their conversation.

"You asked to see me, Lady Rosamunde?"

"Audrey will be attending a tea on Thursday afternoon. Please make sure her wardrobe and her behavior are suitable."

Fear slithered through Audrey. Her stomach rolled like a heavy, oiled ball. She thought of the shiny black beetles Eve had taught her to hold, and tried to summon the courage to face this new challenge.

"Of course, ma'am," Miss Blake replied. "And are there any social events scheduled for tomorrow?"

"Mr. Clarkson and I have a dinner to attend in the evening, but Audrey won't be going."

"In that case, I wondered if Miss Audrey and I could tour London in the afternoon."

"Not in this dreadful weather!"

"Only if the rain stops," Miss Blake said. Audrey tried not to bounce on the chair with excitement at the prospect of seeing the city with Eve. She could keep her promise to take her to the Unknown Warrior's tomb.

"Don't tire her out," Mother said. "I don't want Audrey drooping like a wilted flower at her first tea—or worse, dissolving into hysterics. That will be all."

Audrey and Miss Blake were dismissed. On her way upstairs, Audrey asked the butler to send Eve Dawson up to her room the moment she and the other servants arrived.

Eve bounded into Audrey's room a few hours later, barely pausing for breath as she described her train trip and how huge the London train station was and how crowded the streets were. "I've never seen so many enormous buildings in my life!"

Audrey was bursting to tell Eve the news. "You'll see even more of London tomorrow. I'm taking you to Westminster Abbey and the Unknown Warrior's tomb."

Eve backed up a step and sat down on the edge of Audrey's bed. "Really? Am I really, truly going to see it?"

"Yes! My parents have dinner plans in the evening, so you'll have the afternoon off from cooking. Miss Blake is going to take us."

"I can't believe it!"

Audrey eyed Eve's baggy gray uniform and stained apron. "Do you have something nicer to wear than that?" she asked.

"Well . . . I have my Sunday dress . . ."

"I know! You can borrow one of my dresses!" Audrey bounced to her feet and flung open the doors to her wardrobe, where her dresses and jackets hung in tidy rows.

"If you think I should . . . I mean . . . if mine isn't good enough . . ."

Audrey turned to her. Eve's freckles stood out against her pink cheeks. "I'm so sorry, Eve. I didn't mean to hurt your feelings. I only thought . . ." What had she thought? Fussing about her wardrobe was something Mother would do, and Audrey didn't want to be like her. "I thought we would look like sisters if we dressed the same. And it's such fun to dress up for special occasions. After Westminster, Miss Blake is taking us to see Buckingham Palace and then to Fortnum & Mason for tea."

Eve managed a small smile. "I would like to look my best when I see the Unknown Warrior's tomb."

"Good. Then let's see what fits you. I think we're nearly the same size." She pulled Eve to her feet and towed her to the open wardrobe.

"So many dresses! What do you need them all for?" Eve reached out to touch the clothes, then quickly snatched back her hand. But not before Audrey noticed her chapped skin and broken fingernails.

"I'll be attending parties and teas where I'll be seen—and hopefully noticed—by London's finest families," Audrey said. "It's how people find marriage prospects for their sons. My brother, Alfie, says there's already a mob of girls fluttering around him."

"You mean, you'll be on display to attract a husband? You're only thirteen years old!"

"I know. It does seem silly."

"I would feel like a piece of fruit on a street vendor's cart."

Now it was Audrey's turn to feel embarrassed. She lowered her head for a moment, then drew a breath. "The point is, I have more dresses than I'll ever need, and I would like to share one with you. Please, take your pick." They sorted through Audrey's wardrobe together until Eve chose a simple blue dress and matching jacket. Eve was the same height as Audrey, but more muscular with strong shoulders and sturdy legs from working in the kitchen and running errands. Audrey was annoyed to see that the dress looked better on Eve than it did on her spindly body.

The sun shone in a nearly cloudless sky the following afternoon as they climbed into the car with Williams and Miss Blake. Audrey felt as though she were seeing London for the very first time as she viewed it through Eve's eyes—the Houses of Parliament and Big Ben, the lumbering red buses, the boat traffic on the river Thames. Her friend's enthusiasm was contagious. Audrey felt genuine joy as Eve gripped her hand and gazed through the car windows in wonder.

"Williams, stop!" Eve said suddenly. "I need to buy flowers for the warrior's grave." He pulled to the curb and Eve darted from the car, returning with a colorful bouquet from one of the vendors. A few minutes later, they got out by a small park across from Westminster Abbey. Eve stared up at the two enormous spires as if frozen in place. "It's beautiful!" she murmured. "Like it's made of lace!"

The inside was even more magnificent. A forest of pillars supported the soaring ceiling while light from above flooded the space. A towering stained-glass window sprinkled jewels at their feet. "I feel so small," Audrey whispered.

"I know. This must be what heaven is like."

Miss Blake led the way as they wandered through chapels and

alcoves with ornately carved tombs and past the sepulchers of kings and queens who'd died centuries earlier. Eve grew somber as they walked through the vast, silent space, pausing to view the chancel and high altar, then turning to walk down the broad central aisle to the Unknown Warrior's resting place. In the center of the aisle, a dark rectangle of stone lay flush with the abbey floor, marking the simple grave. Tears flowed down Eve's face as she knelt to place the flowers on it. Audrey was only able to read some of the words engraved on the plaque before Eve's flowers blocked the view:

BENEATH THIS STONE RESTS THE BODY

OF A BRITISH WARRIOR

UNKNOWN BY NAME OR RANK . . .

THUS ARE COMMEMORATED THE MANY

MULTITUDES WHO DURING THE GREAT

WAR OF 1914–1918 GAVE THE MOST THAT

MAN CAN GIVE, LIFE ITSELF . . .

THEY BURIED HIM AMONG THE KINGS BECAUSE HE

HAD DONE GOOD TOWARD GOD AND TOWARD

HIS HOUSE.

In the hush of the vast space, she heard Eve talking softly and leaned closer to listen. "I never got to meet you, Daddy, but your friends told me all about you. Mum loves you very much and I love you, too." She rested her palm on the black stone. "Mum works very hard. And she still loves you, Daddy. Williams asked her to the cinema but Mum says she'll never love anyone else."

Audrey recalled another line of Elizabeth Barrett Browning's poetry: *". . . and, if God choose, I shall but love thee better after death."* She felt empty inside, knowing her own parents had never loved each other the way Eve's had. They didn't even seem to like each other much.

"I hope you're happy up in heaven, Daddy . . ." Eve's voice broke. "Give Granny Maud a big hug for me . . ." She lowered her head and covered her face as she wept.

Audrey started forward to comfort her, but Miss Blake stopped her. An unfamiliar emotion stirred inside Audrey, and she was surprised to discover that it was jealousy. How she envied Eve Dawson! In spite of her hard life as a servant, Eve probably never felt the aching loneliness that filled most of Audrey's days. And Eve's parents loved her and loved each other. Tears of grief filled Audrey's eyes, not for Eve but for herself. She would gladly trade everything she owned to be her.

At last Eve stood and wiped her tears. She looked sad and broken and drained of strength. Audrey remembered the strawberries and wished she had a pocketful to cheer Eve. "Thank you for bringing me here," Eve said. "I've wanted to come all my life."

"You're welcome. Are you ready to leave?"

Eve nodded. But she turned to look over her shoulder at the grave one last time before they walked outside into the sunlight.

"Let's go see Buckingham Palace next," Audrey said. She had to squint in the bright sunlight as they crossed several bustling streets and entered St. James's Park. The path took them alongside a lagoon where children waded near the edge and ducks floated on the tranquil surface. Trees muted some of the city noises, but Audrey missed the peaceful grounds of Wellingford Hall. Nobody spoke as they walked the length of the park and emerged into the broad square in front of Buckingham Palace and the Queen Victoria Memorial.

"The king's palace is enormous, isn't it?" Audrey asked. "Dozens of people could live inside and never run into each other."

"The king must need hundreds of servants," Eve said.

They peered past the golden crests on the iron gates and saw the king's guards in their red coats and bearskin hats. Eve still seemed subdued. Audrey longed to cheer her but didn't know how. "Are you ready for tea at Fortnum & Mason?" she asked.

Eve shook her head. "If you don't mind, I'd like to go back to the town house."

Audrey's emotions had swirled inside her all morning, and now anger rose to the top. She couldn't disguise it as she said, "But I don't want to go home. We still have all afternoon to see the sights."

"Go without me. I'll take a taxi back. I have money." But Miss Blake insisted they both accompany Eve. The lovely day Audrey planned was ruined.

Her temper had a chance to cool by the time they reached the town house. "We'll do all of the other things that I planned tomorrow," she told Eve. Eve simply nodded without looking at her. They climbed from the taxi and Audrey bounded up the steps to the front door with Miss Blake. Eve left them as the taxi drove away and walked around to the servants' door in the rear.

⸎

Eve waited all afternoon and evening to tell her mum about the Unknown Warrior's tomb. They shared a bedroom high up in the attic of the town house while they were in London, and for the first time in her life Eve could talk to Mum every night before bed. But night fell and Mum didn't come. The other servants trudged up the creaking stairs and settled down in their rooms after the long day. The town house grew quiet. Mum's bed remained empty.

When she could wait no longer, Eve lifted Mum's worn flannel dressing gown from the hook on the back of the door, put it on, and padded downstairs in the dark, barefoot. She slipped through the door into the forbidden part of the town house, hoping she wouldn't run into Audrey. They hadn't spoken a word on their way home from Buckingham Palace, and Eve knew Audrey was angry with her for not going to tea. But it seemed wrong to enjoy a fancy tea after mourning at Daddy's grave for the first time.

A ribbon of light shone from beneath one of the bedroom doors. It was ajar. Eve approached quietly, listening for voices, then halted and peeked inside. Mum dozed in a flowered armchair beside the lamp, her head propped on her hand. Eve must have awakened her because she looked up. "Eve! Come here, love. What are you doing up at this hour?" The thick carpet felt soft beneath Eve's feet as she hurried inside and knelt in front of Mum's chair. The aroma of perfume filled the shadowy room, the same scent that trailed Audrey's mother wherever she went.

"I came looking for you, Mum. I wanted to tell you that I went to the Unknown Warrior's tomb today. I bought flowers with the money you gave me and put them on his grave."

Mum took Eve's hands in hers. "What did you think of it?"

"The abbey was so grand and beautiful. It's like God really could live there. And the warrior's grave is in the most important place of all. No one is allowed to walk over it like they do the other graves. He's buried with kings and queens, Mummy!"

"It's wonderful, isn't it?"

"I think the warrior really is Daddy because when I talked to him, it felt like he was listening. Like he heard me."

Mum bent to hug her tightly, holding her in her arms for a long moment. "I'm so glad you were able to go."

"I wish you could have come with me," Eve said when they separated again.

"I know. I do, too. I try to visit Westminster at least once when I'm in London. Maybe we'll have a chance to go together."

Eve thought the heaviness she'd felt all day would lift after she talked to her mum, but it didn't. "I don't understand why Daddy had to die. You and Granny Maud went to church and prayed for him, didn't you?"

"I asked Granny the same question. She was a woman of deep faith, but I could tell she had questions of her own that had no answers. Especially when her husband died so soon after we lost Harry. It seemed so unfair. But then you were born and we knew you were a special gift to us from heaven. A little piece of your daddy lives inside you." Mum traced her finger across Eve's freckles. *Angels' kisses.*

"Tell me about Daddy again," she said as she leaned against Mum's legs.

"Harry was honest and kind and hardworking. And so loving. He enjoyed a pint or two and a laugh with his friends, but he was never a troublemaker. When the war began, he was very courageous and signed up to do his duty. And he was determined to see the good in life in spite of all the bad. When the time comes for you to get married, don't ever settle for anything less than courage and kindness and laughter in a man."

"Audrey told me that the reason they come to London for the Season is so she can start looking for a husband."

"I pity her. I truly do. And I'm glad you can fall in love with anyone you choose. You're so pretty and lively, Eve. The young men are going to buzz around you like bees. But don't fall for the first man who pays attention to you."

"But you never went out with anyone but Daddy."

"That was different. I knew Harry and his family from the village. They were good people, and Harry was steady and solid with both feet on the ground. He wanted a lifelong wife, not a fling. Don't let any man take advantage of you, Eve. If he's honorable, he'll marry you."

Eve stood and took Mum's hand to pull her to her feet. "Come to bed now, Mummy."

Her eyes looked heavy with sleep but she shook her head. "Lady Rosamunde will be out very late tonight with a dinner and then a party to attend. I need to wait up for her until she comes home."

"Why?"

"Because I need to help her get ready for bed, then take care of her clothes and shoes and brush her hair and—"

"Can't she do those things herself?"

"It doesn't matter if she can. This is the way wealthy ladies live. Women like Lady Rosamunde expect their lady's maid to help them with everything."

"It doesn't seem fair that you have to stay up late while she has all the fun. Aren't you tired?"

"I can nap a little while I wait. But this is my job." Eve sank down in front of Mum again, loving the touch of her fingers as she smoothed Eve's hair from her face. "What else did you see in London today?"

"We walked through St. James's Park and saw Buckingham Palace, where the king lives. We were supposed to have tea, but I felt too sad. We might go tomorrow instead."

"I don't think so, Eve. You had the afternoon off because the Clarksons dined out this evening. But Tildy will need your help in the kitchen tomorrow. And the day after that, too. You're here in London to work."

"But Audrey said—"

"*Miss* Audrey," Mum corrected.

"She said we're going to do a lot of things together while we're here in London. She let me borrow one of her dresses to wear today."

Mum leaned forward and cupped Eve's face in her soft hands. "Eve. I'm so glad you enjoyed your day. But listen carefully to me. Miss Audrey will be your friend for only a short time. I don't think her mother knows about your friendship yet, but believe me, she'll never allow it to continue once she finds out."

"Audrey says she can do whatever she wants."

"Not for much longer. You may enjoy her company for now, but never forget that you're her servant. That's never going to change. Young ladies like Miss Audrey don't socialize with their maidservants, especially once they become adults."

"But you're friends with Lady Rosamunde."

"No. We're not friends. She confides in me and tells me personal things because there's no one else she can trust. But I'll never be her friend, Eve. I'll always remain her servant. The same is true for you and Miss Audrey. Even if you become her lady's maid someday, there will always be a gap between you that you can never cross."

"But—"

"Eve, listen to me." Mum took both of Eve's hands in hers. "Enjoy your time with Miss Audrey while it lasts. But please remember that it won't last. I don't want you to be hurt when she casts you aside. And she will someday."

Eve's stomach ached as if she'd eaten too much food. She didn't want to believe that Audrey would stop being her friend, yet deep down she knew Mum was right. After all, Mum wasn't out having fun at the party with Audrey's mother. She was here, staying up until she came home so she could wait on her. If Eve became

Audrey's lady's maid, her role would be the same. She had to accept that. She squeezed her eyes closed as her anger flared, the embers stoked and coaxed into life by the harsh truth. She didn't want to spend the rest of her life as a lady's maid or a kitchen maid or any other kind of maid. "I won't always be a servant," she said. "Especially not Audrey's servant."

"That's right, my love. As soon as you turn sixteen, you're going to take a typing course and leave the manor house and the gentry behind for good."

"You could leave too, Mum. We could take the course together."

Mum gave a slow, sad smile. "You're absolutely right. Maybe I'll do that very thing." But Eve knew she never would.

5

WELLINGFORD HALL, SEPTEMBER 1935

Why were goodbyes so hard? The Sunday worship service ended, and Eve stood with her mum outside the village church, saying goodbye to the people she loved. Everyone in the village wanted to hug her and wish her well before she moved to London to begin her typing course.

"I'm glad to see one of us making good and moving up," Mrs. Ramsay said, gripping Eve's arm.

"I'm not sure if moving up is such a good thing," someone else said. "Seems like the upper crust all wear sour faces. We don't want that for our Eve, do we?"

"You'll never lose your pretty smile, will you, Eve?"

"I hope not," she said, laughing.

"That's our girl."

Eve wiped her cheeks, damp with tears and rain on this drizzly fall morning. Goodbyes were like crossroads where the path divided, places where you could look back at what you were leaving behind yet glimpse the choices and possibilities that lay ahead. Goodbyes were hard because they meant change. Eve knew she would be different the next time she returned, and the people she loved would be, too. The narrow village streets and stone cottages already seemed smaller than when she'd left to work at Wellingford Hall four years ago.

Eve was glad she'd brought her umbrella as she walked the muddy road back to Wellingford with Mum and George. The drizzle had changed to a steady rain, and she needed to keep her Sunday dress dry in order to wear it to London tomorrow. None of them spoke much as they walked with bent heads, dodging puddles. After drying off and changing her clothes, Eve crept down the back staircase and through the forbidden door to the Clarksons' bedrooms on the second floor. She couldn't recall the last time she'd visited Audrey here and didn't know what sort of greeting she would receive. The afternoon teas they'd shared as children seemed so long ago, they might have happened to different people in a different lifetime. In the past three years, their cozy teas in Audrey's room had dwindled from every week to every few weeks and then had stopped altogether. Eve would say goodbye to Audrey, taking another look back before moving forward.

"Eve! Come in!" Audrey said, opening the door. "I'm in the middle of packing, so everything is a bit of a mess." The room looked different to Eve. Along with the usual chaos of packing—a suitcase open on the bed, a steamer trunk half-filled, bureau drawers and wardrobe doors open—she also noticed that new draperies and bed linens had replaced the old ones. Books and a jewelry box had replaced the dollhouse and other toys on the shelves.

"I came to say goodbye," Eve told her.

"I suppose you've heard that I'm leaving for finishing school in London tomorrow."

"Yes, Mum told me. And I'm also off to London tomorrow. I'm leaving service for good and enrolling in a course to become a typist."

Audrey backed up to sit on the edge of her bed. "So I won't see you after today?"

"You can see me whenever you want to," Eve said with a smile and a shrug. "We'll both be in London." When Audrey didn't respond, Eve quickly added, "But I suppose the people in your fancy finishing school wouldn't like you socializing with a working girl like me." Nor would Audrey's mother allow it. When the household went up to London for the Season, Audrey's mother kept her much too busy to visit the sights with her kitchen maid, just as Mum had predicted.

"Wellingford Hall is going to feel deserted," Audrey said with a sigh. "Alfie is studying at Oxford this fall, Mother stays in London most of the time, and now I'm going away, too." As if sensing the strain between them, she added, "If you give me your address, I could write to you from time to time."

Eve smiled and shook her head. "You don't need me anymore, Audrey. You've become very brave all on your own."

"What makes you say that?"

"I've peeked through the baize door once or twice and watched you mingling with all those elegant people your mother invites to her parties. You look perfectly at ease." Eve lifted her chin and held out her pinkie finger as she imitated a fancy lady sipping tea.

Audrey smiled. Then her smile vanished as her eyes welled with tears. "I'm going to miss you, Eve. I'll never forget you."

Eve scrambled for something to say to stop her own tears. She didn't want Audrey to know how much she would miss her—or how hurt she'd been as Audrey had slowly outgrown their friendship. They were both young women now, sixteen years old, and both about to start new chapters in their lives. "I'll share a secret with you if you promise not to tell anyone," Eve said.

Audrey's smile returned at this reminder of their childhood ritual. She placed her right hand over her heart. "Cross my heart and hope to die. I swear by my very life not to tell."

"I'm not always going to be a typist. Once I get a job in a fancy office, I'm going to charm my boss until he falls head over heels in love with me and asks me to marry him. Someday I'll be as rich as you are, and I'll be the mistress of a house just as big as Wellingford. Maybe bigger!"

"I'm sure you'll do it, too," Audrey said with a somber nod. "You'll go far, Eve Dawson."

"Thanks." Eve rarely admitted to anyone, including herself, that she envied Audrey's wealthy, pampered life. She backed toward the door. "Well, goodbye, Audrey, and good luck. Maybe we'll meet again someday." She needed to leave before their farewell turned tearful.

"I wish you well, Eve," Audrey called after her. "And thank you for being a good friend when I needed one."

Eve hurried up the back stairs to her room, wondering if anyone would ever take Audrey's place in her life. She would never forget her friend's quiet dignity and grace and the many things she'd taught her as they'd shared tea together, things she probably never had thanked her for.

Early the next morning, Williams drove Eve to the train station. He offered to let her take the wheel one last time, but she shook her head. Eve looked back only once, not to say goodbye to Wellingford Hall, but for a final glimpse of the woods she'd roamed as a girl. Leaving Mum behind, along with George and Tildy and Williams and Robbins and Mrs. Smith, and all of the other people she loved, had been harder than she'd imagined. They watched out for her, took care of her, but now she was on her own. Alone. If she dared to admit it, she felt afraid.

Williams braked as they rounded a curve in the road, coming to a halt to allow a flock of sheep to cross. The shepherd tipped his hat to them, then used his staff to guide a wayward sheep back to the path. Eve remembered a snippet of the psalm Granny Maud had taught her—*"The Lord is my shepherd; I shall not want"*—and she smiled at this reminder of the Good Shepherd's care. She wasn't alone after all.

A small crowd of passengers already filled the platform at the train depot. Williams got out and lifted Eve's lone suitcase from the boot of the car. "I'm sorry I can't stay and wait for the train with you, but I have to hurry back and load Miss Audrey's things. I'm driving her to London today. Lady Rosamunde wouldn't let me drive you both there together."

"I'll be fine," Eve said around the knot in her throat.

"I know you will, my brave girl. I never met anyone as fearless as you, Eve Dawson. Imagine, coaxing me into teaching you to drive when you could barely see over the steering wheel." Williams sounded as if he had a knot in his throat, too. He paused to clear it. "You still have the directions I gave you for taking the Underground to that new school of yours?"

She blinked away tears and patted her jacket pocket. "I have them. Thanks."

"Well, good luck to you, Eve. I'll miss you, girl." He seemed reluctant to leave.

Eve threw herself into his arms and hugged him tightly. "I'll miss you, too, Williams. Maybe I'll sneak back and visit you once in a while."

"Promise?"

"I promise." She backed away to wipe her tears and saw tears in his eyes, too. "I'll need to practice shifting gears so I don't forget how to do it." He nodded and bowed to her before getting behind the wheel and driving away. Eve watched the car until it turned out of sight.

LONDON, JANUARY 1936

Eve took the steps to her school two at a time and pushed through the door. Several of her teachers and fellow students huddled in the foyer, talking quietly. "Is it true?" Eve asked, panting for breath. "I just heard a newsboy shouting, 'King George is dead! Long live King Edward.' I didn't want to believe it."

"It's true," her typing instructor said. "His Majesty died last night at Sandringham House. Classes are canceled until after the funeral."

Eve wanted to sit down to absorb the news, but the only bench was taken. The hallway seemed oddly quiet without the usual clacking and pinging of typewriters in the background. "I can't imagine England without His Majesty," Eve murmured. She didn't know why, but it seemed like a significant event in her life, the end of an era. Like when Granny Maud died. The other girls continued talking.

"They say King George will lie in state in Westminster Abbey so leaders from around the world can pay their respects."

"I wonder what sort of king Prince Edward will be. He never seems to take his duties very seriously."

"He hasn't even married yet. He has no heir."

"And he's having an affair with a married woman."

"She's twice married! She divorced her first husband and is still married to the second while running all over Europe with Prince Edward."

"It's quite shocking."

"And she's an American!"

"That's enough, girls," the instructor said. "We must show respect for our new monarch."

"Our new monarch." What changes would he bring? The front door opened and closed, bringing gusts of cold air as more students arrived to chew over the news. Eve didn't want to stay and digest this unsettling loss with them. Nor did she want to return to the boardinghouse, where the other girls would be laughing and giggling as they celebrated a few days off from classes. She tied her scarf around her neck again and ventured out into the January morning. Her breath fogged the air as she walked to the nearest Underground station and took a train across town to the Clarksons' town house, hoping to see her mum. Lady Rosamunde lived in London almost year-round now, rarely returning to Wellingford Hall, even for holidays.

"Lady Rosamunde returned home very late last night," Mum said after greeting Eve with a hug. "We'll have plenty of time for a cup of tea before she wakes up." She brewed a fresh pot and poured them each a cup. They sat at the table in the basement while the other servants bustled around with morning preparations. Mr. Clarkson's morning newspaper had announced the tragic news, and the atmosphere downstairs had the subdued hush of a church service. The single, high window near the ceiling allowed scant light on this dismal morning, and the electric bulbs hanging on cords from the ceiling did little to chase the darkness.

"It will seem odd not to have King George on the throne," Eve said. "Nothing will be the same without him."

"He was wonderful to the soldiers during the Great War," Mum said. "Did I ever tell you that he visited the frontline troops?" She had, but Eve wanted to hear the story again. "Your father saw him, and he said it cheered him to see His Majesty mingling with his soldiers. King George walked in the funeral procession when they brought the Unknown Warrior home to London."

"Will there be a funeral procession for King George?"

"On January 23, according to the paper. I'm sure they'll announce the route, too."

"I want to watch it." Eve couldn't explain why but it seemed important. "Come with me, Mum. We should watch it together."

"I'm not sure I can. Lady Rosamunde may need to appear at some of the funeral events, and she'll need my help getting ready. I'm so sorry, Eve."

"I understand." But she didn't. Over the years, hundreds of disappointments had contributed to a thick wall of resentment toward Audrey's mother for commanding all of Mum's time, expecting her to be at her beck and call. Before they had a chance to share a second cup of tea, the jangling bell summoned Mum to Lady Rosamunde's room.

"Don't look so glum," Mum said as they hugged goodbye. "I'm sure the new king will rise to his duties. England will soldier on."

Eve left through the servants' entrance and walked around the row of town houses to the front. A taxi pulled up, the rear door opened—and there was Audrey. Eve might have mistaken her for Lady Rosamunde if she hadn't known she was still in bed. Audrey looked slender and elegant, dressed in a fur-collared coat and stylish hat like the ones her mother wore. Even the languid way Audrey moved and walked was like her mother. But there was no mistaking Audrey's amber hair glowing in the sunlight beneath her hat. Eve hurried toward her before she had a chance to disappear inside. "Audrey! Audrey, wait!"

"Eve? . . . Oh, hello!" She paused on the front step. "How nice to see you. How did you know I would be here?"

"I didn't. I came to see my mum. Did you hear that King George died last night?"

"Yes. They closed school for a few days."

"My classes were canceled, too." Eve looked her friend up and down again, noticing her fashionable shoes this time. "You look really great, Audrey. And so stylish. Like a model in a magazine."

"Thank you." The new Audrey seemed cool and remote. Eve was about to say goodbye and leave, but then the old Audrey emerged with her shy, familiar smile. "It's too cold and wet to stand out here and talk. Come inside so we can warm up with a cup of tea."

"Are you sure?" Audrey's butler opened the front door, but Eve had never entered through it before.

"Of course I'm sure. I want to hear all about what you've been doing."

The butler took their coats, and they went into the morning room, where a fire blazed on the hearth. If the maid who brought their tea was surprised to see Eve Dawson upstairs when she had just been down below with the servants, she didn't reveal it.

"So tell me about your classes, Eve. Have you become a typist yet?" Even Audrey's voice sounded different, clear and precise like a radio announcer for the BBC.

"No, it's only been five months. But my teachers think I'll be ready to apply for a job in the spring."

"Do you like your courses?"

"I suppose. Now that I've picked up the basics, I find the classes a little boring. The only point of them now is for me to learn to type faster and with fewer mistakes. And I hate sitting inside all day."

"You always did prefer roaming the woods," Audrey said with a smile. "Do you have a roommate?"

"Three of them. From my school. We share an attic room in a boardinghouse, close enough to walk to class every day." She sipped her tea, remembering how Audrey had taught her to hold the cup and saucer properly. "How about you, Audrey? Do you still get homesick for Wellingford like you did at your last boarding school?"

"A little. And like you, I also find school boring. I'm learning French, reading English literature, and improving my skills on the piano, but most of our time is spent learning to attract a husband and be a dutiful wife. They don't put it that bluntly, of course."

Eve wanted to laugh but Audrey didn't appear to be joking. "You look smashing, Audrey," she said instead. "I like the way your hair is fixed."

"It looks like you bought some new clothes, too."

"Mum took me shopping for skirts and sweaters so I'll look smart when I go for job interviews." Eve took a few more sips of her tea. It had barely cooled enough to drink and they already had run out of things to talk about. "King George has been on the throne since before we were born," Eve said, remembering what brought her here. "I came to ask Mum to go to the funeral procession with me, but she can't get away. Do you think you'll go?"

"I hadn't thought about it. I only just heard the news."

"I feel like I should go. It's such a meaningful event. Once in a lifetime and all that." On a whim, Eve added, "Come with me, Audrey. Let's watch it together."

She tilted her head as she considered the idea. Once again, the old Audrey broke through the cool exterior. "Yes, let's. I do think I'd like to go."

It took Eve a moment to react to her surprising reply. "Super! I'll find out the processional route from the newspaper and figure out a good place for us to stand."

"Shall I ask Williams to drive us?"

"There will be thousands of people, Audrey. We'll never get anywhere near the route in a car."

"I expect you're right."

They settled on a plan to take the Underground, and Eve quickly finished her tea, deciding she should leave before Audrey changed her mind—or Lady Rosamunde appeared and put an end to their plans. "Make sure you dress warm. It'll be cold outside."

Eve fetched her own coat from the hall tree and headed out the front door without waiting for the butler. She nearly collided with a young gentleman bounding up the steps just as she was leaving.

He caught her in his arms and held her for a moment. "Whoa! What's your hurry?" he asked, laughing. "The town house isn't on fire, is it?"

"No. I'm so sorry." He held her shoulders as if she needed to be steadied. She caught a whiff of his scent, a rich, spicy aroma that reminded her of leather armchairs and warm rum by a fireplace. They hadn't collided very hard, but he was so impressively lordly that Eve couldn't seem to breathe.

"What's your name?" he asked.

"Eve . . . Eve Dawson." She didn't need to ask who he was— Audrey's brother, Alfie. He was very tall, like his father, and had the same strong, patrician nose and jaw. Alfie could have been the model for a bust of someone famous like Alexander the Great or Julius Caesar.

"Hello, Eve Dawson. You must be a friend of Audrey's."

"Yes. We were just visiting."

"I'm Audrey's brother, Alfie, and I'm pleased to meet you." He swept off his hat and his thick shock of hair was the same amber color as his sister's. He looked every bit the gentleman, even dressed in casual tweeds, and was certainly the most refined

man she'd ever talked to—if you could call her nervous stammer-
ing talking.

"Y-yes, I know . . . I mean . . . I figured you were. I've seen—"
She stopped herself before saying she had glimpsed him from
behind the servants' door at Wellingford Hall.

"I hope you aren't in a hurry to leave. I would love to have a
cup of tea and get to know you," he said. Before Eve could reply,
Audrey appeared in the doorway.

"Alfie! Welcome home, darling brother!" Audrey took his hands
as he leaned forward to kiss her cheek. "Are you home because of
King George's funeral?"

"Yes, for a few days. I just invited your beautiful friend for tea.
You're not going to keep her all to yourself, are you, Audrey?"

"Your beautiful friend." His words sent a wave of warmth
through Eve. She longed to follow him into the house, simply for
the novelty of observing his gentlemanly manners up close and listening to the smooth way he spoke. But Audrey seemed annoyed.
She wanted her brother all to herself. "Sorry, but I must be going.
Maybe another time?" Eve forced herself to turn away and stroll
out to the street, looking both ways as she pretended to search for
a taxicab. She would walk to the corner and take the Underground
as soon as Alfie closed the door.

Eve had taken only a few steps when she felt Alfie's hand on her
shoulder. "Eve, wait! I would like your telephone number, if you
don't mind. I would very much like to see you again."

"Very much . . ." "I . . . I would, too . . . I would like to see you,
too, that is."

He held her gaze as he rummaged inside his jacket and produced a small address book and fountain pen. He handed them
to her. Eve couldn't move.

"Did you forget your number . . . ?" he asked, laughing.

"No, I didn't forget." A pleasant wave of warmth spread through her again as she printed the number. "I live in a . . . a flat . . . with some other girls." She was ashamed to admit it was a boarding-house. "Everyone runs to grab the telephone the moment it rings, so make sure you ask for me."

"Oh, I will! Goodbye, Eve Dawson." He grinned and disappeared into the town house.

Eve arrived at the town house a little before ten. Audrey watched her glance around the foyer and peer into the front room as if searching for an umbrella she'd left behind. "Do you think your brother would like to come with us?" Eve asked as the butler helped Audrey with her coat.

"I can't imagine that he would." Nor could Audrey imagine what Alfie had said to Eve the other day after following her down the sidewalk. He'd been very cagey about it. Audrey didn't know why, but the fact that he and Eve had met at all was unsettling, as if the two people she felt closest to shouldn't be allowed to cross paths. But that was absurd, of course.

She and Eve walked part of the way from the town house in the wintry cold, then took the Underground. It was Audrey's first time to ride the subterranean trains, and she found them horribly crowded and noisy. They walked some more until reaching the parade route, where thousands of silent spectators lined the rain-slicked street, densely packed together and bundled against the chill. Eve towed Audrey down the middle of the empty, closed-off avenue toward Hyde Park Corner, and when a policeman on horseback shooed them out of the road, they ended up in the front row with a perfect view of the procession. "Well, that was a clever move," Audrey said. Eve simply grinned.

Audrey hadn't expected to be awestruck by the somber splendor of the king's funeral procession, but she was. In spite of the cold, she was glad she'd agreed to come. She would long remember this day with the banner-draped coffin perched on a gun carriage, the imperial crown, orb, and scepter on top. The queen and princesses, wearing black, rode in a gilded coach, while the new king and his three brothers, the Dukes of York, Gloucester, and Kent, walked behind the casket. Endless lines of uniformed men saluted their monarch for the final time. Aside from the sounds of distant bagpipes and ringing bells and hundreds of feet marching in step, the funeral procession was silent as people paid their last respects to King George V.

"Do you ever think about dying?" Eve asked after the procession passed and the crowd began to break up.

"I can't say that I do. I've never known anyone who died until now. I've never even been to a funeral. Have you?"

"Sure—several of them. Including my granny Maud's." Eve spoke the name with reverence. And love. She lowered her eyes for a moment, then looked up again and linked arms with Audrey. "So we won't get separated," she said as they surged toward the Underground with the rest of the crowd. "Whenever someone in our village died," Eve explained as they walked, "everyone would leave school or stop working and go to the funeral. The vicar always made heaven sound like such a wonderful place that you almost envied the dead person. I guess King George is up there now, too." Eve pointed to the gray, low-hanging sky.

Audrey envied Eve for having been raised in a community that grieved together. Who, besides Alfie and her parents, would attend Audrey's funeral if she were to die? "Do you believe we go to heaven after we die?" she asked.

"Of course! Doesn't everybody?"

"I know very little about heaven. It certainly isn't part of the curriculum at my girls' school. Nor have my parents or Miss Blake spoken much about it. Father took Alfie and me to church on special occasions like Christmas and Easter."

"I know. I used to see you there. The whole village would start whispering whenever you walked in."

Audrey was afraid to ask what they had whispered about.

They slowed as they approached the entrance to the Underground and the crowd had to file down the narrow stairs. Audrey couldn't bear the thought of being jammed together with so many people. "Maybe we should take a taxi instead."

"Ha! Everyone in London is looking for a taxi," Eve said. "But my boardinghouse isn't far. We could walk there and wait until the streets clear."

"At least we'll be out of the cold." Audrey didn't have anywhere else she needed to be. Her coat might have been fashionable, but it wasn't keeping out the January chill, and her silk stockings did nothing at all to keep her legs warm. They walked for what seemed like miles and finally arrived on a block of shabby brick row houses on a narrow back street.

"This is home," Eve said, leading Audrey up the steps and through the door. She towed her into a front room with dusty knickknacks, a threadbare Turkish rug, a pair of overstuffed chairs, and a worn chintz sofa. The fire in the grate had burned low, but the room felt warm compared to the wintry temperatures outside. Eve sank onto one of the chairs, rubbing her hands together to warm them. Audrey sat down on the sofa and removed her kid gloves. "I've been thinking," Eve said. "Whenever someone in our village died, we would mourn their passing at church. But after the burial, everyone gathered at the deceased's home or in the pub to celebrate his life. We should do something to celebrate King George's life."

Audrey felt another prickle of envy. When had she ever felt a sense of belonging? Or celebration? "What do you suggest?" she asked.

"Do you like to dance? There's a little dance hall nearby where my friends and I sometimes go to have a good time and maybe meet some boys." When Audrey didn't reply right away, Eve laughed. "You probably only know the waltz and all those other ballroom dances, right?"

What was it about Eve that always made Audrey feel prissy and stiff? She longed to enjoy life as much as Eve did, to try new things. This time her envy inspired her to action. "I'm willing to learn if you'll teach me. Let's do it, Eve. Let's go dancing tonight."

Eve leaned toward her, staring as if to see if Audrey was joking. When she saw that she wasn't, she jumped to her feet and offered Audrey her hand. "Come on, let's go up to my room and change clothes. You can borrow some of mine this time. They'll know you're not one of us if you're dressed like that."

Once Audrey got used to the dim, smoky dance hall with its loud music and boisterous patrons, she was surprised to find herself having fun. The social events she usually attended were formal and contrived with everyone sizing each other up to an exacting set of standards, trying to gauge how much money they were worth. Eve seemed to be having such a good time on the dance floor that Audrey let her teach her the swing dance and the shag so she could join the fun. The music came from a recording, not a real band, but the lively beat made it impossible to sit still and not tap your toes. The fun seemed contagious. Audrey was even more surprised as young men approached from time to time, inviting them to dance or offering to buy a lemonade.

"You're the two prettiest girls here," one of them said. "Are you sisters?"

"Best friends," Eve replied. "You may have one dance with us, but no more." She leaned close and whispered in Audrey's ear. "It's the only way to get rid of them. Otherwise they'll pester us all night."

It was great fun to hold a young man's hand and swing around the dance floor with the other couples. "I'm very new at this and not very good yet," Audrey explained, panting for breath.

"You're doing great, doll."

Afterwards, she and Eve collapsed onto their chairs, laughing. Audrey wondered if her face was as flushed and beaming as Eve's. "Mother would be appalled if she knew I was here," Audrey said, fanning herself with a paper napkin.

"I'll never tell. Cross my heart and hope to die." Eve made the sign from their childhood ritual, then took a sip of lemonade. "So, tell me, are you and your brother supposed to marry aristocrats or can you marry for love? I don't understand how it works in your world. You're a member of the nobility, right?"

"Well, Mother is, at least. Her brother, Roger, sits in the House of Lords, and their family tree goes back forever. I find all that history boring, and my mother does, too. We rarely socialize with her relatives."

"But she didn't have to marry a nobleman, right?" Eve asked.

"No. My father is wealthy but it's 'new' money. He earned it himself instead of inheriting it. The only reason the snobs don't look down on him is because he has piles of it." Audrey paused as she remembered her mother's confession: *I liked the life he could offer me. And he liked my father's title.*

"So you and Alfie could marry commoners?"

"Yes. But there's no shortage of down-on-their-luck aristocrats who need to marry into a family like ours with new money in order to keep their huge estates going. Why do you ask?" Although she had a feeling she knew.

"No reason." Eve looked away. "You know, our new king is a bachelor. Maybe you'll get to meet him at one of your fancy balls, and he'll give up his affair with that American woman and fall madly in love with you, just like in a fairy tale."

"He's much too old for me," Audrey said with a smile. But her father was sixteen years older than her mother.

"What do you think it will be like to fall in love?" Eve asked. She wore a dreamy look on her face as she watched the swirling dancers.

"I'm afraid I know nothing about it, really, except what one reads in books."

"Everyone says that my daddy was so romantic he could charm the birds right out of the sky. He and Mum fell madly in love. That's how I want it to be for me."

Tears burned in Audrey's eyes. She wanted to believe it was from all the cigarette smoke. She leaped up to dance with the next boy who wandered over, desperate to erase the memory of her parents' story—and the future she likely faced.

Too soon, the lights in the dance hall blinked for closing time. Eve gasped and stared at the clock in horror. "Oh no! I forgot it's a weeknight. I've missed my curfew! My landlady won't let anyone into the boardinghouse after curfew."

"What will you do?"

Eve shrugged as if she didn't care, but Audrey could tell she was worried. "I guess I'll throw stones at the window and hope one of my roommates wakes up and lets me in. And that our landlady doesn't catch us." They fetched their coats from the cloakroom and stepped out into the frigid night.

"Why not take a taxi home to the town house with me?" Audrey asked.

"Well . . . it's better than risking trouble, I suppose. I'm sure Mum will let me sleep in her room."

Audrey hailed a cab and ordered the driver to drop them off at the corner instead of in front of the town house. "Do you mind walking a bit?" she asked Eve. "If our butler sees the headlights, he'll know how late I'm coming home." They were a few yards from the front door when a shiny silver Bentley purred to a halt out front. A dapper stranger left the car idling and dashed around to the passenger door to help a woman from the car.

Her mother.

The man draped Mother's arm around his shoulder, supporting her as he led her to the front door. Mother was as limp as an eel. She began singing "God Save the King" in a loud voice. Shame stole Audrey's breath.

"Shh. You'll wake the neighbors and cause a scandal," the man said, laughing. His voice carried clearly in the still night air.

"That's nothing new. I already have a scandalous reputation, don't you know?" Mother stopped on the front step, wrapped her arms around the man, and kissed him full on the lips. The kiss was like something from the cinema, lasting for half a minute. Audrey averted her eyes as if her mother stood there naked.

"Shh . . . Quiet down, old girl!"

"It's fine for you gentlemen to have a good time. No one even blinks at your indiscretions—even if you're married to some stuffy old wife. But if a woman has a little fling, it's goodbye future. Goodbye reputation. A proper gentleman wants to marry a *good* girl."

"It's time to go to sleep, Rosy dear."

"I'm *good*, aren't I, darling?"

"You're very good," he said with a laugh. "Now toddle off to bed before we wake up the neighbors." The front door opened and the butler helped Mother inside. The man in the Bentley drove away. Audrey longed to sink into the ground, to crawl into a hole and disappear. She felt Eve nudging her forward.

"Let's go in through the back door," Eve whispered. "I know where there's a key."

Audrey barely knew what she was doing as Eve led her around to the rear of the town house and up the servants' stairs. She could hear Mother singing in the hallway, the servants shushing her. She wished she had never seen her mother kissing that man or overheard the ugly truth. How could she ever face her mother again?

"I would like you to leave," Audrey told Eve when they reached the bedroom level.

"Are you sure you want to be alone? Don't you need a friend to—?"

"No. I don't need your pity or . . . or your stupid strawberries. Just go away and leave me alone." She closed the door in Eve's face, then sank to her bedroom floor in a heap. Nausea overwhelmed her. Eve and all of the other servants had witnessed Mother's disgrace. They all knew the truth about her. Did Father?

Audrey wanted to shrivel up and die. Her body shook as she wept tears of shame and humiliation. Then another, darker emotion gradually took control. Rage. For as long as Audrey could remember, Mother had lectured her about proper social behavior and keeping up appearances and being in control of one's emotions. No matter how hard Audrey had worked to please Mother, she had never quite measured up. And now it enraged Audrey to see her mother's secret life exposed. She longed to run far, far away, to be someone other than Lady Rosamunde's daughter, to live a different life.

And yet . . .

In spite of what she now knew, something deep inside Audrey still hungered for Mother's approval. She ached to know she had done well, had obeyed all the rules, impressed all the right people. Most of all, she longed to see pride shining in Mother's eyes when she gazed at her.

Audrey hauled herself up from the floor. She dried her eyes, lifted her chin. Perhaps her own success in London's social world might one day atone for her mother's disgrace. And earn her love.

6

LONDON, DECEMBER 1936

Eve lifted the heavy flatiron from the kitchen range, tested it with a drop of spit on her finger, then gingerly pressed out the wrinkles on her blouse, fearful of scorching it. "I could finish this in a jiffy with an electric iron," she muttered to her roommate, who was washing clothes on the scrub board. Neither of them could afford laundry service at the boardinghouse.

"Why can't Mrs. Russell spend a shilling or two and modernize this place?"

"I know! It's like living in the last century. We don't even have—" Eve paused when the telephone shrilled in the front hallway. The lively chatter in the boardinghouse parlor also stilled as the girls listened, each hoping the call was for her.

"Eve Dawson! Telephone!"

Eve grinned and parked the heavy iron on the stove before hurrying to the phone. "It's a *man*," the girl who had taken the call whispered. She handed over the receiver. Eve couldn't imagine who it might be.

"Hello, this is Eve."

"Hello, beautiful friend of my sister. Alfie Clarkson, here." If Eve had been given a hundred tries, she never would have guessed Alfie. Goose bumps prickled on her arms. "I've been kicking myself these past eleven months for misplacing your telephone number," he continued, "but I just now found it. I realize you likely have dozens of men queuing up at your door, but my fraternity has a formal event at the Savoy on December 10, and I would love to take you."

His words were too much for her to digest, especially in the middle of a boring workweek and while doing a mundane task like ironing. *Alfie Clarkson, the heir of Wellingford Hall, was inviting her on a date. To the Savoy!* He might as well have been King Edward, inviting her on a trip to the moon.

"Hello? Eve? Are you there?"

Her surprise came out as a burst of laughter. "Sorry. You caught me off guard. The Savoy is very posh, isn't it? Are you trying to impress me?"

"Oh yes. Very much so. Will you come? I realize you don't know me very well, but I'm certain Audrey will provide a character reference."

Eve laughed again. She was certain Audrey would be appalled and would do whatever she could to stop them. Eve longed to accept his invitation. If the mere sound of his upper-crust voice on the tinny phone sent a shiver through her, what would spending an entire evening with him be like? Yes, she very much wanted to go. But could she pull it off—faking fancy manners, pretending to be a wealthy socialite? What would she wear? The nicest dress Eve had was the one she wore to church every Sunday. The Savoy was intimidating all on its own, let alone for a formal event. She tried to picture Alfie Clarkson walking up the crumbling boardinghouse steps in his tuxedo to collect her and couldn't. She needed to charm him into falling in love with her before he learned the truth about her—because she would surely give herself away the moment she tried to hobnob with the aristocrats at the Savoy.

Eve threaded the telephone cord through the stair rails and sat down on one of the steps to steady herself. "I don't need a character reference, Mr. Clarkson. I'm perfectly happy to accept your invitation."

"Wonderful!"

"But since we're practically strangers, I think we should have tea together first and take a stroll in the park so we can get to know each other a little better before our big night at the Savoy." She winced, aware that she had just asked Alfie Clarkson on a date. The chatter in the lounge had stopped. Eve pictured the other girls straining to hear, gasping at the mention of the Savoy—and at her audacity for suggesting a date for tea. They all knew she didn't have a steady bloke. Eve held her breath, releasing it only after she heard Alfie chuckle on the other end.

"I must say, Eve Dawson, you are a marvelously mysterious woman. Now I want to meet you more than ever. Where do you suggest we have tea? And when?"

"How about Sunday at three in Piccadilly Circus? We can meet beneath the statue of Eros." Would he be shocked by her boldness in meeting beneath the god of love?

"Done," he said. "Sunday at three. *Au revoir.*"

Eve could barely concentrate on the vicar's sermon on Sunday, her mind a swirling, churning mixture of excitement and fear. Dating Alfie Clarkson was the opportunity of a lifetime, a chance to move up in the world. It might be the only step up she would ever get.

The winter day turned out to be cold yet sunny, perfect for

strolling London's streets. Alfie stood waiting beneath the statue of Eros when Eve emerged from the Piccadilly Circus Underground station. If only the winged god would fire an arrow and make Alfie fall madly in love with her. He stood out from the common crowd, dressed in expensive tweeds and fine leather shoes, but he wore them with casual indifference, as only the privileged class could. He smiled as he greeted Eve, swooping off his hat and bowing to kiss the back of her hand as if she were a princess.

"Even more beautiful than I remembered," he said, bringing a surge of warmth to her cheeks. "Shall we go? There's a tea shop right around the corner." He resettled his hat on his thick amber hair and tucked her hand in the crook of his arm. They started walking.

Eve struggled to think of something witty and charming to say, but every thought fled from her mind, replaced by the thrilling awareness of Alfie Clarkson. Imagine, Eve Dawson, a common serving girl from the village, stepping out for tea with the young master of Wellingford Hall.

"How long have you known my sister?" he asked.

"Since we were twelve. Our mothers have known each other for years. But you don't want to talk about them, do you?"

"Fair enough. What shall we talk about?"

"Well, I'm very curious about something. You must know dozens of girls who would love to go with you to the Savoy. Why did you choose me?"

He stopped in the middle of the sidewalk, grinning as he gazed down at her. "To tell you the truth it was because of your freckles."

"Oh no!" Her hand flew to her face as if she might feel them sticking out. "Do they show? Do I need to powder my nose again?"

"Please don't," he said with a laugh. "I noticed your wonderful freckles the day we met on my doorstep. They reminded me of cinnamon on warm, buttered toast and made you seem very . . . unique."

Eve remembered now. It had been a school day, but classes were canceled because of the king's death. She never wore cosmetics to school—they were too dear to waste.

"And you weren't wearing a ridiculous feathered hat like all the other women do," he continued. "Some hats look as though a bird has perched on the foolish woman's head."

Eve laughed at the picture he drew. She didn't tell him she couldn't afford a fancy hat on her typist's salary. "Somewhere in the world are flocks and flocks of featherless peacocks and pheasants," she said, "shivering in the cold."

"Yes, poor things. I must say the feathers look much better on their original owners." They started walking again. "I also recall that your hair was blowing free and natural, like it is today, not all kinked up into those silly waves that are all the rage. I knew then and there that I wanted to get to know you."

Eve didn't know how to reply. Should she explain that she couldn't afford a curling iron or a fancy lady's maid to arrange her hair? Before she could say anything, Alfie slowed to a halt. "Here's the tea shop." He opened the door to a warm, cozy shop with wooden floors that creaked beneath their feet and a scattering of mismatched tables and chairs. The tantalizing aromas of coffee and chocolate filled the air. Alfie chose an empty table near the window and they sat across from each other at a table so tiny their knees touched. Could he feel hers trembling? He was miles above Eve in all the important ways—wealth, social standing, intelligence—and yet he said such lovely, charming things. Would everything change once she told him the truth about herself?

Eve held on tightly to the thread of conversation as Alfie ordered tea for her, coffee for himself, and scones with jam for both of them. "I daresay not all men would share their opinions on women's fashions so freely," she said after the waiter left.

"I usually don't. But I already feel as though I can speak my mind with you. You're different. Not at all like Audrey's other friends."

"How so?" Her pulse quickened. Could he tell she was a common working girl?

"I can't imagine any of Audrey's friends suggesting tea and a Sunday stroll. They're more likely to suggest champagne and a ride in my automobile."

"I grew up in the countryside. A walk in the park is the closest thing there is in London to remind me of home." Eve would stick as close to the truth as possible as they got acquainted without revealing that she'd once been the scullery maid at Wellingford Hall.

"So do you live in London now?" he asked.

"Yes. I finished school last June and I've been living here ever since." She chose the word *finished* as a subtle reference to finishing school. Let him think what he wanted, for now. It was time to steer the focus away from herself and ask a few questions of her own. "Audrey tells me you're at Oxford. What are you studying there?"

He made a face. "Boring things. I'm convinced that universities were invented by fathers to keep their sons out of their hair until they're ready to hand over their businesses to them."

"Is that what you'll do someday? Work in your father's business?"

"That's his plan. But I'm not ready to settle down yet. I'm having too much fun to spoil it all by going to work every day."

Eve smiled as if she knew exactly what he meant. But she couldn't imagine a life where she didn't have to work every day— if not as a servant or a typist, then running a home as a wife and mother. She decided to change the subject, consulting the mental list of topics she had prepared ahead of time. "I would love to know what you think of King Edward's affair with Wallis Simpson. Do you think he'll marry her?"

Alfie's smile vanished. He looked as solemn and serious as Audrey. "The king will create a constitutional crisis throughout the commonwealth if he does marry her. He is the Supreme Governor of the Church of England. A twice-divorced woman like Wallis Simpson is morally unsuitable to be the wife of a monarch—not to mention the mother of his heir. He's a fool to allow her to control him the way she does. He needs to be rid of her once and for all and get on with the business of ruling Britain."

"Does it also matter that she's a commoner, with no royal blood?"

"Absolutely. But that's the least of her many faults."

Their food arrived, interrupting them as the waiter arranged cups and plates and cutlery on the tiny table. Eve took a bite of her currant-studded scone and decided it was the best she'd ever tasted. Alfie's vehemence on the subject left her with few illusions that he would make the same foolish mistake and marry someone from a different class. She faced a choice. She could end this flirtation now before she fell hopelessly in love with him and had her heart broken when he tossed her aside. Or she could go along for the ride for as long as it lasted, enjoying posh dinners at the Savoy, hoping that maybe, just maybe, Alfie would fall in love with her. After all, Alfie's father wasn't an aristocrat.

"What do *you* think of this mess the king's gotten himself into?" Alfie asked, breaking into her thoughts.

"If he marries her, he will shatter all the rules. Anyone could marry a prince."

"Exactly! It will be the end of order and tradition in this nation." He had misunderstood her. It was just as well.

"I want to know what Wallis Simpson's secret is," Eve said.

"She charmed two husbands into marrying her, and now she has bewitched the king of England. Do you think she's beautiful?"

"Not at all. Especially compared to you." His smile returned. He reached across the table to rest his hand on top of hers.

Eve laughed. "Flatterer!" She enjoyed the warmth of his palm and was pleased when he let it linger there.

"I wouldn't give up my place at the table for Wallis Simpson, let alone my crown," he added.

"Some say King Edward might abdicate."

"If he thinks so little of his duty and his heritage as the Sovereign King of Great Britain, then he should abdicate. I say, good riddance."

"I like a man who gives an honest answer."

They talked of lesser things as they finished their food, then left the shop to stroll through St. James's Park. The afternoon turned cold as the wind blew off the Thames River, and Eve shivered in her roommate's coat. "I should go," she said when she had exhausted her entire list of topics for conversation. "Thank you for tea and the delightful afternoon."

"You're welcome, lovely Eve," he said with a little bow. "So did I pass the test? Will you come with me to the Savoy next week?"

"Of course! I already told you I would . . . but I have one condition."

"Name it."

Her heart hammered. "You have to meet me there."

"That's outrageous!" He tried to look shocked but couldn't erase his smile. "A gentleman always calls for a lady at her home. He might want to bring her a bouquet of flowers or pin a corsage on her gown. And I have a smashing new car."

"Sorry—that's my condition."

He crossed his muscled arms, the fabric of his jacket pulling tight against them. "It almost seems as though you don't want me to know where you live."

"I prefer to remain a lady of mystery awhile longer."

"Might you be Cinderella? Will you dash away at midnight and leave your glass slipper behind?"

"You have a wonderful imagination, Mr. Clarkson." She briefly touched his arm. "I'll see you at the Savoy at seven. And thanks again for a lovely afternoon." Eve waited for him to leave so he wouldn't see her taking public transportation. She floated down the stairs to the Underground with a smile.

She liked Alfie Clarkson. Far more than she had planned to. There was no question of guarding her heart against being bruised. Her heart had escaped from her control, fluttering and skipping and hammering dangerously the entire time they'd been together. She couldn't wait to see how it felt to be held in his arms while they danced. And if the touch of his hand on hers had made her melt inside, what would his kiss do?

Eve just missed a train back home to her boardinghouse. As she waited on the platform for the next one, she changed her mind and crossed the platform to take a train to the Clarksons' town house instead, hoping her mum would be there—and that Alfie and Audrey wouldn't be. She found Mum reading in her bedroom on the top floor.

"What a wonderful surprise, Eve! What brings you here on this wintry afternoon?" They hugged, and then Eve sat on the bed across from Mum's chair.

"I need your help. A very respectable gentleman asked me on a date—and it's at the Savoy. Can you help me find a dress and do something with my hair?" She ran her fingers through it, untangling the snarls the wind had made. She hoped Mum would be happy for her, but she looked worried.

"Are you certain this man isn't married? Some gentlemen are scoundrels in disguise and they take pretty young mistresses from the working class when they get bored with their wives."

Eve blushed, remembering the warmth of Alfie's hand on hers. "I know for a fact that he's single."

"Well, even single gentlemen have been known to use working girls for their pleasure and then discard them."

"I know," she said, staring at the floor. "It isn't serious between us yet. And he doesn't know that I'm just a working girl. I'm sure that will be the end of it when I tell him. But before I do, I would love to have just one unforgettable night to live like a princess and enjoy dinner and dancing at a posh place like the Savoy."

"I understand. But please be careful, Eve. Don't fall into the trap of envying the rich. For all her money, Lady Rosamunde is a very unhappy woman. I'd rather be poor and happy and in love with an honorable, hardworking man than be rich and miserable."

"I'll be careful, Mum. I want to marry for love." But that wasn't entirely true. Wasn't she already dreaming of being the mistress of Wellingford Hall, dressed in diamonds and furs, with handsome Alfie Clarkson by her side? Yet why choose one over the other? Was it out of the question that she and Alfie might fall in love? Mum had once warned her that Audrey would outgrow their friendship—and she'd been right. Alfie and Audrey were very different, but they were raised in the same household by the same parents. And like Lady Rosamunde, Audrey never seemed to be truly happy. Would that be Eve's fate if she married Alfie?

Mum rose to sit beside her on the bed, wrapping an arm around her. "What other dreams do you have for your life, my darling girl, besides finding true love?"

Eve sighed, playing with a loose thread on the bedspread as she searched her heart. "I dreamed of taking the typing course for so long . . . and then I dreamed of getting a good job and being on my own. Those dreams have come true, Mum. I have all of that, now—a nice job, independence, a shilling or two of my own to spend as I please. But I don't really know what's next. I'm not ready to marry and start a family."

"Of course not. You're barely eighteen. I married young but times were different back then."

"Sometimes I go dancing on Saturday night, and while the other girls all try to attract a bloke and pair off with him, none of those fellows appeal to me." Eve twisted the loose thread around her finger. She suspected they would be even less appealing after an evening with Alfie. "They're so loud, and they make crude remarks after a few pints. That's why I accepted this gentleman's invitation to go to the Savoy. For just one night, I would love to be Cinderella." She looked up at her mother, hoping she would understand.

Mum hugged her tightly, then stood. "Lady Rosamunde discards gowns the way we discard old newspapers. I can take one or two of them apart and resew them into something lovely for you. And if you come here beforehand, I'll pin up your hair for you." She lifted Eve's hair off her shoulders and loosely shaped it on top of her head before letting it fall again. "You'll be beautiful."

Joy bubbled up inside Eve. Maybe fairy tales really did come true.

⁂

The soft, beaded gown Mum sewed fit Eve like a dream, hugging her torso, then falling loose from her hips in swirls of swishy fabric. Instead of kinking Eve's sandy hair in waves, Mum draped it loosely on her head so it looked sophisticated yet natural—the way Alfie preferred. None of Lady Rosamunde's shoes fit Eve, so

Mum snuck into Audrey's room and borrowed a pair. "I've talked to Williams," Mum said when Eve was ready, "and he insists on driving you to the Savoy to meet your mysterious date."

"That's so sweet of him." She would have to get out at the corner so Alfie wouldn't see her arrive in his parents' car.

The other servants applauded when Eve descended the back stairs to leave. Tildy had tears in her eyes as she hugged her. Williams did, too. "You are a beauty, Eve Dawson," he said as he helped her into the car. "But we knew that all along, even when you were scrubbing pots in the scullery." He spent the entire journey to the Savoy giving Eve fatherly advice about the dangers of men in general and of rich men in particular. "Hold your head high, darling girl," he said as he helped her from the car. "You're somebody special."

She timed her arrival so she would get there before Alfie, hoping he didn't catch her gaping at the ornate ballroom in naive wonder. Rich girls walked into splendid palaces like the Savoy cool and aloof, immune to gold-embellished ceilings and pristine marble floors, the dazzling tables set with heavy cloths and candles and sparkling china and silver. Wealthy girls didn't hold their breath to better hear the rich, warm sound of the string orchestra.

"Beautiful!" Alfie said when he saw her. "I think I'll simply stand here and gaze at you all evening. That would be feast enough for me." Eve had no idea what to say, so she merely smiled. If she could bottle up all the joy she felt at that moment, it would last a lifetime.

The dinner was like many she had helped to prepare but like none she had ever tasted. Wine and champagne flowed like water, but Eve drank very little, knowing from experience that it rushed to her head and made her dizzy. She wanted to keep her wits and enjoy every glamorous moment of this once-in-a-lifetime evening.

Alfie seemed capable of drinking gallons of champagne and not being affected at all.

After dinner and a brief program, the dancing began. Eve allowed Alfie to hold her close, reveling in his spicy scent as she rested her head against his shoulder. How she loved being held in his arms, strong and muscled from rowing on Oxford's crew team. He told her all about his crew races and rugby games. "You should come up to Oxford sometime and cheer me on," he said. Eve smiled and nodded, knowing it could never happen.

The storybook evening was a wonderful dream until Alfie suddenly gestured across the room as they waltzed together and said, "Look, there's Audrey! I didn't know she was coming, did you?"

"No!" The word came out in a strangled croak. Fear stiffened Eve's limbs as the dream became a nightmare. She hadn't spoken to Audrey since the night Lady Rosamunde came home drunk and Audrey ordered Eve to leave. She longed to release Alfie's hand and run before being exposed as a real-life Cinderella.

"Let's go say hello." Alfie took her hand and led her across the crowded dance floor to where Audrey sat at a table with her date and two other couples. They all shared the same bored, aloof expression, as if fighting migraine headaches. Eve's heart raced. Her secret would be exposed in front of Alfie and everyone else the moment Audrey said, *"Alfie, why have you brought our scullery maid to the ball?"*

But that didn't happen. Audrey acted as though it were perfectly natural to see them together. "I saw you two come in," she said after all the introductions. "You make a smashing couple." The smile she gave Eve seemed forced and didn't reach her eyes. "It's been a while, Eve. How are you?"

"I've been good. You look gorgeous, Audrey." And she did, wearing a gown that would cost Eve three months' wages. She wondered if Audrey recognized her mother's salvaged gowns or her own shoes on Eve's feet. If so, would she comment on them? Eve fidgeted in place, the urge to bolt from the room growing stronger.

Alfie chatted with the other men while Eve waited, stiff and silent with fear. Then, thankfully, the orchestra started up again. "Come on, Alfie, let's dance," she said, tugging him toward the floor.

"Did you see the way the other men looked at you?" he said when she was safely in his arms again. "They're all thinking I'm the luckiest man here. You outshine every woman here, Eve Dawson."

Eve didn't know how to respond to his compliments. Were they true or just flattery, fueled by all the wine he'd swallowed? She decided to believe they were true and to enjoy being a mysterious fairy-tale princess for just a little longer. Audrey would surely tell her brother the truth tomorrow, so Eve better confess before the evening ended. But no matter what happened after that, she would remember this wonderful evening forever.

Much too soon, it was time to leave. As they waited for a servant to fetch their cloaks, Alfie took both of Eve's hands in his and looked into her eyes. "I have two requests, darling, and please don't refuse either. The first is, may I see you again?"

She couldn't help smiling. Was this love—this wonderful euphoria that made her dizzy and giddy and bursting with happiness? Was it love that made her long to stay in Alfie's arms forever? Mum's warnings tried to elbow their way into her thoughts along with Williams's fatherly advice, but Eve pushed them all aside. "I would like that very much."

"And second," Alfie continued, "please say you'll let me drive you home. I can't leave you here all alone. Please, let me have a few more moments with you." Eve looked at the floor, hesitant to reply. Alfie lifted her chin. "You can trust me with your secret, Eve."

"I know," she murmured, then drew a deep breath. Audrey would surely tell him the truth, so she might as well do it first. "Here's my secret, Alfie. I'm a working girl. A typist. I live in a boardinghouse with a dozen other working girls."

"That's all?" he asked, laughing. "You never murdered anyone? You're not a foreign spy or a French cancan dancer?"

"Sorry to disappoint you," she said with a smile. "I don't mind working for a living. It's a good job. And I like being on my own."

"I wouldn't change a thing about you, hardworking, independent Eve Dawson. Now, tell me how to deliver you home, please."

Eve nestled beside Alfie in his car for her last few minutes with him. Then they halted in front of the boardinghouse and the marvelous spell shattered like a crystal champagne glass on a marble floor. She had wrangled special permission from Mrs. Russell to stay out past her curfew, and the porch light illuminated the crumbling steps, the peeling paint on the railing. Eve sighed and said, "It's been a wonderful evening, Alfie Clarkson. One I will never forget. Thank you."

"Well, I enjoyed your company, too, but the event was a little too stiff and sedate for my taste. Next time I'll take you to a livelier place that's more my style. They'll have a swinging dance band instead of an orchestra."

"Next time," she repeated, her heart in her throat.

Alfie gazed at her as if unwilling to move. "I know you only gave me permission to ask two questions, but will you allow me just one more?"

"Your wish is granted."

"May I kiss you good night?"

"No." She grinned at his surprise. "I think I'll kiss you first." She leaned toward Alfie and did what she'd been longing to do all evening.

⟨◦◦◦◦◦⟩

Audrey slept late after her evening at the Savoy. When she awoke to another dreary winter day, her first thought was the disturbing image of Eve Dawson dancing in her brother's arms. She groaned and closed her eyes again. It was wrong for them to be together for so many reasons. Yes, Eve had looked beautiful. In fact, Audrey hadn't recognized her until she'd heard Eve's unmistakable laughter. Audrey's date and all of the other gentlemen at her table stared in slack-jawed admiration as Alfie introduced Eve. Audrey watched the pair whirl around the ballroom floor together, smoothly attuned to each other's steps, and wondered how in the world this ill-suited duo had ever come together. She would ask Alfie about it today.

Her own date for the evening had been bland and disappointing, both of them bound by the social expectations that turned the evening into a chore. Audrey had been relieved to say good night. *My daddy was so romantic he could charm the birds right out of the sky,* Eve once told her. Audrey's date would cause the birds to drop dead from boredom. Even from across the crowded ballroom, Eve exuded a warmth and vitality that women of Audrey's class were taught to carefully suppress. Ladies must be genteel and cool, never laughing out loud with delight the way Eve had. Jealousy slithered through every inch of Audrey's body, and she hated herself for it.

She rose and dressed before the spiral of self-pity pulled her down any deeper. The servants had spread a buffet breakfast on the sideboard in the dining room and she fixed herself a plate. She was eating alone at the long, polished table, the other eleven chairs silent and empty, when Alfie bounced in. "Morning, Sis. Enjoy your evening last night?"

"Not really." Conflicting feelings battled in a tug-of-war. Audrey loved her brother, and deep down, she felt Eve wasn't good enough for him. He was an Oxford student, and Eve had dropped out of the village school at age twelve. Yet aside from Alfie, Eve was the closest friend she'd ever had. "How was your evening?" she asked in return, dreading his reply.

"Splendid! I like your friend a lot."

Audrey hesitated, knowing she would sound like a jealous shrew if she exposed Eve's secret. But Eve was wrong to deceive her brother by pretending to be someone she wasn't. "Eve isn't right for you, Alfie. She's a working girl, a typist in an office somewhere."

"I know. She told me." He speared a sausage and put it on his plate beside his eggs and toast. The casualness of his reply infuriated her.

"Did she also tell you that her mum is our mother's lady's maid? And that she—"

"It doesn't matter, Sis." He cut her off before she could add that Eve was once their scullery maid. He set his plate on the table and sat down across from her, diving into his food as if the conversation were over. Audrey couldn't let it go.

"It will matter to our parents. Mother will be furious. She forbade me to be friends with Eve, so I can well imagine how she'll feel about you courting her. And Father has high hopes for you to marry a titled woman so he can move up another rung on society's ladder."

"I don't really care what Mother thinks. And Father is the last person who would dare to complain about Eve's working-class background. I like Eve. I plan to see her again."

"Is she your act of rebellion? Is that why you'll keep seeing her?"

Alfie grinned as he lifted a forkful of eggs. "I'll keep seeing her because she's beautiful, in case you hadn't noticed. And because she's fun. There isn't a snobbish bone in her body."

"Not a drop of blue blood, either."

"Don't be unkind, Audrey. I thought she was your friend."

"She is!" Audrey closed her eyes, picturing the expression of adoration on Eve's face as she'd waltzed in Alfie's arms, like a starving woman eyeing a banquet table. "She is my friend," she said softly. "Eve is naive and trusting and loving . . . Please don't hurt her, Alfie. You know a romance with her can't go anywhere. But Eve doesn't know it, and she won't believe me if I tell her. She believes in fairy tales. She doesn't know that people like us rarely live happily ever after."

"You sound so jaded, Sis."

"I suppose I am. It's hard to find a man who's interested in me and not our father's money. I would like to fall in love with an unforgettable man who would love me even if I were as penniless as Eve Dawson. I long for a romance that will last a lifetime, not a convenient arrangement like our parents have." She wondered if Alfie knew the truth about their mother. Audrey still wished she could forget that terrible night.

"So you believe in fairy tales too?" Alfie asked.

"I would very much like to. Do you suppose people like us are allowed to believe in them?"

The butler entered before Alfie replied. "Excuse me, sir . . . Miss Audrey," he said with a bow. "You may wish to switch on the wireless. King Edward is making an important announcement."

They left their food on the table and hurried into the morning room. The king had already begun to speak when Alfie switched on the set, but Audrey quickly caught the gist of it. "He's abdicating his throne!" she said. Alfie nodded. *Abdicating!* Laying aside his crown as the sovereign monarch of the British Commonwealth for the sake of love! Audrey sank down on the sofa, stunned, as she listened to King Edward's sad, weary voice.

"I have found it impossible to carry the heavy burden of responsibility and to discharge my duties as king as I would wish to do, without the help and support of the woman I love."

Alfie switched off the wireless with an angry gesture when the broadcast ended. "There's your fairy tale, Audrey. The king is giving up the throne of Britain for love. Don't you think the old boy is just a little bit of a fool?"

"Perhaps." Audrey would never tell Alfie what she really was thinking—that it must be wonderful to be so beloved by a king that he would sacrifice everything for her.

7

USA, 1950

Audrey sank down on Eve's kitchen chair, struggling to control
her tears. They had arrived at Eve's tiny bungalow only minutes
ago, and the air inside was sweltering. Audrey had left her home
in England and endured a long, wearying journey to America to
meet her husband's parents, hoping to find a new home and begin
a new life. But nothing was turning out the way she'd planned.
Eve Dawson was here in her place, telling Audrey she had to leave,
that she didn't belong. Eve's angry words rained down on her like
a hail of shrapnel:

"For as long as we've known each other, you've had all the
advantages and I've had none. You're Audrey Clarkson—the
spoiled rich girl, the aristocrat! You went to a fancy school to learn
how to marry a wealthy husband, so surely you can find a man
in London who'd be willing to marry Alfred Clarkson's rich little
daughter. A man who could buy you a house twice as big as this
one—twice as big as Wellingford Hall!"

106

Audrey closed her eyes to shut out Eve's words. Then she bent forward and covered her face, reminded again of the bitter truth. "I'm not his daughter," she mumbled.

Eve froze in place. The room went still except for the hum of the rotating fan that Eve had switched on when they'd arrived. A fly buzzed against the window screen. Eve opened the freezer and stuffed the treats she'd been carrying back inside. "What did you say?" she asked.

Audrey pulled a linen handkerchief from her pocket and wiped her tears, then blotted perspiration from her forehead. She never should have blurted the truth about her father. Eve planted her hand on her hip as she waited for an explanation "I—I'm sorry," Audrey mumbled. "Sorry." She heard Mother's disparaging voice: *"Oh, for pity's sake, Audrey . . ."*

Bobby noticed her tears and started crying too, clutching a fold of her skirt in his fist. "I w-want to go home, Mummy. Can we go h-home?" Audrey needed to calm him before he gave way to hysterics. This long, joyless trip was supposed to have a happy ending with Bobby's grandparents pulling him into their arms and embracing him with their love. She and Bobby were supposed to have a home at last. But the dream had taken a nightmarish turn. Eve and her son had stolen their places.

Audrey hugged her son tightly, murmuring, "I know, darling. I know you do."

"What do you mean you're not his daughter?" Eve asked as if finally running out of patience. Audrey wished she hadn't spoken.

"Let's talk about it later. Please?" She gestured to Bobby, still hiccuping tears. "Why don't you show us around and maybe we can find something for the boys to do while you and I talk."

"The grand tour will take all of two minutes," Eve said, her impatience obvious as she stalked from the kitchen. "The dining room is here . . . the living room there . . ." They were one L-shaped room, with a picture window facing the front garden and comfortable sofas and chairs arranged around a coffee table. A small, round table with four maple chairs nestled in the dining alcove. Rainbow-hued dishes filled the matching hutch. "This hall goes to the two bedrooms," Eve continued, leading the way. "Mine and Robbie's." Eve's bedroom was pleasant, if small. It had a double bed with matching spread and curtains, a dressing table with a mirror—all pretty and feminine but crowded into a tiny space. "Bathroom's in the hallway . . ." Audrey had never seen pink tile and fixtures before—tub, sink, and toilet, all pink. The black-and-white tile on the floor resembled a tiny chessboard. "Robbie's room is here." It had wooden bunk beds with a matching dresser and a bookshelf cluttered with cars and toys. More toys littered the floor.

"Wanna play with my cars?" Eve's son asked. He spoke the easy, sloppy American way, rather than with crisp British diction, reminding Audrey of Robert.

"Yes, darling, why don't you play with him?" Audrey nudged Bobby forward, but he shook his head, unwilling to release his hold. He'd always been a shy, timid boy, content to play quietly by himself. But the long trip from Wellingford Hall—the only home he'd ever known—had transformed him into a clinging, weeping child who sometimes cried out in his sleep and wet the bed at night. She must get him settled into their new life as quickly as possible.

Eve ended the tour back in the tiny kitchen with its white metal cupboards, electric stove, and round-top refrigerator. "That's all there is to see except the cellar and the back garden." Eve gestured out the window at a grassy, fenced-in space with a single sapling in the middle. The neighborhood was so new that trees hadn't had time to grow, and houses crowded in on all sides as if sharing secrets. For the space of a heartbeat, Audrey pictured Wellingford's beautiful formal garden, the way it was before the war with box-wood hedges, colorful flowers, and gravel walkways. She blinked and the vision vanished.

"I couldn't picture this house when Robert sent me the floor plans and brochures," she said.

Eve gave a mirthless laugh. "This entire house could fit inside Wellingford's drawing room. And how many bedrooms does Wellingford have?"

"A lot." Audrey looked away, not certain she knew. She couldn't bear to think about Wellingford. "When will Mrs. Barrett return home?" she asked. "I'm eager to meet her."

"I'm not taking you back to the Barretts' house, Audrey. We'll have to sort this out between the two of us, right here and now."

Audrey sank down on a metal kitchen chair again, her skirt sliding on the red vinyl seat. She pulled Bobby onto her lap and he sagged against her, thumb in his mouth. "We have no place to go, Eve. We've traveled a long way and we're both very tired, and . . . and we have no other place to go."

Eve released a huge sigh before opening her freezer again and grabbing one of the Popsicles. She peeled off the paper and gave it to her son. "Eat it out in the garden, please," she told him, opening the screen door. He skipped outside, letting the door close behind him with a slap. Eve sighed again and sank down at the table across from Audrey. "You and your son can sleep in my bedroom tonight. I'll share with Robbie—unless you'd rather go to a hotel."

"Here will be fine. Thank you." This was her house, after all. Eve was the intruder.

Eve gestured to her car outside in the carport, loaded with Audrey's suitcases. "Did you bring everything you own?"

"I've made arrangements for the rest to be shipped once we're settled here."

"Settled *here*?" Eve shook her head. "You can't stay, Audrey. There isn't room for both of us."

Audrey didn't reply, struggling not to cry again, unwilling to upset Bobby any more than he already was. "Will you make us a pot of tea? I would love a cup."

Eve rose and bustled around the kitchen, pulling cups and saucers from the cupboards, warming the teapot, boiling the water. "Don't expect it to have much flavor," she said. "It's impossible to find decent tea over here. Everyone drinks coffee."

"At least you can get tea. We still have shortages back home, even though the war ended five years ago."

By the time Eve arranged everything on the table with the tea brewing in a pot, Bobby was asleep in Audrey's arms. Eve sat down across from them. "Now explain what you said, Audrey. What do you mean, you're not your father's daughter? Did he disown you for marrying a Yank?"

Audrey stared at the tabletop, regretting that she'd blurted the truth. She took a moment to reply, swallowing her sorrow. "No, he didn't care that I'd married Robert. I think he rather hoped I would move far away to America." She met Eve's gaze. She had nothing left to lose by telling the truth—nothing at all, including her pride, which had withered away long ago. "Father called me into his study—what was left of his study—and told me to pack my things. He was selling Wellingford Hall and moving back to the north country where he came from. I could tell he'd been drinking, even more than usual, so I said, 'You don't really mean that.' But he cut me off with a shout. 'It's done!' he said. He had already spoken to an estate agent. Wellingford was cursed and he never wanted to see it again." She swallowed, then drew a shaky breath to continue.

"Father had been depressed for months. He'd never recovered

from the war, and he'd lost all interest in life. I'd been waiting for him to decide to live again, but he holed up in his study, day after day, year after year, until it became a hoarder's lair, with—" She halted, unwilling to disgrace him further by describing the piles of newspapers, discarded clothing, and filth-encrusted dishes. The mounds of dust and garbage that accumulated when he refused to leave the room, refused to allow the maids inside. "Father rarely left his study, taking his meals there, even sleeping there. When I tried to talk to him, he acted as if I were invisible. He became a recluse, Eve. But I never imagined he would sell Wellingford. When he told me that he was, I said, 'What about your grandson? Wellingford Hall is his inheritance. You can't sell his family home.' He said, 'I don't have a grandson.'" Audrey paused, barely clinging to her composure as she remembered.

"I wondered if he'd become senile, so I reminded him that I had a son, Bobby. He said, 'I know who you mean, Audrey. I haven't lost my mind. But that boy is *not* my heir.' I was certain that he was merely confused, so I said, 'I'm your daughter—' But he shouted, 'No, you're not! You're not my daughter!'"

Audrey would never forget that terrible moment. She felt as if he had slammed her against a wall—like the aftershock when a bomb explodes. Father had worn a sick smile on his face as he'd stared at her.

"He told me I was the product of one of Mother's many *dalliances*. An unfortunate *accident*." Shame consumed Audrey as she remembered. And Eve would surely remember the shocking sight of Mother kissing a stranger on the town house steps. Audrey hurried to finish her story, her grief as fresh as on that terrible day. "All I could think was, no wonder he'd never loved me."

Audrey looked up at Eve, trying to read her expression, dreading her pity, but Eve's thoughts were unreadable. "I was so desperate, Eve, that I dropped to my knees and begged. You know what he said? 'Go find a rich, gullible fool to live off like your mother did.'"

Audrey paused as the pain rocked through her again. Her beloved home was sold. She was alone. Everyone she loved was gone. No, not everyone. She still had Bobby. She pulled him tighter against her chest as he slept, both of them damp with their mingled sweat. "You were right, Eve. I should have brought Bobby here to America to live with his grandparents right after Robert died." But the fear of being rejected by them, the fear of leaving England and the home she loved, had been too overwhelming. Besides, she was the reason that Robert was dead. How could his parents ever forgive her?

"I'm sorry, Audrey," Eve said softly. "I truly am. Your parents didn't deserve children like you and Alfie. . . . But I've made a new life here for Robbie and me. I didn't steal it from you. I only took what you threw away when you decided to stay at Wellingford Hall."

"But if I had known—"

Eve slammed her hand down on the porcelain table, making Audrey jump. "I can think of a lot of different choices I would have made if I'd known the future! Now it's too late. We—" She halted as Robbie breezed through the back door, his face and tummy smeared with the dripping remains of his purple Popsicle.

"Can I have another one, Mommy?"

Eve rose as if unaware of what she was doing and fetched another Popsicle from the freezer, peeling off the paper. "Take it outside, love."

Robbie flashed Audrey a huge grin before leaving with his prize. He seemed like such a happy child, so contented, so . . . at home. Audrey's heart broke for her own son. *Fight for him!* a voice inside her said. *Fight for what's rightfully his! And yours!* She had learned all about fighting during the war.

Eve sat down again and drew a breath. "Suppose it was the other way around, Audrey. Suppose I suddenly appeared at Wellingford Hall and announced that Alfie was Robbie's father, that Robbie was the rightful heir, and I told you to get out. Would you and your son cheerfully step aside for us and move away, just like that?" She snapped her fingers. "You would never move out for Robbie and me, and you know it! You were happy when we finally left."

Audrey didn't want to argue. She simply wanted . . . what? A home? A family? She wanted what Eve Dawson had. Hadn't that been true all of her life? "What do you suggest we do?" Audrey asked.

"I suggest that you and your son go back home to England so I can get on with the new life I've made here."

Audrey closed her eyes. She could think of no reply. None at all. *Fight! For Bobby's sake!* the voice said again. Only softer this time.

8

Eve threaded her way through the mobbed train station searching for Alfie, her stomach a fist of anxiety. His height alone should make him easy to spot, along with his thick amber hair and noble profile. The mere sight of his lazy grin never failed to make her breath catch in her throat. But uniformed soldiers crowded the station, all dressed exactly like Alfie. Spotting him would be like finding one particular sheep in an entire flock.

The children added to the melee, thousands of them squirming in endless queues. Solemn-faced children, clutching hands and suitcases, their gas masks tied in cardboard boxes around their necks, name tags pinned to their shabby coats. Government posters and leaflets picturing the horrors of the anticipated bombings blanketed London, persuading worried parents to evacuate their children to the countryside for safety. Most of the poor little things were leaving home for the first time, taking the first train ride of their lives. Eve gulped as she remembered leaving her home in the village and walking the long gravel road to Wellingford Hall.

And the mothers . . . Eve couldn't bear to look at the children's mums, standing so bravely as they said goodbye, holding back their own tears to give their children courage. She couldn't imagine the impossible choice they faced—sending their toddlers and schoolchildren far away to live with strangers, or risk seeing them blown to pieces by Nazi bombs. London was a prime target, capital of the vast British Empire, the nation's largest port, center of transportation and industry.

England was at war. Again. A mere twenty-one years after the first war—the span of Eve's life. It wasn't supposed to happen. The agreement reached in Munich a year ago had assured her and everyone else that it wouldn't happen. The war that killed her daddy was called "the war to end all wars." He'd given his life so Eve and Mum never had to experience the horror of another one. And so that Eve would never relive her parents' story—saying a tearful goodbye to the soldier she loved as he headed off to fight. No, none of this was supposed to happen. But it had.

One of the children on the platform let out a wail, quickly setting off a chain reaction of cries like air-raid sirens throughout the station. The no-nonsense chaperones in their sturdy shoes and tweed skirts set about silencing the tears with brusque assurances that the children would love the countryside. Yes, they would soon see.

Eve checked the time on her wristwatch, a farewell present from Alfie. Where was he? She spotted a knot of men in drab-green uniforms on the next platform and moved toward them. The fist of worry punched her in the gut again as she remembered last night. What if he wouldn't acknowledge her or speak to her, wouldn't accept her feeble apologies? She remembered Mum's warnings. Hadn't Eve feared all along that this would happen?

Eve inched close enough to see the group of soldiers, laughing and punching each other as if they were off to a cricket match instead of the living hell of the battlefield. Alfie wasn't among them. Their laughter brought memories of the happier times she and Alfie had shared these past three years. They'd never attended another posh event at the Savoy, but Eve had fallen deeply in love as Alfie called from time to time and took her out. They'd driven down to the coast to spend the day on his boat. They'd danced until the early hours in London's glittering nightclubs and at private parties. She'd watched Alfie drink to the point of stupor, then took away his keys and drove both of them home in his car. "You can even drive a car, darling Eve?" he'd asked in drunken wonder. "What an amazing girl you are!" She loved being with him. Alfie knew how to have fun. Eve enjoyed their passionate embraces in his car as much as he did. But last night he had asked for more.

"I'm going away to war, Eve. Anything could happen to me. Can't you give me one night to remember forever?"

Eve had longed to give in. She couldn't deny the desire she felt for Alfie or his desire for her. She loved him. And yet . . .

Her mother's warnings came unbidden, dousing the flames. Eve was still unsure of Alfie's intentions. He had never said he loved her. Had never talked of marriage. She knew there were other girls in his life. Would spending the night be a way to bind him to her forever or was he just using her? Alfie made it clear he wasn't ready to settle down to a responsible adult life. He'd told her so, again and again. He'd returned to London for a brief leave before heading to Europe to fight with the British Expeditionary Force and asked Eve for one night of passion to remember. And she refused. Had she lost him forever?

Eve stood on tiptoes in the middle of the swirling mob and

surveyed the station again. The children had boarded the waiting train, and it started forward with a hiss of steam. Little ones hung from every open window, bravely waving goodbye. Eve heard a cry of anguish from the crowd of mothers and turned to see them huddled together, consoling each other's tears. They wouldn't know where their children were until after they'd arrived in the countryside and mailed the postcard each of them carried. But at least they were out of London. They were safe.

"Eve! Eve, darling!" She turned and there he was, pushing his way toward her, duffel bag slung over his shoulder, his grin lighting the dismal station.

"Alfie!" She reached for him and they held each other tightly before exchanging a kiss more appropriate for a dark corner than a public place. Eve didn't care. He had forgiven her. And she loved him. "I didn't think I would ever find you," she said when they came up for air. "How long until your train leaves?"

He consulted his expensive wristwatch, a graduation present after Oxford. "Only ten minutes. I was a little hungover this morning and overslept. Walk with me to the platform." Alfie took her hand and cut a smooth path for them—a knife through butter—as people instinctively stepped aside for him in his officer's uniform. "I've been telling the other lads how beautiful you are, and now they can see for themselves."

She didn't want her last moments with him to be spent among a crowd of soldiers, but there was no helping it. Eve longed to tell him she loved him and hear him say he loved her, too. She wanted him to promise to come home safely, promise they would always be together, grow old together. *Cross my heart.* But too soon it was time for Alfie to board.

"Send me your address as soon as you get there, Alfie. I'll write every day."

"Righto. And keep your gas mask with you, darling." He tugged the cord around her neck that held her boxed mask.

"You, too!" She'd seen the wheezing, gasping veterans of the first war, some with missing limbs. *Not Alfie. Please, Lord.*

He held her tightly one last time. Kissed her one last time. And just like the departing children, he and the other soldiers boarded the train, heading off in a hiss of steam, their lives about to be altered forever by the demands of war.

WELLINGFORD HALL

Audrey stood on a ladder, stretching as high as she could to pin the thick black cloth to the back of the dining room drapes. "Here's the next piece," Mrs. Smith said as she bustled into the room. "Oh, do be careful, Miss Audrey. Maybe you should let Robbins do those tall windows."

Audrey lowered her arms, rotating her aching neck and shoulders. "I sent him into the village to see about borrowing a wagon for the children. Do we have enough cloth to finish before they arrive?"

"We ran out. And the dry goods store doesn't expect more from London until next week."

"I'm not surprised," Audrey said as she stepped down. "Every cottage and mansion and flat in England needs yards and yards of it." Making blackout curtains for all of Wellingford's windows was proving to be an enormous task. And even though it was a necessity of war, Audrey was determined to do a neat job of it and keep the mansion looking elegant, not dim and funereal.

"When we finish this room and Mr. Clarkson's study, all of the windows on the first floor will be done," Mrs. Smith told her. "Robbins was able to tape the largest ones so they won't shatter."

"What about the second floor?"

"All the bedrooms that are in use are finished. Robbins thought it best to use the remainder of the cloth to do the servants' rooms on the third floor."

"I suppose that's wise. The wardens will pay us a visit one of these nights to see if we've complied, and the servants will want to use their rooms after dark." The few servants who were left, that was. The footmen and undergardeners had all enlisted. The cook had moved to the London town house, leaving only her assistant to prepare meals. Miss Blake had taken a civilian post with the Royal Navy in Liverpool. The butler, Mrs. Smith, George the gardener, and a handful of very young chambermaids were the only ones left.

"We also blacked out the windows in the former nursery and the schoolroom where the children will sleep," Mrs. Smith added.

Audrey's nerves jangled like a thousand bells at the reminder. "Is everything ready for their arrival?"

"I believe so."

Audrey had no idea what to expect. An unknown number of children of undetermined ages and family backgrounds would arrive from London by train this afternoon to be housed in the village. The newspapers had called it "an exodus of biblical proportions" with more than 800,000 schoolchildren and 100,000 teachers billeted in the English countryside. Every family was taking in a child or two, and Audrey realized they might be expected to house several at Wellingford Hall. Perhaps as many as ten? Fifteen? Audrey's mother wanted nothing to do with the scheme and decided to take her chances in London, vowing to continue with some semblance of her normal life there, war or no war.

Audrey and Mrs. Smith worked with the local branch of the Women's Institute in the village to prepare cots and bedding for the children. They had closed off as many formal rooms and spare bedrooms as possible, storing Wellingford's valuables. The work had been exhausting but fulfilling. Audrey much preferred being mistress of Wellingford Hall over life in London, where streetlights and automobile headlamps weren't allowed, and the streets were so black at night that it was hazardous to venture out. She had no desire to sit in the darkened town house with Mother, waiting for the bombs to fall, as they surely would.

Alfie had driven to Wellingford Hall to say goodbye, and it had been one of the worst moments in Audrey's life. Their father's, too, she suspected. Father mentioned a possible draft exemption for Alfie but he'd refused. Fear for her brother drove Audrey to her knees beside her bed at night and to the village church to pray on Sunday. Eve Dawson had always known so much more about God than she did, and Audrey wished she could talk to her about her faith. No doubt Eve was praying for Alfie, too. At least they were united in that.

Mrs. Smith bustled away again, leaving Audrey alone in the huge dining room. The children wouldn't eat in here, of course, but perhaps someone would—someday. Audrey knew it was irrational, but she wanted to keep the room ready for guests, just in case. Beyond the French doors, the beautiful formal gardens looked as they always had, with neatly trimmed boxwood hedges and the last of the summer roses blooming. The gravel walkways formed intricate geometric designs that bisected the gardens and encircled the fountain in the center. "One would never know we're at war," she murmured as she stepped outside.

The war was bringing countless changes to Audrey's life, and she hated change. This orderly garden had become her place of refuge, her one quiet place of retreat. But even as she walked the peaceful paths, she heard the ominous drone of airplanes overhead. She looked up, shading her eyes against the sun's glare. The droning grew louder, closer. The planes flew low in the sky, three of them, and she released her breath when she saw the RAF insignia. *They're ours.*

Back inside, she found Robbins in the entrance hall, returned from his walk into the village. "I arranged for a wagon to transport the children and their baggage, Miss Audrey." He mopped his brow, then tugged his waistcoat into place. "Horse-drawn, I'm afraid, but it was the best I could do. You'll need to speak with Mr. Grayson, the station porter."

Audrey was becoming accustomed to the mile-long walk into the village. Williams, their driver, had joined the Auxiliary Fire Service in London, and no one else at Wellingford knew how to drive except Father, who refused to serve as chauffeur. Audrey wished Williams had taught her to drive before he left, the way he'd taught Eve. Perhaps she should buy a bicycle.

"Thank you, Robbins. Is that the London paper?" she asked, seeing it tucked under his arm.

"Yes, Miss Audrey. However, you may not wish to read it today. Rather gruesome news, I'm afraid."

She steeled herself as she reached for it. "Thank you for the warning, but I would like to see it, just the same. I'm afraid one must get used to gruesome news. I'll take it to Father when I'm finished."

Reports of atrocities in Poland horrified Audrey and were another reason she'd fled to the safety of Wellingford. Nazi airplanes mowed down civilians like wheat as they fled Warsaw. And Alfie, who was always on her heart, was somewhere in Belgium. *"The Maginot Line will hold,"* he'd assured her. *"It's impossible for the Nazis to get past it."*

Audrey sat on the hall bench and unfolded the paper. The British ocean liner *Athenia* had been torpedoed on its way to

Canada with 1,400 passengers on board. A civilian ocean liner! She lowered the newspaper to her lap. Envisioning the horror those people must have endured would fuel her fears. It was bad enough that she carried the nagging, aching fear for Alfie with her, day and night. Especially at night.

She refolded the paper and took it into her father's study. He stood in front of the window, staring out at the formal gardens. "Here's the London paper," she said. "The news isn't good, I'm afraid." He didn't turn or acknowledge her, so she laid it on his desk. "I heard airplanes flying over today—they were ours, thankfully. But it reminded me to speak with you about putting in an Anderson shelter. Shall I ask the gardener to choose a good spot for it, perhaps behind the house?"

"Waste of time. I won't use it."

"Perhaps for the servants' sakes, Father. It might give them peace of mind to know there's a safe shelter from the bombs." She waited. Should she tell him she wanted it for herself as much as for the servants?

"I won't have my gardens dug up for nothing. The servants can huddle in the wine cellar if it makes them feel better."

She let the matter drop and went to change her clothes to meet the train in the village.

It was warm for September, and Audrey arrived at the station weary and overheated, her feet blistered from the long walk. She wondered again about buying a bicycle. A large crowd gathered to meet the train, every woman in town, it seemed, young and old, waiting to house evacuated children. When the train finally steamed into the station, the ruckus was like nothing she'd ever heard before. The older children emerged from the cars shouting and brawling, the little ones wailing for their mothers. Hundreds of children poured from the train and milled around the platform like a nest of ants that had been disturbed. The village billeting officer waded into the melee, trying in vain to restore order, but the children were having none of it, thrilled to run free after the long ride from London. Audrey waited in the shade beneath the station's overhanging roof as the officials gradually herded the children into groups and sent them off to area cottages and farms. There seemed to be a great crowd of them left over. The officer turned to Audrey. "The rest are yours, Miss Clarkson. We've assigned thirty children to Wellingford Hall along with their teacher, Miss Bristol."

"Thirty! But . . . but we don't have enough beds! Or food! We're only prepared for half as many."

"Come now, Miss Clarkson. It's your patriotic duty for the war effort. Everyone in the village is boarding children, and you can see for yourself how small some of their cottages are. Wellingford Hall is enormous in comparison. It shouldn't be a hardship to find a few empty bedrooms." The man's disdain for Audrey's family was clear. She knew it was caused in great measure by Mother's obvious disdain for the villagers. She had long ignored her responsibilities as lady of the manor. Audrey tried to make up for that lack, but she was still a long way from being accepted, much less admired, by the local people.

She surveyed the swirling, simpering mob that was hers for the duration. *Thirty of them!* Nothing in her experience had equipped her for this task. She drew a breath, remembering how Eve had once taught her to be brave, remembering the scratchy tickle of dead beetles in her hand. "Very well. Would you please let Mr. Grayson know we're ready to leave? He agreed to drive us to Wellingford in his wagon."

The wagon wasn't large enough for thirty children, so the oldest ones followed behind with their teacher while Audrey rode on the seat beside the driver. The novelty of country life proved a huge distraction for the older boys, and rather than keeping up with the wagon, they climbed trees and scampered over fences, scaring a flock of sheep and stampeding the dozing cattle. Audrey had no idea how to restore order. She decided to leave the wandering ones to their teacher and attend to a crying toddler in the wagon behind her. Audrey pulled the girl onto her lap, making shushing noises to soothe her. "We're nearly there, little one. It's just a short ride, now. Goodness, you must be hungry." Would there be enough food to feed thirty children? And where would they all sleep?

The child on her lap continued to fuss in spite of Audrey's efforts, crying in a steady, high-pitched whine that scraped Audrey's nerves. She couldn't bring herself to use her own handkerchief to wipe the girl's running nose. She smelled as though she needed a bath and had grains of rice in her greasy hair. One of the grains hopped.

Head lice!

It required all of Audrey's willpower not to toss the girl off the wagon. She shivered with dread for the rest of the journey, her skin crawling as the girl perched awkwardly on her lap. "Drive around to the back of Wellingford Hall, please," she told Mr. Grayson. If only his horse would gallop down the lane instead of this slow, leisurely plodding.

Audrey scrambled down from the seat as soon as the wagon halted and set the infested child on the ground. The other children jumped down as well, hooting with delight as they scattered in all directions across the estate. Mrs. Smith and two chambermaids came out to welcome them, and they looked appalled as they viewed the invasion. Audrey hurried over to them. "We have to bathe these children and douse them for lice. We can't allow them inside until we do."

"There are so many!" Mrs. Smith said. "How will we manage?"

"This isn't even all of them. The rest are following on foot." Audrey fought to control the panic clogging her throat. It wasn't supposed to happen this way. She had imagined a few clean, orderly children boarding in her beautiful home, not this rabble. "Send one of the maids into the village for soap and . . . and for whatever else the chemist recommends. Their clothing will be contaminated, as well. And probably everything in their satchels."

"But the laundresses don't come until next week, Miss Audrey."

"Will you beg them to come sooner? I'll pay whatever they ask."

"What will the children wear in the meantime?"

Audrey didn't reply. She had no idea. Would it be horrid to billet the children in the carriage house? She felt selfish and spoiled to even entertain the idea, but she wanted all of these children to go away!

By now the stragglers had caught up to the wagon and were chasing each other through the vegetable patch. The gardener ran out of the shed, brandishing a rake and threatening to brain them with it. The boys laughed as they danced around him, treating it as a game. "Can't you control them?" Audrey asked their teacher.

Miss Bristol was still panting from the long walk and didn't reply. She was a stern-looking woman, probably in her fifties, with a thick waist, thick cotton stockings, and shoes like a pair of bricks. Her trek from the village had exhausted her, and it was clear that the children were beyond her control.

Suddenly Audrey's father emerged from the house with his hunting rifle. "Get off my property!" he bellowed. "Now!" He fired a shot into the air and the boys ran from the garden and crouched beneath the wagon to hide. The smallest children began to wail.

Audrey hurried over to him. "They're here by government order, Father. Housing them isn't voluntary."

"We'll see about that!" He stormed back into the house, muttering about calling his MP and maybe even Neville Chamberlain himself. Audrey imagined the boys running wild through Wellingford Hall the same way they'd run through the garden, and hoped her father succeeded in ringing up the prime minister. She resisted the urge to follow Father inside and bolt all the doors. She asked herself what Eve would do.

Eve would take control. She wouldn't let these children run wild. Audrey summoned all her courage and shouted, "Quiet! All of you!" She was amazed when they obeyed. "This is my home and you will either respect it and obey my rules or you'll get off my property!" She saw one of the bigger boys mocking her in pantomime but she ignored him. "Anyone who doesn't obey doesn't eat. Anyone who doesn't behave inside my home will sleep in the carriage house or out in the woods with the other animals. Do you understand?"

One of the girls raised her hand as if in school. "I'm hungry. When are we going to eat?"

"As soon as you settle down." Audrey turned to Mrs. Smith and the two maidservants. "Put together some sandwiches. We'll feed them out here and prepare their baths while they eat. I won't let them into my house in their current condition." Mr. Grayson had unloaded the baggage and was preparing to leave with the wagon. Audrey shouted for him to wait. "Go with him into the village," she told one of the maids. "Ask the chemist what we'll need to delouse thirty children." The girl scampered to board the wagon as if offered a reprieve.

With help from a very reluctant Robbins and a still-fuming George, Audrey managed to corral the children into small groups on a grassy stretch of lawn to eat their sandwiches. Afterwards, the servants separated the boys from the girls and gave them all baths, using every tub and basin in the manor house and gallons of hot water and soap. Then Audrey set the children and servants to work with the fine-tooth combs the chemist had recommended. "He said it was the only surefire way to treat lice and nits, ma'am," the maid had reported. Audrey lacked the stomach for dealing with vermin and took the teacher, Miss Bristol, aside to speak with her.

"I think it would be best if the children attended school in the village every morning. There are too many distractions out here, and they'll never be able to concentrate on their studies. Perhaps the walk into the village and back will help use up some of their energy."

"Is the school large enough to hold them all?"

Audrey knew that it wasn't, but she wouldn't change her mind. She wanted the children out of her house for at least part of the day. "I'll ask the vicar about using the church hall. We'll find room somewhere."

At bedtime, the small measure of order that Audrey had managed to create slipped into chaos. "Do you have any advice for me?" she asked Miss Bristol. "We don't have nearly enough beds."

"Many of these children are siblings. Divide them into families and make the older ones take care of the younger ones. That's what they do at home. I'm sure they share beds, too."

Her advice proved useful, and the children eventually settled down for the night with their siblings. Audrey assigned a servant to each room to prevent the children from escaping, then made her way down to the housekeeper's sitting room to thank her for all she had done. "We may not need more beds after all," she told an exhausted Mrs. Smith. "It seems many of them aren't used to sleeping in a bed and prefer to sleep on the floor. One of the girls told me that beds are for dead people. Imagine!"

"These children are the poorest of the poor. I would feel sorry for them if there weren't so many of them."

"Well, I can't thank you enough for all your help. Hopefully the days ahead will get better."

There was a knock on Mrs. Smith's door and Robbins poked his head inside. "Excuse me, Miss Audrey, but two ARP wardens would like to speak with you outside. They asked for Mr. Clarkson, but he doesn't wish to be disturbed."

The wardens were waiting on the front steps. Audrey recognized the tall, thin man with the stooped shoulders as one of the deacons from church. The plump woman beside him was his wife. "Good evening, Miss Clarkson," he said, removing his cap. "I'm sorry to say you have a bit of a problem. If you'll kindly step outside and close the door, you'll see what it is."

She resisted the urge to sigh and did what he'd asked, closing the front door and following him a few steps away from the house. The fall evening was cool and damp, and she wished she had a sweater. The clouds shielding the moon and stars threatened rain. *Rain!* She tried not to panic at the thought of thirty children cooped up inside her home on a rainy day.

"As you can see," the warden said, gesturing to the manor, "you have light leaking everywhere. It's imperative that the countryside remain in pitch-darkness so our enemies have no signposts to follow on their bombing raids."

Slivers of light spilled from behind windows on all three floors, including Father's study. He hadn't allowed anyone into his lair, and the light shone like a beacon in the featureless night. Beyond the manor, the countryside was pitch-black as far as Audrey could see, causing the leaking light to shine even brighter. "I'm very sorry, but we ran out of cloth." Was it only this morning that she'd stood on a ladder to pin it into place? "Wellingford has so many windows, you see, and—"

"You'll have to paint them. And you'll need to do it right away. Tomorrow, in fact."

The thought of splashing ugly black paint on Wellingford's beautiful mullioned windows pained Audrey. "Yes, I understand. But I'm not sure we can get to it tomorrow. We just received thirty evacuated children today—more than we'd planned for, you see— and it's been a bit chaotic as they've settled in. We'll do better with the blackout in the future, I promise." The warden looked so grim and serious that she fought the giddy urge to add, *Cross my heart and hope to die.*

"We've taken in children as well," the female warden said with a lift of her chin. "And we don't have servants helping us, do we?"

"Of course. I'm sorry." Audrey couldn't have said why she was sorry, but she felt the need to apologize.

"It's going to be a different sort of war, Miss Clarkson," the husband added. "We're all in the fight this time, not just the soldiers. Women and children too. Like it or not, everyone must do his bit for the duration because we have to win. Otherwise . . . well, it's unthinkable to have Nazis goose-stepping through our village and taking all our food like they're doing in Poland."

She thought of Alfie again, enduring the untold horrors of war, and her stomach did a slow turn. "Yes, of course. I do understand. Thank you."

"I'm afraid I'll have to fine you for failing to comply," he said, handing her a piece of paper. "And there will be another fine tomorrow night if you don't get it done. Good evening, Miss Clarkson."

She watched the wardens head back to the village, shuffling

slowly, heads lowered as they plodded home in the utter darkness. She remembered yelling at the children today and demanding that they obey and knew she would have to become much tougher and braver if she was going to survive the days to come. No matter what, Audrey would make sure Wellingford Hall still stood in all its glory when she welcomed Alfie home from the war.

9

"Kindly wait for me," Audrey told the taxi driver. "I won't be long." Clouds filled the late-afternoon sky, mirroring her mood as she hurried up the crumbling steps to Eve's boardinghouse. She searched for a doorbell and, not seeing one, pounded on the front door. Nothing happened. What if Eve didn't live here anymore? More than four years had passed since Audrey had come here with Eve after King George's funeral. *Please, please,* she silently begged. She regretted not staying in touch with her. In spite of their many differences, she still considered Eve her closest friend, the only person who truly knew her without the facade Audrey was required to keep in place.

Voices drifted from inside. She pounded on the door again. The girl who finally opened it looked annoyed. "You don't have to knock, you know. Just come in." The tinny sound of a news broadcast echoed in the front room. The girl seemed eager to hurry back to it. "Who are you looking for?" she asked over her shoulder.

"Eve Dawson."

"In here." She pointed to the crowded parlor, where girls huddled around the wireless, filling the chairs, the sofa, and every inch of floor space. "Eve, someone's here for you."

Eve looked up from the middle of the group and the color drained from her face. "Audrey! What's wrong? Is it Alfie?" She sprang up and picked her way through the seated girls as gracefully as she'd once hopped from stone to stone to cross the creek. "Have you heard from Alfie?"

"He's fine as far as I know," she said when Eve reached the parlor doorway. "He was in Belgium with the BEF the last we heard, but now that they're in retreat, we have no idea what's become of him."

"I haven't heard, either. He hardly ever writes. And even when he does, he can't say where he is."

"Listen, I spoke with my uncle who's in the House of Lords—"

"Shh!" one of the girls hissed. Audrey drew Eve into the foyer, peering outside to make sure the taxi was still waiting. It was. She needed to hurry while there was still enough light to drive.

"Have you heard what's happening in France?" Audrey asked.

"Of course! It's horrible, isn't it? The Nazis are crushing Europe. We're the only ones left."

"I don't have time to go into all the details, but could you please, please drive me down to the coast in our car? The taxi won't take me that far. Please, Eve. I'm desperate to help Alfie and the other soldiers, and you know how to drive."

"Is this for the rescue operation they're talking about?"

Audrey lowered her voice so the other girls wouldn't overhear. "The public doesn't know how dire the situation is, but my uncle says our troops are pinned down on the French coastline with their backs to the channel."

"I can't drive you all the way to France, Audrey." Her grin was typically Eve. "I may not have finished school, but I do know my geography."

"Just take me down to the coast. Father keeps a boat there. They're asking for every available ship to help evacuate our soldiers—fishing boats, ferries, even pleasure craft like ours."

Eve nodded as she seemed to grasp the situation. "Alfie took me out on your boat a few times. Let me grab my coat and my purse." She bolted up the stairs and returned moments later, shoving her arms into her jacket sleeves. Audrey's fear eased slightly. She had an ally to help rescue Alfie. For the first time, she was grateful for Eve's relationship with her brother—whatever it was. They hurried outside and climbed into the taxi. "Where are we going?" Eve asked.

"Back to the town house to get the car." Audrey willed herself to remain calm. They would have a long drive ahead of them to get to the sea. "There's so little real news in the paper or on the BBC that I've been going mad with worry up at Wellingford. My uncle says the Nazis have driven our army and most of France's army to the coast. The men are surrounded and pinned down on the beach and will be taken prisoner or killed unless we bring them home. When I heard about the evacuation, I immediately thought of our boat. The Navy can use it if I can get down there and turn it over to them. But Father is away, making sure his factories and railroads are running at full steam, so it's up to me. I need your help, Eve."

"They were asking for boats on the radio right before you came."

The taxi arrived at the town house, and Audrey told the driver to take them around to the garages in back. Alfie's car and the one Williams drove were parked side by side in the former stables. "Can you believe it?" Audrey asked. "Two perfectly good cars sitting here and none of our servants know how to drive them. That's why I thought of you. I used to watch from my bedroom window when Williams gave you driving lessons." She glanced at Eve and saw a ghost of a smile. "Don't say it, Eve."

She laughed, the same warm, bubbling laugh as on the first day they'd met in the woods. "Don't say what?"

"That Williams would have taught me, too, if I wasn't such a coward."

"I wasn't thinking that at all. I was thinking you had no reason to drive because Williams took you everywhere. Have you heard from him, by the way? Mum told me he joined the Auxiliary Fire Service."

"No, I haven't." She fought the urge to apologize for not knowing more about her former driver, for seeming not to care. "Which car do you want to take?"

"Not Alfie's. He'll murder us. Besides, I have more experience driving Williams's car." Eve opened the door and slipped behind the wheel, taking a moment to settle in, running her hands around the steering wheel, adjusting the mirrors. She started the engine, released the brake, and rolled out of the garage. Audrey closed the garage door behind them and jumped in. "Do you know how to get down there?" Eve asked as she pulled into the London traffic.

"I think so. We should have enough petrol coupons since no one has used our cars since Alfie left. The boat is docked in Folkestone, and hopefully the Navy will have people there. I'm sorry, but we may need to spend the night in Folkestone. Unless the sky clears and there's a moon, we won't be able to drive home in the blackout." Nervous energy and fear fueled Audrey's babbling. Eve seemed calm, as usual, concentrating on the road and the busy traffic. Silvery barrage balloons hovered in the sky above them, swaying from their tethers as Audrey directed Eve southeast through London.

"I never drove this car in the city before," Eve said, dodging around a red bus. "Just so you know."

"I trust you." Rain began falling as they reached the city's outskirts. "Oh no," Audrey moaned. "Rain will slow us down even more." The whir and swish of the wipers grated on her nerves as if whispering, *Hurry, hurry, hurry, hurry!* According to her uncle, Great Britain would be forced to surrender if the Army wasn't rescued.

Eve leaned forward in her seat as if trying to get a better view of the road through the steady rain. "Alfie used to speed down to the sea in less than two hours," she said. "He drove so fast he scared me half to death! It's no wonder nothing looks familiar to me—the countryside used to go by in a blur."

"Thank you for agreeing to drive me. You—" Audrey started to say she considered Eve a good friend, someone she could always count on, but the words died on her tongue with the realization that she hadn't been a very loyal friend to Eve. She probably wasn't doing this for friendship's sake. "You must care a lot for Alfie to just drop everything and do this for him," Audrey said instead.

"I'm in love with him." Eve said the words so softly that Audrey barely heard them above the roar of the motor and the noisy wipers. "I would gladly spend the rest of my life with him if he would ask, but I don't think he ever will. I know he sees other girls besides me."

"I'm sorry for not being more helpful. I honestly can't think of a better wife for him than you." Eve gave her a questioning look before turning back to the road. "I mean it, Eve. My brother deserves the best, and you have so much more character and . . . and vitality than the other girls he knows. And certainly more courage. But to be perfectly honest, he would have to defy both of our parents in order to marry you. Mind you, Alfie always does what he pleases. And he gets away with a lot, knowing he's the heir. But he will likely cave in to their pressure in the end. I don't want to see you get hurt."

"It's too late for that. I already love him. Whatever happens now, when it finally does happen, it's going to hurt." She pulled a handkerchief from her coat pocket, and Audrey thought she was going to use it to wipe away tears. Instead, she cleared moisture from the inside of the windscreen.

"Let me do that," Audrey said, taking the handkerchief from her. "Listen, I hate to sound trite, but surely there must have been a queue of other men interested in you before they all went off to war. You're so beautiful, Eve." It was true. Eve had an unspoiled beauty that didn't require cosmetics and hair waves, a girlish innocence enhanced by her wild sandy hair, clear gray eyes, and endearing freckles.

"Well, your charming brother has ruined all other men for me," Eve said. "I'll hold out for him as long as there's hope, even though I know he'll probably never marry me. I never finished school, my mum is a maidservant, and I work as a typist with a dozen other girls who are going nowhere." She released a sigh, then said, "What about you, Audrey? Is there a man in your life?"

"Hardly. The courtship process in my world is so artificial that it's impossible to fall madly in love. And that's what I want to do— fall madly in love with a man who loves me and not my father's money. It's very hard to distinguish the difference, I'm afraid, since the men I know have been trained to go through all the proper motions and say all the right things. Alfie flouts the rules, and I hope he finds true love someday, but his peers are afraid to stray from the narrow field of women their parents have chosen for them." And in the end, Audrey would dutifully marry the man her mother chose for her.

"Mind if I open my window a bit?" Eve asked, turning the crank. "It's getting muggy in here."

"No, go ahead. The air might keep the windows from fogging." Audrey had been wiping steadily for several minutes with Eve's soggy handkerchief.

"So what's going on at Wellingford Hall these days?" Eve asked. "The last I heard you were housing evacuated children from London."

"We did house them. Thirty, at one point. The village was thick with them, too. But all of ours are gone, now." *Thankfully,* she wanted to add. "And most of the ones in the village, too."

"What happened to them?"

"The war didn't seem to be going anywhere, so they all drifted home. Within four months, we were down to only eight children. Some of them got homesick—they said it was too quiet in the country. Some were called home because their mums missed them. But a lot of them went home because their parents were required to pay six shillings a week for their board, and why waste all that money when the bombs weren't falling as everyone feared?"

"Well, we're in for it now. We're the only ones left to fend off the Nazis."

"Which we can't do without an army. We have to rescue every man we can." Again, Audrey forced back her panic, willing herself to be calm. Fear twisted her stomach into so many knots these days that she could barely eat. She drew a steadying breath, releasing it slowly. "Sorry, but I never asked how you've been, Eve. You mentioned working as a typist?"

"Right . . . but I'll probably be sacked when I don't show up for work tomorrow."

"Oh, Eve! I'm so sorry! I never should have presumed you could get away on such short notice."

"It doesn't matter. To tell you the truth, I hate my job. It's dead boring. All I do is type memos and invoices all day. I hate being cooped up inside all day. At least as a scullery maid I could nip outside once in a while and wander George's gardens—Wellingford's gardens, I should say."

Audrey sympathized but knew her murmurs of pity would sound false. She hated city life too and longed to return to the peace and quiet of Wellingford Hall. But at least she *could* return.

The road grew darker and murkier as night approached, the lowering clouds thicker near the coast. The reality of war struck Audrey as they passed spiky strings of barbed wire and piles of sandbags blocking off side roads and farmers' fields. Guards stopped them at three different checkpoints to search their car. By the time they reached Folkestone, where the boat was moored, the car had slowed to a crawl, the road barely visible. Twice, they stopped to ask directions to the marina. Audrey recognized it once they arrived, and exhaled in relief, glad to have accomplished her mission. "We'll hand over the boat and be done."

Eve parked and cut the engine. She leaned back in her seat, rolling her head as if to relieve the tension in her neck and shoulders. The air was cool and thick with moisture as they got out of the car. Audrey tasted salt on her lips.

"I recognize this place now," Eve said. "Looks like a lot of activity down there by the water's edge." They walked toward the dark shapes milling near the dock, and Audrey was relieved to see men in Royal Navy uniforms. The officer issuing orders looked weary and disheveled, as if he hadn't slept or shaved or changed his clothes in days.

"Excuse me, I'm Miss Clarkson and this is Miss Dawson. We

heard the appeal for ships and came down from London to offer my family's boat. It's berthed in this marina and is large enough to ferry quite a few men."

"Thank you, Miss Clarkson. We're just now putting a flotilla together. I trust you can sail it as far as Dover for us?"

"Well . . . no . . . I—I—"

"We're very short on captains, you see."

Audrey couldn't reply. Someone from the Navy was supposed to take it from here. Her fear surged like the waves that were crashing against the pier at the prospect of sailing it herself.

"Of course we'll sail it," Eve said, stepping forward. "Tell us what to do."

"If you could bring it alongside these other boats, you can join the flotilla. It's only a dozen miles to Dover from here. Shouldn't take long. We'll wait for you, if you wish."

"Yes, thank you," Eve said. "We'll fetch the boat and be back straightaway." She linked arms with Audrey before she could protest and pulled her toward the slip where the boat lay moored alongside several dozen others. "You know how to sail it, don't you?" Eve asked as they stumbled along. "Alfie said he taught you how."

"I don't think I can—"

"You have to try, Audrey. This was your idea, remember? We have to rescue Alfie and his mates. They're stranded over there."

"I—I can't." She had been dragging her steps the entire time, but when she halted in place, Eve grabbed her shoulders and gave her a little shake.

"Don't be such a coward, Audrey! You told me yourself how desperate the situation is. This is more than just saving your brother's neck. Who's going to guard England and your precious Wellingford Hall if all our men are captured and killed by the Nazis? We're the only free nation left and we'll be next!"

"I know, I know, but I don't have your courage."

"Then tell me how to start the ruddy boat and I'll do it myself."

"Eve, you can't!"

"Watch me." She marched forward and stepped onto the float-ing dock, peering in the darkness at the gently rocking boats, mere silhouettes in the gloom. Audrey hesitated, then followed, less sure of her steps. "This is it, isn't it?" Eve called. "The *Rosamunde*?"

"Yes." Audrey tried to remember a time when her mother had sailed on the boat named for her, a time when the four of them had sailed together as a family—and couldn't. Eve had already leaped across the gap from the pier to the deck by the time Audrey got there. Eve held out her hand. "Come on, jump. I'll catch you."

Alfie had always helped Audrey on board, and the memory of her brother's tanned, smiling face impelled her forward. She crossed the rolling deck to the wheelhouse and sank down in the captain's chair behind the windscreen. The boat seemed bigger than Audrey remembered. Alfie had taught her the steps to take in order to start the engine and navigate it out of the slip, and she struggled to remember what they were.

She felt victorious when the engine sputtered and rumbled to life with a belch of oily smoke. Eve cheered. She seemed to know how to unfasten the ropes from the bollards and push away from the dock. Audrey felt the boat drift free. She peered out at the black sky and dark water, indistinguishable in the gloom, and gasped. "Oh, my! I can't see a thing!"

"I'll look for a torch." Eve ducked belowdecks and Audrey heard her rummaging around in the dark. She emerged topside again, carrying a battery-operated light.

"I know there's a blackout," she said, crawling forward onto the bow, "but I think this qualifies as an emergency."

"Shout if you see something before I do," Audrey called to

her. With the dim torchlight shining down into the water ahead of her, Audrey was able to inch the boat forward and reach the pier where the officer and the other boats waited for them, dark shapes outlined against the churning water. She and Eve were the only women.

"Good show, ladies," the officer said as Audrey cut the engine to neutral. "I'll put you in the middle of the flotilla, shall I? There will be someone ahead of you and behind you all the way to Dover. Just keep one of the other ships in sight and you shouldn't go wrong."

A dozen other engines sputtered to life and they began moving away from shore into the channel. Audrey shivered from raw nerves and the cold wind. Neither she nor Eve was dressed warmly enough, but then she'd never imagined she would captain the boat herself. Eve went below again and returned with two blankets, wrapping one around Audrey before wrapping the other around herself. "What else do you need me to do?" she asked.

"Sit beside me and help me stay close to the others," Audrey said through chattering teeth. Her fingers felt numb from gripping the wheel with bare hands. She'd hoped they would hug the shoreline all the way to Dover, but the flotilla picked up speed and headed away from land toward the open sea. The bow reared up and down as the boat plowed against the thudding three-foot waves, and Audrey had to resist the urge to slow down, to turn back. She longed to close her eyes and wake up in her bed in Wellingford Hall, where there would be no war, and Alfie would be asleep in his room down the hall. Instead, she was living a nightmare.

"You're doing great, Audrey," Eve said, a dark shadow beside her. Audrey nodded and gripped the wheel tighter.

She could do this. She had to.

Eve kept her gaze fixed on the boat ahead of them, a dim, bobbing shape in the darkness that retreated from sight as the front of Audrey's boat heaved up and down in the waves. They were out in open water now, far from shore, and Eve was terrified. She never should have forced Audrey to do this. Eve clung to her seat for dear life, fighting the urge to vomit over the side, silently reciting every Bible verse she could remember from her Sunday school lessons in the village. *"The Lord is my shepherd . . ."*

"How will we get back to our car from Dover?" Audrey asked, interrupting her thoughts. If Eve was terrified, Audrey must be half-dead with fright. Was she even strong enough to handle this big, powerful boat? Eve hadn't considered that when she'd pressured Audrey to sail it. She'd thought only of Alfie and hadn't wanted to give up the idea of rescuing him after motoring all the way down from London in the rain.

"I guess we'll have to wait until morning and try to hitch a ride back," Eve shouted as the wind and the engine's roar snatched her words. "We can walk if we have to."

"I'm getting quite good at walking," Audrey said. Eve leaned closer to hear her above the drone of the engine and the pounding waves. "You'd never believe it, but I walk from Wellingford into the village and back at least once a day, sometimes twice."

"Well, if you can drive this boat, you can drive a car, you know. I'll teach you on the way back to London."

Audrey offered a weak smile before fixing her gaze straight ahead once more. Her face was as pale as death, her knuckles white as she gripped the wheel. Eve needed to keep her talking so she wouldn't faint. Hours had passed since they'd left London and they were both growing tired. Neither of them had eaten anything. "By the way, 'Good show, Miss Clarkson,'" she said, imitating the naval officer's accent.

"Thanks. My brother loves this boat. He'll never forgive me if I sink it."

"You won't. You're doing great. I knew you could do it." The boat jolted as they hit a large wave, dashing salty spray into the wheelhouse. "Tell me about Alfie," Eve said to distract both of them. "What have you heard from him? I write to him all the time but he rarely writes back."

"He's terrible at writing letters. I don't hear much from him, either. And when I do, he just whines about all the things he misses from home and how cold and miserable he is on the Continent. Though he does mention the good French wine."

"Alfie loves a good time," Eve said, then wished she hadn't, remembering Lady Rosamunde staggering home, drunk. Eve had seen Alfie in the same condition many times. Would there ever be good times again? The Nazis had goose-stepped across Europe at the speed of lightning, with no army able to stop them, including Great Britain's.

"Where does your courage come from, Eve?" Audrey suddenly asked.

"Me?" She gave a nervous laugh, grateful that Audrey couldn't read her mind. "I'm not courageous. I'm merely thickheaded. I just blunder ahead and do what needs to be done without thinking about it. Your problem is that you're much smarter than me, Audrey. You overthink everything, imagining what might happen and worrying about all the things that could go wrong. You can't help being brilliant any more than I can help being dense."

"You aren't dense. You're every bit as smart as me. You've just lacked the advantages and opportunities I've had. Remember my governess, Miss Blake? She used to marvel at how quick you were to learn and how curious you always were. I consider us equals."

"In spite of our class differences? Isn't the system based on the notion that blue bloods are better in every way than the servant class? We've been told it's useless to try to better ourselves because it's impossible to change what we are."

"Many people might feel that way, but I don't. Miss Blake said the first war knocked holes in the class system because aristocrats and workingmen had to fight and die side by side for the same cause. I have a feeling this war is going to destroy the system altogether."

Eve smiled into the darkness. "I hope you're right. Then there might be hope for Alfie and me." She took her gaze off the shadowy boat in front of them for a moment and looked into the distance, wondering how much time had passed since they'd left shore—three-quarters of an hour, maybe? Lightning flickered on the far horizon, followed by the faint rumble of thunder. That was all they needed, for it to start raining again. She was already wet and half-frozen. Then she realized what the faint bursts of light really were. *The war.* They were that close to it. She pulled her blanket around her, feeling small and vulnerable, hoping Audrey didn't glance at the horizon.

The boat they followed appeared to be changing direction, arcing slightly to the left. "I think we might be heading inland again, Audrey. Maybe we're almost there."

"I hope you're right."

"You deserve a long, hot soak in the tub after this. Your teeth are chattering."

"So are yours. And you're right—we are turning back toward land. I wonder how we'll ever see the shore in the blackout."

"We'll just have to trust the man who's leading us." For some reason, Eve thought of Granny Maud's stories about the Good Shepherd. *A shepherd always leads his sheep; he doesn't drive them. If they follow him, they'll make it safely home. But if they go their own way, they're sure to get lost.* Eve closed her eyes and prayed for Alfie. And for Audrey. If only all three of them could make it safely home.

Then, like a miracle, the clouds thinned from thick wool to filmy gauze. The gauze parted to reveal a glorious half-moon shining down. Moonlight gilded the churning waves and revealed the dark outline of the shore in the distance. "We're going to make it, Audrey! It won't be long now." The scuttling clouds tried to erase the moon, but it shone through long enough to bring the flotilla into the port of Dover.

"We're the volunteers from Folkestone," one of the captains called to the Royal Navy officer onshore. "We have some ladies piloting that vessel, over there. Let's get them tied up first."

"Bring it right up here," the officer called back. They were landing beside a wall, not a dock, with dozens of other boats only a few yards away. Eve stood, letting her blanket fall, and moved onto the deck.

"I don't remember where reverse is," Audrey moaned. Sailors stood above them on the wall, ready to grab the ropes. The engine sputtered, then died as Audrey struggled with the controls.

"Don't worry about it," Eve told her. "I'll throw them a rope." It took three tries, but Eve finally managed to toss it high enough for the men to catch. She felt like cheering when the boat gently bumped against the floats cushioning the wall.

"We made it!" Audrey sighed as if she'd been holding her breath the entire way. She slumped forward, resting her arms and head against the wheel. The deck rocked as two young sailors jumped down to help tie the boat fast. The other ships from the flotilla pulled in close all around them.

"Need a hand up, miss?" one of the men asked Eve.

"Let my friend go first," she said. "But I think she needs a minute."

"I'm all right," Audrey said, raising her head. But it took her two tries to stand on the swaying deck. Sailors helped them climb the iron ladder to the top of the wall. Eve's knees threatened to buckle as she stepped onto dry land. She linked arms with Audrey so they could steady each other.

"We must look like a pair of drunks," Eve whispered.

"What's going on with our navy that they have to send women to war?" she heard one of the seamen say. He was an older man in patched clothing, tanned and grizzled as if he'd spent his entire lifetime at sea.

"They didn't send us," Audrey told him, her voice surprisingly strong. "We volunteered. We couldn't leave the men we love stranded across the channel when we happened to have a boat."

"You must have a shilling or two to own a pleasure craft like that one," the man replied.

"Yes. I suppose I do."

Eve's eyes slowly adjusted to the darkness onshore, and she realized that the shadowy figures she saw jamming the lanes and alleyways around the docks were soldiers in round tin helmets, loaded down with gear. Hundreds of men. Most sat on the ground, leaning against walls and barrels and anything else they could find. Some wore bulky, square life vests. Some smoked cigarettes, shielding the glowing tips with their helmets. Many were asleep.

"Are these our men?" Eve asked.

"The last of them for today," the seaman replied. "Just got here before dark. They're waiting for the train."

LYNN AUSTIN · 147

"We need to find Alfie," Audrey said.

"I had the same thought. But right now, we need to sit down and get warm." Audrey was trembling from head to toe and likely couldn't walk a single step without Eve holding her up. She had concentrated on her task for more than an hour, half-frozen and rigid with fear.

"You ladies come into my shack and warm up," the old seaman said. He gestured to a square black shape a short distance away. "Have a cup of tea. Might even find you a sandwich or two."

"I need to find my brother."

"Those soldiers aren't going anywhere. Come in and have a seat." He led the way inside, then turned up the wick on his lantern once the door was shut. The shack's only window had been painted black. Eve blinked in the dim light and looked around before sinking down on a low wooden bench beside Audrey. Fishing nets and wooden floats and various other equipment that Eve didn't recognize filled the tiny space. It smelled strongly of fish, and with her stomach still queasy from the boat ride, she politely refused the sandwich the man offered. But it was warm inside the shack, out of the wind and salt air. A kettle of tea simmered on a hot plate. The man poured them each a cup. It was very strong and very hot—and easily the most delicious cup of tea Eve had ever tasted.

"That ought to revive you," he said, pouring a cup for himself. "You girls deserve a medal or something. It's hard enough to navigate in the dark, let alone with waves like those out there. Anything could've happened."

"We'll suffer a much worse fate," Eve said, "if England has to surrender and the Nazis take over."

"You're right about that, miss."

She looked at Audrey, still shivering as she sipped her tea, both hands clenched around the chipped cup. Her wonderful, timid, fainthearted friend was afraid of black beetles and sometimes her own shadow. But tonight, Audrey had shown courage in spite of her fear. And Eve had never loved her more.

10

"Thank you for the tea," Audrey said when they'd finished a second cup inside the seaman's shanty. "Is there someplace nearby where we can stay for the night? Our car is in Folkestone, you see." She stopped short of adding that both she and Eve could use a long soak in a hot bathtub, if possible.

The old man frowned and raked his fingers through his bristly hair. "I don't think you'll find anything around here. If it hasn't been boarded up and sandbagged, it's being used by the military."

Tears filled Audrey's eyes before she could stop them. *"Oh, for pity's sake,"* her mother's voice whispered.

"There now, miss . . . Don't cry . . . ," the old man said. She was ashamed that he'd noticed her tears, but his voice softened as he added, "You might try the stone church down the street. They've been working hard, bringing tea and sandwiches to the soldiers. Might find a quiet corner in there where you could sleep."

Audrey pulled Eve's damp handkerchief from her pocket and blew her nose. "Thank you so much. That's what we'll do, then. Which street is it on?"

"Dunton. But it won't do you any good to know that. All the

signs are down so the Nazis can't find their way. Turn left outside the door, cross the next road, and keep going. Dunton twists and turns a bit, but you'll soon see the church."

"Thank you so much." The tea had steadied Audrey's nerves and she was able to stand and walk outside without Eve's help. The train hadn't arrived for the soldiers yet, and men filled the streets and alleyways like a lumpy, olive-drab carpet. "I want to look for Alfie. Would you mind terribly?"

"I was just thinking the same thing," Eve said. They slowly felt their way across the street to where the closest group of men lay huddled.

Audrey couldn't imagine her brother sleeping on the hard ground and hoped that officers like him were billeted someplace with real beds. She wouldn't mind sacrificing a room for the night if Alfie needed it. As near as she could tell, most of the men were asleep, but one of them opened his eyes as she and Eve approached and nudged his mate.

"Look, Clyde. We must have died and gone to heaven because here's two angels coming for us."

"Don't be daft. Angels got wings and they don't."

"We're looking for my brother, Lieutenant Alfred Clarkson," Audrey said. "Do either of you know him? Have you seen him?"

"Never heard of him," the one named Clyde replied. "But you're not going to go walking through here and waking everybody up to ask about him, are you?"

"Well, I'd hoped—"

"Don't do it, lady. Most of us ain't slept in three days. This is the first we've closed our eyes without worrying about Nazi planes screaming down from the sky. And us with no place to hide."

"You have no idea what we been through," the other soldier added.

"We're very sorry," Eve said before Audrey could reply. "We'll come back tomorrow. I'm glad you made it home." She tugged Audrey's arm, pulling her away. "Come on. Even in daylight it would be like finding a needle in a haystack."

They walked close to the wall of houses and shops on one side of the street, feeling their way in the unfamiliar town, stumbling over cobblestones and sandbags. The half-moon still fought to shine through the clouds, and Audrey spotted the church steeple silhouetted against the sky. Once inside, they followed the sound of voices to a makeshift kitchen behind the sanctuary, where three women chatted as they washed dishes and swept the floor. The one with the broom spotted Audrey and Eve.

"Well, hello, there. Do you need something?"

Eve quickly explained their errand, the long drive down from London, the frightening boat trip in the dark. "And now we're wondering if we could sleep on one of your pews for a few hours before walking back to Folkestone tomorrow."

"You can come home with me, duckie, if you don't mind sleeping two-to-a-bed."

Audrey was uncertain about going home with a stranger, but Eve wasn't.

"That would be lovely," she said. "Thank you."

Audrey yanked her arm. "But—"

"They must be good people to be up at this hour, helping our soldiers," Eve whispered. "Isn't there something in the Bible about offering kindness to strangers?"

"I suppose. . . ." Audrey didn't know enough about the Bible to say for certain.

"We heard your church is offering tea to our soldiers and we would like to do our bit," Eve added. "Could you use some extra help in the morning?"

"We could use all the help we can get," the woman at the sink said. "There's thousands of our boys needing it."

"My name is Margery," the woman with the broom said. "Give me another minute to finish up and I'll take you home. It isn't far."

Audrey clung to Margery's apron strings with one hand and to Eve with the other as they made their way to Margery's cottage in the dark. Audrey hoped they wouldn't take a wrong step and fall in the harbor as they skirted past it. Margery's little cottage was clean but very primitive, and Audrey decided not to ask for soap and a towel after seeing how very little the woman had. Margery herself looked exhausted as she led them up the steep wooden stairs to an attic room. It had only enough space for a narrow bed and a chair, but Audrey was grateful for it. "It's my son Ralphie's room," Margery said, setting the candleholder on a windowsill. "He's one of the boys they're trying to bring home from France."

"We'll pray that he makes it," Eve said.

"Thank you so much for taking us in, Margery," Audrey said. "Will you wake us, please, so we can help you in the morning?"

"It'll be before dawn," Margery said. "We fix jam toast and tea to give out as soon as the boats arrive."

Eve stripped to her underwear and snuffed out the candle, falling asleep almost instantly. Audrey stayed in her clothes, lying awake for a long time as the harrowing boat trip played over in her mind. Her stomach felt as tightly clenched as a fist. The lumpy bed sagged in the center, and whatever they'd used to stuff the mattress made her skin itch. Or maybe it was the rough cotton sheet. Eve was accustomed to sleeping this way, and so were the London children who had stayed at Wellingford. They'd been content to sleep two and three to a bed or even on the floor. Audrey knew she was spoiled. If this war toppled the barriers between the classes as Miss Blake predicted, would Eve be raised to her level, or would she be reduced to Eve's? Audrey doubted if anyone would be content to meet in the middle.

Audrey's head ached when she awoke the next morning. Margery fed them weak tea and thick porridge before leading the way back to the church. Airplanes droned overhead in the dawn light, dozens of RAF planes flying south toward the Continent. The train must have come for the soldiers during the night because they were gone, the streets emptied. They neared the seaman's shack and the wall where Audrey had tied up her boat last night.

"We'll catch up with you at the church," she told Margery; then she walked with Eve to the water's edge. The flotilla was preparing to leave with all sorts of ships, from ferries and tugboats to paddle steamers and fireboats. Audrey spotted hers in the middle. She recognized the harried naval officer from last night walking toward her and wondered if he'd slept at all.

"Good morning, miss," he said, tipping his hat. "I didn't have a chance to warn you last night, but you should know it's possible your boat may be damaged before we're through. I'm sorry, but the channel is mined, and the Luftwaffe will attack our ships from the air. Mind you, the RAF will give them a run for their money, but enemy planes still hit some of their targets."

"I would hate to lose our boat," Audrey replied, "but there will be little need for it if we're forced to surrender."

"You're right about that."

Audrey felt useless at the church when it came to slicing bread and brewing gallons of tea, so she helped spread jam on the toast. They left for the dock just as the first ships neared the shore. Audrey stared in amazement at the sight. Soldiers in round tin hats and bulky life vests filled every inch of deck space on the vessels. A vast forest of men in olive drab, thousands and thousands of them, moved from ship to shore in long, silent lines like colonies of ants. Their faces had the weary, haggard look of beaten men. "Where do we even begin?" Audrey breathed.

"The most important thing," Margery told her, "is for the men to see your pretty faces and smiles. They've been to hell and back, shelled while on land and attacked from the air. Your job is to welcome them home."

Audrey waded into the stream of weary men, smiling as she passed out jam toast from her basket, searching the sea of unshaven, dirt-smudged faces for Alfie's. Eve stayed beside her, pouring tea from a large kettle into the soldiers' mess cups. "How will we ever find Alfie?" she asked Eve. "He won't stand out among so many!"

"No, but we'll stand out. He'll see us, Audrey. If he's here, he'll recognize us."

The soldiers' dazed expressions all looked the same, numbed by shock and fear. And shame. Armies were supposed to fight, not retreat. *It isn't your fault,* Audrey wanted to tell them. No one ever dreamed the Nazis would be so powerful. Or that the combined armies of Europe would be unable to stop them.

"Welcome home," she repeated again and again to hundreds of murmured thanks.

"Is that blood on your face?" Eve asked a soldier as he reached for a piece of toast. "Do you need medical attention?"

He absently wiped his cheek. "The blood isn't mine. It's my mate's. They bombed the beach and we had no place to hide. Men were blown to bits all around me. Guess I'm one of the lucky ones."

"Ever hear the screaming sound the Nazi dive-bombers make?" the young man beside him asked.

"No, I—I . . ."

"It sounds like a siren coming down out of the sky. They dove straight at us with their load of bombs. I kept thinking, *This is it. I'm done for now.*"

"Right, and just when we're thanking God for not being hit, back they'd come to have another go at us."

Audrey didn't hurry the men along, letting them talk, unloading their horror. Some of the men were shell-shocked, staring straight ahead as they walked past the refreshments, trembling like palsied men. Some needed help to hold the cup of tea and lift it to their lips.

"Where are you from?" Audrey asked to put them at ease. They named places she'd never heard of.

"I felt like a sitting duck," she heard a soldier telling Eve. She was much better at getting them to talk. "Our destroyers couldn't get close to shore, so they used smaller ships to ferry us out to them." That was probably what Audrey's boat would be used for. Many of these working-class men would be boarding a boat like hers for the first time.

"They had this long pier-like thing that stretched out into the water," another soldier said, "and we all lined up, waiting for a ship to pull alongside it so we could board. I was next in line when they told me no more room. I watched the ship move away, carrying my mates and leaving me behind. . . . Then, out of nowhere— boom! A Nazi plane got through and bombed the ship. I stood there watching it burn and sink, smoke boiling up, men jumping off into the water." His voice broke and he started to weep. "It might have been me!"

Eve shoved her kettle into Audrey's hands and pulled the soldier into her arms to let him cry. It was such a natural thing for her to do, so like Eve—and so foreign to Audrey. It wasn't that she felt no compassion for the man—his story brought tears to her eyes. But she'd never experienced warmth or consolation for her own tears and had no idea how to offer it to a stranger. Eve had once comforted her with a handful of strawberries.

The soldier thanked Eve and wiped his smudged face. He moved on. Audrey pasted on a smile and served the next soldier and the next as airplanes droned overhead and the sounds of battle rumbled in the distance.

Eve had looked into the faces of thousands of men, served hundreds of cups of tea, but hadn't seen the face she was searching for. Late that afternoon, she and Audrey became separated, so after emptying the last drop from her kettle, Eve went to find her. Audrey wasn't cut out for this work, physically or emotionally. She had a tender, sensitive heart, which she guarded behind an icy wall. But when Eve finally found Audrey, she was speaking to a group of French soldiers in their language. "We're rescuing their soldiers, too," she told Eve. "Isn't it wonderful?"

"Yes, and I'm glad to see your fancy education is finally being put to good use." Eve was relieved when Audrey laughed.

"I never imagined that speaking French would prove useful."

"My kettle is empty again. Let's go back to the church."

"I've looked everywhere for Alfie," Audrey said as they walked, "but I haven't seen him."

"Neither have I. But I have to believe that he's here somewhere."

"Let's stop by the dock where we left the boat," Audrey said. "I want to see if it's back." They pushed through the crowd of soldiers lining the shore and found the old seaman from last night standing outside his shack. There was no sign of the *Rosamunde*—or of any other boats, for that matter.

"Heard you ladies might be looking for a ride back to

Folkestone," the man said as they approached. "There's a fellow here who can take you in his lorry."

"We can't leave yet," Audrey said. "We need to stay and help."

The man rested a thick hand on each of their shoulders. "Go on home now, girls. I'll make sure your boat gets put back where it belongs."

Eve knew they had done enough. Audrey looked exhausted and there was little hope of finding Alfie among thousands of soldiers. "He's right, you know," Eve said. "We'd better go while we have the chance. And if we leave now, we might be able to get back to London before dark. Alfie might already be there."

Their car was in the same place where they'd left it in Folkestone. Eve jumped into the passenger seat before Audrey had a chance to. "What are you doing?" Audrey asked.

"Get behind the wheel. You're driving home."

"You know I can't drive."

"It's time you learned."

"Eve . . . please . . ."

"You'll thank me for it someday. Get in and let's go home."

Audrey was a terrible driver at first, bouncing the car like a kangaroo until she got the hang of the clutch and shift lever. Eve nearly changed her mind about trying to teach her. But after the first hour, she did well behind the wheel. Once again, they passed miles of barbed wire, fortified military installations, and dozens of signs warning them to *Keep Out*. "It's a relief to know that our coastline is well armed and ready to defend against an enemy attack," Audrey said.

"The first attacks won't come from the sea, though," Eve said. "The Nazis will attack us from the air like they have in all the other countries."

Audrey stared straight ahead, her gaze riveted to the road. "I'm scared, Eve."

"So am I."

Audrey glanced at her. "But you're always so brave," she said before turning to watch the road. Eve didn't reply.

Back in London, Eve asked Audrey to drop her off at the boardinghouse. She climbed from the car, stretching her weary limbs, then walked around to the driver's side to say goodbye to her friend. "You'll let me know as soon as you hear from Alfie, won't you?" she asked. "You still have my telephone number, right?"

"Yes, you gave it to me," Audrey replied, patting her purse.

"Promise you'll ring me up the moment you hear?"

"I will. Cross my heart and hope to die." She smiled as she traced an X over her chest. "Now let me get going while there's still enough daylight to find my town house."

Eve felt reluctant to let Audrey go, wondering when she would see her again. "What's next for you, Audrey? Are you going home to Wellingford?"

"I plan to, yes. If they give Alfie leave time, that's where he'll want to come."

Eve thought otherwise. After hearing what the men had endured in France, she guessed that Alfie would seek comfort with a whiskey bottle in a London nightclub. Eve studied her friend and wondered if she looked as ragged as Audrey did. Suddenly Audrey flung open the car door and leaped out, pulling Eve into her arms for a hug. They held each other tightly; then Audrey released her and got back into the car, grinding the gears as the car lurched away.

"Keep practicing, Audrey," Eve called with a grin.

Eve found the other girls in the parlor of the boardinghouse, still gathered around the wireless where she'd left them the night before. One of her roommates leaped up when she saw her. "Eve! Where in the world have you been? We've been worried sick about you, taking off like that."

"Have you heard what's happening?" another roommate asked. "The news is calling the evacuation from Dunkirk a miracle. They say if it hadn't taken place, we would've been forced to surrender to Hitler!"

"I heard." But Eve didn't say that she'd been part of it. She couldn't find words to describe her experience yet, but she was proud to know that she and Audrey had made a difference.

On June 4, everyone gathered around the radio as a news announcer described in grim tones how some 250 ships of various kinds and sizes had been sunk in the channel. *Was one of them Audrey's?* He told how the RAF had downed numerous Luftwaffe aircraft and had suffered heavy losses themselves. Thank heaven Alfie wasn't a pilot. Some 300,000 men had been ferried to safety across the channel, thanks to hundreds of civilian volunteers. The number astounded Eve.

Then the room grew hushed as Prime Minister Churchill spoke. "Wars are not won by evacuations," he said in his gravelly voice. Eve closed her eyes, picturing everything she'd witnessed, the weary, discouraged men, wounded and shell-shocked. She didn't open them again until Mr. Churchill reached his stirring conclusion: "We shall not flag or fail. We shall go on to the end, we shall fight in France, we shall fight on the seas and oceans, we shall fight with growing confidence and growing strength in the air, we shall defend our island, whatever the cost may be, we shall fight on the beaches, we shall fight on the landing grounds, we shall fight in the fields and in the streets, we shall fight in the hills; we shall never surrender."

Never, Eve silently repeated. She walked out of the parlor and up the stairs. This was only the beginning of the war, not the end. She didn't want to type memos while she waited to hear from Alfie. She wanted to fight back. On Monday, she would go to the War Office and apply for a job.

11

Eve barely slept. It was more than just the discomfort of a restless night in the summer heat, sweating on the narrow bunk in Robbie's room. What kept her awake was the unanswerable question of what to do about Audrey. She couldn't send her former friend away with no place to go. Audrey had been part of Eve's life, on and off, since they were children, sometimes growing very close, sometimes distant. Yet if Audrey stayed, then Eve and Robbie would have no place to go. And they couldn't live together, two women and their sons sharing the same names. All of Eve's lies would be exposed. Her life would unravel.

She lay in bed with her eyes open, watching the sky beyond Robbie's cowboy curtains slowly grow light. The bunk reminded her of the one she'd slept on as an Auxiliary Fire Service volunteer. She peered at her watch. A few minutes after six. Eve tried to crawl down from the top bunk carefully but the movement awakened Robbie. He sat up, rubbing his eyes.

"Mommy?" He would never go back to sleep now. Eve opened her arms and he went into them for a hug. She loved his sticky warmth, his little-boy smell. "I'm hungry, Mommy," he murmured into her shoulder.

Had they eaten supper last night? Eve vaguely recalled cooking beans and sausages—hot dogs, the Americans called them—but she couldn't recall eating any. Her stomach felt the way it had aboard the *Rosamunde* during the evacuation of Dunkirk, as her mind swirled with thoughts of what to do about Audrey. She wished they would simply vanish. *Poof!*

Eve needed help with this dilemma, someone to confide in, and the first person who came to mind was Tom Vandenberg. Whenever Louis and Robert talked about the Famous Four, they called Tom their conscience. He'd become a trusted friend to Eve during the past four years, and if her life was about to disintegrate, perhaps he could tell her how to fight back or where she could go or what she should do next. Maybe he'd help her pick up the pieces—if he didn't turn against her for lying to him all this time.

"We need to get dressed very quietly," she whispered after releasing Robbie, "so we don't wake up our guests. Then we'll ride out to Uncle Tom's farm and see his new baby lamb. Would you like that?"

"Yeah!" The wooden bed frame creaked as Robbie bounced up and down.

Eve held her finger to her lips. "Shh . . ."

"Shh . . ." He grinned, imitating her. Eve threw on the clothes she'd worn yesterday and helped Robbie into a clean pair of shorts and a striped T-shirt. She was dying for a cup of tea but couldn't risk waking Audrey. After scribbling a quick note telling Audrey to help herself to breakfast and promising to return soon, Eve grabbed a banana for Robbie and hurried out the door, speeding away in her car like a bank robber fleeing the scene of the crime. She had to find a solution to this problem. For Robbie's sake.

The twenty-minute drive through the rolling countryside calmed her, as did the sight of Tom's sheep dotting the green hillside beyond the barn like tufts of cotton wool. Eve rolled down her window and inhaled the scents of hay and manure, the scents of her childhood. Tom's farm had become a place of refuge for her, the only place where she felt free to be herself. Tom was coming out of his barn with his dog at his side as she pulled into the driveway.

"You're up with the chickens this morning," he said with a grin. Eve had never seen Tom without a smile. He reminded her of the film star Jimmy Stewart, with his tall, angular frame and thick hair. He walked with a noticeable limp from a shrapnel wound, but it didn't keep him from running his family's dairy farm. She looked away from him to quench the impossible attraction she felt as Robbie ran up to him for a hug. Mum and Granny Maud would have adored Tom. Mum had told Eve to never settle for less than courage, kindness, and laughter in a man—a description that fit Tom perfectly.

"I suppose we are rather early," Eve said. "I wanted to apologize for being so short with you yesterday. My guests arrived unexpectedly and . . . and I guess they threw me a little off-balance." She swatted at the ever-present flies that buzzed around the barnyard.

"No problem. You looked a little frazzled yesterday."

"Are we too early to watch you feed the new lamb? I don't want to interrupt anything."

"Not at all. The cows are all milked, and that new lamb will want his bottle right about now. Want to help me, Robbie?"

"Yeah!" He hopped up and down with excitement.

"Come in the house while I fix it."

Eve followed Tom through the screened-in back porch, waiting while he stopped at the porch sink to wash his hands. The aromas of coffee and frying bacon drifted from the kitchen along with the smell of something wonderful baking in the oven. They stepped into the kitchen, where Mrs. Vandenberg stood at the cast-iron range, pans sizzling as she cooked breakfast. Tom's father sat at the kitchen table drinking coffee. The room was cozy and warm with blue-checked curtains and whitewashed wainscoting and a worn linoleum floor that groaned when you walked across it.

"Good morning," Eve said. "I'm sorry we're here so early. We heard there's a new baby lamb to feed."

Tom's mother turned, spatula in hand. "Well, good morning, Audrey. I'm just fixing breakfast. You want some?" She was a sweet, white-haired woman who reminded Eve of Granny Maud. "The eggs are fresh. Gathered them myself this morning."

"We don't want to be a bother."

"You two are never a bother," she said matter-of-factly.

"Guess what, Grandma Van!" Robbie said. "I'm going to feed the lamb!" Mrs. Vandenberg had told Robbie to call her Grandma Van after he'd struggled to say her name.

"Come here and give me a hug, sweetie pie." She bent down as Robbie hurtled toward her, then folded him into her arms. A wave of longing for Granny Maud's soft arms washed over Eve. If she told the truth about who she was, all of this would be snatched away from her son. He had a family here in America. He was loved. Mrs. Vandenberg was a fine churchgoing woman who would be horrified to learn what a liar Eve was, how she'd deceived her and won her heart by pretending to be someone else. Facing Grandma Van's disappointment would be like facing Granny Maud's. Eve could never confess—to her or to Tom. She would have to find another way out of this dilemma.

"That's wonderful, Robbie," Grandma Van said, returning to her cooking. "We sure could use your help with that lamb. Get out two more plates, Audrey honey, and some silverware." Eve was familiar enough with the farm kitchen to do what she'd asked. Tom poured a cup of coffee for himself and one for Eve, then dragged an extra chair to the table.

"You take cream, right, Audrey?" he asked, setting the pitcher near her plate. Eve was certain Tom could read her guilt. She nodded, then quickly turned away.

"What's baking in the oven?" she asked. "It smells wonderful!"

"I made a batch of biscuits." Mrs. Vandenberg gestured to a wire rack on the counter where plump white mounds, lightly browned on top, were cooling. "Try one," she said, "then go ahead and put the rest in that basket." They looked like coconut macaroons, but the bite Eve tasted wasn't sweet at all. Instead, it was buttery and floury and seemed to melt in her mouth. Tom had explained once before that British "biscuits" were called "cookies" in America. What his mother made, he'd insisted, were *real* biscuits.

"You and Robbie sit down now," Mrs. Vandenberg said. She carried the skillet to the table and dished scrambled eggs onto everyone's plate. Guilt ripped through Eve's heart when Tom's father bowed his head and prayed aloud. God knew the truth about her. Granny Maud said He kept a record of her sins in His book. Her page must be full. Robbie folded his hands and closed his eyes, too, his little legs dangling, his chin level with the table. He loved it here. Loved Uncle Tom and Grandma Van as much as he loved Nana and Grandpa Barrett. And so did Eve. It didn't seem fair that Robbie would be punished because of her lies.

Eve struggled to smile and act nonchalant while they ate, flinching inside each time someone called her Audrey. After breakfast, she helped wash the dishes while Tom and Robbie fixed a bottle for the lamb. Then the three of them walked out to the barn, Robbie skipping ahead with the bottle, the dog at his heels. Eve gazed up at the blue sky and white clouds and knew, deep down, that her secret would be found out. Audrey was here in America and she wasn't going away. And Eve also knew that it was more noble to confess than to be caught in the act. But she simply couldn't bring herself to confess—not to Tom or anyone else. Not yet. Not until she exhausted every other possible way out of this mess. And she would find a way out. She had to.

"Come on, Mommy," Robbie called from the barn. "Hurry! The lamb is hungry!"

"We're coming." Tom led them to a little pen he'd made inside the barn, opening the gate for Robbie to step inside. Tom crouched down, wincing slightly as if his leg felt stiff. He showed Robbie how to hold the bottle. The lamb dropped to its front knees to suck, its white tail whirling like a flag in the wind.

Don't cry, Eve told herself as she watched them. *Whatever you do, don't let Tom see your tears.* He would ask about them and she would have to pour out her story. "What happened to the lamb's mother?" Eve asked instead.

"The ewe had twins and rejected the smaller one," he replied. Robbie giggled as the lamb pushed against the bottle, guzzling greedily. Her son needed this, needed Tom's strong arms around him, teaching him things only a father could. She wouldn't let Audrey take this from him.

"Hey! He drank it all!" Robbie said a few minutes later. "Can we give him another bottle, Uncle Tom?"

"No more until lunchtime, I'm afraid." Tom ruffled Robbie's hair as they both stood. "And the lamb is a girl, not a boy. What do you think we should call her?"

"Um . . ."

"You don't have to decide right now. Think it over and let me know."

"Okay." He handed the empty bottle to Tom and ran out into the sunlight with Tom's dog.

"We need to go home," Eve said. "Thanks so much for letting him do this."

"What's your hurry?"

"My visitors are still here. But I wanted to apologize again for yesterday."

"There's really no need . . . Are you all right, Audrey? You seem—"

"I'm fine." She felt tears burning and fought them back. "Just tired. We got up much earlier than we usually do."

"Cloudy!" Robbie suddenly shouted. "The lamb's name is Cloudy because she looks like a cloud."

"Cloudy it is," Tom said with a grin.

Eve used the twenty-minute drive home to rehearse what she would say to Audrey, barely listening to Robbie chatter on and on about Uncle Tom's dog and the new lamb. Audrey was sitting in the living room, her son asleep on her lap, when Eve arrived. She looked rumpled and bleary-eyed, as if she hadn't slept well either.

"I fed Uncle Tom's lamb," Robbie announced in a loud voice. "He said I could name her anything I wanted, so I called her Cloudy 'cause that's what she looks like. Wanna come out to the farm and see her?" he asked Audrey's son, who had awakened. He shook his head.

"Have you eaten?" Eve asked. "Would you like breakfast? I can fix some toast or eggs . . ."

"Neither of us are hungry," Audrey replied.

"Maybe some tea, then?"

"We need to talk, Eve."

She couldn't stall any longer. Eve sat down on the sofa, perched on the very edge, and drew a deep breath. "Listen, Audrey. If you

need money, you can have all of Robert's life insurance money and
the trust fund his parents set up. All of it, if you'll just—"

"If I just what?"

"Go back home. Please, I'm begging you!"

"I told you, I don't have a home."

"Then I'll sell this house and give you the money to buy one. And
I'll send you more money every month, as much as you need—"

"I don't care about the money, Eve. I didn't come here for the
money. My son is Robert's child, and he deserves to know his
grandparents and to have a real family. I don't have any family
left and—"

"Neither do I! All I have are the people I've grown to know and
love here. Please, let Robbie and me get on with our lives. He loves
all these people, too."

"I know what happened to your family back home, Eve, and
I'm so sorry for you. But this is my son's family, not yours. I want
Bobby to grow up surrounded by them, celebrating his birthdays
with them, Christmastimes."

"And I want the same thing for my son!" And for herself. How
many times had Eve started all over, forging a new life when the
old one ended? She couldn't do it again. The loss would undo
her. She cleared her throat, forcing herself to talk quietly so she
wouldn't upset the boys. "I'm sorry, Audrey, but you can't have this
life back. It's too late. We're settled here. I'm sure we can figure out
a different plan for you, a different road to take—"

"I've reached the end of the road, Eve. I'm not going any further. *I* belong here, not you."

Eve stood as her fear of losing everything made her desperate.
"Listen, the war taught us a lot of things, most of all, how to live
day to day. We never knew during those long, endless months and
years what would happen tomorrow, whether we'd be dead or alive

by morning, so we both tried to grab a little happiness wherever we could find it and—"

"I tried to warn you about the poor choices you were making, but—"

"Don't lecture me, Audrey! I'm not your servant anymore!" She was shouting now. "The war did away with all the barriers between us and made us equals. I'm sorry your father sold Wellingford Hall. But you threw away your chance to have this life when it was offered to you four years ago. It's too late to change your mind!"

"It's your fault for—"

"Don't you dare blame me for the way things turned out! If you're going to blame anyone, blame Hitler. He ruined our lives the day he invaded Poland. Or blame the Americans for not coming to help us until it was nearly too late. We did the best we could, Audrey, making the best decisions we could, trying to survive the bombs and the rockets, living on a pound of meat a week and a few ounces of sugar and a pinch of tea, if we could get them. Remember?"

"Of course I remember. How could I ever forget?" The determination Eve saw in Audrey's eyes, the strong tilt of her chin, startled her. "But Bobby and I are not going anywhere. We're staying here." Audrey had found her courage at last.

Eve closed her eyes as she faced the reality of what she was about to lose. She pictured Granny Maud standing in front of her, wagging her finger the way she always did when Eve misbehaved. *The Good Book says that when you sin against the Lord, you may be sure that your sin will find you out.* Were the losses she now faced God's punishment for her sins?

There had to be another way out. But Eve had no idea what it was.

12

WELLINGFORD HALL, JUNE 1940

Audrey opened the French doors that led from Wellingford Hall's drawing room to the garden and searched the gray sky for the airplanes thrumming overhead. The sound interrupted the serenity of her peaceful estate as planes took off and landed at the new airfield nearby. The Royal Air Force had built dozens of airfields, radar stations, and repair sheds all over the once-peaceful countryside, making it commonplace to hear their activity. Audrey always looked up to see if they were RAF, having learned to tell British Hurricanes and Spitfires from German Junkers and Messerschmitts. Not that she'd seen a Luftwaffe plane flying above Wellingford—yet. But after what she and Eve had witnessed in Dover a few days ago, she feared it was only a matter of time.

The jangling telephone echoed through the foyer. She closed the drawing room doors and hurried to answer it before Robbins did. She lifted the receiver with hope and dread. "Wellingford Hall. Miss Clarkson speaking."

Her brother's laughter greeted her on the other end. "Are things that bad at home, Sis, that you have to answer the phone yourself? Has our butler joined the Army, too?"

"Oh, Alfie! Thank God you're alive!" Her vision blurred as she sank onto the hall bench, weak with relief. "I've been waiting for days to hear from you!"

"Yes, I'm alive. And grateful to be off that hellish French beach."

"Where are you? Are you coming home? Shall I fetch you at the village station?"

"I'm not at the station—"

"Then I'll drive to London straightaway. I need to see for myself that you're all in one piece."

"I'm not in London, either. I'm not supposed to say where I am, but I'm back on British soil and digging in to defend us from the Hun."

"Oh, it's so wonderful to hear your voice! I've been frantic with worry ever since driving home from Dover—"

"What were you doing in Dover? Do you have a driver again? Is Williams back?"

"They put out a call for ships of all sizes for the rescue operation, so I went to London and got Eve Dawson. She and I drove down to Folkestone to offer the *Rosamunde*. We sailed it to Dover ourselves and loaned it to the Royal Navy. Then we stayed and helped serve tea to all the soldiers. We searched and searched for you, but there were so many men!"

Alfie whistled in admiration. "I'm proud of you, Sis."

"I got word from the marina yesterday that the *Rosamunde* made it back safely."

"That's good to know."

"Eve gave me the courage to sail it by myself. And she even taught me to drive the car on the way back to London. She's a good friend, Alfie. And she cares so much for you. Does she know you're all right? Did you telephone her?"

"I didn't think you approved of me seeing Eve."

"Of course I do, but Mother and Father won't. Please don't hurt her, Alfie. I know you have no shortage of girlfriends, but Eve is—"

"Hang on a minute, Sis . . ." Audrey heard muffled voices in the background, and Alfie speaking to someone. Then, "I have to go, Audrey. Tell Father and Mother I'm well. Call Eve for me, too, will you? Hope to see you soon." He rang off.

As soon as she hung up the telephone, Audrey doubled over on the bench and wept for joy, her days and sleepless nights of worry over. For now. Alfie was safe.

When she scrubbed her eyes and looked up, Robbins and Mrs. Smith stood in the doorway to the servants' quarters, waiting as if steeled for bad news. It embarrassed her to be seen weeping. "It's good news," she told them. "Alfie is alive and well and back in Britain."

"Thank God," Mrs. Smith breathed. Their relief seemed nearly as great as her own.

"Yes. We must thank Him straightaway!" She would ride her secondhand bicycle into the village and go to the church and . . . and she wasn't quite sure what she should do once she got there but perhaps the vicar would know. She started to rise, then remembered that she'd promised to call their parents and tell them the news. And she must call Eve. "Do you know how to contact Father?" she asked Robbins.

"He left some numbers where he might be reached."

"Please call him for me and relay the news. And . . . and will you call Mother at the town house, too?" She couldn't explain her reluctance to speak with her mother, but she couldn't deny it, either.

"Yes, Miss Audrey. They will be very happy to hear that Master Alfred is well."

"I have to make one other call first, but I'll need to run upstairs and fetch the number from my room." Eve was at work when Audrey called the boardinghouse, but the landlady promised to give her the message. Audrey scribbled a quick letter to Eve in case she didn't get the phone message, then rode into the village to post it. Afterwards, she propped her bicycle outside the church and went up the front steps, longing to say something or do something to show the Almighty her gratitude for sparing Alfie's life.

The small stone church was cool inside and whisper-quiet. She paused in the vestibule near a message board overflowing with pinned notices and meeting schedules and ARP bulletins. She felt like an intruder. And she was unsure how one went about thanking God properly. The notices reminded her of the church in Dover where she and Eve had volunteered. The women there worked as a team, and she had so enjoyed helping them.

Audrey slipped into the silent sanctuary, tiptoeing down the long aisle to the front, reluctant to disturb the Almighty or anyone else. She sat in the Clarkson family pew, where she and Alfie used to sit with Father on special occasions such as Easter and Christmas, her brother fidgeting to contain his boundless energy, jiggling his foot and squirming in his seat. Father never reprimanded him and seemed just as eager as Alfie to hurry away when the service ended. Audrey couldn't recall Mother ever attending with them.

Alfie was safe! She rested her forehead on the pew in front of her. "God, thank You . . . thank You!" It was all she could manage before dissolving into tears. Mother would be appalled at her lack of control. Proper ladies didn't parade their emotions in public for all to see. But how else to convey her enormous gratitude and relief to God?

Audrey lifted her head when she thought she heard footsteps. She turned, recognizing Rev. Hamlin in his dark suit and clerical collar, hesitating in the doorway behind her. She quickly wiped her eyes and sat up straight. "Good afternoon, Vicar."

"Forgive me, Miss Clarkson. I didn't mean to disturb you, but if there's anything I can do, I'm happy to help." He was a lean, pleasant-looking man in his fifties with curly white hair that reminded her of lamb's wool. From his sermons in the few months she'd been attending church regularly, Audrey thought him an intelligent, caring man. His tanned, muscular arms and work-worn hands hinted that he was unafraid to share his parishioners' labors.

"Thank you for your concern, Reverend. I just heard from my brother, Alfie, who'd been on the Continent with the BEF. He's fine, thank God, and I wanted to . . . to thank Him."

"Indeed. That's very good news. I'll leave you, then." He turned to go.

"Wait. If you have a moment, I would like to ask you how I can help. In the village, I mean. I know my family hasn't been very active, and I apologize for that. But I would like that to change. My parents are away for the time being, and I'm now the lady of the manor, you might say, and I see on the notice board that there's much to do here in the village. For the war effort, I mean. And to . . . to serve God." She was rambling, her words stumbling along like a drunkard on a crooked path, but the vicar smiled kindly.

"No need to apologize, Miss Clarkson. We'll simply go forward from here. There is, indeed, much to do as we prepare for the defense of England. We welcome all the help we can get."

"I would like to do more for the church, too. I know I haven't been very involved, but I've seen the work that other churches in England are doing, and I very much want to be. Involved here, I mean. To show my gratitude for Alfie. The message board is a bit overwhelming."

The vicar nodded and sat down in the pew in front of her, crossing his legs and resting his arm on the back of the pew as he faced her. "I can describe some of the ways the other villagers are involved and you can decide what suits you. Fair enough?"

"Yes, thank you."

"We always need volunteers to take shifts as rooftop spotters to look for enemy aircraft. This is especially important since an invasion is imminent and will likely include Nazi paratroopers dropping from the sky. The battle for Britain has already begun, and our valiant RAF fighter pilots are doing a remarkable job of keeping the enemy at bay. But the Nazis will have an advantage once France falls and the Luftwaffe takes control of their airfields thirty miles across the channel. I'm told they'll try to knock out our air defenses first, as they prepare to invade us. And as you know, our village is quite close to several airfields."

"Yes, I see." Audrey hadn't imagined enemy paratroopers landing near Wellingford. She found the idea frightening.

"If you aren't squeamish," Rev. Hamlin continued, "the government offers first aid classes so we'll be mobilized to help in the event of an emergency. It's expected that the enemy will begin massive bombardments to try to weaken us by destroying our war industries and crippling our ports to prevent shipping and cause slow starvation. If the Nazi invasions of other nations are any indication, we can expect aerial bombing raids quite soon. Once they begin, the need for air-raid wardens, civil defense workers, fire brigade volunteers, and medics will skyrocket."

"Oh, dear." Audrey felt the color draining from her face as he brought the war vividly to life, right in her backyard. She could tell that the vicar saw her fear, too.

"I'm sorry, Miss Clarkson. Have I been too blunt? My wife often accuses me of it."

"Not at all. I did ask. Please, go on."

"Many of the villagers qualify for the free bomb shelters the government provides, but there's always a mountain of paperwork involved with these endeavors, and we could use help sorting through the government red tape. We also lack the manpower to get the shelters dug with so few men remaining behind. It's vitally important to ensure that everyone has access to a safe shelter when the invasion comes."

Audrey nodded, feeling numb. Father had refused to provide an Anderson shelter for their servants, but perhaps she should look into it while he was away. A few holes in the back garden would be well worth saving their lives.

"Then there's the Women's Voluntary Service," he added. "They're preparing to help out in almost any home-front situation one can imagine. In fact, they're meeting in the village hall at this very moment, if you'd like to listen in."

"Yes, please. I would." She stood, and they walked to the village hall together, the vicar wheeling her bicycle for her. "What about helping at church?" she asked. "I would like to convey my gratitude to God by helping to serve there in some way."

He studied her for a long moment and she wondered if he was scrutinizing her motives. Or was she being overly sensitive? "My wife leads a prayer group every evening before curfew," he finally said. "You're welcome to join us anytime. Right now, and for the immediate future, I believe that the work of Christ's church will be exactly those things I have just outlined. It's more important than ever that we serve as the hands and feet of Christ in every way we can during these troubling times."

They stopped outside the door to the village hall, which stood open. The murmur of women's voices drifted outside. The vicar paused before saying, "I hope you won't feel offended, Miss Clarkson, if the villagers seem a bit cool at first. I suspect there is some resentment toward your family for seeming to ignore the village's needs all these years. Once they see that you would like that to change, I'm certain they'll welcome you and your efforts. But please don't be put off until they do."

Audrey drew a steadying breath, determined to be useful instead of hiding in Wellingford Hall for the duration of the war. "I'm grateful for the warning. I know my family's faults as well as the villagers do, and I shall try to be thick-skinned."

They slipped inside and sat down in the back row, listening as a middle-aged woman in a tweed skirt and cardigan described plans to help a village family whose son had died on one of the rescue ships that sank near Dunkirk. She followed with the story of a young wife and mother whose husband was taken prisoner in France. Two other women from the village struggled to cope alone with their husbands away. In every instance, women from the group pledged their help and support. Eve Dawson grew up in this village and likely knew all of these families, people who had helped Eve and her mother after her father died in the first war. Audrey longed to stand up and apologize to all of them for her family's long indifference. Instead, she turned to the vicar and asked, "Where is God in all these tragedies? Why does He allow evil to triumph and cause such suffering?"

Rev. Hamlin sighed. "Much wiser men than I have tried to answer that question. One can only hope that when all is said and done, God will use this war to draw us closer to Him and make us better people. I fear, however, that it may have the opposite effect in many cases."

Audrey thought it an odd thing to say. There was so much she didn't understand about God. In fact, she barely knew where or how to begin to understand Him. She stood. "I'll be back," she promised, then went outside and climbed onto her bike for the mile-long ride home to Wellingford.

She was within sight of the manor house when she heard the roar of an airplane approaching from the south, flying lower than usual. She braked and looked up, shielding her eyes, straining to see the insignia on the fuselage and wings, dreading the sight of a Nazi plane. The roaring engine grew louder, closer. Her heart pounded as she recalled the vicar's ominous words about an invasion of paratroopers.

The plane came into view at last, just above the woods, the engine stuttering now. A plume of dark smoke trailed behind. Audrey spotted the bull's-eye emblem on the RAF Spitfire and could breathe again. But the plane flew much too low, barely skimming the chimney tops as it soared over Wellingford Hall. It was going to crash on the lawn. Audrey leaped onto her bicycle and pedaled as hard as she could toward home, as if she could do something if she got there in time, as if she could prevent the stricken plane from crashing.

But of course she couldn't.

The explosion, when it came, rocked through her, nearly knocking her from her bike, moments before she reached Wellingford's front door.

LONDON, SEPTEMBER 1940

"I have no idea if my mum will be here or not," Eve warned her friend Iris as they walked to the Clarksons' town house. "I hope she and the rest of the servants have all gone back to Wellingford Hall. But if she's here, Mum will be getting Lady Rosamunde ready for a Saturday night out."

"A night out?" Iris asked. "Who would go out with a war on?"

"Lady Rosamunde won't let a silly little thing like a war keep her home." Which was why Eve worried about her mum. Audrey was at Wellingford, and Alfie was somewhere in the north, and Eve wished Mum could leave London, too.

The sun felt warm on her shoulders as Eve walked with Iris to the servants' door, passing the ungainly hump of an Anderson shelter dug into a bare patch of ground between the town house and the garages. It hadn't been there in May when Eve had come with Audrey to fetch the car. Fresh earth lay mounded over the top and sides to cover the shelter's corrugated roof. It resembled a tomb and looked much too small to house Lady Rosamunde and all of her servants.

"Your mum is upstairs," Tildy said after hugging her. Eve led Iris up the steep servants' stairs, feeling out of breath when they reached the top floor.

Mum pulled Eve into her arms, holding her tightly. "What brings you here, love?"

"I came to tell you my good news. I have a brand-new job as a typist for the Ministry of Information."

"That's wonderful!" Mum's hands lingered on Eve's shoulders, caressing them.

"The pay is better, and I feel like I'm doing my bit for the war effort instead of typing invoices all day. Iris works there, too." She gestured to her new friend, a pretty, black-haired girl who also came from a working-class background. Iris was the pride of her family for escaping the poverty of London's East End with a good job as a typist. She and Eve sat side by side at the Ministry of Information in an office crammed with clacking, pinging typewriters.

"Iris needed a fourth roommate for the flat she just rented and asked me to move in with her. No more dreary boardinghouses for us! I came to give you my new address and telephone number."

"You're doing so well for yourself, Eve," Mum said, hugging her again. "I'm so proud of you." The familiar room where Eve once slept looked unchanged. The photograph of Eve's daddy still sat on the bedside table. Granny Maud's picture of the Good Shepherd hung on the wall above the bed. Mum owned so little—but then so did Eve. "Let's go downstairs," Mum said. "I'll make tea and we can visit."

"No, please don't fuss. We can't stay long. I'm going with Iris to the East End to visit her grandmother."

"Granny takes her tea with mounds of sugar," Iris explained, "and she can never get enough of it, with rationing and all. I take my lot to her whenever I can. I'm getting used to going without," she finished with a laugh. Her cheerful, generous spirit was one of the reasons Eve liked Iris. She was so unlike serious, moody Audrey.

"That's very kind of you, Iris," Mum said. "I'm sure your granny appreciates it."

"Why are you still in London, Mum?" Eve asked. "The Season is over—if there even is such a thing with the war on. I was hoping you'd be back at Wellingford, by now, where it's safe."

"Lady Rosamunde has decided to stay in London. She finds it too boring in the country. All her friends are here."

"But . . . Audrey is at Wellingford, isn't she? And Mr. Clarkson?"

"I don't know where Mr. Clarkson is these days, but Audrey is there, yes."

"You should quit and go home to the village, Mum. You could easily find work there. I can send you some of my pay every week. They're saying the Nazis will bomb London any day."

"So are you leaving London and going where it's safe?" Mum asked.

Eve looked away. "No. My work is here." She didn't say so, but

Eve would stay as long as there was hope that Alfie would come to London on leave.

"My work is here too," Mum said.

"I don't understand why you're so loyal to her, Mum. Lady Rosamunde demands so much from you, working all hours of the day and night, yet she doesn't have an ounce of consideration for you."

Mum sighed and sat down on the edge of the bed. "It isn't easy to explain, Eve. I suppose . . . I suppose it's because of what the vicar once said in one of his sermons. He read a Bible passage that said servants should do their work joyfully, as if serving the Lord. Jesus said if we're ordered to go one mile, we should go two. And I feel sorry for Lady Rosamunde. For all her wealth, she is a sad, lonely woman."

"It's her own fault if she is."

"You're right. But she gave me a job at a time when I badly needed it to support you. So I've always thought that God must have a reason for wanting me to work for her." Eve shook her head, unable to persuade her. "Don't worry, Eve," Mum added. "There's an Anderson shelter out back where I can go if there's an air raid. I hope your new apartment has one, too."

"There's a public shelter nearby," Iris said. "We'll be fine, Mrs. Dawson."

They spent a few more minutes visiting, but Eve could tell that Iris was eager to get to the East End and home again before the afternoon grew too late and the blackout began. Eve hugged her mum, promising to visit longer the next time, and they left.

London's East End was a warren of densely packed houses and tenements, yet Eve felt at home among its poor, hardworking people. They were much like the villagers she knew back home. Iris's grandmother, a tiny, white-haired woman with a bent back and gnarled hands, reminded Eve of Granny Maud. She sat crocheting in the dark cottage where Iris had grown up with her three older brothers, all now off fighting the war. Threadbare furnishings and well-worn possessions filled the tidy room. "Where's Mum and Dad?" Iris asked.

"At work, putting in extra shifts at the motor works. Would you girls like tea?"

"Not for me, thank you," Eve replied. The fire in the range had gone out on this warm September day, and besides, she knew how dear tea was in these days of ration books and pinching pennies.

"Oh, you've brought pure gold!" Iris's granny exclaimed when Iris gave her the packet of sugar. "God love you for it, darling." They carried a chair outside for her, and Eve and Iris sat beside her on the stoop, watching the swirl of activity in the street while they told her about their new jobs and three-room flat. Few people owned cars in this neighborhood, nor could they afford the petrol to drive them, but bicyclists and pedestrians strolled past, enjoying the lovely fall afternoon. Barefoot children played in the streets. A year ago, children had stood in long queues in the train station waiting to be evacuated. Now here they were, back home again.

The sun slipped lower in the sky. The damp, fishy odor of the nearby Thames drifted on the breeze. "We should probably be on our way," Eve finally said, standing and stretching. "It must be after four thirty." That's when they'd planned to leave, but Iris had lingered, hoping her parents would return.

Then, above the clamor of children at play, Eve thought she heard a rumbling sound, like a distant waterfall. She remembered that sound from her time in Dover with Audrey—the hum of airplanes. Her pulse quickened.

She hurried out to the middle of the street, wading into a lively game of tag, and looked up. High in the distance, hundreds of airplanes filled the sky, glinting in the waning sunlight like a swarm of silvery insects. The children stopped playing and looked up, too. "Surely they're ours," Eve murmured as the rumble grew louder. But their shape was all wrong. And there were so many of them. Eve stood frozen in place, not with fear exactly, but with astonishment. Was this really happening?

"What is it?" Iris called to her, but before Eve could reply, the dreaded siren began to moan, shivering up Eve's spine like an electric current. *Wailing Winnie*, people called it. The sound swelled as it rose in pitch, screaming a warning—loud and urgent. Eve's instincts demanded that she run, like the children who were scattering in every direction. There had been air-raid warnings in London before, followed by small raids and a few clusters of bombings, but never such an enormous cloud of aircraft as this.

She sprinted toward Iris, shouting, "Where's the shelter? We have to get to a shelter!" *Ten minutes.* Once an air-raid warning sounded, that was all the time they would have to get to safety. Iris's granny stared as if she didn't understand. She hadn't seen the deadly swarm of enemy planes, but Eve had. She took the old woman's arm and lifted her from the chair. "Where's the nearest air-raid shelter? Do you know where one is?"

"Can't we just go in the house?"

Eve glanced at the little shanty with its sagging roof and crumbling chimney. It resembled a cottage in a children's fairy tale that might blow over with a huff and a puff. "No, it isn't safe here," she said. "Come on, we have to go!"

They followed the crowds of panicked people running down the street. Eve hoped they knew where to go. Iris's granny couldn't move very fast, so Eve and Iris slowed to match her pace. A squat, brick shelter crouched at the end of the block, and the mob funneled through its narrow door. Women screamed as loud thumps from falling bombs began sounding in the distance. Eve glanced over her shoulder and saw plumes of smoke rising in billowing columns. And still the planes kept coming. They would surely bomb the nearby docks along the Thames. The gasworks. And the Ford Motor Works, where Iris's parents worked. Factories and warehouses filled London's East End, which was why so many families packed the neighborhood.

Clanging fire bells added to the chaos as fire brigades sprang into action. Volunteers from the Auxiliary Fire Service poured from their homes in helmets and boots, turning in circles as if wondering what to do in this first test of their meager training. One of the barrage balloons, tethered from steel cables to entangle low-flying aircraft, exploded with a loud blast, bringing a shower of debris raining down. Eve felt the push and crush of people and wrapped her arm around the older woman's waist as she and Iris tried to hurry her along, all three of them mute with fright.

They reached the public shelter at last. Why wasn't it underground? Frightened people jammed the interior. More fought to cram inside. Iris found a place for her granny to sit and they huddled beside her as if they could protect her from the accelerating thumps and booms outside. Children clung to their parents. Women moaned and prayed. An old man shook his fist at the ceiling. Above the clamor, the roar of planes kept coming and coming. They were overhead now.

A bomb fell through the sky right above them with a deafening scream. Eve lowered her head and gritted her teeth, preparing to die. When it struck nearby with a tremendous roar, the ground trembled. Another followed and another. Hundreds of bombs, one after the other, until the building shook and shifted. Plaster sifted from the ceiling like flour, coating everyone with white dust.

Eve had never known such terror. She was going to die, and she didn't want to. She wanted to live, get married, have children, grow old. She closed her eyes as she hunched in place, silently pleading with God to spare her life. To spare Mum and the other servants in the Anderson shelter. Audrey at Wellingford. And Alfie, wherever he was. She wanted to beg for mercy for the people she loved, yet she had nothing to bargain with. Nothing to offer God in return for her pitiful pleas. She was helpless. Utterly helpless.

Overhead, another bomb screamed through the sky, and she braced herself for the hit. When the explosion came, the suction tingled through her. The very air seemed to shake. Why was this shelter aboveground? No one would live through this onslaught. All around her, people whimpered and wept. Eve silently vowed that if she ever had to endure this again, it would be in an underground shelter.

On and on the bombs fell, the explosions booming and roaring until Eve lost all track of time. The ringing in her ears was so loud she didn't notice, at first, that the hum of planes grew fainter, replaced by the clamor of racing fire engines outside, the shouts of rescue volunteers. The bomb blasts tapered off.

"Dear God, is it over?" she whispered. A hush fell over the room as everyone waited, holding their breath. Time passed. Eve's limbs ached as she sat cross-legged on the floor, bracing for more, straining to listen for approaching planes. When the all clear sounded its steady, two-minute note, she slumped with relief, unsure if she had the strength to move.

"Are you both all right?" she asked Iris and her granny. Plaster dust coated Iris's black hair, making her look like an old woman. Iris nodded and swiped her tears, smearing more dust across her face. Eve must look the same. Iris's granny stared straight ahead as if in shock, her gnarled hands clenched into tight fists.

There was another scrambling race to get out of the shelter.

Eve looked at her watch. Six thirty. Nearly two hours had passed since they'd sat in the sunshine in front of Iris's house, enjoying the afternoon. Two hours of relentless bombing.

Iris helped her granny to her feet and they all followed the others outside. Eve had feared the worst, but the sight that met her eyes was beyond imagining. She stepped out into hell itself. "Dear God . . . dear God . . . ," she breathed.

Bombs had demolished the neighborhood, leaving mounds of lath and beams and bricks where tenements and houses had stood two hours ago. The sky above the nearby docks resembled a wall of flame. The smoke stung Eve's eyes and clogged her throat. If the fire spread this way, they would never outrun it.

Fragments of wood and belongings lay strewn everywhere. A wooden table leg. The back of a splintered chair. A spoon. Broken glass crunched beneath her feet as Eve walked forward in a daze. Farther down the street, a row of tenements still stood, but all the windows had blown out, leaving gaping black holes like unseeing eyes.

Streams of water and tangled fire hoses filled the streets. Injured, bleeding people begged for help. Civil defense workers shouted to each other as they shoveled through the rubble, searching for survivors. Eve wanted to help. She needed to do something. But what?

"Our home . . . ," the old woman mumbled. "Where's our home?" She looked disoriented, in shock.

Iris was in shock, too. Her voice trembled as she said, "Please stay here with Granny, Eve. I'll run home and see." Eve kicked aside some broken glass and helped Iris's granny sit down on the curb. They waited in silence. Nothing Eve said could console her in this nightmare.

Suddenly a dark stream of movement streaked toward her—a

swarm of rats fleeing from the burning docks. Eve screamed, unable to move as they raced past, then disappeared into the debris. She shivered in horror.

Hours seemed to pass before Iris returned, carrying a few of her family's belongings in a scorched pillowcase. "The landmarks are all gone," she said, her voice hoarse with smoke. "I could barely find our house. Then I couldn't find my way back."

"But your house . . . ?" Eve asked.

Tears filled Iris's eyes as she shook her head. "Gone. It's gone." She sank down beside her grandmother, clinging to her, weeping. "I'm sorry, Granny . . . I'm so sorry!" Eve thought of the sugar packet, the errand that had brought them to the East End. Iris's granny would be dead if they hadn't come.

"We can't go home, Granny," Iris wept. "I tried to save a few of our things . . ."

"There must be someplace we can take her to find food and shelter for the night," Eve said.

"I know, but where? And I need to find Mum and Dad."

"Stay here with her. I'll find someone in charge." Eve waded through the endless chaos, asking anyone and everyone if they knew where people who'd lost their homes could spend the night. No one knew. Surely plans had been made for this disaster. Everyone expected London to be bombed. But those plans had been blown to pieces amid the horror of the devastation. The most immediate needs were to rescue the injured, locate survivors among the wreckage, and clear the streets to allow stretchers and ambulances to get through.

At last, Eve learned of a local school a few blocks to the east that was a temporary shelter for bomb victims. Night had fallen, but fires lit the streets like daylight as she made her way back to Iris. Eve helped them both to their feet and tried to get Iris's granny walking, but she was still dazed and shaken. They had shuffled only a few yards when the chilling wail of the siren sounded once again, slicing through the night.

"No . . . Oh, God, no!" Eve moaned. She couldn't see the approaching planes in the smoke-filled sky but she heard them. They would find their targets easily, the night illuminated by fires from the first round of bombings. "We have to get back to the shelter!" she said above the siren's shriek. They hadn't walked very far from it. They turned and hurried back.

Fallen bricks lay all around the building. The foundation seemed to have shifted. "It doesn't look safe," Iris said. "Are you sure we should go in?"

"I don't want to, but there's no other choice."

Ten minutes. Maybe only eight minutes now. Eve relived the nightmare for a second time, holding her breath as bombs shrieked toward earth. Bracing herself for each impact. Breathing again after each explosion. And the next and the next. All around her, people wept and prayed. She tried to pray, too, but as the endless raid wore on, she could only mumble, "Please, God. Please . . ." as the world exploded around her. She battled waves of panic, feeling trapped and helpless in the windowless shelter. She wanted to get out—had to get out! But she didn't dare.

At midnight, there was still no end to the bombing. The shelter had been designed for short-term raids, a place for residents to wait an hour or two until an attack ended, not a place where hundreds of people could huddle through a long night of continuous bombing. There were no washroom facilities, no beds, and not nearly enough seats. No provision had been made for the elderly or small children. There was no food or drinking water, no way to fix a comforting cup of tea. The electricity cut off when the second raid began, and no one had thought to provide emergency lighting in the windowless building. Eve sat on the floor in the darkness as the hours passed with nothing to occupy her mind except fear. Her heart pounded and tripped over itself as her panic soared. She couldn't breathe. She had to get out!

She couldn't get out.

The attack continued until dawn. Eight straight hours of bombing. Eve's ears rang from the blasts. Nothing would be left outside. Where was the Good Shepherd? Didn't He care about His suffering sheep?

By the time the all clear sounded, Eve felt numb. Once again, she emerged from the shelter with Iris and her granny into a world of impassable streets, pocked with craters, strewn with debris. A woman sat on a pile of rubble with a limp child in her arms, crying in a low, endless wail. She refused to let the volunteers near her. Everywhere Eve looked, civil defense workers frantically dug through debris, pulling out bodies, loading the injured into ambulances, their faces weary and hopeless. Flames and smoke filled the horizon above the docks. Eve felt the heat, saw it shimmering in the air. Someone said the Ford Motor Works had been hit. She wondered about Iris's parents.

"Where are we supposed to go?" Iris asked. Everyone asked the same question. People called out names of missing family members, questioning everyone they met. Iris did the same, asking about her parents and the factory. Soot blackened many of the faces Eve passed; others were white with plaster dust. How would Iris recognize anyone?

A canteen truck arrived from the Women's Voluntary Service with tea and sandwiches. Eve gobbled one down, weak from hunger. She and Iris hadn't eaten since lunch yesterday. One of the volunteers confirmed that there was a temporary shelter being set up in the school a few blocks away. "If you wait there," she told them, "the government will send buses to take you to a permanent facility with food and clothing. They'll find you a place to stay until your homes can be repaired or you find new ones."

"Let's take your grandmother back to our flat," Eve said. "This is no place for her."

"No, you go home, Eve. I'll take Granny to the school and wait to hear from my parents. If the Ford factory was hit . . ." She couldn't finish.

"Oh, Iris! Let me stay and help you. What can I do?"

"Nothing. There's nothing anyone can do. Go home and make sure your mum is safe."

She was. The area of London where the town house was located hadn't been damaged. Eve fell into Mum's arms, unable to find words to describe what she'd endured on her endless night in the East End. Mum let her weep, then drew her a hot bath. Eve thought of Iris as she soaked in the tub, and of all the people who no longer had bathtubs. Or running water. Or gas to boil a pot of tea. It took a long time for Eve to stop shaking.

"I don't think anyone ever imagined this," Eve said later as she sat in Mum's room, cradling a cup of hot tea. "If the soldiers on the battlefront endured this horror during the first war, it's no wonder they came home shocked and broken. Now the battlefront is here, in our own streets. Every one of us is a soldier. But how do we fight back?"

"Don't worry about that right now," Mum said. "It's Sunday morning, and we should go to church and thank God for sparing your life last night. We'll pray for Iris and her family, too."

Eve closed her eyes as tears spilled down her face. "I don't know if I can face God. I'm still so angry. You didn't see what happened in the East End last night."

"Try to get some sleep. We'll talk when I get back."

Eve did manage to fall asleep in Mum's bed for a few hours, but nightmarish visions filled her dreams. They didn't spring from her imagination like most nightmares, but from what she'd seen and experienced. When she awoke, Mum had Eve's breakfast on a tray. "Tildy made you eggs and toast. Everyone downstairs is thanking God you're all right."

"I'm going to volunteer for the Auxiliary Fire Service," Eve said as she ate. "I watched them work yesterday, and I want to help."

"Oh, Eve. You're not big enough or strong enough to handle heavy fire hoses. I would be worried sick about you. You're all I have!"

"Well, I can't just cower inside a shelter until the war ends. I felt so trapped sitting there! The fire service must have other jobs I can do besides handle a hose."

"Pray about it. Please, love. I know you're angry with God, but talk to Him. This isn't a good time to walk away from Him."

Tears filled Eve's eyes as she looked up at Granny Maud's picture of the Good Shepherd. It had comforted her as a child. She had trusted Him. But where was He now? How could He allow this terrible war to happen?

Eve spent the afternoon with her mum, and they ate a light supper downstairs with the other servants. The horror Eve had endured slowly began to fade. She might be able to close her eyes tonight without seeing flames and rubble or the image of the mother cradling her dead child. "I should go," she finally said. "I need to get back to my flat before the blackout." She stood by the back door, preparing to leave, when the air-raid siren began its terrible wail, rising in pitch with a wobbling scream. Fear rippled through Eve. *Ten minutes.*

"Oh, God, help us," Mum breathed. "Eve! Get in the Anderson shelter with the others. I'll run upstairs and help Lady Rosamunde."

"No, don't leave me!" Eve said, clinging to her.

Mum pushed her toward the door. "Go with the others, love. I'll be there in a minute."

Nine minutes. The evening air made her shiver as she followed the other servants outside. The shelter was so tiny, an underground hole designed for six adults. Her heart pounded with panic at the thought of being buried alive. She had to bend over to crawl inside. It smelled of damp earth and worms. Eve and the others sat on ledges across from each other, knees touching, a jumble of arms and legs. Waiting.

Five minutes. Half the time had passed by now. Above the sound of the siren, the taunting drone of enemy airplanes rumbled. Where was Mum? *Hurry! Please, hurry!* Eve was about to leap up and run back inside the town house to find her when the flap opened and Mum crawled inside, breathless. Eve made room for her, gripping her hand as she sat down.

"Where's Lady Rosamunde?" the housekeeper asked.

"She wouldn't come. She said she refused to be buried alive in a nasty hole before she's dead. I hated leaving her there all alone, but . . ."

The explosions began. The nightmare returned. It didn't seem real. The blasts were more distant than last night's, but the thumps and crumps of falling bombs terrified Eve nonetheless. She had witnessed their destruction. She couldn't breathe. She had to get out!

She couldn't get out.

As the other servants talked softly, she tried to gauge how far away the blasts were. What the targets might be. Which part of London was getting the worst of it. It sounded like the East End. Again. She tried to draw deep breaths but couldn't. A heavy weight sat on her chest.

Hours passed and nothing changed. Eve sat in the shelter with her mum throughout another long night as the ground shuddered and London burned. She prayed for Iris and her family. She prayed she and Mum would survive another endless night.

13

The telephone awakened Audrey just after dawn, jangling its dire alarm. She grabbed her robe and stuffed her arms into the sleeves as she hurried downstairs. Robbins answered it, and he held out the receiver to her. "It's the vicar, Miss Audrey."

"Hello, Rev. Hamlin. This is Audrey."

"I'm sorry to disturb you, Miss Clarkson, but there was a horrific bombing raid on the city of Coventry last night. They're asking for help. Will you come?"

Her heart thumped faster. She knew the vicar well enough to recognize the urgency in his voice. "Yes, of course. What can I do?"

"We need blankets. Food. Old bedsheets to tear into bandages. Clean drinking water."

"Right. I'll meet you at the church as quickly as I can."

"And, Miss Clarkson . . . ?" he added before she rang off. "I'm told that Coventry is a scene from hell. Nazi planes bombed the city for eleven straight hours. Devastated it."

"Oh, dear God . . ."

"They even destroyed Coventry Cathedral."

Audrey closed her eyes. That beautiful fourteenth-century cathedral. Gone.

The vicar cleared his throat. "Everyone will understand if you stay here while we deliver aid to the survivors."

"No," she said. "No, I would like to help." Eve had taught her to be courageous, forcing her to pilot the *Rosamunde* for the evacuation of Dunkirk, insisting she learn to drive a car. She could do this. She would do this.

Audrey ran up the stairs to her room to dress, praying for the people of Coventry, for the men and women who labored to help them. She'd learned to pray in the past few months as she'd become more involved in the village and in the life of the church. It was simple, really, the vicar said. A matter of talking to the Almighty and believing that He heard. That He cared. She'd also taken a first aid course to learn how to apply a tourniquet and administer basic medical help. Now, as she and one of the chambermaids gathered blankets and sheets from Wellingford's bedrooms, then raided the linen cupboard for more, she thought of how different she was from the shy, tearful girl she'd once been.

Mrs. Smith and Robbins boxed up all the food they could find and filled spare containers with drinking water. George helped load everything into the car. "I would like to come with you, Miss Audrey," he said. "They might need me to help dig . . . you know . . . for survivors."

Audrey feared he was too old for such grim labor, but she wouldn't deny his request. "Yes, of course, George. Put your shovel in the boot with the rest of the things."

They stopped at the village church to pick up more supplies and volunteers. Then, with the car fully loaded, Audrey followed the vicar's car across the tranquil countryside to Coventry. With such dire news these past weeks, Audrey wondered, at times, if England would survive. Italy had entered the war on the side of the Nazis. France had surrendered less than three weeks after the evacuation of Dunkirk. Nazi troops occupied Britain's Channel Islands, a few miles away. Nearly all of Europe had been defeated. Eve's letters detailed the ongoing fear and destruction in London as the Nazis bombarded the city night after night. Would anything be left?

Meanwhile, Audrey's family was separated. Mother insisted on staying in London in spite of Audrey's pleas. Alfie would be shipped out soon, traveling through U-boat-infested waters aboard a transport ship. Father was overseeing his factories in Manchester, with no plans to return to Wellingford. And Eve worked in London during the day and slept in a bomb shelter every night. Audrey longed to gather together all of the people she loved and stash them in the shelter George had dug in Wellingford's back garden, but she couldn't. They were all fighting this war in one way or another, and she wanted to help, too.

Three miles outside Coventry, a dense cloud of oily black smoke filled the horizon, tinted with a reddish glow. The city was on fire from end to end. Their convoy halted beside a group of dazed refugees, staggering away from the stricken city as if sleepwalking. George fetched his shovel and went ahead with the vicar to help in the rescue operation, while Audrey climbed from the car to distribute food and water and blankets to the refugees. She dug out her first aid kit to bandage wounds and burns. Many survivors had cuts from broken windows, shattered by the explosions. Audrey and the other women of the WVS worked nonstop as victims with smoke-reddened eyes and sooty faces continued to come throughout the morning.

Eventually, Audrey and the others got back in their cars and drove toward the city, where the real horror began. When they could go no farther, the roads blocked by debris, she and the other women got out and walked, passing out food and water to the workers digging for survivors in the rubble. She couldn't bear to look at the bodies lined up in rows outside the remains of their homes. Shards of glass splintered beneath her shoes as Audrey offered water and bandaged wounds, accompanied by the roar of distant flames, the clang of ambulance bells and fire engines, the cries and moans of survivors. She wanted to sit down in the dust and weep over the tragedy and destruction she was witnessing. Instead, she silently prayed for the strength to continue for as long as she was needed. And she was badly needed.

She had no idea how much time passed—hours? Days? She knelt on the ground, offering water to an elderly man, when someone called her name. Rev. Hamlin stood over her. George stood beside him, his shoulders slumped, his hands and tan, whiskery face covered with soot. "We've done all we can for today," the vicar said. "It's time to go home." He offered his hand to help Audrey to her feet. Somehow, the other volunteers from the village made their way back to the cars, now emptied of supplies, their strength exhausted.

Audrey's eyes burned from smoke as she drove. She would never forget this day for as long as she lived. And the war was far from over. What more would people be forced to endure? Would her nation hold firm or fall to the Nazis as so many others had? There were no answers. Only endless questions and agonizing uncertainty. *God, help us,* she silently prayed. *Please . . . please . . . help us all!*

LONDON

Eve cleared off her desk and slipped the cover over her typewriter for the night. She had just enough time to hurry home and eat before changing into her Auxiliary Fire Service uniform and reporting for night duty with the other volunteers.

She laid her hand on Iris's typewriter in silent tribute. Iris's desk was still unoccupied. She had never returned. When Eve last saw her, Iris was heading to an East End school with her grandmother to wait for a government bus to take them to a shelter. Eve knew from the memos she'd typed at the Ministry of Information that there'd been a mix-up. The buses never arrived at the school. While Eve had huddled in the Anderson shelter all night with Mum and the other servants, a bomb struck the school. Sixteen hundred people were injured in that nightlong raid. Four hundred and thirty had died. Eve longed to return and search for Iris and her family, but London's East End was so utterly devastated, she knew she would never find the block of houses where Iris's little cottage once sat.

Eve hunched her shoulders against the November wind that blew through her jacket as she left the ministry building. She hurried to the stairs to the Underground, the streets crowded with jostling people heading home after work. Life went on in London in spite of the widespread damage and destruction. The Nazis had bombed the city relentlessly every night for the past month, striking countless historic landmarks—St. Paul's Cathedral, Westminster Abbey, Mansion House, the Law Courts, even Buckingham Palace.

The Nazis dropped incendiaries first, igniting fires to guide their bombers through the blackout. Sandbags lay piled on every street to douse the fires. Every home and business had a stirrup hand pump, and everyone in London knew how to use it.

Eve detoured around a cordoned-off street, passing an apartment building with its outer wall sheared off, leaving people's belongings dangling on tilting floors. She shuffled down the stairs to the Underground with hundreds of others. The station platforms, the stairs, and even the rails would soon fill with people who didn't have an Anderson shelter in their yard or a public shelter nearby. Some people had already lined up to stake claim to their nightly spot. They were supposed to stay behind the yellow lines until after the evening commute before settling down to endure another night of terror, but many ignored the rules.

A rush of stale air preceded the train. Eve pushed her way on board, gripping a strap for the rattling ride home. Weary Londoners stared straight ahead or perused the daily newspapers. She wished she could read their thoughts.

Twenty minutes later, Eve exited at the station near her flat. She slept down here with her roommates when she wasn't on duty with the fire service. They'd become a community of sorts, laying their bedding in their customary places, mothers reading bedtime stories to their children, elderly women knitting socks for the soldiers. The long night always began with sirens. Always. How Eve hated that sound! On some nights, the thud and crump of bombs sounded very close, shaking the ground. No one knew what the landscape would look like at dawn.

Eve climbed the steps to her flat and found her mates eating a quick supper before gathering their things for the shelter. "Are you coming with us?" asked her new roommate, a girl named Mabel, who'd replaced Iris.

"I'm on fire duty tonight. I'll see you in the morning." She fixed beans and toast, then changed into her Auxiliary Fire Service uniform, slipping the strap of her gas mask over her head and donning her steel helmet. Audrey had begged her to come to the safety of Wellingford Hall, but Eve wouldn't flee London. She felt a solidarity with the other volunteers who fought back against the enemy. She worked every other night from 9 p.m. to 8 a.m., manning four emergency telephones with another volunteer; then she would return to her flat to change clothes, eat breakfast, and go to work.

Tonight, the other volunteer was a middle-aged housewife named Edith who had settled her children and her mother on the Underground platform for the night before coming to volunteer. "I see the telephone lines are back up," Edith said. "They were knocked out by the bombing the last time I worked here."

"I guess the fire lines are always a priority. My flat hasn't had telephone service all week."

They talked in between emergency calls, sirens wailing in the darkness above them along with the roar of enemy planes, the rattle of British antiaircraft fire, the hail of shrapnel. Whenever a call came in that an incendiary bomb had ignited a fire, they found out how many fire engines were needed and dispatched equipment from various fire stations.

"You can go to sleep," Eve said when Edith began to yawn. "It's slow tonight and I'm wide-awake for some reason." They would take turns sleeping on bunk beds, waking whenever the telephones rang.

The night wore on. The sound of distant booms continued overhead, accompanied by Edith's soft snores. Eve was good at judging how far away the bombs were and which areas of London were hit.

She was beginning to feel sleepy when the telephone startled her. Eve listened with growing horror as the caller described a direct bomb hit in a London neighborhood, civilian injuries, a spreading fire. The Clarksons' town house was in that neighborhood.

Mum!

Eve's voice trembled as she grabbed a telephone and called for multiple fire engines. Emergency vehicles.

Not Mum! Please, God, not my mum!

Once help was on the way, she woke Edith. "I—I need to go. You'll have to take over."

"You can't leave! We're both supposed to stay here until the next shift arrives."

"The street where my mum lives was bombed!" Eve donned her jacket, slung the straps of her purse and gas mask over her head, and bolted up the stairs.

It was too far to walk. She grabbed one of the yellow bicycles that AFS messengers used. Eve longed to race as fast as she could, but it wasn't safe in the pitch-darkness of the blackout. She usually took the Underground to the town house, so the overland route was unfamiliar to her. And London's street signs had been removed to confuse enemy spies. Sirens blared all around her. Antiaircraft guns hammered the sky. Searchlights probed for airplanes. Whistling bombs fell with thuds and explosions. Eve pedaled as fast as she dared through it all, begging God to spare her mum.

She neared the neighborhood at last. The glow of flames lit up the night from several blocks away. She got off her bike and walked with it, picking her way through rubble-filled streets and snaking fire hoses. Firefighters blocked off the area, but her AFS uniform and bicycle allowed her inside the barricades. Her chest ached as she labored to breathe. Her heart pounded with fear and fatigue as she rounded the corner.

The sight that greeted Eve made her cry out in horror. The entire block of town houses was a flaming pile of rubble. No one inside could possibly have survived. The bicycle fell from her grip and clattered to the pavement. Her knees gave way and she dropped to the pavement in shock. *No! Oh, God, no! Mum!*

"Miss? Are you all right, miss?" A volunteer tried to help her to her feet. Eve's legs wouldn't hold her.

"M-my mum . . ." She couldn't breathe. "Is anyone . . . ? Did everyone get out?"

"They're digging for survivors."

"Th-there's a . . . a shelter . . . an Anderson . . . behind the town house." Her lips wouldn't move right, her thoughts wouldn't form. *Oh, God!* "People . . . there might be people inside." *Please, God . . . Please, please let Mum be one of them.*

"We'll get to them, miss, as soon as we can get back there. Why don't you wait over there?" But Eve shook her head and gripped the frame of the fallen bicycle like a life raft.

Cries and moans came from the rubble. Faint calls for help. Workers dug frantically, moving the precarious piles of debris, shoveling, shoveling. Eve wanted to dig with them, but she couldn't move, watching through a haze of smoke and tears. Watching. Waiting. Hoping. Her heart thrashing against her ribs.

Please, God, let them all be safe! Not only her mum, but Tildy, the butler, the housekeeper. Her friends. And Audrey's mother. For Audrey's sake, Eve prayed that Lady Rosamunde had gone into the shelter too. But God seemed very far away. He must have turned His face from His creation to allow this death and destruction to go on and on, night after night.

When Eve was sure her legs would hold her, she stood and wandered through the crowd of workers and victims, searching the faces of pajama-clad people. She drew a shuddering breath before looking at the bodies lying in the street. She didn't recognize anyone. She waited some more, watching the digging, the suspense agonizing. The workers shook their heads. Were they giving up?

Maybe Mum wasn't even in London. Maybe she and Lady Rosamunde had returned to Wellingford Hall after all. Eve ran to find the nearest phone box, clinging to a thin strand of hope. "You shouldn't be out, young lady," a policeman hollered as she sprinted past. "Get to a shelter!"

Eve ignored him and kept running. Good thing she'd remembered her purse. She dug inside it for coins when she reached the phone box. She could barely insert them into the slot, her fingers shaking with fear and cold. She deposited all she had. The operator said it wasn't enough.

"Reverse the charges, then."

"Whom shall I say is calling, please?"

"Um . . . Rosamunde Clarkson."

The operator placed the call. Eve heard it ringing, ringing. "Sorry, no answer, ma'am."

"Keep trying! It's a huge house. They need time to get to the phone in the middle of the night."

At last she recognized Robbins's voice, thick with sleep. "Hello? Wellingford Hall. Who's calling, please?" Eve started to reply but the operator interrupted, asking if he would accept a collect call. There was a pause. Then, "Yes, Operator. Yes, I will."

"Robbins! This is Eve. I'm sorry for saying I was Lady Rosamunde but this is an emergency. Is my mum at Wellingford?" The wait for his reply seemed interminable.

"No, she's at the London town house."

A wave of nausea washed through her. She had to lean against the side of the phone box. Surely Mum was safe inside the Anderson shelter even if Lady Rosamunde refused to go. Mum had to be safe. She *had* to be.

"Hello? Hello?" Robbins said. "What's going on, Eve?"

"Is Audrey there?"

"She's asleep."

"Go upstairs and wake her. She needs to come to London straightaway. A bomb destroyed her London town house tonight."

"Oh, dear God . . ."

"It's in ruins. I don't know if . . . whether anyone . . ." An ambulance raced past in the darkness. It halted near the ruins. Eve's stomach twisted with dread. Helpless. She was so helpless.

"Hello, Eve? Are you still there?"

"I need to go. Tell Audrey to come to the town house . . . um . . . to where it used to be. I'll be waiting for her."

She hung up the phone and sprinted back to where the ambulance idled. The attendants had a stretcher out and were loading someone onto it. Eve pushed past the ARP wardens who tried to restrain her, shouting, "No! Let me through! Let me see my mum!"

It wasn't her.

Eve was trembling so violently she could barely stand. She had to get around to the back, to the Anderson shelter. Surely Mum was inside it. All of the servants were. They had to be! She tried to make her way down the street, around the chaos, but the workers wouldn't let her through. She stammered an explanation, desperate to make someone understand, but her thoughts and words jumbled together.

"We'll get back there as soon as we can, miss," they assured her.

Eve stumbled back to where the ambulance stood. One of the attendants made her sit down and wrapped a blanket around her shoulders. It didn't help. Eve couldn't stop trembling. Her entire body was going to shake into pieces. She watched the activity swirling around her as if from a great distance, as if time had slowed to a crawl and the minutes ticked by like days, weeks. Why didn't they hurry?

Please, God . . . Please don't take my mum . . .

⟨⟐⟩

Audrey stood in her bedroom doorway in her robe, wondering if this was a bad dream, wishing it were. Robbins was in the darkened hallway in his pajamas, saying that Eve had called. The town house had been hit. Audrey needed to come at once. She gripped the doorframe as the room tilted. She'd seen what Nazi bombs had done to Coventry.

"I would like to go to London with you, Miss Audrey," Robbins said. "I don't like the idea of you going alone."

"Thank you, Robbins. I would be grateful for your company. We'll leave as soon as we're dressed." She needed to stop trembling. She must pull herself together and be strong. It would take hours to get to London, inching along in the darkness, unable to use headlamps in the blackout.

She had begged Mother to leave London and come to Wellingford. "I won't let the Nazis scare me from my home," Mother had replied.

"Wellingford is your home, too," Audrey had said. She'd heard Mother's bitter laughter and imagined her shaking her head. Mother didn't love Wellingford the way Audrey and Alfie and Father did. To them, it would always be home. But not to Mother.

The sun was beginning to rise when Audrey and Robbins reached the outskirts of London. It had been the longest drive of her life. The longest night. A pall of smoke hung above the city, and she could taste the scorched air—the same as in Coventry.

The destruction filled her with dread as they neared the town house. Rubble. Police and fire barricades. A woman in uniform telling Audrey she couldn't go any farther. Audrey wanted to rage at her but managed to reply calmly. "My town house was bombed last night."

"You'll have to walk. You can't drive any closer. Emergency vehicles only."

Audrey parked, and she and Robbins got out. Her distress grew with each trembling step, dodging bricks and shiny chunks of shrapnel, twisting fire hoses. Audrey halted in silent horror when she saw the crumpled, smoking ruin. Robbins groaned and gripped his forehead.

All but one of the town houses had collapsed. The front of that unit was sheared off, and Audrey saw inside her neighbors' rooms as if peering into a dollhouse. Pictures hung crookedly on the walls. Furniture and rugs lay jumbled in heaps. The floors tilted, ready to collapse. Her family's town house had stood in the middle of the row. Audrey couldn't move. Couldn't think.

"Audrey! . . . Audrey!" She heard her name as if from a great distance, the way one hears it when being awakened from a nightmare. "Audrey!" She turned and fell into Eve's arms. The strength of her grip pushed all the air from Audrey's chest, but she clung to her, longing to draw from Eve's strength.

"Oh, Eve . . . dear God . . ."

"They haven't found anybody, yet."

Audrey couldn't grasp what she was saying. "They have an Anderson, don't they? In back?"

"They're still trying to dig it out. The garages—" Eve halted. She released her and ran toward a fireman leading a group of dazed survivors from the alleyway. Robbins took Audrey's arm as they followed. The cook and the housekeeper were hugging Eve. Weeping. Mother wasn't with them. Neither was Eve's mum.

"Where's my mum?" Eve shrieked. "Isn't she with you?"

"No—"

"What do you mean, *no*? She has to be!" Eve gave the housekeeper a shake as if forcing her to change her reply. The cook's words came out between sobs.

"We were all in the shelter except Lady Rosamunde. Your mum went back inside to persuade her to come down where it was safe. Then . . . then the bomb hit."

Eve collapsed to the ground and wept.

Audrey didn't know what to do. She hesitated, then crouched beside her, feeling Eve's loss as much as her own. "They're still searching, aren't they, Eve? Let's not lose hope."

Hours passed as they waited, holding tightly to each other's hands, watching the rescue workers dig. A canteen truck arrived with tea and sandwiches but neither of them could eat. Audrey heard her servants talking, weeping, and Robbins comforting them like a father.

Every now and then Audrey would recognize a broken bit of furniture or a fragment of a rug or a vase as workers shoveled debris into the street, and she had the crazy notion that if she could just gather up all the shattered pieces and put them back together again, everything would be all right. Mother would be all right. She imagined her mother emerging from the rubble, strong and proud and beautiful, dusting dirt from her sequined dress and sniffing at all the fuss—then frowning in displeasure at Audrey's tears of relief. Audrey wished she could cry but she felt strangely numb as she fought to hold herself together. It was what Mother would have wished.

Shortly before noon, the workers found two bodies. ARP wardens laid the lifeless forms on stretchers. As Robbins went forward to identify them, one of Mother's cigarette holders rolled out of the ruins at his feet. Audrey saw his expression and knew the answer before he spoke a word.

"NO!" The scream rose up from deep in Audrey's soul before she could stop it. It couldn't be true. Mother couldn't be dead. She was larger than life, a proud, beautiful woman who held Audrey's world together. She'd never been the mother Audrey longed for, but she was the mother she needed—now more than ever. How would she navigate the rituals of the aristocracy without her? There

were rules and customs she still needed to learn, standards one must live up to, the right people to meet. For as long as Audrey could remember, she had clung to the hope that if she managed to do everything right, married a suitable husband, socialized in the proper circles, perhaps Mother would finally love her. Because in spite of Mother's aloofness, in spite of the dark truth of her infidelity, Lady Rosamunde was her mother. And Audrey loved her.

Eve's cries were as soul-deep as her own as she wept alongside her. Audrey turned to her. They shared an unimaginable loss. But Eve stepped back. "This is your mother's fault!" Her face twisted with anger and grief. "She was too selfish to go into the shelter where it was safe. She wouldn't leave London, so my mum had to stay here, too. She didn't think of anyone but herself!"

Eve's anger stunned her. But the accusation was true. "I know. I know what Mother is like . . ." What she *was* like. Mother was dead. A chasm of grief opened before Audrey, and she covered her face and wept as hours of pent-up fear and sorrow overflowed. Eve turned away from her into the cook's arms. None of the servants moved to comfort Audrey.

14

Eve gripped Alfie's hand as she watched George and Robbins and Williams—men who had been like fathers to her—lower Mum's coffin into the ground behind the village church. The villagers she'd known all her life surrounded her, sharing her grief, murmuring about Mum's tragic death. Throughout the long hours of the wake, the funeral, and now the burial, Alfie and Audrey had remained by Eve's side, holding her up, helping her through these terrible days, even though they were also grieving. Lady Rosamunde's funeral would be tomorrow at Wellingford, once Mr. Clarkson returned home.

"If there's anything I can do," Rev. Hamlin said. "Anything at all . . ." Everyone had loved Ellen Dawson. Her fierce loyalty to Lady Rosamunde baffled the villagers as much as it did Eve. She still blamed Lady Rosamunde for Mum's death. If not for her stubbornness, Mum would be alive. The Anderson shelter had kept the others safe. Yet Eve tried not to direct her anger at Alfie or Audrey.

It wasn't their fault. They'd suffered from Lady Rosamunde's self-ishness, too.

Tears blurred Eve's eyes as Mum's coffin came to rest at the bottom of the hole alongside Granny Maud's grave. The two people she loved most in this world were gone. When Granny died, Eve thought the ache in her heart would never heal. Her life had changed that day, yet the world spun on, the sun rising and setting. *"Rain or shine, just take the day the Lord gives you,"* Granny Maud taught her. With Mum to console her, the painful wound of grief had slowly healed. This time, Eve's grief seemed bottomless, swallowing her alive, blocking off the sunlight.

How could she live her life without Mum? Who could she confide in when she fell in love? Who would share her hopes and dreams, her joy on her wedding day? Who would teach her how to be a mother? Mum had worked so hard, sacrificing so much to raise Eve to adulthood and now she would miss the rest of Eve's life. And Eve would miss the warmth of Mum's arms, her gentle words of advice, her love. It wasn't fair! Her grief was a wound too deep to ever heal.

After the funeral luncheon, after the last of the villagers and servants had consoled her and wept with her, Eve returned to Wellingford with Alfie and Audrey. She had no other place to go besides her flat in London. She would sleep in her old room tonight.

"Let's go out and get drunk together," Alfie said as they climbed Wellingford's front steps.

"I can't do it, Alfie. Getting drunk won't help. That's not how I grieve."

"Are you sure? It always helps me forget. For a little while, anyway." Did Alfie know about his mother, how much she drank? About the men in her life? This wasn't the time to ask.

In the end, Alfie ordered the servants to build a roaring fire in the sitting room—one of the smaller of Wellingford's rooms—and he and Eve cuddled together on the brocade sofa until well past midnight. Audrey joined them for part of the time, and when she finally went to bed, Alfie doused the lights and opened the drapes so they could gaze at the windswept November sky. "Aren't you worried that the ARP wardens will fine you for opening your curtains and letting the firelight escape?" Eve asked as he settled beside her again.

"I'll give them a piece of my mind if they try."

He'd opened a bottle of his father's whiskey, but he was the only one drinking it. Straight from the bottle. Eve liked Alfie better during the first part of the evening when he was still himself, before the drink turned him into someone else, someone acting the part of a happy man. She leaned against his shoulder, dreading the thought of saying goodbye, the thought of him returning to war. Would God take Alfie from her, too? Was He that cruel?

"Thanks for helping me get through today," she said, exhaling. "My entire family is gone now. I'm all alone."

"How can I cheer you? I miss the lively girl you were before the war. You were always so vibrant and . . . untamed. So full of life. I used to think you could have fun in an empty room."

"This war changed all that. It destroyed my hope of ever having a future. It seems like the war will just go on and on until there's no one left on either side." She paused. "And now you're going off to fight again, too."

"Don't remind me." Alfie lifted the bottle and took a swig. He wiped his mouth. "But it has to be done."

Eve leaned away from him and waited until he looked at her. She would say what she longed to say, no matter the outcome.

"I want you to know that I love you, Alfie. I do. With all my heart. You're the only man I've ever loved, and you've set the bar so high I don't think I could ever love anyone else as much as you."

He pulled her close. Held her tight. "I have a confession to make. I'm in love with you, too."

"Y-you are?"

"Mm. I have been for a long time. I've met plenty of girls, but none even comes close to you, Eve Dawson."

She pulled free to look at him, searching for the truth in his eyes. They shone with tears in the firelight. "That's the first time you ever told me."

"I know. I never told you because—" He stopped. She waited. "Because I'm afraid to love you, Eve. Afraid I'm going to hurt you. I don't believe in marriage after the way my parents' marriage turned out. It's safer for both of us if I don't give away my heart. If I don't have any expectations for myself or for you. We can just be together, having fun." He started to raise the bottle, but Eve held on to his arm.

"I don't know what a marriage looks like, either. My daddy died before I was even born."

"See? I couldn't bear the thought of loving you, finding joy and happiness with you—and then losing you. That's why . . . this . . ." He waved the whiskey bottle.

"You hide behind it, Alfie. What if you decided not to hide and you were just yourself?"

"I don't think I would like what I saw if I had to face myself sober."

"Why? You're a wonderful man."

"No, I'm not," he said with a bitter laugh. "I'm shallow, Eve. I like money and nice things. Fast cars. Loud parties where I can get lost among all the other shallow people. I'm like my mother in that respect. I would lose that life if I married you."

Eve closed her eyes and looked down as an arrow of pain pierced her heart. Alfie loved her. He thought about marrying her. But he never would.

"See?" he said, lifting her chin. "I've already hurt you. And that's the last thing I ever want to do." He set his bottle on the floor and took her hand, holding it between his. She wanted to pull away yet she wanted him to hold it forever. "I'm sorry, Eve, but that's the truth about me. Father wants me to marry into an aristocratic family. He's been working toward respectability all his life, and the fact of the matter is that I'll lose my inheritance if I don't please him. And I don't want to lose it."

In that moment she hated Alfie. Hated his brutal honesty as her hope bled away. "So given the choice between love and wealth, you'd choose wealth?" she asked, her voice stiff with anger.

"I already confessed that I'm shallow, Eve. I'm sorry."

"And I'm very sorry for you. A simple life with someone you love can be every bit as wonderful as a life with . . . all of this." She gestured to the opulent room. "Do you think your parents' wealth made them happy?"

"I know it didn't." He lifted the bottle and took a long swallow, grimacing as he lowered it again. "I know I can't expect you to wait for me. But if you're willing . . . if you let me remain a bachelor until I get my inheritance, then I'll be free to marry you."

"What sort of man will you be by then?"

"I don't know. I don't like myself very much now, so what's the difference? That's why I need this." He held up the bottle for a moment. "And it's why I need you."

"If you need to drink in order to live with yourself, what good is it to be rich?"

"You're asking impossible questions. Just kiss me, Eve. I'm a better man when I'm with you." She let him pull her close and kiss her, tasting the whiskey on his breath. And for a few beautiful, floating moments, nothing else mattered. She loved him. And Alfie loved her. She lost herself in the sheer joy of it.

When the kiss ended, she caressed his face, loving the rough feel of his whiskers. They glinted like amber in the firelight. "You're a better man than you think, Alfie."

He shook his head. "When I was in Belgium, every day seemed like my last. I was certain I was going to die. I watched so many others die, better men than me . . . The truth is, I don't think I'll survive this war."

"Don't say that!"

"That's why I'm determined to make the most of every day I have." He set the bottle on the floor again and cupped her face in his hands. "My leave is nearly over. Can't we share one precious night of happiness together?"

"You mean sleep with you?"

He nodded. Eve couldn't deny the passion she felt for him, burning bright and hot like the coals in the fireplace. She imagined her joy in being engulfed in each other's arms, each other's love. So many people already had died in this war, and who knew if she and Alfie would survive it? Why not give this last night to each other? Oh, how she longed to! And yet she couldn't. She shook her head. Tears slid down her face as she tried to explain. "All I have is myself, Alfie. I can't give that to you or to any man unless I know I'm getting all of him in return. It wouldn't be a fair exchange. I would give you everything—and I'd have nothing."

"It wouldn't be like that."

"You just told me that you love something else more than you love me. You admitted that I don't have all of your heart."

"Eve, listen—"

"I need to go to bed, Alfie. I'm returning to London tomorrow."

She wiggled out of his embrace and stood. "I'm going to believe that you'll change. That you'll find yourself and choose love in the end, not money. For now, it's enough to know that you do love me, even if I take second place in your heart."

He grabbed her hand to stop her. "Will you be at Mother's funeral tomorrow with Audrey and me?"

"I can't. My mum died because of her. I already told Audrey I wasn't coming. She understands. You need to be with her, Alfie, not me. She loves you so much. You're all she has. Please be good and kind to her. Don't start drinking until you get back to your Army base."

"So we're saying goodbye now?"

"Not goodbye—until next time." She bent and wrapped her arms around him, kissing him as if it were the last time, praying it wouldn't be. "I'm going to write to you every chance I get, even if you hardly ever write back. I love you so much, Alfie."

He didn't try to follow her as she crossed to the door. She turned for one last glimpse of him and saw him lift the bottle to his lips.

⟨◦⟩

Audrey rose before dawn and dressed quickly. Eve was leaving early this morning, and there were things she wanted to say to her. Things she needed to say. She found Eve down in the basement kitchen having a cup of tea.

"You're up early," Eve said.

"I want to drive you to the train station."

Eve shook her head. "Thanks, but I would rather walk. I need time to think . . . and to say goodbye to this place."

Audrey sat down beside her on a wooden chair. "I'm so sorry for the selfish choices my mother made. I know my words can't change anything, but I am truly sorry. Please, stay here at

Wellingford with me for a while, Eve. You need to get away from the madness in London and take time to grieve. We both need—"

"I'm not going to run away and hide in the country."

"That's not what I meant. Just stay for a few days and—"

"We're very different, Audrey. Your reaction is to scurry back to safety. Mine is to fight!"

Audrey wanted to deny it but knew Eve was right. "I pleaded with Mother to come to Wellingford, where it was safe, but she refused."

Eve didn't seem to hear her as she stared at her empty teacup. "War has taken everyone—first Daddy and now Mum. I have no one left. At least you still have your father and Alfie."

"Oh, Eve."

"Well, I'm fighting back! I've been thinking about it for a while, but now my mind is made up. I'm enlisting."

"I thought you already were volunteering."

Eve waved her hand as if canceling Audrey's words. "I sit beside a telephone for the fire service. It isn't enough! I'm going to join the ATS and drive an ambulance or a lorry or . . . or something! I'm not going to sit in an office and type all day, then huddle in a shelter all night. I need to fight!"

Anger stirred inside Audrey, too. Her mother was dead, her town house in ruins. If Alfie and Eve could do their bit, then she could, too. Passing out blankets and bandaging cuts no longer seemed like enough. She could be courageous with Eve beside her. "I'll enlist with you."

"Ha! That I'd like to see!"

Audrey could forgive Eve's disdain. Her grief was speaking.

"I mean it, Eve. I don't want to sit in Wellingford Hall all alone until the war ends."

"If it ever does."

"We've both lost our mothers. We both should fight back. Together. Like we did at Dover during the evacuation. And you aren't all alone, Eve. You still have me. And Alfie."

Eve stared at her for a long moment. Then she pulled Audrey into her arms and they wept together. "I'm sorry, Audrey . . . I'm so sorry for the things I said . . ."

"Never mind. We'll get through this together. We'll grieve together. From now on we're sisters. We'll stay together no matter what. In the good times and the bad. Until the war ends—and forever after that."

"I can't imagine an 'after.'"

"I can't either. But whatever happens, Eve, we'll face it together."

⟨◦✐✐◦⟩

Eve's mind raced with all of the things she needed to do as she walked to the village train station. Unless Audrey changed her mind, they would enlist together in the Army's Auxiliary Territorial Service next week. In the meantime, Eve needed to resign from her job at the ministry and as a fire service volunteer, pack her meager belongings, and say goodbye to her flatmates.

The train arrived, crowded with men in uniform. If only the Army would let women fight with real guns and weapons. Eve would be fearless like her daddy had been. After all, she had nothing left to lose.

She was still thinking about her daddy as the train chugged into Victoria Station in London, and mourning the loss of his photograph in the rubble of the town house. Granny Maud's picture of the Good Shepherd had also been destroyed along with any faith Eve might have had in Him. The ARP wardens promised she would be allowed to pick through the ruins but she wasn't hopeful of finding anything.

Eve had planned to take the Underground to her flat, but she rode to the Westminster station instead. Big Ben chimed the half hour as she emerged into the cold daylight and crossed busy Bridge Street to Westminster Abbey.

She felt alone in the vast hall as she made her way to the Unknown Warrior's grave. She gazed down at the dark slab, dry-eyed, emptied of tears.

"You're all together now, Daddy," she murmured. "You, Granny Maud, and Mum."

She'd visited this grave often since moving to London and always sensed that her daddy was near, that he was listening. But not today. Today, the grave was merely a black marker in the middle of the vast stone floor. She was alone.

15

ATS MOTOR TRANSPORT TRAINING CENTER, DECEMBER 1940

Audrey pricked her finger yet again on the sewing needle, drawing blood. She fought to control her tears. In the week that she and Eve had spent in the ATS training camp, Audrey was always fighting tears. She hadn't imagined anything could be this hard. It was bad enough that on their first day in the Army they were marched into the latrine, six girls at a time, and given only sixty seconds to finish what they needed to do. But the snickers and lewd comments from the lower-class girls, who had pegged Audrey at first sight as an aristocrat, made the experience worse.

"Just shut up and leave her alone!" Eve bellowed at the worst offender. "She's doing her bit like the rest of us, isn't she?"

"Thanks for standing up for me," Audrey told Eve later.

"You could do it yourself, you know."

"I don't know how. I didn't know how in boarding school, either, and those girls were all from the gentry. Remember how miserable I was? This is even worse."

"It'll get better. Once we survive basic training, we'll have something useful to do."

Audrey wasn't certain she *would* survive. In the past seven days, they had stripped her to the bone of everything familiar and comforting, everything that told her who she was. Physicians poked and prodded her during humiliating medical examinations. The screaming sergeant major bullied and harassed her until she dreamed of "left-right, left-right" in her sleep. She wouldn't have made it this far without Eve.

"You're much better at adjusting to change than I am," Audrey said when they'd finally collapsed onto their narrow cots that first night. They slept in the former dormitory of a bleak boys' preparatory school. Eve had to show Audrey how to put sheets on the bed. The scratchy fabric felt like sacking. The ugly Army-issue pajamas would fit a girl twice Audrey's size. Prison must be like this.

"The only reason I can adjust to poor conditions is because I've been poor all my life," Eve had replied. "At least you can go back to your posh life after the war ends." Audrey wanted to assure Eve that her life would also be better after the war when she married Alfie, but neither of them truly believed that Eve's romance would have a happy ending.

For now, Audrey's only reminders of her former life were the civilian clothes she'd worn to the training center, now stowed inside the locker by her bed, and the framed photograph of herself and Alfie on top of that locker. The picture had been taken on board the *Rosamunde* the last summer she and Alfie sailed together, the sun in their faces, the wind blowing their hair. Eve also had a photograph of Alfie on her locker, looking handsome in his uniform, a carefree grin on his face. The ATS had stripped everything else from Audrey, including her own underwear and brassieres. The Army-issue ones were ghastly.

"These frumpy old things look like something our grannies would wear!" one of the girls said, holding up a baggy pair of the long-legged underpants.

"Our grannies wouldn't be caught dead in those knickers!" someone else shot back. Every girl in the dormitory received the same-size brassiere, whether they were plump or thin, well-endowed or flat-chested, and was told to make it fit. The girls joked about sharing the surplus or stuffing the cups with socks. As the other girls stripped without a care, the lack of privacy humiliated Audrey. It was one of the things she'd despised about boarding school.

The food in the dining hall of the former boys' school required another adjustment. "I can't even guess what kind of meat this is, can you?" she asked Eve as she sawed into a rubbery brown lump.

Eve shrugged off her concerns. "I don't care. I'm eating a lot better than my flatmates and I did before I enlisted. None of us had time to stand in queues all day with our ration coupons. All the meat would be sold by the time we got home from work." Audrey had lost weight, not only from the inedible food but from the endless marching, day after day, and the requirement that they run from place to place rather than walk. Her blistered feet spoke of how unaccustomed she was to such rigorous exercise—and of the awkwardness of her clunky Army-issue shoes. She remembered how gracefully Eve had skipped barefoot across the rocky stream the day they'd first met, and how she'd climbed down from the tree as if she'd been born to do it. Yes, Eve fared much better in the Army than Audrey did.

Now she sat on her bed in the few remaining minutes before lights-out, using her regulation sewing kit to alter her brassiere and various other items in her uniform kit—jacket, skirts, pullovers, slacks, shirts, and ties. The sleeves and hems were miles too long for her and Eve's petite frames. The thick stockings resembled the ones her housekeeper wore. Everything needed to be labeled with her name and number. And she still had to shine her shoes and uniform buttons before she went to bed. They'd issued her a cleaning kit for each task, and Audrey hadn't known what they were for. Her shoes and clothing would appear in her wardrobe at Wellingford as if by magic, clean, polished, ironed, and brushed. Audrey had never sewn in her life, and now she sucked blood from the latest prick to her finger. Yes, Army life required a bigger adjustment than she'd ever imagined. How had Alfie endured it?

"I would like to see the girl they designed this uniform to fit," Eve said. She sat on the bed across from Audrey as they sewed. "She would have to be six feet tall, with arms like a chimpanzee and a huge bosom. One size does not fit all!"

"It's such an ugly uniform too," Audrey said with a sigh. "What are all these pleated pockets for? And the belted jacket makes everyone's bottom look enormous. We should have joined the Wrens. The famous fashion designer Edward Molyneux designed their uniforms."

"Spoken like a true aristocrat! You obviously never had to wear a scullery maid's uniform. Believe me, this is a huge improvement."

"I can't help who I am, Eve. You don't have to rub it in." She sucked her injured finger, still oozing blood.

"You can still change your mind about enlisting, you know. I don't think it's too late. Joining up was my idea, not yours."

Everything in Audrey longed to quit, but Mother's taunting voice—"Oh, for pity's sake, Audrey"—strengthened her resolve. She vowed to continue, to measure up to the standards expected of her, just as she'd been doing all her life. They weren't Mother's expectations that she must live up to now, but her nation's. And Audrey also longed to please God. "I'm not going to quit," she replied.

She would stow away her personality and individuality for the duration of the war and become like everyone else, right down to her Army-issue toothbrush and hairbrush. She resumed sewing.

One of Audrey's biggest tormentors, a loudmouthed girl named Irene who didn't seem interested in making her uniform fit, roamed the room looking at the framed photographs on the other girls' lockers. Audrey bristled when Irene picked up Alfie's photo. She was about to ask her politely to put it down when Eve kicked her foot, then held a finger to her lips.

"Hey, have a look at this, girls," the bully said to the others. "Tweedledee and Tweedledum over here share the same boyfriend!" Everyone looked up as if something interesting was about to happen.

"Handsome fellow, isn't he?" Eve said calmly. She continued to sew.

"He sure is!" Irene replied. "I wonder how many other girls have his picture. Maybe I could get one." She got what she was after—mocking laughter.

Eve kept her voice even. "Look a little closer, Irene. He could be Audrey's twin, right? He's her brother—and my boyfriend."

"You're having me on! You're never stepping out with the posh girl's brother!"

"Cross my heart and hope to die if I'm lying," she said, making the sign over her chest.

"Didn't your mum warn you that the gentry's sons want only one thing from girls like us? And it isn't marriage." There was more laughter.

Eve didn't seem perturbed. "Think whatever you like," she replied. "I know the truth."

Irene stared at the pictures for another moment, then seemed to lose interest. She set them down none too gently and moved on to her next victim. Audrey released the breath she didn't know she'd been holding.

Eve slid off her own bed and stood over Audrey. "You okay?" she asked.

"I suppose. Although I'm not getting anywhere with this sewing. I keep knotting the thread."

"Let me," Eve said, taking it. "I'll finish your sewing if you polish my shoes."

"Thanks." Audrey found it much easier to polish shoes than to try to sew. "How did you learn to handle the taunting?" she asked Eve.

"The boys in school used to torment us girls all the time. I learned that if I didn't react, they'd lose interest." She snipped the sewing thread with her teeth, then added, "And the ones who didn't lose interest found out that I could hold my own in a brawl."

Audrey smiled. "You're my hero, Eve."

"Listen," she said, leaning closer to whisper. "I know how you can win over Irene and all the other bullies."

"How?"

"I'm told our pay packets come with a chit for cigarettes from the canteen. You don't smoke but Irene does."

The tiny measure of power helped Audrey sleep soundly that night.

She rose early the next morning for a day that began like all the rest, scrambling to get everything in order for "kit parade." She must lay out her belongings on her properly made bed, the blanket folded just so, jacket buttons and shoes polished to a shine. Audrey stood at attention at the foot of her bed, not daring to move, praying she would pass inspection. Failure meant scrubbing the latrine floor on hands and knees. With Eve's help, Audrey always passed. After inspection, they quick-marched to the parade ground to practice drilling until the sergeant major was satisfied. Audrey couldn't see the point of inspections or understand how she could serve her country by marching in perfect squares. "Are we ever going to start driving?" she whispered to Eve as a misty rain began to fall.

"Let's hope so. I know they're desperate for ambulance drivers."

"All right, listen up," the sergeant major barked when the drilling ended. "Before you begin your driving courses, everyone must pass the gas drill."

"This doesn't sound good," Eve mumbled. She had confided her fear of enclosed spaces to Audrey, her dread of being buried alive. Even donning her cumbersome gas mask made Eve feel trapped. It was the only fear Audrey had ever known her to admit.

"Everyone must suit up in her gas mask," the commander explained. "We'll go into that hut over there and the gas will be turned on. When the red light flashes, take off your mask and wait until it stops flashing. Then make your way to an exit door and run out."

"Just don't panic, Eve," Audrey whispered as they pulled their masks from their cases and slipped them on. "Obviously, the gas won't be lethal."

"It's this mask that's terrifying!"

"Whenever I need to stay calm, I recite the Lord's Prayer. You can do this, Eve." The role reversal was new to both of them.

With her mask in place, Audrey crowded into the windowless hut with Eve and sat down beside her on one of the benches, noting where the two exits were. She took Eve's hand as the lights went out and the room filled with an eerie gray fog, so thick she could barely see her hand in front of her face. Her fingers ached from Eve's grip. Hours seemed to pass before the red light flashed, painting the fog with its glow. Eve released Audrey's hand and ripped off her mask. Audrey did the same, fighting the urge to inhale a panic-stricken breath. The light flashed forever. Audrey feared her lungs would burst. She heard one of the other girls cry out. Several began to cough. The moment the flashing stopped, Audrey grabbed Eve's hand and towed her through the pushing, shoving mob toward the nearest door, grateful in the pitch-darkness that she'd noted where it was. She found the latch and flung open the door. The chilly rain felt wonderful as she lifted her face to the sky and breathed.

"We passed!" Eve said with a shaky grin. But it took several minutes for the color to return to Eve's face and for Audrey's heart to slow down. A corporal rounded up the choking, weeping girls who'd failed the test, including the bully, Irene.

Afterwards, the corporal assigned Audrey and Eve to a squadron of twenty-five women. "For the next few weeks," their new leader explained, "your training course will consist of vehicle driving, vehicle maintenance, first aid classes, anti-gas drills, and map-reading tests."

"Driving will be easy for us," Eve predicted with her usual confidence. Audrey thought so, too. But neither of them had counted on the difficult double-clutching that the lorries and ambulances required. The practice vans were mounted on blocks so students could learn to handle the transmissions without moving anywhere, and Audrey ground through a lot of gears on the vehicles before getting the hang of it.

As if the uniforms weren't bad enough, they were issued ugly gray dungarees to wear for the vehicle maintenance classes, taught in garages so cold Audrey feared her fingers would freeze off. She and Eve learned to change tires and perform routine maintenance and repairs on their ambulances. Map reading taught them to navigate in their assigned districts without signs. They learned to travel on the worst types of roads, at night, with hooded headlamps, in the pitch-dark of the blackout. Through it all, Audrey was bullied, insulted, shamed, and—once in a while—praised.

"We're fighting for our homes," their instructor reminded them after a particularly discouraging day when everything went wrong. "There's no time to cry for your mum." Audrey risked a glance at Eve as she blinked away tears, wondering if Eve would shout that they'd both lost their mums, thanks to Hitler's bombs. But Eve remained stoic.

After weeks of the most grueling work she'd ever accomplished, Audrey and the others faced a final test—driving their ambulances at night down an assigned route, wearing a gas mask and full gas-protection gear. Eve clearly grew increasingly nervous with each piece of equipment she donned. When she peered at Audrey through her gas mask, Eve had fear in her eyes. "You can do this," Audrey said, though she wondered if Eve even understood her with her mask-garbled voice. They studied their maps a final time, then each drove away on their assigned routes.

Audrey's eyes strained to the limit as she drove. She wouldn't think about all the disaster stories she'd heard—crashing into cows or vehicles in the dark, driving off the road into swamps and fields. Seated beside her, the instructor gave no hint of how well or poorly Audrey was doing until they came to a final stop back at the training center.

"Very good, Miss Clarkson. You may remove your mask." The instructor made no move to get out of the vehicle as she scribbled on a form, so Audrey didn't either. "Of course, you realize, Miss Clarkson, that this isn't your final test."

Audrey's perfect, inbred posture failed her for a moment as her shoulders slumped in disappointment. "It isn't?"

"No. You won't know if you've passed the real test until you're called to a disaster site for the first time. That's something we cannot simulate, nor can we truly prepare you for it. Do you think you can handle the sight of severed limbs scattered around a bomb site or dead bodies burned beyond recognition?"

Audrey swallowed, searching for a reply. "I couldn't say. One would be foolish to speculate. I hope to keep my mind on the fact that I'm there to do my job and transfer the living to hospital."

"I wish you luck, Miss Clarkson."

"Thank you." Audrey ran her hand through her sweaty hair, matted and itching from the gas mask. She no longer resembled the girl who'd grown up in Wellingford Hall, the debutante who'd had an audience with the queen. That Audrey was gone. It was just as well—she never liked her much anyway.

"I noticed that you signed up for the same postings as Eve Dawson when you leave."

"Yes, ma'am." She wondered how Eve had survived the confinement of her gas suit.

The instructor gave Audrey a hard look. "Wouldn't you rather partner with someone from your own class?"

The question startled her. "Um . . . No, ma'am, I wouldn't. I would much rather partner with Eve Dawson."

The woman opened her door with a sigh as if to convey to Audrey that she was making a terrible mistake. "If that's what you wish. I hope you won't regret it."

JANUARY 1941

Eve awoke to the sound of distant explosions. Bright flashes like lightning pierced the edges of the blackout curtains. The Nazis were bombing Liverpool again. The roar of destruction filled the night even though the ATS ambulance base where she and Audrey were posted was several miles from the city. Eve sat up and peered at the watch Alfie had given her. Two thirty in the morning. She rose and put on her uniform and a warm jersey, knowing they would surely be called out into the cold night. Audrey rolled over and squinted at her.

"What are you doing? What time is it?"

Eve held up her hand. "Listen . . ." The rumbling was continuous, like an unending thunderstorm. "The Nazis are bombing Liverpool. It sounds bad. They'll be calling us any minute, so we'd better get dressed."

Audrey rubbed her eyes, then stood to put on her clothes, as well. They shared the former hotel room with two other girls, who also climbed from their beds to get ready. The knock on their door came a few minutes later. "Oh, good. You're all ready," the night supervisor said when she saw them. "Let's go."

Eve had driven on several ambulance runs in the two weeks since she and Audrey had qualified as drivers. So far, their work involved evacuating civilian patients from Liverpool hospitals to safer ones outside the city. Judging by tonight's powerful explosions, this run would be different.

"No wonder they made us run all the time at the training center," Audrey said as they jogged from the hotel to the vehicle garages. The streets were empty except for drivers and medical orderlies racing to their ambulances. Inside the call center, telephones shrilled incessantly and volunteers hurried to copy down urgent assignments.

"I have a feeling this is going to be bad," Eve said. "Are you ready, Audrey?"

"I think so. How about you?"

"I'd rather do this than sit in a bomb shelter."

They assigned her and Audrey to the same site—a technical college on Durning Road in Liverpool. Eve quickly pored over her map, waiting for the medical orderlies to arrive—young men exempted from fighting as conscientious objectors.

"Remember the night we sailed from Folkestone to Dover?" Audrey asked as they hurried toward their assigned vehicles. "We had no idea that it was only the beginning of our war adventures, did we?"

Eve recognized a tremble of fear in Audrey's voice. "You'll do well, Audrey. You've become very courageous since that night."

"I'll see you there," Audrey said.

Eve quickly scribbled her name, destination, and the time into the vehicle logbook, then started the engine. She set off toward Liverpool, aware that the city was the Nazis' number one target after London. It was a port city, vital for deliveries of food and war supplies from across the Atlantic. The Nazis attacked nearly every second night. Now she and Audrey drove into the thick of that battle, the city already engulfed in smoke and flames.

Eve's progress slowed as she neared the city, bumping over fire hoses, dodging piles of rubble in the streets, detouring around craters that devoured the road. At last she turned on to Durning Road. ARP wardens and AFS volunteers who'd cleared a path for the ambulances waved her forward. Eve's heart stopped when she saw the enormous pile of rubble that once had been the technical college, recognizable only by a dangling sign on a fragment of wall. Swarms of workers frantically tunneled into the debris. Eve parked her vehicle as close as she dared and climbed out. Audrey pulled up behind her as a civil defense worker hurried forward.

"We think there are close to three hundred people trapped inside," he said. "See those two trams?" He pointed to what was left of them, half-buried beneath the collapsed building. "When the alert sounded, they stopped here so the passengers could get to the public shelter in the basement."

"Dear God . . . ," Eve whispered. Buried alive. Her greatest fear.

The orderlies unloaded stretchers from the ambulances. "Where have they put the casualties?" one of them asked.

The worker shook his head. "We haven't found any yet. Any living ones, that is. We're still digging."

"Got an extra shovel?" the orderly asked.

"Follow me."

Eve grabbed her first aid kit, and she and Audrey waded into the melee. Above them, Nazi planes continued their attack, splitting the air with the screams of falling bombs, shaking the ground with the thunderous roar of explosions. Searchlights crisscrossed the skies along with the deafening reply of antiaircraft guns. Eve had experienced the horror of battle in London's East End, but Audrey hadn't. She startled and flinched with every blast, instinctively ducking and covering her ears, but she bravely continued forward to where rescuers had tunneled into the basement bomb shelter, and workers and civilian volunteers pulled bloodied, mangled bodies from the wreckage. Hundreds of bodies. Some mere children. Crushed beyond recognition. None of them alive.

The grisliness halted Eve in her tracks. Her first aid kit fell to the ground as it slipped from her grasp. She was going to be sick. She couldn't do this. But then Audrey was beside her, leaning against her, trembling and weeping with her as they held each other up. "I'm sorry, I'm sorry," Audrey sobbed. "I didn't want to fall apart. . . . I wanted to be strong . . ."

Eve hugged her tightly. "Go ahead and cry, Audrey. You've always had a heart as big as the ocean."

"But Mother hated it when I blubbered. People in our class never do. One must control oneself, you see."

"Do you really want to be like your mother?" Eve asked.

Audrey pulled back to stare at her for a moment, then fell into her arms again. "Oh no, Eve! This is how they suffered and died, isn't it? Our mothers . . . like these poor people."

A dam inside Eve burst and she began to sob, too, weeping for her mum, for these dying, suffering people, for all that her country had endured and would continue to endure. She wept for the never-ending nightmare that she and Audrey lived through and for the future she still couldn't see or imagine. The din of battle raged around them, uncaring. Unceasing.

Suddenly a shout came from inside the wreckage. "This one's alive! Bring a stretcher!"

Eve and Audrey parted, wiping their eyes. They had a job to do. What neither of them could do alone, they would do together.

16

USA, 1950

"Bobby and I are not going anywhere, Eve. We're staying right here." Audrey didn't know how she had summoned the courage to say it, but she meant it. She could tell by Eve's expression that she had surprised her. Yet Eve was the one who had taught Audrey to be courageous.

She turned away from Eve's angry glare, rocking Bobby gently as she gazed through the wide living room window at the neighborhood where Eve lived. It was an alien world to Audrey, just coming to life on this warm summer morning. Dogs were barking; children were tossing balls and riding bicycles and scooters. The houses were painted different colors but were otherwise identical, built on tidy squares of green grass. The shutters on their windows didn't seem to do much except serve as decoration. Audrey remembered the shuttered cottages on England's seacoast where she and Alfie had sailed every summer, their breezy shabbiness and random sizes and shapes. Back home, London had still been rebuilding when Audrey left, even though the war ended five years ago. One didn't have to venture far to see signs of destruction. There were still shortages of food and clothing in many places.

Eve's American neighborhood seemed untouched by the war. But while everything looked neat and clean and orderly, it seemed barren. The sparse trees and bushes would take decades to grow. Audrey missed the stateliness of Wellingford Hall, the beauty of its spacious rooms and wooded grounds.

She turned to face Eve again. "Do you have any idea how difficult it was for me to leave England behind and come here? And to face Robert's family after turning away from them four years ago? Especially after the way Robert died . . ." She paused to swallow the choking grief that still welled up whenever she thought of him. "You know how much Wellingford has always meant to me, and I thought I would always live there. The reason I came to America . . . the reason I'm here is because I had no other choice."

Eve sighed and passed her hand over her face. "Listen, we can figure out a way for you to get a new start here. There are plenty of nice little towns where you can live. You can have all of the Barretts' money—"

"I don't want money! I've had money all my life and it never provided what I needed the most. Or what my son needs. We want a family, Eve. The one you've stolen from us."

"You threw it away—!"

"Yes! Because I was grieving! But that still didn't give you the right to take it!"

They'd reached an impasse. How long were they going to stare at this roadblock before one of them gave in and tore it down? It would have to be Eve. Audrey wasn't going to budge.

Bobby stirred in her lap. "I don't feel good, Mummy," he murmured. He looked pale and listless, his eyes red-rimmed as if he had cried all night. She brushed his dark hair from his eyes. His forehead felt warm. Was it the summer's heat or was he feverish? She wished Wellingford's housekeeper were here to advise her.

"You need to eat something, darling." He shook his head and buried his face against her shoulder. For some reason, Audrey thought of her brother. She often wished that her son had Alfie's spark of humor, his mischievous streak. Instead, Bobby was quiet and reserved like his father had been, often gazing into space as if pondering deep mysteries. Did Eve miss Alfie as much as she did? Audrey knew she and Alfie had enjoyed an extravagant life when they were Bobby's age, and they had taken it for granted. She closed her eyes, silently praying the way Rev. Hamlin had taught her, asking God to show her the solution to this dilemma. His solution.

"Hey, you wanna play in my sandbox?" Eve's son asked, tapping Bobby's shoulder. Bobby moved away from him, squirming deeper into Audrey's arms.

"He doesn't feel well, I'm afraid."

"What's wrong?" Eve asked.

"I don't know. He feels warm to me. Can you tell if he's feverish?"

Eve stood and placed her hand on his forehead. "He does feel warm."

Audrey's fear spiked. Reports of infantile paralysis filled the newspapers back home and struck fear in every mother's heart each time her child ran a fever.

"My tummy itches," Bobby said with a moan. Audrey lifted his pajama top. He was covered with tiny pink spots.

"Is there a physician we can call?" she asked, her heart pounding.

"I'll phone Mrs. Barrett. I'm sure she knows someone who will come out to the house."

"You don't think it's polio, do you?"

Eve waved away the question as she walked toward the kitchen telephone. "I'm guessing it's measles—which means Robbie will probably catch them, too. We'll be stuck in this house for a week!"

Audrey listened as Eve dialed the telephone, then chatted with Mrs. Barrett with easy familiarity. "Hi, Mom, it's me. Sorry I've been out of touch but my visitor from London is still here. . . . Yes . . . yes, we served in the Army together. . . . Listen, her son is running a bit of a fever and has a rash. . . . Mm, I thought it might be, too. Do you know of a doctor who—? . . . Thank you. That would be super. Thanks. . . . No, you'd better not visit us, Mom. Robbie is sure to catch them, too, and we'll need to keep the boys quiet and in bed. . . . Yes . . . Yes, I'll call and let you know what he says. . . . Bye for now." Eve returned to the living room and heaved a sigh. "Mrs. Barrett promised to send a doctor. There are dozens of them at her country club."

"You call her 'Mom'?" Audrey asked.

"It's what she asked me to call her."

Audrey felt astonished and angry at the same time. And cheated, all over again. Eve had stolen her son's family. Her family. Yet Audrey doubted if she would ever be able to call Robert's mother *Mom*. That word held an entirely different meaning for her than it did for Eve. "Well. It seems we're going to be your prisoners for a few more days," she said, exasperated.

Eve sank down onto the chair across from her again. "Can't you try to see this from my point of view?"

"I'm finding it very hard to do that. And I could ask you the same thing, Eve. When you left Wellingford four years ago, you fell off the face of the earth. I had no idea what happened to you. I've been worried about you all this time, hoping you were all right, wishing you would call or write. I prayed for you every single day. I didn't come here to ruin your life. When Father sold Wellingford Hall and I left for America, I had no idea I would find you here."

"Would you have come if you'd known?"

"I have no other place to go! Don't you understand that yet? I know you don't want us here, but where else can we go? Tell me, please!"

Eve stood. "I'd better make a path so the doctor can get through the door." Audrey watched as she hauled the trunks and suitcases from the tiny entryway into the bedrooms. She knew Eve well enough to know that she was doing it to defuse her anger. And to avoid answering her question. "Robbie and I had breakfast out at the farm," she said when she finished, "but I'll fix you something if you tell me what you'd like."

"Why did you change his name to Robbie? You named him Harry, after your father. I remember that very clearly." Eve simply stared at her as if the answer were obvious. She supposed it was. "I'm sorry, but I still don't understand how you could do this, Eve. Or why you did it. From anyone's point of view, your deception is monstrous. Don't you feel at all guilty for lying to Robert's parents, deceiving them into thinking Harry is their grandson? Taking their money, this house?"

"I never intended to stay! My plan was to use the tickets you threw away to come to America. Harry and I would have a new start. I was going to leave town once I found a job and figured out how to make it on our own. But coming here was like stepping into a snare. I was trapped. The Barretts were devastated by Robert's death, as you can well imagine. They made me feel like I was doing a wonderful thing by staying here and giving them a family again. You have no idea how happy they were to welcome Harry and me into their lives. How fully they embraced us. You were far away and out of touch and, I assumed, getting on with your life. I knew how much you loved Wellingford Hall. I never imagined you would change your mind and decide to take back what you so callously threw away."

"I was unable to make any rational decisions when I threw those papers away."

"If anyone has done something monstrous, it's you—refusing to even visit the Barretts or let their grandson be part of their life."

"I was certain they blamed me for Robert's death. I didn't want to upset their lives."

"You're upsetting their lives all over again by showing up now!"

"That's unfair, Eve. I had no idea you were here, impersonating me. I didn't come here to hurt you or them. Can't we find a solution to this mess?"

Eve huffed again. "I'm going to make tea. Do you want some?"

"No thank you. I think I'll put Bobby to bed."

Audrey sat on the edge of the bed, rocking him in her lap until the doctor came an hour later. His diagnosis was roseola. "The rash usually lasts three to five days," the doctor said. "He should feel normal in about a week." Eve had been standing in the doorway, but Audrey saw her turn and walk away at his words. They would be trapped here together for a week. "Keep him quiet and in bed," the doctor continued. "He should rest and avoid activity. Have him drink plenty of fluids. Give him half of an aspirin tablet for his fever."

Audrey sat by Bobby's bedside after the doctor left, waiting until he fell asleep. She was returning to the kitchen for the promised cup of tea when she overheard Eve's son say, "Can we go swim in Nana's pool now? I'm hot!"

"Not today. We have company."

"Well, when are they going away?"

"I don't know . . . The little boy is sick and has to stay in bed."

"That makes me mad!" The back door slammed. When Audrey ventured into the kitchen, Eve was sitting at the kitchen table with her head in her hands. She looked up.

"You have to understand, Audrey, that when I was Harry's age, I had all of this." She gestured to the kitchen, the back garden. "Not the Barretts' wealth, certainly, but a cozy home and a mum and granny who loved me. I lived in a village where everyone looked out for each other, and I was free to play and explore . . . and to just be a child! I wanted those things for my son. Does that make me a monster?"

"I never had any of this," Audrey said. "Only the wealth. That's why I couldn't imagine this life when the Barretts offered it to me. Especially without Robert. I can barely imagine living here now, but I have no other choice. What I wanted for my son was the life that Alfie and I had at Wellingford Hall. But the war we fought to preserve that life ended up destroying it." She sat down at the table across from Eve. "And it also made us sisters, Eve. Remember?"

"Yes. . . . Maybe I could tell everyone you're my sister," she said with a weak smile.

"And keep living a lie?"

"I don't know what else to do! It's like there's a huge mountain in my path and I don't know how to climb over it or go around it. I'm thirty-one years old and I've already climbed so many mountains that I don't have the will or the strength to try."

"You were the one who always kept me climbing, Eve. Even when I wanted to quit."

"Well, maybe I'm tired of being the strong one."

"Remember how hard that year was after our mothers died?" Audrey asked. "If anyone had asked us what we hoped for once the war ended, we wouldn't have known what to say."

"I couldn't imagine that it would ever end," Eve said, running her fingers through her sandy hair. "One by one we watched our dreams being destroyed along with our country. There was no chance to ask ourselves who we were or what we wanted in life. We lived day to day, driving ambulances, picking up broken people, taking them to hospital down pitch-dark roads. Sometimes I lost hope that my life would ever be different."

"I know. The years when most girls plan and dream of the future were stolen from us. All we knew was to get through each day, doing without all the things that gave us our identity and helped us know we were women."

Eve gave a mirthless laugh. "Remember that shapeless ATS uniform? Those ridiculous undergarments? We looked like old crones."

"We had no idea what life would be like when the war ended— when we either won or, God forbid, were forced to surrender. So why dream? Why plan?"

"And then the Americans came," Eve said with a little smile. "Pearl Harbor was bombed just like England had been. Finally the Americans entered the war. There was a ray of hope at last. I remember feeling glad that the Japanese attacked them—and then hating myself for thinking it."

"I remember thinking that it truly was a worldwide war now. I pictured that little globe Alfie and I had in our schoolroom and it chilled me to know that nearly every place on the planet felt the war's effects. It was overwhelming! Like something from the last pages of the Bible."

"And then the invasion came, remember? Not the Nazi one we'd long dreaded, but the American invasion. All those fresh-faced GIs. Nearly two million of them!"

"One of them was Robert," Audrey murmured.

"Yes, and one was Louis. They made us remember who we were. They made us feel like women again."

Audrey could only nod. Not only had Robert made her feel like a woman, but like the woman God created her to be. Where had that woman gone?

17

Eve was eating supper in the mess hall with Audrey when the sergeant major walked in. The woman stood for a moment, gazing around the hall as if searching for someone in particular. Eve groaned. "Oh no. Hide under the table, Audrey. Quick!"

"Why?"

"The Mouse just walked through the door and I think she's looking for a victim." Eve scrunched lower in her chair, keeping her head down, even though it probably wouldn't help if the Mouse was searching for them. Audrey's glorious amber hair and aristocratic posture set her apart from all the other women.

"She can't make us drive on our weekend off, can she?" Audrey asked. "We've been driving every night for two weeks!"

"She can do whatever she wants. Duck your head, Audrey."

"Too late. Here she comes."

The woman strode across the room, shoes squeaking on the linoleum floor. The telltale sound had earned her the nickname

Mouse, even though Bull would have better fit her build and personality. Eve looked up in dread as the squeaking halted beside their table.

"I've been looking for you two. You have tonight off, right?"

"We did . . . ," Eve mumbled.

"Yes, ma'am," Audrey said. "We have the weekend off. For the first time this month, in fact."

"Good. There's a dance in the village hall tonight for some American officers. You two girls need to be there."

"Sorry, but I can't go, ma'am," Eve said in her most contrite voice. "My boyfriend, who is fighting in North Africa, wouldn't approve."

"And I don't dance very well," Audrey added.

"I'm not asking you to marry them. Just show them some British hospitality for an evening. They're saving our necks, for heaven's sake. Would you rather be sitting in a pub entertaining Hitler?"

"No, ma'am," Audrey replied.

"Good. Spiff yourselves up, then. The lorry will pick everyone up at seven thirty. I expect to see both of you there."

"I'd rather drive an ambulance across the English Channel," Eve said as the woman stalked over to her next victim. Audrey eyed her curiously.

"I thought you liked to dance."

"I do. But not with a bunch of loudmouthed Americans."

"Remember the dance you took me to after King George's funeral?" Audrey asked.

"That seems like ages ago. In a different lifetime."

"You taught me to dance that night. And we had fun, didn't we? It helped us forget that the king had just died and that everything was changing."

"What's your point?"

"Maybe we need another night of dancing to help us forget."

The other girls in their dormitory seemed thrilled with the idea. Eve listened to their chatter as they crowded around the mirror, giggling as they primped. "Every American I've seen is as handsome as a film star," one of them said.

"Even their uniforms are glamorous. Not like the drab, baggy ones our men have to wear."

"I hear they give away cigarettes."

"And lovely silk stockings."

"Do you know how long it's been since I've worn a real pair of silk stockings?"

"Since 1939!" someone shouted. Everyone laughed.

Eve had to admit that the band sounded great. She tapped her feet and sang along to all of the American big band tunes and her favorite Vera Lynn songs. She was glad she'd been coerced into coming after all and was content to sit at a table with Audrey and enjoy the music. Let the other girls flirt with the Americans. "I miss Alfie," she said as she watched the couples dancing. "He's a wonderful dancer." *Until he gets drunk,* she added to herself.

The hall was so crowded that she didn't notice the two Americans approaching until they halted in front of her. Both of them were, in fact, as handsome as film stars. One had blue eyes and ginger hair, the other dark eyes and ebony hair. Both were tall and well-built. The ginger-haired one would need to duck to clear the doorframe, and the dark-haired one was only an inch or so shorter.

"You gals look lonely over here," the ginger one said. "Wanna dance?"

"No thank you," Eve replied.

"Come on. Just one dance. That's all. We aren't looking for true love." His cocksure American boldness made Eve's blood boil.

"My friend and I aren't interested in you American GIs," she said heatedly. "We don't need your chocolate bars or your nylons or your cigarettes. You spin a fancy line but you're here today and gone tomorrow."

"Geez! Take it easy!" he said, holding up both hands. "I only asked if you wanted to dance!"

"Please excuse my friend," Audrey said. "We've heard stories about love affairs with American servicemen. Most have ended badly."

The ginger one slid into an empty seat at their table, his long legs barely fitting beneath it. "What kind of stories?"

Eve was about to order him to leave when she saw the Mouse standing a few feet away. Eve huffed in frustration. "There was a girl we knew who believed all your love talk. She ended up in the family way. Next thing she knows, the American father gets himself transferred out of here. No forwarding address. Now, what's she supposed to do?"

Ginger gave a long, slow whistle. "Geez . . . that's tough."

The dark-haired one gestured to the second empty chair. "May I?" he asked politely. "Would you mind? We've been on our feet all day."

"Of course not," Audrey replied. He pulled out the chair and sat.

"You know what they're saying about you Americans?" Eve asked. "You're 'overpaid, oversexed, and over here.'" Ginger laughed and the sound was warm and friendly, not at all mocking.

"I'm very sorry for the way that some of our fellow Americans have behaved," Dark Hair said. "My friend Louis and I are just looking for a night off, away from all thoughts of the war."

"I'm a married man with a baby back home," ginger-haired Louis said. He held out his left hand to show Eve a gold band on his finger. "Want to see pictures?"

"Yes, in fact, I do," Eve replied, calling his bluff. He looked too young to be married—in his early twenties like she was, she guessed. He was very fair-skinned with deep-blue eyes and a smile that looked like an advert for tooth powder. Oh yes—as handsome as a film star.

He reached into his back pocket for his wallet. Eve studied the black-and-white photograph of a young woman holding a bundled baby. She handed back the photo. "Being married doesn't stop most American men from behaving badly. They think British girls owe them something for coming to our rescue."

Louis ignored her comment as he returned his wallet to his pocket. "My friend Bob here is practically married. He has a long-time girlfriend waiting for him back home. Wanna see her picture, too?"

"That's not necessary," Eve replied. "Just so you know where you stand. I would show you a picture of my boyfriend but I don't have one with me. He's fighting in North Africa." She felt a fist in her stomach at the thought of Nazi artillery shells raining down on Alfie. *I don't think I'll survive this war,* he had said.

"Well, this is a very good arrangement, then," Louis said, tilting his chair back on two legs. "We'll all have a good time, you won't have to worry about us making a move, and our girls back home won't need to worry about you. Can we agree to be friends?" He stuck out his hand for Eve to shake. She hesitated for a moment, then reached for it. The warmth and strength of it made her ache for Alfie's touch.

"Deal," she said, clearing her throat. "Just friends."

"So what are your names?"

"I'm Eve Dawson and this is my best friend, Audrey Clarkson." She wondered what Audrey thought of these Americans as she gave them her shy smile and shook hands.

"Pleased to meet you, Eve . . . Audrey. I'm Louis Dubois and this is my friend Robert Barrett. We're best friends, too, ever since grammar school."

"From what we've seen over here," Robert said, his voice a soft contrast to Louis's booming one, "this war has been very hard on you ladies."

"It has been," Audrey replied, just as softly. "My home in London was destroyed during the Blitz. Eve and I both lost our mothers."

"That's terrible," Robert said. "I'm so sorry. That must have been awful for you."

Eve didn't want to think about what they'd suffered and lost. She wanted to listen to the music and forget about the war and her grief for one night. Louis must have felt the same way because he asked, "Can we get you ladies a drink?"

"I'm set," Eve said, pointing to her half-finished one.

"No thank you," Audrey said. "I don't drink."

Eve knew why, and it was another bitter reminder of Lady Rosamunde's selfishness and the loss it had cost her. She rose to her feet. "You know what, Louis? Maybe I'll take you up on that offer to dance." Audrey and Robert could sit by themselves and talk about morbid things if they wanted.

Louis stood and took Eve's hand. "Great! I like this song." They wove through the press of people and swing danced to three fast tunes in a row, enjoying every rollicking minute. Then the music slowed. Eve went into Louis's arms as if it were the most natural thing in the world to do. He was an excellent dancer—better than Alfie, if she dared to admit it. She closed her eyes as Louis held her close, and she pretended he was Alfie.

"My boyfriend's name is Alfie," she told him. "What's your wife's name?"

"Jean."

"I'll bet she misses you. And your baby's name?"

"Karen. She won't know who I am when I get home."

"Where are you from in America?"

"Connecticut. Not far from New York City. And you're from London?"

"No, I grew up in a little village out in the country, then moved to London to work. I don't really know where home is, nowadays. The ATS keeps moving us all around, wherever we're needed."

"Is your boyfriend from your home village?"

The question startled Eve. Alfie was, and yet he wasn't. They'd grown up worlds apart.

"Alfie's home was about a mile from mine." It was the simplest answer she could give. It would seem like a Cinderella story to describe Wellingford Hall and explain how she'd once been Alfie's scullery maid.

"Is that where you and he hope to settle when the war ends?" Louis asked.

Tears filled Eve's eyes. She knew as she swayed in this handsome American's arms that Alfie was never going to marry her. She was a fool to imagine that she would ever become Mrs. Alfred Clarkson, mistress of Wellingford Hall. Not while Alfie's father was alive. Her mind knew it, but her heart refused to believe it. "Yes," she lied. "That's the plan. . . . Tell me, what do you think of my sad little country?"

"I wish the sun would shine more often, but other than that, I think it's swell. We never traveled much when I was a kid, so it's pretty exciting to get out and see the world."

"Even with Herr Hitler trampling across it, shooting at you?"

Louis's laugh made her smile. "He does take some of the fun out of it. Especially crossing the Atlantic in a troopship, dodging U-boats."

Eve and Louis danced to one number after the next. She was having fun, and she couldn't recall the last time that had happened. Meanwhile, Audrey and Robert seemed deep in conversation, which was unusual for the normally shy Audrey. Eventually the band took a break, and Louis led Eve to the refreshment table. "Wow!" she said. "Look at all this food! It must have come from you Americans. We haven't seen chocolate or fruit or these wonderful sugary cakes in years!"

"Fill your plate, then. I'll go save our table so Bob and your friend can get some, too." They all sat down at the table to eat, and as Eve filled up on sponge cake and fruit tarts, she was glad that the Mouse had ordered them to come.

"You two seem like really good friends," Eve said after listening to Louis and Robert banter back and forth like a lively game of tennis. "How long have you known each other?"

"Since we were seven or eight years old," Robert replied. "We played Little League baseball together. Louis's dad was our coach."

"We played together on every sports team you can name, after that," Louis added. He had a habit of twisting his wedding ring as he spoke, as if it fit too tightly. "Then two other buddies, Tom and Arnie, joined us when we were in junior high. The four of us played everything—baseball, football, basketball—you name it."

"But our favorite is basketball," Robert said. "The four of us—Louis, Tom, Arnie, and I—were on the greatest team our high school ever produced. We won the state championship two years in a row."

"Everyone called us the Famous Four," Louis said. "We all went to college on basketball scholarships, then joined the Army together after Pearl Harbor."

"It's a bit of luck for Louis and me to end up here together, considering how far-flung this war is, and all the places we could have been sent."

"What did you study in college?" Audrey asked.

"Bob is destined to become a lawyer," Louis said, answering for his friend. "His filthy-rich father and grandfather won't settle for anything less, right, Bob?"

"So it seems," he said quietly.

"I studied business. My father owns an insurance company, so I've always figured that's what I'd end up doing. Especially now that I'm married."

Eve felt a growing uneasiness with the conversation, fearing it would lead to questions about her education. "What about your other two friends?" she asked to prevent them from questioning her.

"Tom's family owns a dairy farm," Robert said. "He's the bashful one, especially when it comes to girls."

"He never had time for girls," Louis said, "working as hard as he did, helping out his folks. We used to joke and call him 'Father Tom,' as if he was a priest or something, because he's the kind of guy you can confess all your troubles to, you know? And he'll tell you the right thing to do. He's stationed somewhere in the Mediterranean, at the moment. And Arnie is the opposite—a real playboy. He worked as a lifeguard at the country club every summer, showing off his tan, getting all the girls to swoon over him. My kid sister was one of them."

"Arnie would go steady with a different girl every hour," Robert said, smiling. "You ladies would really need to watch out for him."

"Where is Arnie now?" Eve asked.

"I'm not really sure. He studied to be a veterinarian, so the Army decided he should become a medic or something."

"Arnie also understands German," Robert added, "so I'm sure Uncle Sam will put that to good use."

Eve swallowed the last bite of cake and stood. "Let's dance, Louis. Want to?"

The band had returned from their break and the dancing resumed in full swing. Then, as the clock inched closer and closer to midnight, the music slowed. "If I give you a compliment," Louis said as they danced to "When the Lights Go On Again," "you won't smack me for it, will you?"

Eve grinned. "Why, do I seem like the smacking type?"

"You were a little scary when Bob and I first came to your table."

"Go ahead. Compliment me. I'm immune to American sweet talk."

Louis stopped dancing and smiled down at her. "You have the most beautiful freckles I've ever seen in my life. They remind me of those little spots on a baby fawn." For the second time that night, tears filled Eve's eyes. She turned her head away but it was too late. Louis had already seen them. "Hey, I'm sorry, Eve. Go ahead and smack me if I've said something stupid."

"You didn't," she said, wiping them away. "It's just that my boyfriend loves my freckles, too."

"And you're missing him?" Eve nodded. Louis pulled her close for a brief hug. "I understand. Sometimes I can barely remember what Jean's laughter sounds like or how it felt to hold her in my arms. This stupid war has messed up everybody's life, hasn't it?"

"Let's not talk about the war," Eve said, putting on a brave smile. "Let's just dance."

◦◦◦◦◦◦◦

Audrey couldn't get over how easy Robert Barrett was to talk to. She had never felt this relaxed with a man in her life, especially one she had just met. Maybe it was the fact that neither of them had any expectations. She wasn't being appraised or analyzed as a potential match among her mother's social contacts. Robert knew nothing about Wellingford Hall or how wealthy Audrey was. He wasn't interested in her aristocratic lineage or her father's financial holdings. Robert was intelligent and well-spoken and seemed, from what he'd told her, to come from a well-to-do family. His dark good looks and olive-black eyes would set any woman's heart aflutter, but he didn't seem aware of how handsome he was. He had a quiet intensity and a way of focusing on Audrey as he listened that made it seem as though he could peer into her soul. She'd never met anyone like him.

"So what do you do in the Army?" he asked after Eve and Louis returned to the dance floor.

"I drive an ambulance."

"Really!" He seemed taken aback.

"We also drive lorries or escort fancy officers around in their staff cars if needed, but we both prefer driving ambulances."

"And the Army taught you to do this? Surely you didn't drive for a living before the war."

"No, I didn't do much of anything before the war except try to please my mother by socializing with the aristocracy. My parents' goal was for me to attract a husband who was a good social match—nothing less than an earl, mind you. Now I can change tires and do routine maintenance and repairs on any vehicle in the fleet. And I also drive casualties to hospital, of course."

"Forgive me if I sound rude, but if you came from an upper class, weren't there other jobs the Army could have given you? You seem too petite and delicate to be changing tires."

"I could have had a desk job, but Eve and I wanted to drive. Army service was voluntary when we enlisted. Conscription began in December of '41, and service is now mandatory for all unmarried women between the ages of twenty and thirty. In fact, King George's daughter, Princess Elizabeth, enlisted in the same branch as Eve and me. She wears a uniform and changes lorry tires just like the rest of us."

"That's amazing."

"I think it's more an indication of how desperate England is. We're fighting for our very lives, so every able-bodied man and woman must do their bit. Even the aristocracy."

"You didn't mention a boyfriend, but I imagine that a woman as lovely as you must have one."

Audrey blushed at his flattery. He didn't seem the type to make a pass at every girl who walked by. His compliment felt genuine. "No boyfriend, I'm afraid. It turns out I'm hopeless at making small talk with earls and dukes—much to my mother's dismay. As you may have guessed, Eve is the outgoing one and I'm the tagalong."

"It's the same with Louis and me. He plows forward and I follow in his wake. And the reason I haven't asked you to dance is because I'm terrible at it."

"I'm hopeless at dancing, too. Louis mentioned you have a longtime girlfriend back home?"

"Right. Linda." He paused and Audrey waited for him to say more. Most people lit up with gushing smiles when asked about the person they loved. It seemed unusual that Robert didn't. "Linda and I have been together since junior high school. Our parents are old friends. Everyone has always assumed we'd be married, someday."

"You don't seem too enthused by the idea. May I ask . . . are you in a situation similar to mine, needing to meet parental expectations?" He hesitated again, so Audrey quickly said, "I'm sorry. It's rude of me to pry into your personal life."

"No, no. It isn't that. It's just that no one has ever asked me that question. Even Louis, and he's my best friend. Everyone just assumes that Linda and I will always be together . . . It's what she wants, what our parents want . . ."

"But you aren't sure."

"I've never even kissed another girl. I used to see Arnie with a different girl every few minutes and I would wonder what it would be like to get to know someone else besides Linda. I once told her that I wanted to take a little break, and—I never told anyone else this—but she was almost suicidal. She said she didn't want to live without me."

"Robert, that's no reason to—"

"I know, I know. But there was a lot more to it than that. You're right—it's that whole business of parental expectations. If we broke up, her family and mine would work overtime to make sure we got back together. I know that must make me sound weak-willed, but—"

"Not at all. I know exactly how it is. I've been trying all my life to please my parents, even at the cost of who I am and what I want. They've never been pleased with me, of course, but I continue to try. My mother died in the Blitz, but the funny thing is, I'm still not free. I find myself doing the things that would have pleased her and earned her approval. It's the only thing I know. If this war ever ends, I'll probably end up marrying the second son of some earl who I don't love and who has nothing in common with me, and we'll carry on with our separate, empty lives."

"That's what I'm afraid of with Linda. We want different things in life. When no one else is around and we try to talk about important things, we have nothing in common. She loves the country-club life, fancy clothes and cars, and I want more. I don't really want to be a lawyer but that's what's expected of me. I'll be the fourth generation to join our family's law firm."

"Why can't we seem to speak up for ourselves and break free?"

"Because the pull of family is even stronger than the force of gravity. . . . I did manage to speak up once, and it bought me a reprieve of sorts. Linda wanted to get married before I went away to war. She wanted to have a baby in case anything happened to me. She was even making wedding plans, but I panicked. I just wasn't sure. I don't even know who I am or what I want out of life, so I'm certainly not ready to choose a wife and settle down. To be honest, I don't even know if I love Linda. I've never experienced all those feelings of euphoria and rapture that people in the movies describe when they fall in love—have you?"

"Hardly! I rarely even like the men who are chosen for me."

"Exactly. Linda seems like my parents' choice, not mine. Of course, she was furious when I wouldn't get engaged before I left for basic training, let alone married. Especially after Louis and Jean got married. But she didn't want to break up with me, either. She writes me long letters with news from home and tells me how much she misses me and loves me. I never know what to write back. I would like to be able to share my thoughts about the war and all of the deep spiritual issues it raises—but I've never been able to talk about my faith with her. To Linda, Christianity is a tradition, a comforting ritual, but for me it has become much, much more—especially as I grapple with what I've seen and experienced over here. My faith—" He halted abruptly, a look of embarrassment flooding his face. "I'm sorry, Audrey. This is supposed to be an evening for fun and I've been yapping on and on about all these personal things—"

"Please don't apologize. Aside from the vicar back home, you're the only person I've ever talked with about things that really matter. You and I are similar in so many ways, and I think . . . I think we understand each other. This war has raised endless questions about faith."

"I can well imagine that you'd have questions after losing your mother. It must seem like your world is on the brink of extinction."

"That's exactly how it feels. Oddly enough, the vicar seems to think that God can use the war to bring about something good. He said that most of us muddle along with our mundane lives without ever contemplating life and death or the God who created us and loves us."

"There are no atheists in foxholes."

"I think that's true. To be honest, my religion was a lot like Linda's before the war. I never thought much about God. I never read the Bible at all."

"Me, either. After I enlisted, the Army was passing out Bibles to anyone who wanted one, so I took it, even though religion has been little more than a formality for most of my life. Inside the cover was a letter from President Roosevelt. I'll have to show it to you sometime. He recommended that everyone in the armed services read the Bible, said it has offered wisdom and strength and inspiration to people throughout the ages. I've been reading it ever since."

Audrey couldn't reply, stopped for a moment by Robert's words: *"I'll have to show it to you sometime."* He assumed they would see each other again. Perhaps he even hoped they would. And Audrey was very surprised to discover that she hoped so, too. She was still struggling for words when the bandleader announced they would play one final song, "We'll Meet Again."

Robert stood and extended his hand. "I would love to dance this last one with you, Audrey. I apologize in advance for stepping on your toes."

She felt herself smiling as she stood and accepted his hand. "Believe me, I won't feel a thing through these monstrous Army shoes." She went into his arms as if she had been there before.

Perhaps it was the deeply personal things they'd shared this evening that made Audrey feel at home with Robert. And safe. But she also felt sad. Because Robert Barrett was one of nearly two million American soldiers on her island, and when "We'll Meet Again" ended and she and Eve climbed into the lorry to return to their base, she would probably never see him again.

18

"I can't believe it!" Audrey stared at the ATS message board in amazement. "We have a two-day furlough!"

"Where should we go?" Eve asked.

"I don't know . . . I don't fancy London. Do you?"

"Definitely not. They say the city is packed with Americans, like pilchards in a tin. Agnes got her bottom pinched a dozen times when she was there. She got so tired of hearing, 'Hey, baby!' that she came back to the base a day early."

Audrey felt a longing for home that hadn't surfaced since she'd enlisted two and a half years ago. "What do you say we go to Wellingford Hall on our leave?" she asked as they walked back to their room. Wellingford wasn't far. She and Eve were based near Southampton now, ferrying wounded soldiers who arrived on hospital ships. Their injuries broke her heart. She offered up prayers for Alfie with every ambulance journey she made.

"I thought the Americans took over Wellingford," Eve said.

"Most of it, yes. But Robbins kept some spaces private in case Father or Alfie or I came home."

It was decided. They took the train to the village, and after Eve greeted some of her longtime friends and promised to return for tea, she and Audrey walked the last mile to the manor house, hauling their duffel bags. Audrey was unprepared for all of the changes to her home. The Land Army now cultivated the fields and grasslands bordering the road. They'd erected fences to pasture cows and sheep, slicing Wellingford's elegant property into ugly farm lots. "Robbins told me the Land Girls were farming some of our property, but I never imagined they would ruin so much of it," Audrey said. It grew worse as she passed through the stone entry gates. A vegetable patch replaced George's stately formal gardens. Heavy vehicles left the driveway rutted and muddied. Three American jeeps were parked out front and a group of soldiers stood on the steps smoking cigarettes. *My home!* she wanted to cry out. *What have you done to my beautiful home?*

"Let's go around to the back door," Eve said.

"No." Audrey felt unaccountably stubborn. "This is my home. Yours too, considering all the years you and your mum worked here. We're going to use the front door."

"Good job standing up for yourself," Eve said with a grin. "I hope you're prepared to be ogled and pinched."

"They wouldn't dare. And I'd better not hear any *Hey, baby*s, either." They marched forward. The men stopped talking and watched them approach. Audrey stared straight ahead, her chin lifted, refusing to meet their gazes.

She was almost to the door when a soft masculine voice said, "Audrey? Is it really you?"

She turned in surprise. "Robert! What are you doing here?"

"I'm stationed here," he said with a little laugh. "I'm assigned to the new airfield they're building a few miles away. What are you doing here?"

"I live here. That is, I do when I'm not in the Army. Wellingford Hall is my family's home. I grew up here. Eve and I have a two-day furlough, so we decided to come home."

"Gosh, it's good to see you again." He looked as though he wanted to embrace her but they both held back. "I didn't think we'd ever meet again. They transferred Louis and me a few days after I met you."

"Are you enjoying Wellingford Hall?"

"It's beautiful! . . . I mean, I can see that it used to be beautiful before the war."

"I'm appalled by all the changes, and I haven't even been inside yet."

"Allow me," he said, opening the heavy door. "And I apologize in advance for what my countrymen may have done to your home."

"No, don't. England might well be lost by now if it weren't for you Americans."

The Americans kept the blackout curtains closed all the time, and the foyer was very dark, as were the sitting and dining rooms on either side. For a moment, Audrey felt disoriented in the gloom. Then Robbins appeared, and he seemed cheered to see her. "Miss Audrey! Welcome home. When you called to say you were coming, we were all pleased. Very pleased. And, Eve—" Before he could say more, Eve dropped her duffel and went to him for a hug, making Audrey envious. "How are you, Eve, my girl?"

"I'm super. I hope you don't mind me using the front door. Audrey said I could."

"Nonsense." He picked up their duffels. "I'll carry these upstairs and we'll get you both settled in. Mrs. Smith made up your bedroom, Miss Audrey."

"Thank you," she said as they climbed the stairs. "I can't wait to put on civilian clothes. And what about Eve? Perhaps she'd like Alfie's room?"

"If you don't mind," Eve said before Robbins could reply, "I think I'd prefer my old room on the third floor. If no one is using it, that is."

"Are you sure?" Audrey asked. "It isn't necessary, you know."

"I'm hoping Mum left a few of her things. I couldn't bear to look after the funeral, but now I'm hoping that she didn't take everything with her to London."

"You're welcome to it, Eve," Robbins said. "We haven't changed a thing in there."

"Good. But first I want to get out of this uniform and go for a walk in the woods like I used to do when I was a girl. Do you think it would be all right? With the Americans, I mean? They aren't tromping through there shooting rabbits for target practice, are they?"

"As far as I know, they've left the woods untouched," Robbins replied. "We billeted the American officers in the west wing, not this side of the manor."

"Want to come to the woods with me, Audrey?"

She shook her head. "I think you'd be happier alone."

"See you later, then." Eve left Audrey outside the door to her room and hurried to the servants' door to the third floor. Audrey heard her footsteps racing up the wooden stairs.

"Is there anything else I can do for you, Miss Audrey?" Robbins asked as he carried her duffel bag inside.

"No thank you. I'm fine." He nodded and left the room, clos-ing the door. Her childhood bedroom should have felt familiar to Audrey but it didn't. The books and keepsakes on the shelves seemed to belong to a different person. She opened the doors to her wardrobe and found it filled with clothes more appropriate for her former life than for wartime. She used the washroom to freshen up from her trip, then changed from her uniform into a pair of wool slacks, a silk blouse, and a cashmere sweater, the most casual clothes she could find. She glanced out the window and saw Eve striding across the cultivated field toward the woods. Audrey closed her eyes and whispered a prayer that Eve would find the carefree, young girl she'd once been. When she opened them again, she caught a glimpse of herself in the mirror. Audrey saw a stranger. She quickly looked away, frightened by the unfamiliar image.

She took a moment to hang up her uniform and unpack her bag, tasks she would have let the servants do in the past. When she finished, she wasn't quite sure what to do with herself. She should have asked Robbins which rooms downstairs she was allowed to use. She'd been disoriented after arriving, and everything had happened so quickly that—

Robert! She had walked rudely away from him without even a proper thank-you or "It was nice to see you again." And it had been nice to see him. She'd never forgotten the wonderful evening they'd spent together at the dance. She crossed to another window and looked down to see if the jeeps were still parked outside. They were. Audrey ran a brush through her hair and hurried downstairs to find him. Robert stood at the bottom of the steps as if waiting for her.

"Robert! Hello again. I'm sorry for dashing off so abruptly—"

"Not at all. I can only imagine how good it must feel to be home again."

"It is nice, yes. Although no one else in my family is home at the moment. And everything is so . . . different."

"You've been invaded, Audrey. Thank goodness it wasn't by the Nazis."

"This is the first time I've been home since Eve and I enlisted. It was such a nice surprise to find you here. I so enjoyed talking with you the night we met."

"I did, too. And now that you're here, I hope we can talk some more. Maybe even right now, if you're free."

"I would like that very much. But aren't you supposed to be working? I'm not keeping you from anything, am I?"

"I'm off duty today and tomorrow, as it happens. Louis and I almost went to London but decided to stay here. Now I'm glad we did."

"I am, too. Shall we go someplace and catch up? How about Father's library?"

"That's one of the rooms that's off-limits to us. I confess that I've peeked inside, though. I couldn't resist all those books. But I didn't touch any of them."

"Come through, then. You'll be my guest." They scanned the shelves as they roamed the room, using the library ladder to peruse the highest shelves. They shared the same tastes in poetry and literary classics. And history.

"I could spend years in here and still not read everything that I'd like to," Robert said when they finally sat down in Father's club chairs by the fireplace.

"I'll tell Robbins to let you borrow books whenever you'd like."

"Thank you. What a spectacular inheritance you have, Audrey—this house, these books and furnishings, your distinguished family. I assume all of the grand portraits in the foyer are your ancestors?"

"Hardly! I'm a fake aristocrat, actually." She surprised herself by admitting the truth to this virtual stranger. Yet something in Robert's gentle manner, his honesty and attentiveness, convinced Audrey that she could trust him. "My father came from a middle-class family and made his own fortune through shrewd business ventures. He bought this estate from a down-on-his-luck aristocrat who'd gone bankrupt. All of the portraits and antiques and books came with the house. The sterling silver, too. My mother was the true blue blood. Their marriage was one of convenience. She gave Father respectability and he gave her enough wealth to keep any woman happy. I don't suppose there are many situations like theirs in the United States."

"You'd be surprised. We don't have an aristocracy, but an old family name and a good reputation are still highly valued, especially in families like mine that have been around since before the Revolution. There's a lot of pressure on the sons—especially only sons like myself—to follow in the footsteps of their fathers and grandfathers. I'm expected to attend Yale Law School after the war and join the family practice."

"That's what struck me the last time we spoke—how alike we are. I don't know if you feel trapped, but I sometimes do. Yet when one spends their entire lifetime trying to please one's parents, disappointing them is out of the question."

"I understand, believe me. But just for a moment, let's try to imagine what we would do if we truly were free from all of those expectations. You go first."

"I don't know! . . . I haven't dared to imagine . . ."

"Okay, it wasn't fair to spring the question on you. I'll go first because I've been thinking about it ever since I started basic training. Joining the Army turned my life upside down, ripping away all my usual props. It forced me to rethink everything I once knew—"

"Yes! That's exactly how I've felt since enlisting. Army life is so opposite the life I'm accustomed to that my identity felt pared down to the bone. I still don't know who I am. Just now, I felt like an intruder in my old bedroom. The girl who once lived here wasn't me. I even hung up my own uniform—something I would have left to the servants in the past."

"So why not try to imagine a new future? During all those long hours coming over here on the troopship, I watched the other guys playing poker or sleeping and I tried to imagine what I would do if I didn't have to go back to the life mapped out for me—marrying Linda, joining the law firm, adding my name to the distinguished line of Barretts."

The idea made Audrey feel even more lost and alone. Who was she? What did she really want her life to be like? The questions frightened her, just as seeing the stranger in the mirror had. Yet Robert's ponderings intrigued her. "What did you decide you would do?" she asked.

"If I could have my wish? . . . When I first started asking that question, I felt a little like the rich young man in the Bible who asks Jesus what he should do. Are you familiar with that story?"

"Yes. Rev. Hamlin preached a sermon on it. Jesus told him to sell all that he had—"

"And give the money to the poor. Right. It struck me that Jesus didn't say to *give* everything away. He said to *sell* it. That involves taking an inventory of what he had, analyzing its value, getting the most out of what it was worth so *then* he could offer the profits to the poor. The lesson for me was to take a close look at how God created me and all the assets I've been given—and then generously invest it all for His Kingdom. That's the opposite of following everyone else's expectations for me, living the life that's been decided for me. Instead, I should live the one I was created for."

His words intrigued her, excited her. Yet frightened her. "But how do we know what we were created for?"

"That's the key question." He sat forward on his chair as he

faced her, his dark eyes intense. "I still don't know in my particular case, but I think the broader answer can be found in the
second half of Jesus' command—give to the poor. In other words,
I'm to give all that I am to help others so that God is glorified.
Rich people usually don't sell everything they have and give away
the proceeds. There would have been a lot of questions and a lot
of amazed people if that rich young man had actually done it.
People would want to know what motivated such a sacrifice—and
he could point to Christ and say that his love for his Savior had
changed him."

"That's profound, Robert. You could be a minister."

"I don't think so," he laughed. "I don't have answers for why
good people suffer or why there's evil in the world and men like
Hitler and Mussolini."

"When I lived at home before joining the Army, I felt com-
pelled to do something to help people. A lot of my motivation
sprang from guilt. My family had so much, yet they ignored the
needs of the villagers. And I also wanted to show God my gratitude for bringing my brother safely home after Dunkirk. The vicar
said something similar to what you're saying. That the work of the
church is serving Christ in any way we can with what we've been
given."

"I think he's right. I admit, though, that I'm still a lot like
that rich young man. I'm still saying no and backing away from
what Jesus asks because I fear the unknown. There's safety in my
familiar life and in my family's expectations. I know I can probably
please them and still have a great life."

"And that's why I've never dared to think of another future. It's
why I came home this weekend. There's safety in what's familiar.
Thank you for challenging me."

"No, I'm the one who's grateful. I've been holding all these thoughts inside with no one to share them with." He moved to the edge of his chair and reached for her hand. The warmth of it startled her, then quickly spread through her with a sensation that was much like sinking into a steaming bath. "Please tell me if I'm out of line, Audrey . . . but if I may presume . . . could we talk some more while you're home?"

Audrey squeezed his hand. She felt none of her usual cold reserve with Robert, and that surprised her. "I would love that. I know the tide of this war is changing and I finally dare to hope it will end. So I do need to think about how I want to live afterwards."

"And maybe . . . ," he said, still holding her hand, "maybe we could write to each other after your leave ends and keep this conversation going."

Audrey felt a moment's hesitation, remembering Robert's girlfriend, Linda. But Robert wasn't asking for love letters.

"I would like that very much," she said. "Very much."

⟨◦◦◦◦◦⟩

Eve found the glade in the woods where she'd first met Audrey and the little island in the stream where they'd had their picnic. They were unchanged, just as she'd hoped, offering comfort in a world that was changing much too quickly. Today the woods were bursting with life, the leaves the deep-emerald color that was her favorite. Ferns and wildflowers had pushed their heads through the ugly brown leaf mulch, declaring that the season of death was over, new life had come. If only the same could be true of the rest of the world, and the season of death and loss were nearing an end. She was tired of death, tired of living nearly every moment of every day with the awareness of war, weary of seeing bloodied reminders of it everywhere she looked.

She leaped from stone to stone to cross the swollen creek and sat down on a rock on the island thinking, *This is where I belong.* If she closed her eyes, she could be a girl again, believing that the world might cycle through its appointed seasons without ever really changing. She could have the faith of an innocent lamb from her Sunday school lessons, trusting the Good Shepherd to keep her safe and secure. Her eyes shot open as she remembered calling on God in the bomb shelter in the East End—and then emerging into a scene from hell when the all clear sounded. She remembered praying that Mum would be safe as she'd raced to the town house on a yellow bicycle, only to find her prayers in ashes. Eve struggled to breathe as the woods seemed to close in on her. She quickly looked up to see blue sky through the bright-green branches. Her panic slowly subsided.

She breathed deeply again, listening for the peaceful rustling and buzzing of the forest. But even that stillness had been altered by the war. Airplanes droned overhead. Army vehicles shifted gears as they bumped and rattled down the lane to Wellingford Hall. A tractor rumbled to life in the field she'd just crossed, a field that had once been a pleasant meadow. Tears brimmed in Eve's eyes as she picked up a stick and used it to scrape mud off the soles of her shoes, shoes worn by a girl who had roamed these woods barefoot. Maybe it had been a mistake to come to Wellingford Hall. It was Audrey's home, not hers. Eve no longer had a home, not even in these woods.

She brushed aside her tears and stood, refusing to give in to sorrow. She followed the trail through the woods to the village, emerging in the cemetery behind the church. After climbing over the fieldstone wall, she wove among the markers and tombstones, stopping at the plots where Mum and Granny Maud lay buried, side by side. Eve would keep fighting this war for their sakes, for the hopes and dreams they'd once had for her future. They'd sacrificed so much for her, hoping she would have a better life than theirs. She wouldn't disappoint them.

When she'd said her goodbyes at their graves, Eve went out through the church gate and walked up the street toward the village green. She spotted a group of American soldiers coming her way, and her instinct was to turn down another street to escape their leers and comments. But then she recognized the tall one in the middle of the group, the one who laughed the loudest. The one with ginger hair. She halted, waiting to see if Louis would recognize her in civilian clothes. As she'd expected, all of the soldiers ogled her as they drew near, appraising her from head to toe. One of them gave a wolf whistle. Then Louis grinned.

"Eve? What in the world are you doing here?"

"Hello, Louis. It's good to see you again." It was the truth. She had enjoyed every minute of their time together and often wished she'd run into him again. The other soldiers teased Louis, asking to be introduced to this "pretty little dish" and reminding him that he was a married man.

"Go ahead without me," he said, waving them away. "Eve doesn't want to meet any of you loudmouthed Americans, right, Eve?"

"Right," she said with a smile. Louis shooed them off, and he and Eve sat on the low stone wall in front of the manse. "Fancy seeing you here," she said with a grin. "I was just with Audrey at the manor house and we ran into Robert, but he didn't tell us that you were here, too."

"You mean, Wellington or Welling-something Hall?"

"Wellingford Hall. Yes."

"Bob and I got transferred there right after I met you at the dance. We've been there ever since, helping to get the new airfield operational. But how did you end up here?"

"I grew up in this village. Wellingford Hall is Audrey's home. We had a two-day furlough and decided to come home."

"I've been here for about two months now, and I have to say that aside from our work at the airfield, it's been pretty boring. It's a little too quiet for me at that grand old house."

"Then you probably haven't found it much livelier here in town. Where are you headed?"

"Just to the pub for a game of darts—I'm the reigning champion, by the way—and to drink warm beer. Haven't you British discovered refrigeration yet?"

"We like it warm."

He grimaced and shivered dramatically. "Hey, come to the pub with me, Eve. You're much easier to look at than those other goofs I'm with."

Eve took a moment to consider his offer. Louis made her laugh. And laughing helped her forget. She wasn't likely to have many laughs with Audrey at the manor house. The village was where she really belonged, not Wellingford.

"If I come for a drink, do you promise to protect me from those 'goofs,' as you call them? I could have gone to London on my furlough if I wanted to be leered at and groped."

"I'll be your guardian and protector." He held out his arm and she took it, smiling up at him as they walked to the pub. It was stuffed with Americans, laughing loudly, drinking pints, playing a rowdy game of darts. Louis was chivalrous as he fended off his fellow Americans. Eve greeted the pub owner, an old friend who gave them free pints, before taking Louis to a small corner table to talk. Two elderly farmers who had known Eve's daddy stopped by the table to greet her on their way out, and she made a mental list of all the other friends and neighbors she wanted to see during her visit, villagers she'd known forever and who'd been kind to her when Mum died. She had been too numb with grief at the time to thank them.

"Hey, your fiancé doesn't have spies here in town, does he?" Louis asked after the farmers left. He leaned across the table to speak softly. "He's not going to send his henchmen after me for sitting with you, is he?"

"No, you don't need to worry about Alfie." Her eyes suddenly filled with tears. She couldn't explain why.

"Oh no. Did I say the wrong thing, Eve?"

"Not at all. It's just that . . . Alfie and I aren't engaged. And the truth, which I'm slowly learning to accept, is that we probably never will be." She took a sip of her drink, desperate to think of a way to change the subject. Nothing came to her. She remembered how uneasy she felt walking through the front door of Wellingford Hall earlier, yet how good and natural it was to greet Robbins with a hug. Audrey had offered her Alfie's room but Eve couldn't sleep there. Her room on the third floor was home. Her friends in the village, not Alfie's friends, were the people she belonged with.

"Did you break up with him or something?" Louis asked. His concern seemed genuine as he studied her with his clear blue eyes. "I'm willing to listen if you want to tell me." With no one else to confide in, she decided to trust Louis.

"I used to work at Wellingford Hall," she said with a sigh. "As a servant. My friend Audrey grew up there. It's her family's home. Her daddy has more money than King George. We're good friends, though, in spite of our different backgrounds."

"I can tell that you are. Like Robert and me. And his family has way more money than mine does."

"Then you'll understand if I tell you that my boyfriend, Alfie, is Audrey's brother."

Louis gave a low whistle as he leaned back in his chair. "But that shouldn't be a problem if you love each other, should it?"

"Before he shipped overseas, Alfie told me he loved me. But he won't marry me as long as his father is alive because he would lose his inheritance."

"He sounds like a jerk."

"That's not completely fair. Alfie wouldn't know how to live without his money. He and the rest of the gentry grew up in huge manor houses with dozens of servants. He would be at a loss without them. There's the idea that blue bloods are somehow above the masses of people like me. Before the war, King Edward had to choose between marrying an American divorcée or reigning as the king of England. He chose love. But the aristocracy has shunned him for it ever since. Alfie would face the same rejection if he married me. I was his family's scullery maid, for goodness' sakes."

"And yet you stay faithful to him?"

Eve nodded. "I love him. And I guess, deep down, I still hope that he'll change. In many ways, the war is slowly destroying his way of life. He and Audrey are forced to live and work alongside people they once considered beneath them. They've learned to make do without the finer things they once took for granted, like warm baths and five-course meals. I feel sorry for them. Their family is so cold and unfeeling that neither one of them really knows what love is. Alfie can't imagine that love would be enough to sustain him if he gave up his wealth. Money is all he has to give his life meaning."

"Audrey is different?"

"I think so. The hardships of war have knocked some sense into her. She'll be okay. Although I would hate to see her return to that cold, drab way of life when the war ends. I hope she finds true love." She paused to take another sip of her drink, then asked, "What about you, Louis? What will your life be like after the war?"

"I'll join my father's insurance business. Support my wife and daughter . . . But I want to ask you one more question, Eve. If you're right and things don't work out with Alfie, what will you do when the war is over?"

"I have no idea. Live day to day, I suppose. Find a job, share a few laughs with friends. Wait to fall in love again." She shrugged as if hoping she could shrug away the pain. "I honestly don't know. After four years of war I feel like the shell-shocked people you see wandering through bombed-out ruins in a daze. All the familiar landmarks are gone, and they have no idea where they'll go or how they'll live, so they just stand around waiting for someone to come along and tell them what to do."

"You're so young. You'll have plenty of time to figure it out."

She tried to smile. "You're right. I will." Eve felt drawn to this man, comfortable with him. Too comfortable. She needed to change the subject. "Tell me about your wife."

Louis took another slug, grimacing at the taste or maybe the temperature. Eve recognized the move as something Alfie did to stall for time. She waited for Louis to swallow, wanting to hear all about the woman who'd captured the love of such a warm, sensitive man as Louis.

"Jean and I were pretty young when we started dating. Only sixteen. We went steady all through high school. Then I went off to college to study business and Linda took a job in her uncle's department store. Her father didn't want her to go to college, saying it was a waste of money since all she really wanted to be was a wife and mother."

"And is that what she wanted?"

"I guess." He shrugged as if he'd never considered the question before. "After Pearl Harbor, we knew I'd have to go off to war, and we were both a little scared of what the future might bring. Jean had a cousin who'd died on board the USS *Arizona*, so that hit pretty close to home. In those last weeks before I had to leave, Jean and I . . . well . . . we went a little bit too far, if you know what I mean."

Eve looked away, remembering Alfie's pleas. She knew.

"Just our luck, Jean got pregnant," Louis continued, idly twisting his wedding ring. "She wrote and told me about it while I was in basic training. We got married when I came home on leave. After that, the Army shipped me all around for more training, so we've never lived as a married couple in our own place. It seems funny to think that she's my wife. Jean and the baby live with her parents. Karen was born while I was stationed in California, but I got to see her once before I shipped over here. The first time I held her, it scared me to death to think I was responsible for such a tiny, helpless human being. I was a carefree college student and a jock one day, a husband and a father the next. And now a soldier. Like it or not, I'll have to settle down and be responsible when I get home. One night of youthful passion and now all my choices have been made for me."

"Do you love her?"

He gave a little laugh. "I loved her a little too much, wouldn't you say?" Eve wanted to shake her head and say that passion and love weren't the same. She knew from experience with Alfie. She also knew how hard it was to deny passion when you loved someone. Eve didn't regret her choices, but Louis obviously did.

"When Jean told me she was pregnant," he continued, "I asked Tom and Bob what I should do. They advised me to do the right thing. The honorable thing. But I felt like I messed up my life pretty badly and probably Jean's life, too. She should be out having a good time with her friends instead of being tied down with a baby. Sometimes I wonder if she feels as trapped as I do."

"Would she tell you if she did?"

He slowly shook his head. "No, probably not. And I would never hurt her feelings by telling her what I just told you. We've made our bed, as they say, and now we have to sleep in it."

"Listen to us," Eve said, summoning a smile. "Let's not talk about dreary things anymore. Do you Americans ever hold dances around here? Maybe we could go to one. You're a terrific dancer."

"They post notices about dances at the base all the time, but Robert never wants to go, and I didn't have a charming partner like you to go with."

"Let's go tonight. Want to?"

"There's nothing I'd like better."

"Super!" she said, springing to her feet. "You find out where the dance is, and I'll meet you in Wellingford's foyer, ready to go."

Louis stood as well. "Are you going there now? I'll walk back with you."

"No, there are a few people here in town I'd like to visit first."

"Swing by here and get me when you're ready to go. In the meantime, I'd better defend my championship title at the dartboard."

19

Eve's envy stirred when she saw two letters for Audrey on the hotel's front desk and none for her. She trudged up the stairs to their room, leaving Audrey behind to open them. After a long night with numerous ambulance runs, Eve longed to take a hot bath and collapse in bed. Their accommodations in this aging guesthouse had a marvelous bath. Too bad the tub had a red line painted around the inside to remind her that she was allowed only five inches of water. How could anyone enjoy a satisfying bath in five inches of water? Eve followed the rule, nonetheless, and when she returned to her room, wrapped in a towel, she found Audrey sitting in bed, still reading her letters. Either they were very long letters, or she was reading them more than once. The smile Audrey wore was so rare and so lovely that Eve wished she could take a photograph.

"Are both letters from Robert?" Eve asked.

"Yes." Audrey didn't look up.

"And didn't he send two letters last week, too?"

"Uh-huh." Audrey laid the letters down with a sigh and stood to rummage through her dresser drawer for stationery and a pen. "Do you mind if I keep the light on for a while?" she asked. "I want to answer Robert before I go to sleep."

"That's fine," Eve said, brushing her hair. "Maybe I'll write to Alfie." But Eve sat with the blank page in front of her, unable to think of anything new to say. Meanwhile, Audrey filled page after page, smiling to herself. Her bliss was striking. Was she falling in love with Robert Barrett? They'd spent a great deal of time together during Audrey's furlough at Wellingford. Eve had gone dancing with Louis both nights and didn't know how Audrey and Robert spent their time, but in the months since then, they'd written letters to each other regularly. Lots of letters. If Audrey was falling in love, Eve would do everything she could to make her friend's romance end happily.

"Audrey . . . ?" Eve waited for her to look up. "I checked the board today and there's an ATS post near Wellingford that needs drivers." Audrey stared at her, a million miles away. "We should take it. You could go home whenever you have time off."

"Would we go together?"

"Absolutely. I had fun dancing with Louis." And for just a little while, Eve had been able to stop worrying about Alfie being in danger and about her uncertain future with him. She could dance with Louis and have fun and forget the war. Louis didn't ruin each evening by drinking too much. He was always a perfect gentleman, always faithful to his wife and daughter. "You could see Robert more often," Eve added, testing her reaction. Audrey smiled. Her face shone brighter than the bedside lamp. Oh yes. Audrey might not realize it yet, but she was falling in love with Robert Barrett.

The pair continued writing to each other in spite of the busy-ness of the war and the move that Eve and Audrey made to the new post. After settling in and finally earning a two-day leave, they went to Wellingford. Both Robert and Louis arranged a day off and the four of them decided to take the train to London. "We'll give you a guided tour of all the sights," Audrey promised. She and Robert had their heads together the entire journey, planning what they would see and do. Eve watched them closely, her certainty growing. They cared deeply for each other.

Everyone claimed to have a grand time, but for Eve, the visit to London felt bittersweet. She remembered her first trip to London and seeing the Unknown Warrior's tomb with Audrey. And like that visit, which had changed from excitement and anticipa-tion to overwhelming sadness, this journey began to change for Eve, too. The sorrow she felt wasn't only for her daddy and for her mum, who had died here in London, but also for the city itself, so ravaged by war. Eve hadn't taken three steps from the train station before seeing signs of destruction from Nazi bombs and incendiaries. Craters and rubble and broken, boarded win-dows. Antiaircraft guns and barrage balloons. Piles of sandbags. Shattered glass. The grand department stores all suffered from the bombing and from lack of merchandise. Nearly every landmark they visited had sustained damage, from St. Paul's Cathedral to Buckingham Palace, from the Guildhall to the Chamber of the House of Commons. Bombs had even damaged Eve's beloved Westminster Abbey. And everywhere—on the streets, crowded onto buses, in the tea shops, and seated at lunch counters—were American soldiers and American MPs in their white helmets and gaiters, trying to keep the GIs in line. This wasn't the London Eve knew. She felt like a stranger here, and she longed to go home. But where was home?

In spite of the cold, wintry day, Audrey decided they should walk through St. James's Park to Buckingham Palace. As Eve strolled along the edge of the icy pond, the others laughed at something funny Louis said, their breath visible in the cold. But Eve felt tears stinging her eyes. When they reached the plaza in front of the palace where the Queen Victoria Memorial used to be, she left the others and walked toward nearby Green Park, trying to decide what the odd white lumps in the once-lovely park were. Approaching on one of the paths, Eve realized they were sheep. Sheep! In London! Grazing untended on the wintry-brown grass. She didn't understand. Where was the shepherd? Had he abandoned his sheep in this perilous, stricken city? She longed to shout her question out loud—*"Where is the Good Shepherd in all of this suffering and loss?"* She felt as abandoned as these sheep, deserted by Him. Eve turned away, wiping her tears. She shoved her hands deep into her pockets as she rejoined the others, determined not to let them see her pain and confusion.

The train compartments were all crowded on the journey home, mostly with American soldiers. Unable to find four seats together, they split into two pairs. Audrey and Robert sat together, deep in conversation. Eve leaned against Louis's shoulder and closed her eyes, tired from walking and still upset by all the destruction. And by the sheep.

"Look at the two of them," Louis murmured after a while. "They look like two lovebirds, don't they?"

Eve opened her eyes. She sat up. Audrey and Robert bent close, their faces radiant even in the darkened railcar.

"You're right. They do!" Eve's sadness had driven away all thoughts of Audrey falling in love, but here was proof, right in front of her. And it also was obvious that Robert was in love with Audrey. "Louis, tell me about Robert's girlfriend back home."

"Linda? She and Robert have been together forever. I can't remember a time when they weren't."

"Are they happy? Do they seem well suited for each other?"

"Well . . . Jean and I are good friends with Bob and Linda, you know? I'd hate to talk about them behind their backs . . ."

"Louis, look at Audrey and Robert. They're glowing! Did he and Linda ever look like that?"

Louis gaped at them. "Um . . . not that I can remember. To tell you the truth, they never seemed well matched to me. Linda is moody. She can be happy and full of fun one day, flying high as a kite, then she crash-lands and lies in bed for days on end and won't go anywhere. Bob was always trying to figure out what he did wrong and how to make it up to her. Because when Linda gets mad—watch out! I never told Bob, but in a way, I would hate to see him stuck with her for the rest of his life."

"But he loves Linda, doesn't he?"

Louis was thoughtful for a moment. "I never heard him say it in so many words. But he's a gentleman and much too nice to tell her to get lost. I know that both sets of parents hope they'll get married someday."

"But look at him now, Louis. I've known Audrey for a long time, and I've never seen her this happy. She's always been so serious. But she beams like a searchlight when she gets a letter from Robert. Did you know they've been writing to each other?"

"I've seen him writing letters but I figured they were to Linda."

Eve shook her head. "Audrey gets at least two letters a week from him. And she actually smiles as she writes back to him."

"They sure look happy now."

"Yes, Louis, my friend. They do." And Eve decided to do something to nudge Audrey along the path of love. The train pulled into the station and they all linked arms to keep from stumbling in the dark as they walked up the road to Wellingford Hall. Inside the foyer, Robert took both of Audrey's hands as they parted and kissed her cheek. She closed her eyes as if savoring rich, sweet chocolate. "Did you see that?" Eve whispered to Louis.

"Wow! I guess I've had my head in the sand. I'd better have a talk with Bob."

"Wait." Eve grabbed Louis's arm to stop him. "Whose side are you going to be on when you have this talk—Audrey's or Linda's?"

"I'm on Bob's side," he said with a mischievous grin. He paused, leaving Eve in suspense. "Which means I'm rooting for Audrey."

"Me, too."

They all said good night and goodbye, knowing they wouldn't see each other again before Audrey and Eve returned to their base in the morning. Eve trailed Audrey up the main staircase to her room, then followed her inside instead of continuing up to the third floor. "We need to talk," she said, closing the door. Eve had been inside Audrey's stately room before, but tonight she felt uncomfortable for some reason, as if the room didn't belong to either of them and they were intruders.

"Talk about what?" Audrey still wore a dreamy, satisfied expression on her face from Robert's kiss, like a cat that had just awakened from a long nap.

"Sit down," Eve ordered, gesturing to the bed. Audrey obeyed, perched on the edge, her spine straight. Eve crawled onto the bed and sat cross-legged, facing her. She drew a deep breath and said, "You're falling in love with Robert, aren't you?"

"What? No . . . I . . ." Audrey's pink cheeks gave her away. "We all agreed that the four of us would be friends, didn't we?"

"Louis and I agreed because I'm in love with Alfie and he's married to Jean. But Robert has a girlfriend, not a wife. The two of you are both free to fall in love with each other. And I think you have."

"You're wrong about Robert. We're just friends."

Eve decided to try a different approach. "What were you talking about on the way home tonight?"

Audrey brightened as if an electric light had switched on inside her. "All sorts of things. Robert talks to me the same way you and I talk, not in an artificial way like all the other men I've known. Tonight, we discussed our favorite poets—Elizabeth and Robert Browning in particular. Robert has some of his favorite lines memorized and he recited them."

Eve laughed out loud. "Come on! Can't you see it, Audrey? You two are in love."

"I . . . I don't think so. . . . Robert has a girlfriend—"

"How does it make you feel when you imagine him going off to war? When you think about him being in danger? Or being killed?"

"Eve, that's horrible! Don't talk that way!"

"How do you feel about him going back to the United States and marrying his girlfriend and never seeing you again? He won't be able to write any more letters, you know. How will it be to live the rest of your life without him? Are you willing to say goodbye to Robert forever and settle for one of the men you used to date before the war? Or maybe you'll become an old maid like your governess—what was her name?"

"Miss Blake. Why are you saying these horrid things?"

"Because you're in love with Robert and he's in love with you, and if you're smart, you'll melt that wall of ice that has separated you from people all your life and give him your heart! Fall in love, Audrey. Enjoy the wonder of it. It's like nothing you've ever experienced in your life, isn't it?"

Audrey seemed deep in thought for a moment. Her face glowed. "Even if you're right and what I feel for Robert is love, I wouldn't know what to do about it. I've never received anyone's affections before or given away my own. I've never learned how one goes about it."

"Oh, Audrey . . ." Eve longed to embrace her, but Audrey sat so stiffly Eve feared she might break. "There's no right or wrong way to love someone. Just do what comes naturally. Let go of your reserve and give away your heart. Don't keep it all locked up inside and protected."

"I've had to. It's the only way I can keep from getting hurt. I envy you, Eve. I always have. Everywhere you go people love you. I'm afraid to love as spontaneously as you do."

"You need to let go of your fear and take a chance while you still can. Robert may be going into combat soon. We both know the invasion is coming with the promised 'second front.' We know why they've been massing troops and piles of equipment. None of us knows what tomorrow may bring. We could all be dead and forgotten. In the meantime, why not take a chance on love?"

"Where . . . how does one begin?"

"Tell Robert how you feel. Tell him that your friendship has become something more to you. Tell him you want to be with him every single moment you possibly can."

Audrey looked down at her lap. "I could never do that. It's not the way I was raised. One doesn't boldly speak one's mind that way."

"Look around you, Audrey. Look what's become of your beautiful home. And remember what London looked like today? Does anything you see resemble the way you were raised? Did you ever think you would wear an ugly uniform and drive an ambulance and eat in a mess hall and shower with a dozen other women? The war has erased the rules and traditions we grew up with. England is never going to be the same again. And neither are we."

"You're right, you're right. . . . I know I've changed. . . . But what if Robert doesn't feel the same way about me?"

Eve rolled her eyes. "He does, believe me! Haven't you noticed the way he looks at you? Doesn't it make your insides melt?" Audrey looked away, blushing. "And why do you think he writes so many letters? I don't write to Alfie as often as you write to Robert, and Alfie is thousands of miles away, not forty."

"But . . . what if he doesn't love me?" she asked in a tiny voice.

Eve huffed in frustration. She was trying to be patient, but she didn't want her friend to miss her chance at true love because of fear. "Even if he does reject you, you'll be no worse off than you are now. You can still remain friends. But if I'm right, and he is in love with you, then you'll never be sorry that you took a chance."

"What about his girlfriend, Linda?"

"It's up to Robert to worry about her. She has nothing to do with you loving him."

The peaceful look on Audrey's face had vanished, replaced by a furrowed brow and pinched lips. "Did you tell Alfie how much you love him?" she asked. Audrey was stalling, but Eve indulged her.

"I told him that I love him, yes. And he claims he loves me. But he also admitted that he loves your father's money more."

"That can't be true. He looks so happy when he's with you."

"Alfie hides behind the same wall of ice that you do. He's just better at masking it with a show of affection. He's as scared and unfamiliar with relationships as you are. Where would he have learned to be a good husband? Or to have a loving marriage? Not from your parents. Alfie doesn't know how to love any more than you do."

"Yet you love him and hope to marry him?"

"I love him, yes. But he isn't going to marry me and risk his inheritance. At least he was honest enough to admit it. The war is changing all of us, so for now, I'm hoping our darling Alfie will come home a different man, with different values. I hope he'll see that love is the most important thing in the world. And right now, I'm trying to get you to see the same thing. Hasn't this war changed you, Audrey?"

"When I look in the mirror, I hardly recognize myself. I've learned to do things I never imagined I would be brave enough or strong enough to do."

"Then tell me this—do you want to live your life after the war according to your mother's rules? Do you want to be a socialite, marry a rich man you don't love? Let the servants do everything for you, including raising your children?"

"I don't. No."

"Then take a chance, Audrey. Melt the wall of ice and tell Robert you love him. I guarantee you'll never regret it."

"But what if—?"

"Don't even think about all the what-ifs. Because even if things don't turn out for Alfie and me after the war, I will never regret loving him."

⁂

Audrey didn't have a chance to see Robert the next morning before she and Eve had to hurry back to their base. She hadn't slept well, unable to stop thinking about Eve's words. Her feelings for Robert were so new and unfamiliar that she had no way of knowing what they were. She had merely floated along like a ship on calm seas, enjoying every moment with him. But Eve was right. What she felt was love. She was in love with gentle, brilliant, kind Robert

Barrett. The possibility of losing him terrified her. What if he was killed in battle? What if he returned home to America and she never saw him again? What if he didn't love her as much as she loved him?

What if he did?

For more than a week, Audrey silently debated these questions, sometimes so deep in thought that she would arrive at her destination and not remember driving there. Should she confess her love or play it safe? Maybe she could ask Louis if he knew how Robert felt before making a fool of herself. The only bright spots in her endless hours of transporting the injured to hospital were Robert's letters—long, wonderful letters that brought Audrey joy every time she read them. And she read them again and again. But if Robert was in love with her, he never said so on those pages. Audrey knew it would be cowardly to confess her love for him in a letter. If she took the leap, she needed to do it in person so she could see his face when she said, *I love you.* But, oh, how it would hurt to see rejection in his eyes.

Audrey had to wait three full weeks before she finally had a day off. As soon as she and Eve saw their names on the furlough roster, Eve turned to her and said, "We're going to Wellingford."

"But it's only a one-day leave," Audrey said, trying not to panic. "We won't have enough time."

"We can jump on the train as soon as our shift ends. You'll have time. It only takes a few seconds to say, 'I love you.'"

"What if Robert can't get time off?"

"It doesn't matter. We're going. Write to him. Tell him you're coming."

"I'm still not sure I can say it."

"Do you love him, Audrey?"

"Yes . . . I think so."

"Then you'll be able to say it when the time comes. You'll thank me for this someday."

"I envy your certainty."

Audrey wrote and told Robert when she would arrive. He wrote back to say that he would be on duty all that day and wouldn't return from the air base until after midnight. *Can you meet me for breakfast in the morning before you catch your train back?* he asked. Audrey waited up for him instead, knowing she would never be able to fall asleep. She listened from her bedroom window for the sound of his jeep and raced downstairs to the foyer the moment she heard it. He was with two other men, but she saw only Robert.

"Audrey! You waited up!" His smile erased all the weariness from his face and made her heart leap like a wild thing. She nodded, unable to speak past the knot of joy in her throat. She reached for his hand, towed him into Father's library, and closed the door. Before she could utter a word, Robert pulled her into his arms and kissed her. The warmth of his lips spread through her body until she felt as though she were melting. She had never been kissed this way before, and the surge of love and pleasure she felt overwhelmed her.

"Audrey . . . ," Robert whispered when they parted. He kissed her temple, her throat, then found her lips again. "I love you, Audrey," he murmured as he held her tightly. "I love you so much!"

Audrey's tears brimmed, then overflowed. "I love you, too," she breathed.

He pulled away to look at her. "Why are you crying?"

"I don't know. I've been a blubbering mess all my life. And now . . . now I've never felt so happy in my life!"

"Neither have I." His eyes also filled with tears. "It's just like in the movies, isn't it? The joy! The unbelievable joy of being with the one you love."

"I waited up for you tonight because I wanted to tell you that I love you. I didn't want to wait until tomorrow. But you said it first."

"I'm sorry," he said, turning serious. "Go ahead and tell me. I want to hear you say it again."

"I love you, Robert Barrett. More than I have words to say."

"Will you marry me, Audrey? I know we haven't known each other long, but I can't imagine the rest of my life without you."

"Yes. A thousand times, yes," she replied, clinging to him. Audrey didn't even pause to think about asking for Father's approval. It didn't matter. She could walk away from Wellingford Hall on Robert's arm and never look back. They kissed again and her knees felt so wobbly she had to sit down with him on the sofa.

"I know that the process of getting permission to marry will take time," Robert said in between kisses. "I've already looked into all the red tape that GIs have to go through to marry foreign brides."

"You have?" she asked in astonishment.

"Of course! I want to marry you, Audrey, and I hoped and prayed that you felt the same. According to War Department regulations, American soldiers stationed overseas need the approval of their commanding officers two months in advance. My CO is required to interview you, and there are dozens of forms to fill out. I'll have to provide letters from the States to confirm that I have a job back home and the means to support you. In some cases, the Army wants assurance that soldiers' families support their decision. But I'm over twenty-one, so that shouldn't matter."

Audrey felt a shiver of unease. "What if your parents don't approve of me?"

"They may be disappointed that I'm not marrying Linda, but I don't think they'll stand in our way. I'm their only child. They want me to be happy. No, the biggest hurdle right now is that all foreign marriages are forbidden until after the invasion. But I've been thinking about it all day, and if you're willing to marry me, I think we should submit the paperwork right away. We'll stand a better chance of it being approved by the time the war ends."

"Such beautiful words, Robert—us being married and this war finally ending."

"It will end. The Allies are making steady progress. . . . But you look so worried, darling. Is something else bothering you? Am I moving too quickly?"

"No! I would marry you today! But how will you break the news to Linda? What will you tell her?"

"I've been trying to prepare her for this event ever since you and I began writing to each other, because I knew then that I was falling in love with you. I've been very honest with Linda all along, since before I left home. I've told her frequently and emphatically how much I dislike the country-club life, playing tennis and golf, sailing expensive boats, spending money. She keeps saying I'll change my mind. I've been telling her in my letters that I'm becoming more and more certain that I don't want to become a lawyer after the war and live the way our parents do. She says I'm talking nonsense. I've also reminded her that we left our relationship open when we parted and that we're both free to date other people. I even told her that I've been seeing you. She insists I'm the only man she'll ever love. She's living in some sort of fantasy world and believes she's going to get her own way, because she always has."

"I feel sorry for her, Robert."

"I do, too. But now that I've fallen in love with you, I realize that I was never in love with Linda. I never felt this way about her. She and I both would have been cheated if we'd married."

"Is there no other way to soften the blow for her?"

"She's friends with Louis's wife, Jean. Louis knows how I feel about you, so he asked Jean to talk to Linda, help her see that we want different things in life. That we've always wanted different things." He pulled Audrey into his arms again, and it felt so right to be nestled close to him. She never wanted to leave his embrace. "I love you, Audrey. I can't say it enough times. From now on, we're going to dream about a future for the two of us."

"I've been trying to imagine how I would live my life if I was starting over," she said. "If I didn't have to go back to the life my family expects of me. The truth is, I don't think my father cares what I do or who I marry. The only person he has ever cared about is my brother, Alfie."

"Oh, Audrey . . ."

"I don't say that so you'll feel sorry for me, but to tell you that I'm the only one who is putting limits on what I'll do after the war. Mother is gone. I don't have to live up to her expectations."

"Is that a frightening thought for you?"

"No. It's liberating. There's so much uncertainty with the entire world at war. Such horrible things are happening, and we're seeing the depths of evil that man is capable of. Somehow, it seems wrong to be as happy as I am right now. Are we crazy to plan a life together when the future is so tenuous? Only God knows our future."

"You're right—we don't know the future," he said, kissing her again. "But we can continue to pray and trust God. The most hopeful, faith-filled thing we can do is to plan our life together."

That felt right to Audrey. Blissfully, wonderfully right.

20

The knock on Audrey's dormitory door came just as she was waking up. "Meeting for all drivers in fifteen minutes!" She sat up in bed, rolling her shoulders to loosen the knots, pining for the luxury of a long, hot bath. Her ambulance unit had moved to a post near the southern coast to transport casualties from the D-Day invasion. The tension, along with the horrors of what she'd seen, had exacted a toll. She dreamed of clanging ambulance bells in her sleep—when she was able to sleep.

"Fifteen minutes?" Eve groaned as she climbed from her bed. "Good thing we learned to dress quickly in basic training."

"Right. And to use the loo in sixty seconds." Audrey pulled on the same pair of coveralls she'd worn yesterday and they hurried out of the dormitory together.

"Maybe it's good news," Audrey said as they jogged up the street to the ambulance headquarters. The news had been hopeful lately. Rome had fallen to the Allies on June 4. The long-awaited D-Day invasion had finally come on June 6. An armada of airplanes had filled the sky that day, more than Audrey thought existed, some of them from Robert's air base. At the end of those long days of anxiety and bloody warfare, the Allies established a foothold in France for the first time since the Dunkirk evacuation.

"I'm so afraid to hope," Eve said, panting from the uphill climb. "Do we dare believe the war might finally come to an end?"

"But the cost . . . the lives lost. It's horrible, Eve. Horrible! I thank God every day that Robert hasn't left for France yet."

"Do you think they'll transfer us across the channel to follow the advancing Army?"

"Maybe that's what this meeting is about." It would be a dangerous assignment. Even after everything she'd endured, Audrey wondered if she was ready for it. "You and I have been driving the longest, Eve. Before conscription even started."

"Which means we're the most experienced. They'll need experienced drivers."

They squeezed into the former petrol station—now the ambulance command center—for the meeting. The other drivers looked as harried and weary as Audrey felt. Their commander called for everyone's attention, and Audrey held her breath, waiting.

"I know we've all been bracing for Hitler's response to the D-Day invasion. . . . Well, the news is bad. We just learned that he has a new weapon. The V-1 missile resembles a torpedo with wings and is launched directly from bases in France and Holland without a pilot or an airplane. Each missile carries nearly two thousand pounds of explosives and causes enormous damage. They travel so fast that there's no time for warning sirens. And unlike the Blitz, V-1 attacks happen around the clock, even in broad daylight. We haven't discovered a way to shoot them down."

Audrey's already-tense muscles tightened with fear. She glanced at Eve as the other drivers whispered among themselves. If Eve was frightened, she didn't betray it. The officer raised her voice above the murmurs. "The engine that powers each missile makes an odd sputtering sound. Some say it's a bit like a motorcycle with a faulty engine. Others describe a buzzing noise. Just before the missile falls to earth, the engine stops. Nothing else is heard until the explosion." She paused again. This time the room fell silent. "Since firing the first missile on June 13, the Nazis have launched about a hundred a day, every day. With no advance warning, you'll need to stay alert for the sound. If you think you hear one, get out of your vehicle and take cover."

"What if we're transporting casualties?" someone asked.

The officer shrugged. "Now, I'm asking for drivers who are familiar with London and are willing to transfer there. Central London is being hit especially hard by these missiles. Can I see a show of hands from volunteers?" Eve immediately raised hers. Audrey hesitated, then raised hers as well. "Thank you. All those who have volunteered, please remain after everyone else is dismissed."

They were told to pack their belongings and leave immediately for their new post at St. Thomas's Hospital in central London. They would need to memorize the streets and landmarks. Most of the orderlies had followed the troops on D-Day, so Eve and Audrey would receive an emergency first aid course and be assigned to the same ambulance. They would be billeted in nurse housing and be on call when needed. The tension Audrey already felt spread to her stomach. She could barely manage tea and toast before hurrying back to her room to pack.

"Such discouraging news," Audrey said on the train to London later that morning. "Hitler's new secret weapon sounds frightening. There's no warning? No time to get to a shelter?"

"If it's our turn to die, what difference will it make how it happens?" Eve replied. "And you already know how I feel about sitting inside a shelter."

"Yes, I do."

"I volunteered for your sake, you know."

"For mine?" Audrey asked. "What do you mean?"

"You'll be much closer to Wellingford Hall if we're living in London. Closer to Robert." Eve waited for her reaction, and when Audrey managed a smile, Eve laughed out loud. "Isn't love wonderful?" she asked.

Audrey felt herself blushing. "Yes. It is."

They barely had time to settle into their new living quarters at the hospital before their ordeal began. The new weapon with its seemingly random civilian targets had caused morale in the city to plummet again after the success of the long-awaited D-Day invasion. As soon as the report of a V-1 strike came in, Audrey and Eve had to jump into their vehicle and race to the scene, steeling themselves for the grisly sight of mangled bodies and severed limbs. St. Thomas's Hospital was directly across the Thames River from Westminster Abbey, the Houses of Parliament, the Ministry of Defense, the Foreign Office, the Treasury. Buckingham Palace was a little farther on. All prime targets for enemy missiles.

They had just reported for duty at the hospital on a clear Sunday morning a few days later when air-raid sirens wailed. A huge, window-rattling explosion quickly followed. Eve stood, grabbing her medical kit. "Here we go again."

Audrey stood as well, her skin tingling. "That sounded close. On the other side of the Thames, I'm guessing. Where all the government buildings are." The telephone lines sprang to life.

"A V-1 struck Guards' Chapel on Birdcage Walk," the dispatcher told them.

"I know where that is," Eve said. "Right next to Wellington Barracks."

"A worship service was in progress, with soldiers and civilians in the congregation. Casualties will be in the hundreds. Go!"

"That's a stone's throw from Buckingham Palace," Audrey said as she and Eve raced to their vehicle with the other drivers. Every doctor and nurse who could be spared accompanied them.

Eve jumped behind the wheel and they drove across Westminster Bridge, alarm bells clanging. They drove past the Houses of Parliament and saw St. James's Park ahead on the right. A huge plume of dust billowed in the sky above the stricken chapel. Leaves and pine needles littered the roadway, blasted off the trees in the park by the explosion. A cloud of choking dust enveloped the block as they arrived, but it couldn't hide a scene of utter devastation. Guardsmen from the nearby barracks worked to clear a path for the ambulances, directing them to park as close to the demolished chapel as possible. Doctors and nurses leaped from the rear of the ambulances.

"The missile nose-dived straight into the chapel roof," one of the guardsmen said. "The building collapsed on top of the congregation before anyone could get out. There may be as many as three hundred people trapped inside."

"Is there a way for us to tunnel in and tend to the injured?" one of the doctors asked. "We can offer morphine until they're dug out from the debris."

"The main doors to the chapel are blocked. The heavy rescue teams are still searching for a way inside. We'll let you know as soon as they find one."

Audrey stood beside Eve and the medical teams as they waited, feeling helpless. She stared at the toppled walls and caved-in roof, wondering how anyone could possibly survive. She relived the same nightmare that had haunted her dreams since the war began as she gazed at mounds of bricks and stones and jagged timbers and heard shattered glass crunching beneath the workers' feet. And always, she was aware that helpless people were suffering, dying.

The rescue teams signaled for silence. Audrey held her breath as they listened for moans and faint cries for help. Then came shouts from the rescue workers. "Over here!" Guardsmen from the barracks joined the digging, freeing the first victims and carrying the living to the waiting ambulances.

"You drive to hospital, Eve," Audrey said. "It's such a short distance. I'll stay here and help with triage." She knew how to apply pressure to a bleeding wound, fasten a tourniquet, soothe terrified patients. Workers had tunneled into the interior of the chapel, and Audrey watched the courageous doctors and nurses crawl into the debris to administer morphine to trapped victims.

As quickly as survivors were located and dug free, ambulances transported them to hospital, then raced back for more. The task was endless and agonizing, the dead and dying outnumbering the living. When Audrey's composure began to crumble beneath the weight of suffering, she and Eve swapped tasks.

Forty-eight hours passed before the last of the victims were freed and Audrey and Eve had a chance to sleep. The final toll, she was told, included 121 dead and 141 seriously injured. The chaplain from the morning worship service was among the dead, along with several senior British Army officers and a US Army colonel.

Audrey wondered if the suffering would ever end. The V-1 bombs continued to fall on London throughout the month of June, meaning that Audrey and Eve were always on call, working day and night. If they weren't driving, they were keeping their vehicle in good repair, the engine cleaned from clogging dust, the tires checked for punctures from broken glass. Audrey learned to recognize the ominous buzz of the V-1 bombs, which the Londoners had nicknamed doodlebugs. She experienced a new, heart-pounding fear when forced to wait, holding her breath, during the interminable moments between when the stuttering motor halted and when the deafening explosion finally came. No one could predict where or when the missiles would fall. Letters from Robert became her lifeline, short and hastily written, but a joy to read and reread at the end of a grueling day. He was still in England, keeping the air base running and the airplanes flying, providing air support for the battles raging on the Continent.

We've heard terrible reports of the V-1 bombings in London, he wrote. *I worry about you, Audrey, my love.*

She assured him she was safe. *I'm learning to put my sensitivities aside and administer first aid when needed,* she wrote back. *One must get used to the sight of blood to be of any help at all. Perhaps I'll be a real nurse by the end of the war.* As the endless weeks and months passed, she and Robert longed for the day when they would see each other again. Neither of them had any idea when that day would be.

⁓

"You two ladies deserve a break," Eve's supervisor told her and Audrey one lovely September morning. "How would you like to go for a ride outside London?"

Eve longed for the forest, the scent of pine and moss and damp earth. "That sounds wonderful! Where are we going?"

"We borrowed one of our ambulances from another unit and we'd like you to return it. I understand you're both from a nearby village."

Eve couldn't have imagined anything better. She could see her old friends, visit the cemetery, walk in the woods. Audrey would

see Robert, and maybe Louis could get an evening off to go dancing. Eve felt a thrill of anticipation at the thought of laughing with
Louis, dancing in the comfort of his arms.

"I'll drive. You can nap," Eve offered, sliding behind the wheel.
"You don't want Robert to see you with dark circles beneath your
eyes, do you?" Audrey looked bone weary after months of demanding work. She was dozing before they reached London's outskirts.

The familiar countryside soothed Eve. How wonderful to leave
behind the signs of war and ruined lives and the stress of cop-
ing with V-1 missiles. She was driving through an idyllic village,
thinking how untouched by hardship it seemed, when she heard
a motorcycle approaching behind her. She checked her rearview
mirror to see if the driver wanted to overtake her. There was no
motorcycle. Nor was one approaching in front of her. Her heart
stopped when she realized what it was.

Eve jerked the steering wheel to pull over and slammed on the
brakes. "Audrey! Audrey, get out! Get out now!" she screamed.

Audrey looked around, dazed. "What? . . . Why?"

"It's a V-1, Audrey! Get out!" Eve scrambled from the ambulance to take cover, not bothering to shut the door. When she
looked back, Audrey was still inside.

The V-1's sputtering motor halted.

Oh, no!

Eve sprinted to the ambulance and yanked open the passenger
door. She pulled Audrey out. They were staggering away from
the vehicle when the force of the blast knocked them both to the
ground. It happened so fast that Eve had the sensation of slam-
ming into a brick wall. Pinpricks of light danced in her vision like
stars. The shock wave traveled through every inch of her body.
She barely had time to cover her head before a cloud of debris and
dust rained down.

She lay in the weeds, stunned. Deafened. She tried to sit up and her head whirled as if she'd spun in circles. The sensation made her vomit. "Audrey . . . ," she rasped. She could barely hear her own voice. "Audrey, where are you?" She sat up slowly and looked around. Audrey lay in an ungainly heap, her limbs sprawled, her leg twisted at an unnatural angle. She wasn't moving.

Eve heard ringing. An ambulance was coming. *Thank God.* She crawled painfully toward Audrey to see if she was alive, if she was breathing, and found a pulse in her throat. "Audrey! Audrey, wake up!" she begged. Blood matted her forehead and hair. Something was sticking out of her leg. Her own shinbone. Blood pulsed from the wound. Eve pulled out a handkerchief for a makeshift tourniquet, using a stick to twist it tight. It would do until the ambulance arrived. Where was the crew? *Come on, come on!* They must be nearby. The bells were so loud!

Yet all of the other sounds around her were muffled. Eve couldn't hear birds or the wind in the trees or any other noises. She could barely hear her own voice when she cried out for help. They weren't ambulance bells. The ringing was in her ears. And Audrey might be dying. She needed to drive her to hospital.

Eve looked around for their ambulance, praying that the bomb hadn't destroyed it. It sat alongside the road where she'd left it, only a few yards away, the windows blasted out by the explosion. Eve half crawled, half staggered to it, ignoring her nausea and throbbing head. Every movement brought a surge of agony from her left arm, but she managed to open the rear doors. Pull out a stretcher. Drag it to where Audrey lay. Shift her limp body onto it. Drag it back to the ambulance. Audrey didn't moan or move, even as Eve clumsily hauled the stretcher into the rear of the ambulance. She checked Audrey's pulse again. *Weak.* She replaced the handkerchief with a real tourniquet. The exertion made Eve dizzy. She closed her eyes for a second to keep from passing out. She couldn't faint. She couldn't.

Eve grabbed a blanket from the back before closing the doors and used it to cover the broken glass on the driver's seat. A jolt of pain shot through her leg as she depressed the clutch. Another pierced her arm as she grabbed the gear lever. *Oh, God, help me!* She couldn't drive. She had to.

Tears of pain and panic blurred Eve's vision. Only fear and training propelled her forward. Two ambulances raced past, coming from the opposite direction. They sounded miles away even as they zoomed by. She should have waited, searched for other victims. There wasn't time.

At last, at last, Eve pulled up at the hospital's emergency entrance as she had so many times. The engine bucked and died but she was in too much pain to step on the clutch one last time. She'd been trained to keep calm, but she flung open her door and half fell from the ambulance, screaming at the attendants to hurry. Audrey didn't move when they transferred her to a gurney. "Is she alive?" Eve asked as they rushed Audrey inside. She couldn't understand the muffled reply.

A nurse eased Eve onto another gurney. "Let's take care of you," she mumbled. Eve felt a shock of pain before everything went black.

A doctor stood over her when she opened her eyes, listening to her chest with his stethoscope. He said something to her and she shook her head. "I can't hear anything!"

"You're going to be all right," he said, bending close. "Your eardrums weren't ruptured. We'll stitch up the worst of your lacerations, like the deep one in your leg. You suffered bruising and a dislocated elbow, but you'll recover."

Eve tried to sit up. "I need to move the ambulance—"

A nurse held her down. "We already moved it. We have more casualties coming in."

"What about my friend? She has a head injury—"

"We know. We're taking care of her. She needs surgery for a compound fracture in her leg. You lie here quietly, now, so we can get you stitched up."

Eve did as she was told and lay still on the gurney. The pain as they yanked her elbow joint into place was like nothing she'd ever felt before. Then, miraculously, the pain was gone. The cuts requiring stitches contained bits of broken glass, likely from the shattered windscreen. More casualties poured into the emergency room, and the nurses moved Eve to a chair near their station so they could use the gurney for someone else. Eve wished she could help, but she couldn't stop trembling, even with a blanket wrapped around her. Audrey was badly injured, and Eve was terrified for her.

Hours passed before the flow of ambulances and victims halted. Eve's hearing improved, but her head continued to throb. She stopped one of the busy nurses and asked about Audrey. "I'll send a doctor out to speak with you," she promised. At last, the same doctor who'd spoken with Eve earlier crouched in front of her, leaning close to her ear.

"Your friend had surgery for her fractured leg. She's still unconscious. We won't know more about her head injury for a while. In the meantime, you should notify her family."

A wave of nausea rolled through Eve. Audrey would want Robert by her side. Eve needed to call the American air base and Wellingford Hall to locate him. Yet she would never be able to use a telephone until her hearing improved. She pulled herself to her feet, slowly, painfully, and limped over to two ATS ambulance drivers who stood talking near the door. "Will you help me, please?" Eve explained what had happened and begged them to notify Audrey Clarkson's fiancé, Robert Barrett, at the American air base or at his barracks in Wellingford Hall. The drivers wrote down the information and promised not to give up until they got through to him. They helped Eve to her chair at the nurses' station before hurrying away to use the phone.

Eve leaned against the wall and closed her eyes. *God, are You going to take Audrey away along with everyone else I've ever loved? If so, please take me, too.* She drifted to sleep from exhaustion and shock.

When she opened her eyes again, someone was gently shaking her and calling her name. "Eve . . . Eve . . . ?" Louis crouched beside her. Night had fallen outside the emergency room doors. "Eve, are you okay?"

"I think so. . . . I fell asleep." If Louis was here, then Robert must be here, too. "Audrey! Is she all right? Did they tell you anything?"

"She's still unconscious."

"I need to see her." She tried to stand, but Louis made her stay seated.

"She needs to be hospitalized for a few more days. In the meantime, you need to get out of here and get some rest."

"I need to stay with Audrey—"

"Bob is with her. The doctor said I should take you home."

"I . . . I don't have a home." The truth struck Eve like a second shock wave. She covered her face and wept. Louis's arms surrounded her—gently, so gently, as if afraid he'd hurt her. She leaned against him and sobbed. She felt his warmth and strength and never wanted him to let go. "Don't leave me all alone, Louis. Please!"

"I won't." He lifted her into his arms and carried her outside to his jeep. She didn't care where he took her as long as he stayed beside her and didn't leave. He drove to Wellingford Hall. After Robbins fussed over her and Mrs. Smith promised tea and hot soup, Louis carried her up the stairs to her bedroom on the third floor.

"I can walk," she told him, but he wouldn't hear of it. Mrs. Smith brought the tray and stayed with her and Louis while she tried to eat. Eve's stomach felt queasy as if the blast had shaken all of her insides out of place. Louis left the room while Mrs. Smith helped Eve change from her bloody uniform into a nightgown, but Eve begged him to come back and stay with her for a while, if he didn't mind.

"I'm not going anywhere," he assured her. "The doctor said you shouldn't be alone."

Alone. The word terrified her. The only person she had in the world was Audrey. *If anything happened to her . . .*

"Do you remember what happened?" Louis asked, sitting beside her on the bed.

"Audrey and I were delivering an ambulance to our old post . . . I heard a doodlebug . . . Such a stupid name for something so deadly . . . I thought Audrey was going to die!" Her tears began to fall.

"She's not," Louis said, holding her tightly. "The doctors are pretty sure she'll be okay."

"I thought I was going to die, too, and I didn't want to. I needed to live and save Audrey. She's the only family I have left, and if anything happens to her . . . I'll be . . . I'll be alone!" She started to shiver uncontrollably. Louis made her lie down and tucked a blanket around her the way Granny Maud used to do before kissing her good night. "Don't leave me, Louis!"

"I won't. I'm here, Eve." He lay down on the bed beside her and held her again.

"I'm so tired of bombs . . . and living in fear," she wept. "I've been surrounded by death for so long that I feel half-dead myself. I know how thin the line is between life and death—one breath, one heartbeat." She rolled over onto her side to face him, laying her hand on his chest so she could feel his heartbeat. The steadiness of it comforted her. "Do you ever feel afraid, Louis? Tell me the truth. Ever since the war started, I've been trying so hard to be brave. But I need to know that someone else is as terrified as I am." He nodded. He understood.

"When Bob got the call about you and Audrey—" Louis's voice broke. Tears pooled in his eyes. "I thought, *Not them. Please, God. Don't take any more people I care about.* Some of the crews at the air base . . . I'll be eating with them one day, then they're gone the next, shot down, and they're never coming back. I have to gather up their personal effects and notify their loved ones—" He uttered a sob as tears flowed down his face. "I'm sorry . . ." He let go of her long enough to swipe his tears. Eve felt such a longing for this kind, gentle man, such love.

"Don't be sorry, Louis. God knows we have every right to cry. Although He doesn't seem to care."

"My boyhood buddy Arnie is over in Belgium right now. Right in the thick of things. And I just got news that my other friend Tom was wounded in Italy. I'll be transferred to France soon, and we'll have a long, hard fight ahead of us before we get to Berlin, and . . . I've never told anyone this, not even Bob . . . but I have a terrible feeling that I'm going to be next—that I'm going to die—and I'm so scared!"

Eve rested her face against his stubbled cheek and let their tears flow together. His were warm and somehow soothing.

"If we die, Eve, what purpose will it serve? Do the deaths we've seen have any meaning at all? Will ours make a difference?"

"I don't know. I came so close to dying today." A shiver raced through her. Louis held her tighter. "I've been living with death, surrounded by it, for five endless years, and I'm so sick of it. The smell of it, the sight of it. The horror of it. And there's no end in sight. I long to forget about this war, Louis. For an hour—or even for five minutes! I want to forget so I can feel alive again. I don't want to hear the drone of approaching planes or the buzzing V-1s as they fall. I don't want to hear the explosions when they hit and know that people's lives have just shattered into a million pieces. I'm tired of the wailing sirens, the clanging ambulance bells." She pulled back to look into his sorrowful eyes. "Please, Louis. Please help me forget."

Louis gazed at her for a long moment through tear-filled eyes, then cupped her face in his hands. He kissed her. A dam burst inside Eve and she kissed him in return with all of the love and longing that her barricaded heart had stored away. All that mattered was the touch of his lips on hers, the warmth of his arms surrounding her.

At last Louis pulled back and whispered, "I love you, Eve." She looked into his eyes, into his soul, and saw his heart. He was telling the truth. He loved her. "I never meant to fall in love with you, but it happened. I think about you all the time, and I ask Bob if he knows when you're coming to Wellingford again so I can see you. All those hours we spent together, dancing, laughing . . . I've fallen in love with you."

"And I love you," she whispered. His handsome smile, the sound of his laughter, his ginger hair. Love had all but disappeared from her war-scarred world, and she hungered for its healing power. "I've tried to deny it and convince myself that we're just friends, but it isn't true. I love you, Louis. I thought I would never love anyone except Alfie, but I feel closer to you after these months we've spent together than I ever did to Alfie. I could never be sure of him." And Alfie had been right—he was shallow. Louis had substance and depth.

"How did this happen to us?" he asked in wonder.

"I don't know. But kiss me again, Louis. Maybe we can forget that we may not be alive tomorrow." He pulled her close, and Eve offered all her grief and passion to him, surrendering all her pain and fear to his love.

They fell asleep in each other's arms.

Eve awoke during the night and Louis was still beside her, strong and warm and alive. She watched his chest move with each breath he took, and the sound of his breathing soothed her back to sleep. She awoke again when he kissed her softly. He stood over her, dressed in his uniform. Before she could say anything, he slipped from the room.

Loneliness engulfed her. Her arms felt empty, the room cold and bare. Mum was gone. The splendor of Wellingford Hall was gone. And now Louis was gone, too.

She climbed out of bed and moved the blackout curtain to peer outside. Light from the dawning sun flooded the room, blinding her. A tidal wave of guilt slammed into her. *What have I done? Louis is another woman's husband!*

Granny Maud had made her memorize the Ten Commandments. *"Thou shalt not commit adultery"* was one of them. But Granny had also insisted that the Good Shepherd would always be near Eve, watching over her—and He wasn't. Innocent people died by the thousands and hundreds of thousands, and He didn't care. Audrey had almost been one of them. None of what Granny Maud had taught her was true. None of it.

Eve wanted to forget that her night with Louis had ever happened, but she knew she never would. Because for one night, she had finally felt alive again.

21

Audrey opened her eyes to blinding pain. Her head throbbed. She couldn't move. Everything around her was white. A hospital? She tried to speak, but her mouth was dry, her throat raw. She heard a faint rustle, and then Robert stood over her. "Audrey! I thought I was going to lose you." His muffled voice sounded far away.

"What happened?" Her throat felt as if she'd swallowed gravel.

Robert offered her a sip of water. "You were injured by a V-1 rocket. You're in the hospital."

"I don't remember. Eve and I were driving . . . I was so tired I couldn't stay awake . . . then . . . nothing."

"It happened two days ago. They gave you sedatives to keep you asleep so your brain could heal."

"Two days? . . . Eve! Where's Eve?" Panic made it hard to breathe.

"She's fine. Just cuts and scrapes and a dislocated elbow. She saved your life, Audrey. Your leg was fractured and she stopped the bleeding and drove you here."

"Where is she? I need to thank her." Audrey tried to turn her head to look for Eve, then cried out as pain shot through her skull.

"Shh . . . shh . . . Just lie still, my love. . . . Louis took Eve home to Wellingford. She's supposed to rest for the next few days, too."

"Hold me, Robert." He kissed her and lay down on the bed beside her, ignoring the other people in the crowded ward and the scowling nurses. Audrey tried to hug him, but her arms were too weak. "I'm so glad you're here," she breathed before everything went dark again.

She awoke to find a doctor bending over her. "Can you hear me, Miss Clarkson?" She nodded. His voice sounded muffled, but she could hear him. "Your recovery is proceeding nicely. I'm very pleased."

"Where's Robert? Is Robert here?"

"Lieutenant Barrett is just outside. The nurse will send him in when we're finished."

Robert was allowed inside a few minutes later, and the sight of his handsome face was all the medicine she needed.

"Listen, I have good news," he said after he kissed her. "The paperwork we need in order to get married has gone through. My CO expedited it when he found out what happened to you. We can be married whenever you're ready."

His face blurred as Audrey's eyes filled with tears. "That's wonderful!"

"But there's some bad news, too. I'm being deployed to France."

"Let's get married before you go, Robert. I don't want to wait. Life is so short, and it could end for either of us at any moment."

"Won't you need time to plan—?"

"No. Let's ask the vicar to marry us right away. Right here." She surprised herself. Audrey had always been a planner and a plodder, afraid of change. But her narrow escape from death made her determined to live each day fully from now on. "We'll ask Louis and Eve to be our witnesses."

Robert laughed. "Don't you want a lacy white dress and a flower-filled church? What about notifying your father and your brother?"

"You're not trying to back out of this wedding, are you?" she asked, smiling.

"God forbid!" He kissed her again. "I just don't want to rush you."

"Robert. All I need is you."

Eve arrived at the hospital later that morning, wearing a worried look and purple bruises and scrapes. "Oh, Audrey," she said when she saw her. "I was so scared for you. I'm so glad you're alive!"

"I'm glad too, believe me. They say you saved my life."

"You would have done the same for me."

"I owe you, Eve, and I'll never forget it. Thank you. And now I have a favor to ask. Well, two favors, actually."

"Anything."

"Will you contact Rev. Hamlin and ask him to marry Robert and me?" She smiled at the look of surprise on Eve's face.

"When . . . ? Where . . . ?"

"Right away. Right here in the hospital. . . . And the second question is, will you be my maid of honor?"

⁂

Eve envied Audrey's happiness as she stood at her bedside and watched her become Mrs. Robert Barrett. Not in a church as Audrey might have dreamed, but in a hospital ward. Not wearing a fashionable wedding gown as Lady Rosamunde might have wished, but a hospital gown and a white plaster cast on her leg.

And thank goodness it wasn't to some tedious bore from the gentry, but to a man she loved. Eve wondered if Audrey even remembered the shy, fearful girl she'd once been, bending to everyone's wishes but her own. Audrey had gone after what she wanted, and Eve was happy for her. Her new husband looked handsome in his uniform, wearing a smile that told the world he was the luckiest man alive. If only his luck would hold when he faced the Nazis.

Eve gave the vicar the wedding ring she'd safeguarded and reached for Louis's hand as Audrey and Robert recited their vows. The warmth of his palm, the gentle pressure of his squeeze, brought tears to her eyes. The happiness they'd found for one night could last a lifetime if he wasn't married. If only.

She told herself not to be sorry for what she and Louis had done. She had no reason to feel guilty. She hadn't left the Good Shepherd's fold—He had abandoned her! He had ignored her prayers and let Mum die instead of watching over His flock as He'd promised. He had left Eve all alone in the world, with nothing and with no one to love. Why should she obey His rules any longer?

Eve stood alone in the corridor after the wedding, waiting to drive back to Wellingford with Louis and Robert. Louis found her there. They hadn't been alone since their night together, and as Louis groped for words, Eve thought she knew what he was about to say.

"Eve, I hope you don't think . . . I mean . . . what we did . . . I need you to know that I truly am in love with you. I may have been wrong to take advantage of you when you were so vulnerable, and if so, I'm sorry—"

"I'm not sorry. I needed you that night, and you needed me. We love each other, Louis. If I have any regrets at all, they're because you're—"

"I know . . . Listen . . ." He glanced at the door as if worried Robert might overhear. "Will you write to me when I'm in France? I need to know that you're safe. That you're okay. And I need to confide in you about . . . about my fears. There's no one else—"

"Yes, of course." She could hang on to her love for him awhile longer. "Does Robert know about us?"

Louis shook his head. "Does Audrey?"

"I haven't told a soul."

"Eve, I don't know if I'll have a chance to see you again before I leave, but—"

It was all they were able to say before Robert emerged from Audrey's room, looking at his watch. "We need to go. Some way to start a marriage, huh?"

"There will be happier days ahead," Eve said. She didn't really believe it.

Two days later, Audrey was discharged to recuperate at Wellingford with her new husband before he was deployed to France. The servants moved Audrey's belongings into the small sitting room on the first floor and converted it into a bedroom.

Eve spent the remainder of her furlough visiting with Audrey while Robert was at the air base and eating the meals that Tildy prepared from their meager rations. "This is a gourmet meal compared to what we're used to," Eve assured the cook.

When the notice of her reassignment arrived in the post, Eve found Audrey alone in her room, hobbling around on crutches to practice walking. "I'm going away tomorrow, Audrey. My leave is over." She waved the letter from the ATS. "I'll be a staff driver, taking the brass all over London and waiting endlessly for them to finish their important meetings."

Audrey limped to the edge of the bed and sat down. From her worried expression, Eve might have been assigned to a war zone.

312 · IF I WERE YOU

But hadn't London been a war zone for the past five years? "Oh, Eve! The V-1s are falling on London day and night," Audrey said.

"They can strike anywhere, Audrey. You should know that better than anyone. But with any luck, once I'm in London, navigating around all the craters and barricades and closed streets, I'll be too busy to worry about Alfie." *Or to think about Louis.*

"It's going to be quiet around here. Robert ships out in two days."

"Is Louis leaving, too?" Eve's heart plummeted when Audrey nodded. "I guess we won't be dance partners for a while." She remembered Louis's premonition and wondered if she would ever see him again.

"Eve, I'm so terrified for Robert!"

"He'll come back to you. You'll see."

Audrey nodded, but neither of them believed it.

"I need to go pack," Eve said.

"Wait. Will you help me do something first?"

"Of course. What is it?"

"Drive me into the village. I want to go to church and pray for you and Robert and Alfie."

Eve battled to control her temper. She wanted to ask Audrey where God had been for the past five years and why she thought He would start answering her prayers now. Instead, she tried to make light of it to hide her irritation. "I'm pretty sure God can hear your prayers right here, Audrey." *If He's even listening.*

"I feel closer to Him in that little church."

Eve lost the battle as her anger exploded. "And the people in Guards' Chapel probably felt very close to Him before the V-1 fell through the roof and killed them all!"

Audrey appeared startled, as though Eve had slapped her. Then she looked down at her lap. "Never mind. I'll find another ride."

"I'm sorry," Eve mumbled. "I'll drive you. I don't want to leave here with hard feelings between us. . . . But please don't expect me to go inside with you."

Audrey looked up at her again. "I don't understand. I always envied your faith. You went to church with your grandmother when you were growing up. You used to talk about the Good Shepherd and how He would always take care of you. What happened to your faith, Eve?"

"What *happened*? It got buried in the rubble of the town house along with our mothers! My faith was stolen from me by the Nazis—along with Alfie and my youth and all of my hopes and dreams! The bombs blasted it away when they took my friend Iris and her grandmother and thousands of other innocent people! The same bombs that nearly took you!" She clenched her fists, breathing hard as the bitter words spewed out. "God demolished my faith when war took my mum just like it took my daddy. He blasted a huge gulf between us when He abandoned me and left me alone, without even a place to call home!" And now she had widened the gulf when she'd slept with a married man.

"I . . . I don't know what to say . . ."

"I'm glad you still have faith, Audrey. And I'm glad that you and Robert found each other. I'm sure you'll have a wonderful life together in America when the war ends, far away from the ruins of England and all the reminders of what we've lost."

"Eve . . . please . . ." Audrey groped for her crutches and struggled to stand. Eve knew she would try to embrace her, but pity was the last thing Eve wanted.

She turned toward the door. "I'll bring the car around front and meet you outside." Eve would visit the cemetery while Audrey prayed. Take a walk in the woods. Have a pint at the pub. She would not go inside the church.

Eve was still fuming over Audrey's naive faith as she lay in bed that night, staring into the darkness. It was useless to try to sleep. She rose and parted the blackout curtains, hoping there would be a moon and stars so she could see the distant woods. But the sky was overcast, the woods buried beneath a mist of fog. She let the curtains fall back into place. It seemed appropriate that from the very beginning of the war, every home and building in the nation had been shrouded in black as if prepared for mourning. Eve couldn't think of a single person she knew who hadn't lost someone in this endless war.

She was about to climb back into bed when there was a knock on her door. Her heart sank, fearing it was Audrey. She didn't want to see her, unable to bear a prolonged goodbye with her friend. Eve held her breath, hoping Audrey would think she was asleep and go away. The knock came a second time, louder. Then a man's voice. "Eve . . . ?"

Louis.

She opened the door. Louis stood in the narrow hallway, nervously shifting his feet. His face looked ashen. His expression sent a jolt of fear through her. She pulled him into the room. "Louis, what is it? What's wrong?"

"Audrey wanted to be the one to tell you but I told her I would do it."

"Tell me what? What happened?"

"A telegram arrived—"

"What? Is it Alfie? Not Alfie!" Her heart nearly burst with fear. She couldn't bear another loss. Eve grabbed the front of Louis's uniform to shake the news out of him. "Don't take so long to say it, Louis. Just tell me! Tell me!"

"Alfie is missing in action. There was a battle, and the Nazis took prisoners. Right now, he's believed to be among them."

"So he isn't dead?"

"He wasn't identified among the dead or the wounded. The Red Cross requested a list of prisoners. We'll pray that Alfie is on it." She released her hold on his shirt and stepped back, then swayed as a wave of vertigo washed over her. Louis grabbed her and walked her backward to sit on the edge of the bed. "Are you all right?"

She shook her head. This was all her fault for betraying Alfie. She had slept with Louis after refusing to sleep with Alfie. If he was dead, if he could look down on her from heaven, he would know that she hadn't really loved him. That she loved Louis more. But then Alfie had loved his father's money more than her. She looked up at Louis, and the shock of her love for him, the power of it, overwhelmed her. But Louis wasn't hers to love.

She tried to stand. "I should go to Audrey. She'll need me."

Louis made her stay seated. He sat down on the bed beside her, pulling her into his arms. "Bob is with her. She's hanging on to him—and to hope. You can't lose hope, Eve."

She closed her eyes. Why hope for something she could never have? Whether Alfie lived or died, he would never be hers. And neither would Louis. "I loved Alfie . . . ," she said as her tears came. She pulled away and looked into Louis's eyes. "But I'm in love with you. And you're going into battle. You'll be in danger and . . . and I can't bear to lose you, too!"

Neither of them said a word as they yielded to each other's arms.

22

LONDON, MAY 1945

The commotion in the streets below Audrey's window grew louder and more joyous by the minute, but she sat by the radio in her tiny flat, afraid of missing the latest news. Especially if it concerned places where Robert and Alfie were. Victory in Europe would be officially proclaimed today—May 8. VE Day. Victory in Europe. The Nazis were defeated. Thousands of Londoners had started celebrating last night in anticipation. Today, the revelry exploded.

Ever since Robert left last fall, Audrey had remained glued to the radio whenever she wasn't working, anxious for news of the war. The Allies achieved stunning victories and suffered bitter defeats throughout the long winter, keeping her permanently on edge. After the plaster cast came off her leg, Audrey returned to work as a dispatcher in London to be near Eve. "Why didn't you apply for an easier posting?" Eve had asked. "The Nazis are firing V-2 rockets on London now, and they're even deadlier than the V-1 that nearly killed you."

"We've been in this together from the start," Audrey replied, "and we'll finish together, too." Besides, she would hear news from the battlefront sooner in London. The Red Cross still hadn't found Alfie. He wasn't on the prisoner of war list with his mates and was officially missing in action. Surely they would find him now that the fighting had ended.

As the Allies had pushed toward Berlin and news of Nazi atrocities surfaced, Audrey's fear for Robert nearly consumed her. "If anything happens to me," Robert had said before leaving, "I'll be waiting in heaven for you." Audrey prayed ceaselessly for the people she loved, including Eve, who had lost her faith.

Audrey was adjusting the tuning to clear out the static and better hear the broadcast when Eve strode over and switched off the set. "What are you doing?" Audrey asked.

"Come on. We're getting out of this flat. We've waited nearly six years for this day—six long years of our lives! We need to celebrate."

"You're right," Audrey said after a moment. "I'll grab my jacket."

"No, put on your uniform. We played a part in this victory." Audrey dutifully changed into her uniform and cap, then followed Eve down the steps and out into the street. "We'll take the Underground to Trafalgar Square," Eve said, pulling her along. "They're going to broadcast the king's speech from loudspeakers."

People jammed the Underground, all heading to Trafalgar Square. They got off at Charing Cross and made their way through the joyous crowds to the square. Thousands of people filled the streets, cheering and waving flags—Audrey had never seen so many flags! People climbed onto the statues and flower-strewn monuments, rejoicing. Men and women in uniform were everywhere, representing the many roles that citizens had played in this fight, and Audrey was glad Eve had insisted she wear her ATS uniform. She smiled, remembering how she'd hated the ill-fitting uniform when it first was issued to her. She thought of all the bloodstains it had absorbed, including her own, and wore it proudly.

Someone shoved miniature flags into their hands and they joined the waving and cheering. Children rode on their parents' shoulders, little ones who had never experienced peacetime. She saw smiles on people's faces but also tears. Everyone had lost someone. At least no more people had to die. Audrey nudged Eve to get her attention, raising her voice to be heard above the tumult. "This doesn't seem real!"

"Can you believe the war is finally over?" Eve shouted back. Audrey remembered Dunkirk and Coventry. The technical college in Liverpool. The Guards' Chapel in London. The people who'd perished in all those places weren't here to celebrate. But perhaps some of the people she and Eve rescued were.

"I haven't seen the streets this crowded since we watched the king's funeral procession," Audrey said. "Remember?" It had been a cold January day, not a mild spring one like today. The streets had been silent and somber, fitting for royalty. Today was for the ordinary people, the victory they celebrated was theirs. When the loudspeakers in Trafalgar Square broadcast the official announcement, Prime Minister Churchill echoed Audrey's thoughts. "This is your victory," he said. "The war is at an end. Long live the cause of freedom. God save the king!" The war wouldn't end for Audrey until Robert and Alfie were home. The Allies still battled the Japanese, and Audrey feared Robert would be sent to the Pacific front.

A hush fell over the crowd as King George VI began to speak in his soft, halting voice. The king offered thanks to God, "our strength and shield," and said we must "thank Him for His mercies." Afterwards, Audrey and Eve joined the crowd that surged toward Buckingham Palace to cheer him and the royal family. Across the plaza behind the iron gates, the king and queen, along with Princesses Elizabeth and Margaret, stood on the royal balcony waving to the cheering people. King George wore his military uniform, Princess Elizabeth an ATS uniform like theirs. "I daresay her uniform fits her better than ours do," Audrey said, laughing.

Eve grinned. "I'd like to know if she's wearing those horrible regulation knickers!"

People danced in the streets as the afternoon wore on. Eve pulled Audrey into a conga line. Bonfires illuminated the darkness as night fell, turning back the gloomy years of the blackout.

"Ready to go home?" Audrey asked as it grew late. Eve nodded. They walked arm in arm to the Underground to keep from being separated. "I suppose our jobs with the ATS will be ending soon. What then?"

"I'll stay in London and work for as long as they let me," Eve said, her voice hoarse from cheering. "It'll give me time to figure out what to do and where to go."

"Then I'll stay, too, while I wait for Robert."

Three days later, the telephone rang as Audrey prepared for bed. She and Eve didn't get many calls and it unnerved her when it rang. She picked up the receiver, her heart pounding.

"Hello, Miss Audrey? . . . Robbins calling, from Wellingford Hall."

She sat down on the edge of the bed. The tremor in Robbins's voice was a bad sign. She remembered how he'd accompanied her to London after the town house was bombed and how she'd found comfort and strength from his steadfast presence during that long, terrible ride. She held her breath, wishing Robbins were with her now.

"I'm so sorry to tell you, Miss Audrey, but your father received news of young Master Alfred. . . . They have confirmed that he died in battle. . . . I'm so very, very sorry."

Audrey let out a sob. Eve moved beside her and clutched her hand. "How . . . how is Father taking the news? Shall I come? Does he . . . does he want me to come?"

"Your father isn't here, I'm afraid. He left Wellingford after receiving the news. Mrs. Smith and I . . . we thought we should call you."

"Yes, I see." Her father was the only family Audrey had left now, but they would be no comfort to each other. *Alfie was gone.* She couldn't comprehend it. She couldn't picture him dead, but only alive, with his mischievous smile and teasing voice, his hair blowing in the wind as they sailed together. How she loved him!

"We'll be here if you decide to come home, Miss Audrey."

"Thank you, Robbins. . . . I'll . . . I'll let you know." She hung up the receiver as if it weighed a thousand pounds.

"Alfie is gone, isn't he," Eve said.

Audrey could only nod, her throat so tight she could barely breathe.

"I knew he was. I already felt his loss."

Audrey had never been so grateful for Eve as she was in the days that followed the unthinkable news. Eve had loved Alfie too. They grieved together, as they shared memories of him, weeping until their eyes were swollen and red. They had lost their mothers together, and now they'd lost darling Alfie. Audrey would never see him again. Her grief seemed bottomless.

⚬⚬⚬

Four months later, in early September, Robert wrote to say he was returning to London. The war in the Pacific was over, and he would be among the first troops to be demobilized and sent home to America. Audrey hadn't seen Robert in nearly a year. Eve rode on the Underground to Victoria Station with her for the reunion.

American soldiers jammed the train, jostling and laughing and hooting with joy. Audrey watched them pile from the coaches and spotted Louis first, standing taller than the others, his ginger hair shining. And there was Robert, right beside him. Audrey dropped the overnight case she was carrying and ran to him, weaving between the other soldiers. Robert's duffel bag fell from his shoulder as he swept her into his arms. Audrey had never felt such joy in her life.

"I've made reservations in a hotel nearby," she told him after they'd kissed. "We can finally have a proper honeymoon."

"Let's go." They retrieved their bags and walked to the hotel, arms entwined. Audrey never wanted to leave their room again. At last, she knew what it was to be loved.

Later, they talked about their future as they lay beneath the covers and nibbled from the room service tray. "I never asked how you felt about leaving your home and moving to America," Robert said.

"My home is wherever you are."

"My parents promised their support. They're eager to welcome you into our family."

"I admit it will be hard to say goodbye to Wellingford. And it will be horrible to say goodbye to Eve. She's like a sister to me."

"We'll come back to visit. And Eve can visit us whenever she wants."

"I'll tell her that." Audrey smiled at him. But one matter was still unresolved before they could move on. She hated to spoil their bliss by bringing Robert's former girlfriend into the conversation, but she needed to. "What about Linda? Has she adjusted to the news that we're married?"

"It seems so," he said with a sigh. "My parents don't mention her, and Linda stopped writing to me. I hope we can remain friends. Would that bother you, Audrey?"

"Not at all." She nestled against his shoulder, secure in his love. It was the most amazing feeling in the world.

"I don't feel right about ending things with Linda from a distance—even though I sent dozens of letters beforehand explaining my decision. I need to see her face-to-face and apologize if I hurt her. I need to ask her to forgive me."

"That's kind of you, Robert. You have such a tender heart." And so different from the other people in Audrey's family. She would need to learn from him and try to forgive her parents for the ways they'd hurt her. "No one in my family ever talked about their feelings," she said. "Feelings were kept behind closed doors, tightly locked and sealed. It's going to be very different to be able to share them."

"We'll both begin again and make a new life together. I've thought about it a lot, and I've decided to go to Yale Law School after all. I think I would make a good lawyer—but not a cutthroat one. A lawyer who works for good causes. And I won't let it consume my life the way my father and grandfather did. We'll live modestly."

"I would like to study nursing and become a proper one, someday."

"You have my full support, darling." He lifted her hand and kissed it. "Whatever we do, we won't let other people pile their expectations on us. The only ones worth living up to are the ones in the Bible." Robert turned to face her. "When we joined the military, we made a commitment to serve a common mission, the cause of freedom. We followed commands and surrendered our lives and our decision-making to those in charge. We went willingly into battle, prepared to give our lives, if necessary. And you nearly did lose yours."

"Eve saved my life. I'll always owe her for that."

"As will I!" He leaned close and kissed her forehead. "Now I want to make the same commitment to serving God. For the rest of our lives, we can use the discipline we learned as soldiers, and the lessons we learned while fighting the war, to lay aside our own comfort and follow His commands. The fight against evil is far from over."

"That's true. I know people who still need to be set free." Audrey thought of her father. And Eve, who remained bitter toward God. "We'll figure it out together," she said, moving into his arms. "For the rest of our lives, we'll always have each other."

⸙

Eve didn't dare to embrace Louis when he got off the train at Victoria Station. Not with Audrey and Robert and the other GIs standing around on the platform. Everyone knew Louis was married. When Eve dared a glimpse of him, he was gazing at her. The tears of joy in his eyes matched her own. "Where are you headed, soldier?" she asked, smiling up at him.

He grinned. "I don't know. I'm new to this city. What do you recommend?"

"Are you hungry? There's a great fish and chips place not far from here." Audrey and Robert left for their hotel, and after some discussion, three of Louis's mates joined him and Eve for fish and chips. They all sat together, laughing and eating the greasy food, while Eve tried to pretend that she didn't love Louis, that she wasn't dying inside. "So where will you head next?" she asked.

"We're being discharged," one of the men replied. "We're heading home."

Home. Whenever Eve heard that word, no picture came to mind. Not Granny Maud's cottage. Not her room on Wellingford's third floor. She couldn't call the countless boardinghouses and dormitories and hotels where she'd lived these past few years *home.* Even the tiny flat she now shared with Audrey wasn't truly a home, but a temporary rental until her service with the ATS ended. *And then what?* "I'm happy for all of you," she said, summoning a smile. "I imagine you'll be glad to be home."

Louis lingered behind when the others finished their food and prepared to leave. "I'm walking Eve to her subway station," he told them. "I need to keep her safe from roving Americans like you. I'll catch up with you later." Eve ached with love and longing as Louis walked to Sloane Square Station with her. "I'm probably the only GI who's not happy about going home," he said. "It means I'll be leaving you. And I don't want to say goodbye."

Eve took his hand and silently led him down the steps to the Underground. They rode to her stop, got off together, and she led him up the stairs to her flat. Audrey would be away for three days. "It's very tiny," she said when they were inside, "and not very fancy—"

Louis pulled her to him, cutting off her words.

She awoke in the night and stared at him, asleep beside her. She had forgotten to close the blackout curtains and could see him clearly in the moonlight. If only she could sleep beside him every night and wake up beside him every morning. She combed her fingers through his ginger hair and studied his face in the faint light, trying to imagine how she could make that happen, how they could be together for a lifetime. But as the moon slowly set and the sun rose, Eve knew it was impossible. Louis wasn't hers to love.

She climbed from her bed and dressed for work, moving

quietly in the tiny flat so she wouldn't wake him. But her rustlings did awaken him, and he propped himself up on his elbow and watched her.

"Where are you going?" he asked, his voice thick with sleep. "Come back to bed." He moved the blanket aside in invitation.

Eve turned away. "I can't, Louis. I'll be late for work."

"Do you really have to go to work?"

"Audrey has a good excuse to take a few days off, but I don't. I'm sorry."

The bedsprings creaked as Louis climbed out of bed. Eve finished dressing, avoiding his clear blue eyes, inching away from him. Louis wasn't hers. He never would be. She had to leave him. And she needed to do it quickly.

"I don't want you to go, Eve. I love you. Ever since we met, I've been trying to figure out how we can always be together, and—"

"Don't," she said, holding up both hands to keep him away. "There's nothing we can do. You're an honorable man. You can't abandon your wife and daughter." She laced up her shoes, shrugged into her uniform jacket. Found her purse. Any minute now, she was going to fall apart.

"I made a mistake when I married Jean. I don't love her the way I love you. Jean was—"

"Jean is your wife. It's over between us. It has to be. You need to go home to her and Karen." Eve fought back tears, the hardest battle of her life.

"But I love you and you love me—"

"That doesn't matter! We can't see each other again. What we feel for each other, what we had . . . you and I were just two more casualties of war."

"Eve, wait!"

"Lock the door behind you when you go."

23

LONDON, NOVEMBER 1945

The war had ended three months ago. Audrey thought she would never have to sit in a bomb shelter again. Yet here she was, huddling in a damp crypt wearing pajamas beneath her coat. She wrapped her arms around her raised knees to keep warm. She still trembled after being startled from sleep by news of an unexploded bomb in the rubble across the street from her flat. The smell of damp and mold sent a wave of nausea through her. She hoped she wouldn't be sick. She'd wrestled with nausea every day this week until finally admitting the reason for it. She needed to tell Eve the news. Audrey moved closer to her, leaning in. "Eve, listen. I need to tell you a secret."

Eve looked as though she was trying not to smile. "Should I cross my heart and swear on my life not to tell?" she asked.

Audrey drew a shaky breath. "I think I'm pregnant."

For a moment, Eve appeared stunned. Then she pulled Audrey into a hurried embrace. "Congratulations."

"I haven't written to tell Robert yet. I'm afraid to. It was an accident. We took precautions . . ."

"He'll be happy, just the same," Eve said, squeezing Audrey's hands. "Especially if it's a boy. Doesn't every man want a son?"

The baby seemed real to Audrey now, after sharing the news with her best friend. Her thoughts raced ahead. "This morning, with this bomb—I realized how badly I want to stay safe from now on. We risked our lives so many times during the war, and it didn't seem to matter because nobody knew what tomorrow would bring, whether we would live or die, or if the Nazis would pour across the channel and murder us. But the war is over and Robert is safe, and I want to stay safe, too, until it's time to move to America to be with him. I want our baby to be safe."

"So what are you saying?"

"I'm leaving London. I'm going home to Wellingford Hall."

It took Eve a moment to respond. "What about your job? And our flat?"

"I'll give them my notice. Today, even." Her job was no longer important. They weren't driving ambulances, merely pushing government papers around, processing discharge documents for the returning soldiers. Besides, the men would want their desk jobs back. "You won't have any problem finding a new flatmate," she added. "I'm going to miss you, Eve."

"Me, too." Eve stared at the stone wall across from her like a prisoner in a cell.

Later that afternoon as they rode home on the Underground, Eve turned to Audrey as they sat side by side in the swaying train car. "I thought Robert said it would take months for all your paperwork to go through."

"He did. The government's first priority is getting the soldiers home from around the world. It may take as much as a year for them to send for the war brides."

"So what's your hurry? Why quit and leave London? What will you do with yourself at Wellingford while you wait?"

"The Americans left the manor in a bit of a mess, as I'm sure you know. I need to unpack all the items that were stored and take down the blackout curtains. With Father still away so much of the time, he'll need help restoring Wellingford to its former glory. The few servants who are left could do with some supervision and direction."

"Will your father live there all alone after you leave for America?"

"I'm not sure . . . Maybe . . . Wellingford holds so many good memories of Alfie." The train slowed, approaching a station. The doors rasped open and people hurried off. More crowded on. The doors closed and the train started up again. "Father and I have never been close. But all we have left now is each other. And I would like to think . . . well, it's my hope that we can be a comfort to each other in these last months before I leave. Perhaps if I help restore Wellingford and make it a home . . . if he sees how much it means to both of us . . ." She stopped, having no idea what she hoped for. Affection, perhaps? Was it fair to try to build a relationship with him and then leave for America? Audrey had never experienced love before meeting Robert, and she wondered if her father ever had. Aside from his pride in Alfie, he'd never shown love to anyone that she could recall.

They got off at their stop and rode the escalator up to the street. People crowded the sidewalks, all hurrying home from work. Eve didn't speak again until they reached their flat. "We should have stopped at the store," she said after opening their pantry. "There's nothing to eat."

"I haven't felt very hungry lately," Audrey said, resting her hand on her middle.

"When is your baby due?"

"June, I think." Eve merely nodded. She seemed preoccupied. And despondent. Audrey sat down at their tiny table and watched her rummage through tins of soup and canned peaches, wishing she knew what to say, how to help her. "You never talk about your plans after you leave the ATS, Eve."

"That's because I don't have any. Unlike you, I don't have a husband or even a boyfriend. This flat is the only home I have. And not to sound too tiresome, I don't have a family, either. Your father may be distant, but at least you have one."

"Listen, Eve—"

"Whatever you're about to say, don't. The last thing I need is your pity. I'll figure something out." She left the tins on the counter and fetched her coat from the hook by the door, shoving her arms into the sleeves.

"Where are you going?"

"To the park. I do my best thinking when I'm around trees."

"Shall I come with you?"

"Please don't. It's time we got used to being apart. There's going to be an entire ocean between us before long." The lock clicked as the door closed.

Audrey worried that she'd made a mistake in deciding to go home to Wellingford so abruptly. With thoughts of Robert and the baby occupying her mind, it hadn't occurred to her that Eve would be left all alone. Yet Eve made friends so quickly. She always had. Dozens of girls from the ATS would love to share this tiny furnished flat with her. Besides, it was too late—Audrey had given her notice at work. She glanced around the room, deciding what to pack, already homesick for Wellingford Hall.

Eve's trousers were growing tight around the waist when she learned in late January that her job was ending. She would be let go on the first of February. Her boss promised sterling references, but what chance did Eve have of being hired as a typist once the bump in her middle gave away her secret? Still, she had felt the first fluttering of life and didn't regret her decision to let her baby live.

All around her, Londoners picked up the pieces of their lives and rebuilt from the rubble of war, marrying sweethearts, starting new jobs, repairing damaged homes. She must do the same, even though she felt scoured to the bone, stripped of everyone and everything that might provide a foundation to build upon. She had tried to formulate a plan while riding back and forth to work on the Underground every day, but without success. She had walked for miles through St. James's Park and nearby Green Park—the sheep were gone now that the war was over—trying to decide what to do. In the end, the only person she could turn to for help was Audrey. That meant returning to Wellingford Hall. Eve would go there and beg for a job, not for her own sake, but for her child's. Her baby was the only family she had left, the only link to the people she loved—to Mum and Granny Maud. And to Louis. Eve cleared off her desk on the final day of work, packed everything she owned, which wasn't much, and rode the train to Wellingford.

The once-familiar landscape seemed alien as she walked down the road to the manor house with her suitcases. The plowed fields were deserted and overgrown with weeds, the road rutted and scarred from Army jeeps, casualties of war just like her. Like her child. Eve had walked this road with Mum to begin work as a scullery maid. She had left on this road to become a typist, then an ATS driver. She never had imagined that she would return as a servant. But she would do it willingly if Audrey allowed her to stay.

She halted inside the open gates for a moment, setting down her suitcases to catch her breath. She looked up at the imposing stone facade with its mullioned windows. They stared back at her in cold silence, offering no welcome. Wellingford Hall revived memories of Alfie. She'd said goodbye to him here—and good-bye to the foolish dream of becoming his wife and the lady of Wellingford Hall. It also brought back memories of Louis.

Eve sighed and hefted her suitcases again. Mum had worked so hard to make sure Eve had a better life, far from Wellingford. Eve understood now why Mum had stayed, why she'd sacrificed everything for the child she loved. Eve would do the same.

She walked around to the servants' door, back to where she'd started.

⁓⟳⟳⟳⁓

Audrey sat at her desk in the small sitting room, trying to describe to Robert the soft brush of the baby's movements inside her. *They feel like feathery angels' wings,* she wrote. She wished she could tell him in person, but the bureaucratic paperwork that would allow her and thousands of other war brides to come to America moved at a frustrating pace. Some of her fellow "wallflower wives" protested outside the US Embassy in Grosvenor Square, others outside the hotel where Eleanor Roosevelt, the former president's wife, stayed. Audrey missed Robert terribly, the ache of loneliness nearly unbearable at times. His letters offered the only bright spots in her long days of waiting.

She heard a knock and turned to see Robbins in the doorway, a hint of a smile on his face. "Someone to see you, Miss Audrey."

He stood aside and there was Eve, looking cold and weary in her worn wool coat. Audrey hurried forward to embrace her.

"Eve! What a surprise! Oh, it's so good to see you!" And it was good—wonderful, in fact. Audrey had missed Eve more than she'd imagined she would. "Robbins, please take Eve's coat. And will you bring us some tea, please?"

"Yes, Miss Audrey."

"Come through and sit down, Eve. Tell me what brings you here on this cold winter day." Eve didn't reply. Instead, she rested her hand on her middle. On a bump the same size and shape as the one Audrey had. Audrey backed up a few steps and sat down on her desk chair in astonishment. "Eve! A baby?"

"Yes. A baby."

"But who . . . ? How . . . ?"

"Does it matter?"

"How could you do such a thing!"

The words slipped out before Audrey could stop them. She and Eve had heard so many stories during the war about girls who'd gotten into trouble. They'd listened to so many dire warnings about the consequences of having a baby out of wedlock that Audrey believed Eve too wise, too self-confident and ambitious to end up in this condition. Besides, Audrey was with Eve throughout the war. She didn't have any boyfriends besides Alfie. The child couldn't possibly be his.

"I need your help, Audrey, not your condemnation."

"I'm sorry . . . It's just such a shock! I never imagined you would do such a thing!"

"Because you wouldn't? Oh, that's right—you always follow the rules. And you never make mistakes, right?"

"Eve . . . I'm sorry . . ."

"I came to ask for a job as a servant here at Wellingford Hall.

There aren't a lot of other options for women in my condition. Will you hire me or should I apply elsewhere?"

Audrey's reaction had hurt her. She could only imagine how much pride Eve had swallowed in order to come here. "I'm sorry," she said again. "Please forgive my stupid outbursts. Of course you can stay, Eve, of course. Please, sit down."

Robbins returned a few minutes later with the tea tray. The tension had a chance to defuse as he arranged a table between them and filled their cups. Eve looked as uncomfortable as she had the first time Audrey invited her to tea upstairs in the schoolroom. Eve didn't reach for her cup or for the tea biscuits.

"Tell me what else I can do to help," Audrey said after Robbins left. "What will you do after your baby is born?"

"I don't know yet."

"I can talk to the vicar about arranging an adoption. It would be the best solution, for you and the child."

"I have a few more months before I need to decide. For now, I would be grateful for a job and a place to stay. I'm willing to clean, do laundry, and I can cook, of course. I was Tildy's assistant before the war, remember? And if you need a scullery maid . . ."

"Of course you may stay. I'll arrange some work for you. And we have plenty of rooms. I've been putting them back in order now that the Americans are gone. I'll have Mrs. Smith fix one for you."

"I would prefer my old room on the third floor. To be honest, it feels the most like home. And I can make up my own bed."

"Of course. I know you can. I just thought . . . well, you're my friend, and I would rather think of you as my guest than—"

"I need to work, Audrey. At the very least to pay my room and board. And I need to save money for the future." She rested her hand on her middle again.

Audrey sighed and leaned back in her chair. "Remember during the worst of the war, when we couldn't imagine the future? It didn't seem like it would ever come."

"And this isn't what either of us imagined, is it? You off to live in America and me with a fatherless baby?"

"No. It isn't." Audrey lifted her cup and took a sip of tea. It rattled against the saucer as she set it down again. She wanted to ask who the father was, but Eve would tell her in her own time.

"So when do you leave for America?" Eve asked, breaking the awkward silence.

"I don't know. I hoped our baby would be born over there, but if the paperwork takes much longer it's going to be difficult to travel in my condition. There are so many other war brides waiting along with me, more than sixty thousand, they say, in Britain alone."

"Those American GIs were busy while they were here." Eve said it with a smirk. Audrey didn't see any humor in her comment.

"I was encouraged when the first boatload of British brides landed in New York earlier this month. More than 450 women and another hundred or so children. Hopefully, I'll take my place in the queue soon."

"Starting a brand-new life."

Audrey studied Eve in her warworn dress and was uncomfortably aware that there would be no new start for Eve. Audrey found it frightening to give birth so far from her husband and couldn't imagine doing it with no husband at all. Surely Eve would offer the child for adoption. Audrey cleared her throat and searched for something to say. "Robert was surprised to hear that our baby was coming so soon, but he's happy. He sent me some brochures with plans for the house he's going to build for us, but I can't picture it yet. Would you like to see them? I have them right here." She passed the glossy pamphlets with drawings of the little bungalow's exterior and floor plans to Eve. The illustration showed a happy American family inhabiting the two-bedroom house: a smiling father, an aproned mother, two adoring children, and a grinning dog. Audrey couldn't interpret the expression on Eve's face as she looked them over.

"Not quite Wellingford Hall, is it," she finally said. "Where will your servants sleep?"

Audrey's face grew warm. Before she could reply, Robbins entered and refilled her teacup. Eve hadn't touched hers. "Would you like anything else, Miss Audrey?" he asked.

"No thank you." She waited until he glided from the room again, then sighed. "You know me better than anyone else, Eve, so you must know how frightening all these changes are for me. I've never liked change, and now there will be so many of them—leaving home, starting such a different life."

"At least you won't have to do it alone."

"Yes, that's true. I couldn't face any of it if I didn't love Robert as much as I do. But I worry that his parents won't accept me. They wanted him to marry Linda. Her parents were lifelong friends of theirs."

"You're an earl's granddaughter. Your father is richer than King George. It's not like he's bringing home a common servant girl like me."

"Robert says they don't have a class system like ours in America. There is no aristocracy."

"Don't believe it. Someone always wants to be on the top of the heap—and that means someone else has to be on the bottom."

"I'm going to miss Wellingford Hall. And you, Eve. We swore we would always stay together, remember? Like sisters."

"We might have been sisters," Eve said softly, "if Alfie had survived." She refolded the house plans and handed them back to Audrey. "It looks like your new home isn't going to be as luxurious as what you're used to."

"Robert says we'll live a very ordinary life in America. I'll need to learn how to cook and run a home."

"I thought Robert's family was rich."

"They are. But we want to live on our own, apart from their expectations. You already know I can't cook. Maybe you could teach me how."

"I suppose that's one way we can stay occupied while we wait." Eve managed a smile as she patted her middle again.

"And I don't know the first thing about taking care of a baby, do you?"

"Not much. But if we can learn how to change tires on a lorry, we should be able to change nappies." For the first time since she arrived, Eve smiled.

"You haven't touched your tea or the biscuits," Audrey said, gesturing to the tray. "Aren't you hungry?"

"I'm famished. I haven't eaten since this morning."

"Then let me ring for Robbins. I'll ask Tildy to fix you a proper lunch."

"I have a better idea," Eve said, pulling herself to her feet. "Come down to the kitchen with me and I'll give you your first cooking lesson."

"We don't need to start right away. You just arrived."

"I came here to work, not to sip tea with you. Now, do I have a job or not?"

"Of course you do, but—"

"The bride ships are setting sail, Audrey. You'd better learn how to cook for that husband of yours and to take care of that house he's building. There's no time to waste."

The midwife rode her bicycle out to Wellingford Hall on a warm June evening to deliver Eve's baby. Audrey begged Eve to move to a more comfortable room, but she insisted on giving birth in her simple servant's room on the third floor. She asked Audrey to stay beside her through it all. "I'll show you how to do it," she said with a smile, "just like I showed you how to drive a car and how to cook a chicken dinner for your husband."

"You taught me so much more than that," Audrey said as she held Eve's hand between contractions. "You taught me how to be brave."

"And don't forget that I convinced you to tell Robert you loved him."

"Oh, I'll never forget that! I only wish . . ." She started to say that she wished she could help Eve find someone to love, but Eve's groan cut off Audrey's words as pain gripped her again. Eve still hadn't told her who the baby's father was. It wouldn't matter once Eve gave up the baby for adoption, but she hadn't agreed to that yet, either.

"You'll change your mind and go under ether at a hospital after watching me," Eve said when the pain subsided.

"If you can do it, then so can I." But Audrey couldn't deny her fear.

Several long hours later, Eve gave birth to a baby boy. Her joy as she held her son in her arms erased all the lines of pain on her face. "I'm going to name him Harry after my father," she said, kissing his tiny clenched fist.

When the room was put right and the midwife returned home, Audrey pulled a chair close to Eve's narrow bed. "Would you like me to take him so you can sleep?" she asked.

338 · IF I WERE YOU

"I'm too excited to sleep. Look at him, Audrey. Isn't he perfect?" The scrunched red face made Audrey smile. She watched Eve stroke the baby's ginger hair and realized with a shock who Harry's father was. During all those wonderful hours that Audrey spent with Robert, Eve had been with Louis. Audrey had been blind to their affair.

"Is Louis Dubois Harry's father?" Audrey asked. She'd tried not to reveal her shock and disapproval, but judging by Eve's angry response, it had leaked through.

"Yes, Audrey. Of course Louis is his father."

"But . . . but Louis is married. He has a child!"

"Well, surprise. Neither of those things stopped him from fathering another one."

"Oh, Eve. You must see that under the circumstances, the best thing to do is to give the baby up for adoption."

Eve pulled Harry close as if Audrey might snatch him away. "I can't give him up."

"How will you live? He'll grow up in disgrace."

"The war produced a lot of fatherless babies. Little Harry will have plenty of company. Who's to say his father wasn't killed in battle?"

"But . . . what will you put on his birth certificate?"

"I'll make up a name."

Audrey exhaled in frustration. She had to stop her friend from making a terrible mistake, one that would ruin her son's life as well as her own. "You're making a very poor decision, Eve. You'll be forced to lie to your son for the rest of his life. Wouldn't it be better for him to grow up in a home with two parents?"

"A home like yours, Audrey?"

The words stung and brought tears to Audrey's eyes. "Please take some time to pray about your decision."

Eve's response was swift and angry. "Now, why would God answer that prayer when He hasn't answered any of the others? I prayed that He would keep Mum safe, yet she died. Horribly. I prayed that He would keep Alfie safe—and so did you, I might add—yet Alfie died. Also horribly. This baby is the only family I have. Could you give up your child if you were in my shoes?"

"I can't say. I'm not in your shoes. But let me ask you this . . . what would your mum advise you to do if she were here? Or your granny?"

"I don't think either of them would judge me. They sacrificed everything for me. I didn't have a father, but I always knew how much my family loved me. And I'm determined to raise Harry to know the same thing, even if I have to be a scullery maid to do it."

"But if the rest of society doesn't accept him—"

"You followed all the rules, Audrey, all your life. Society may have accepted you, but did you feel loved?"

Audrey rose and left the room. She sat in her own bedroom, sickened, and discovered that she still envied Eve Dawson—as she had all her life. She envied Eve's courage, her certainty, and most of all, the legacy of love that would help her become a loving mother. Audrey could have learned that from Eve, too, if she weren't leaving for America.

Her own labor pains started a few hours later. When the midwife arrived, Eve nestled her son in a laundry basket and carried him downstairs so she could stay by Audrey's side. "I'm sorry I was unkind," Eve whispered as she held her hand.

"I'm sorry for what I said, too."

Audrey's son was born the next day after hours of the worst pain Audrey had ever known. She remembered Eve's question as she held little Bobby in her arms and knew the answer was *no*. She could never give away her son, no matter what.

As soon as she was able, Audrey put through a telephone call to the United States to tell Robert the wonderful news. "It's a boy, Robert! A beautiful, healthy baby boy!"

"I'm wiping tears of joy," he replied. It was glorious to hear his voice through the static. "And are you all right, darling Audrey? I wish I was there with you."

"Yes, I'm fine. Our son reminds me so much of you that it's like having a little part of you here with me. He has lovely dark hair just like yours."

"I hoped he'd have your hair. It's such a beautiful color."

"I love you, Robert. I pray that all three of us will be together soon."

"I'm praying for the same thing. I love you, darling Audrey."

They would always be the most beautiful words Audrey ever heard in her life.

24

It had become a habit—one which Audrey thoroughly enjoyed—to spend a few minutes in the sitting room with Eve and their two sons every morning while Eve took a break from work. The babies, now three months old, were growing quickly and already were as different in looks and temperament as she and Eve were. Audrey's son, Bobby, had Robert's dark hair and eyes and a solemn, sensitive nature. Eve's son, Harry, had his father's ginger hair and blue eyes and was as cheerful as his mother always had been. Motherhood seemed to come naturally to Eve, and she was teaching Audrey how to be a good mother to this child she loved so fiercely. They were laughing together and trying to coax a smile from little Bobby when Robbins brought in the morning post. The sight of a thick packet from the United States government made Audrey's pulse quicken. "Oh, my. They're finally here."

"Are those your immigration documents?" Eve asked, leaning closer to see.

"It looks like them. I guess the wait is finally over." Audrey laid Bobby in his bassinet and carried the package to her desk to open it. Eve followed, bouncing little Harry in her arms. Audrey slit open the envelope with her paper knife, her emotions careening from joy to dread and back again like an out-of-control car. Joy that she and Robert would be together at last. Dread at the thought of leaving her home and starting a new life among strangers in a foreign land. She pulled out the letter, saw her name, *Mrs. Robert Barrett*, and that of her son, *Robert Clarkson Barrett*. She read the opening paragraph, then looked up at Eve. "We've been approved."

"Does it say when you're leaving or where you're supposed to go?"

Audrey scanned the letter. "I'm to report to the former Army camp in Tidworth in two weeks. . . . There will be required medical examinations. . . . Our stay at Tidworth may be as long as three weeks. . . . It doesn't give a final departure date."

"You'd better start packing."

Audrey's hands with the papers fell limp. "I'm scared, Eve."

"You made it through Army boot camp. You captained a boat through rough seas in a war zone in the dead of night. And you survived a V-1 rocket attack! You can do this, Audrey. And don't forget—Robert is the prize at the end of your journey."

"I wish we were doing this together."

"You'll be fine without me. You have a family now. Not only Robert and the baby, but his parents and all of his friends. I envy you."

Audrey stuffed the letter back into the envelope. "You're right. It's silly of me to be cowardly. It's just that I've never quite measured up to people's expectations, no matter how hard I've tried. And I don't want to disappoint Robert."

"He's the only person you need to worry about, and he's crazy about you. Wait until he tastes your cooking and sees what a great mother you are to his son."

"Speaking of our son . . ." Bobby hadn't liked being plopped into his wicker bassinet and was fussing. Audrey lifted him to her shoulder, savoring the soft warmth of him, his milky scent. "I hope this journey won't be too much of an ordeal for him. He's so tiny."

"Babies are pretty adaptable at this age. All he needs is milk, a cot, and clean nappies."

Audrey carried him to her chair by the fire and faced Eve again. "I wish they could grow up as friends, like we were. Like their fathers were." Eve looked away at the mention of Harry's father. Audrey was immediately sorry. She hurried to change the subject. "What will you do after we're gone? Of course you may stay and work here with Robbins and Mrs. Smith, but what about the future? You're capable of so much more than being a servant for the rest of your life."

"I'm not sure. I'll figure something out." Her tone was curt.

"I wish I could help you—"

"You already have." Eve stood. "It's getting late. I have work to do."

"Eve, listen—"

"And then we'd better figure out how to fit all your clothes into your trunks and suitcases." She left before Audrey could think what to say.

They were working upstairs in her bedroom later that afternoon, Audrey's bed strewn with clothing, her bureau drawers and wardrobe doors flung wide, when Robbins knocked on the door. "Telegram for you, Miss Audrey."

"Thank you, Robbins. Do you need something for the delivery boy?"

"I already tipped him."

"Thank you." Audrey ripped open the envelope, wondering if it contained more news about her immigration papers. "Let's hope they haven't botched things up somehow," she said as she pulled out the message.

"Maybe they want you to report to Tidworth even earlier. Good thing we started packing."

The telegram had come from the United States. It read:

THERE HAS BEEN A TRAGEDY STOP ROBERT DIED IN A
CAR ACCIDENT LAST NIGHT STOP WILL TELEPHONE
LATER STOP ROBERT O BARRETT SR

Audrey stared at the words in disbelief. She read them a second time as if they were in a language she hadn't learned. *"There has been a tragedy . . ."*

"No . . . No . . . It can't be true!" The room spun.

Eve grabbed Audrey before she toppled over and led her to the bed. "Audrey, what's wrong? What happened?" Audrey pushed the telegram into Eve's hand. "Oh, Audrey . . . no!" Eve breathed.

A sob rose from deep inside Audrey, strangling her. She struggled to speak around it. "It can't be true. . . . I need to call him. . . . He'll tell me . . . he'll say there's been a mistake!" She tried to stand, but the floor rolled like the deck of a ship. She wished she really were on board a ship and that the ocean would swallow her. "I need to call him."

"Hang on, Audrey. Don't try to stand. I'll run downstairs and ask the operator to put a call through for you. I'll be right back."

Audrey heard Eve shouting to Robbins and Mrs. Smith as if from the end of a long, empty tunnel. Audrey didn't move. Couldn't move. Couldn't feel anything except a searing pain where her heart should be. *Oh, God! Please don't let it be true! Please! Please . . .* She thought of Eve's bitter words that God didn't answer prayer.

What time was it in America? Robert had taught her to calculate the time difference so they wouldn't call each other too early or too late. Audrey couldn't think. She didn't care about the time. All she wanted was to hear Robert's voice, reassuring her that he was fine. That there had been a mistake. *Please, God . . .*

Eve bounded into the bedroom again, breathless. "The operator will ring back when the call goes through." She sat on the bed beside Audrey and gripped her trembling hands. "Do you want me to talk to Robert's parents for you?"

"No . . . I—I'll do it." But how would she speak with a gaping hole in her chest? She could barely draw a full breath past her suffocating fear. *It was a mistake. It had to be.* She would walk to the telephone, which seemed a hundred miles away, and speak to Robert.

"Let me help you," Eve said as Audrey rose on shaking legs. They went downstairs to the foyer, to the telephone. Audrey's head whirled with every step she took. When they reached the bottom, Eve pushed a handkerchief into Audrey's hands, and she wiped tears she hadn't realized were there.

When the telephone finally rang, Audrey flinched, startled. "Are you sure you don't want me to talk to them?" Eve asked as she lifted the receiver. Audrey shook her head. The telegram was a mistake. In another moment, she would hear Robert's voice. She put the receiver to her ear.

"Hello, this is Audrey—" She nearly said *Clarkson.*

"Yes, hello. I'm Robert's father. . . . I'm sorry we didn't call. . . . When we sent you the telegram, the police still weren't sure what happened. We were waiting until we knew more details, but now . . ." His voice crackled with static and faded for a moment.

"Hello? Are you still there?" Audrey asked.

"Yes . . . Can you hear me?" He sounded as if he were speaking into a tin can.

"I can hear you. Speak louder, please." Her heart pounded so violently she feared it would burst.

"We're still reeling . . . Linda, Robert's former girlfriend, came to the house and asked Robert to run an errand with her. She was driving the car, and she . . . she . . . Witnesses say she was going at a very high rate of speed. The police believe she deliberately steered into the bridge abutment, killing herself and Robert."

Audrey gasped. The phone slipped from her grip as her knees buckled. Eve grabbed her and held her up as Robbins slid the bench beneath her. "He—he's gone? . . . He's really gone?" Audrey's son began wailing in his bassinet upstairs as if mourning for his father.

Eve picked up the receiver. "Shall I finish for you?" she whispered. Audrey shook her head and reached for it again. Every breath she drew felt crushing, as if she lay buried beneath tons of rubble.

"I'm afraid it's true," Mr. Barrett said. "I'm so sorry. . . . We're making funeral arrangements . . ." His voice broke. Audrey waited, listening as he struggled for composure. "My wife will write to you. . . . I need to go."

The phone went dead. Robert was dead.

Dead.

And Audrey wanted to die with him. "It was all my fault," she mumbled as Robbins replaced the receiver. Eve crouched in front of her.

"How could Robert's death thousands of miles away possibly be your fault?"

"Linda caused the car accident. She killed him and herself."

"No . . ."

"If I hadn't told Robert I loved him, if we hadn't married, he would have gone home after the war and married Linda. He would still be alive."

"Are you saying he'd be better off married to a woman capable of killing him?"

"I don't know what I'm saying. But Robert would still be alive!"

"But you wouldn't have a son. Robert's son."

Her son. He was crying. The sound of his wails caused a dam inside Audrey to burst. Grief poured out in a scream that rocked her body with its force. She screamed and screamed, unable to stop. If Eve hadn't held her tightly, Audrey would have shaken into pieces.

Time stood still. Audrey had no idea how long she screamed, how much time passed before the village doctor arrived and administered a sedative.

She had no memory of climbing the stairs to her room, but she must have because she awoke in her bed, her throat raw, her eyes swollen and burning.

Eve was sitting beside her. She was weeping, too. "I don't know what to say, Audrey. I'm so sorry."

"Where's Bobby? Is he all right?"

"He's downstairs with Mrs. Smith. Shall I bring him up to you?"

"No . . . I can't . . ." Her tears started falling again. She wanted to go back in time and wake up on a different day, a day when Robert was still alive, when she could call him and hear his voice. Hear him say, *"I love you."* But she would never hear those words again. Audrey closed her eyes and welcomed the darkness, praying she would never have to open them again.

She didn't know how many days of darkness followed. Her grief was a mountain she had no idea how to climb. She couldn't get out of bed. She forgot she had a son. Eve and the other servants ran the household and cared for Bobby while Audrey drifted in a stupor. Eve talked to her whenever she brought meals to her room, meals Audrey couldn't eat, but none of her words made sense. Eve tried to coax Audrey from her bed, but all she wanted to do was swallow another pill and sleep forever and never wake up.

"The pills are gone," Eve told her one morning. She flung open the curtains, flooding the room with light, making Audrey's swollen eyes ache. "You need to get up so we can change your bed linen. I'm drawing you a bath. Come on, I'll help you." Audrey allowed Eve to undress her and lead her to the tub, just as Eve's mum had done for Mother. The hot water made her skin tingle, and she longed to sink beneath the surface and let it swallow her. "You have to eat something, Audrey. You're skin and bones."

"I'm not hungry."

"Lean back and I'll wash your hair." Audrey obeyed, letting the water flow over her head. "Remember during the war when we were only allowed to bathe in five inches of water?" Eve asked.

Audrey didn't reply. The long, horrible war was over and Robert had survived. Yet now he was dead.

"I know it must seem impossible, Audrey, but you need to start living again. You have a child to think about."

"Robert was my life. He was all I had, all I wanted. I can't go on without him."

"I know. But you have to. Robert wouldn't want you to stop living."

"I didn't think I would survive the pit of grief when Alfie died, but Robert was here with me. He kept me from drowning."

"And now I'm here."

Audrey shook her head. She didn't want Eve. "You can't understand what it's like. I have no one left!"

Eve rose from where she knelt beside the tub. "Did you forget who you're talking to? Who do I have, Audrey? I've lost everyone, too. But we'll manage, somehow. Both of us. We have no other choice." When Audrey didn't reply, Eve laid the towel on the edge of the tub. "I'll let you finish by yourself."

Audrey wanted Eve to stay, yet she wanted to be alone. Eve turned to her again when she reached the door. "Get back in the fight, Audrey. If not for yourself, then for Bobby's sake. Do you want the servants to raise Robert's son the way you and Alfie were raised?"

Audrey couldn't reply, couldn't make any decisions for a life that no longer included Robert. When she finished her bath, she dressed for the first time in nearly two weeks. She found Eve downstairs in the sitting room, feeding Bobby a bottle. The servants had switched him to formula while Audrey mourned, her breast milk dwindling to nothing when she refused to eat. "Here, you finish feeding him," Eve said, handing her the baby. For a moment, Bobby felt awkward in Audrey's arms, a warm, wiggling, unfamiliar weight. Then her son looked up at her with his olive-dark eyes. His father's eyes.

Audrey hugged him close to her chest. She wasn't alone. She held a little piece of Robert in her arms. A precious piece. She would hear her husband say, *"I love you"* every time she looked at their son. She understood, now, what Eve meant when she'd urged her to get back in the fight for her son's sake. Audrey focused on his sweet face as he finished his bottle and slept in her arms.

"A letter came for you from the Barretts," Eve said when she returned to the room to tend the fireplace. "It's on your desk."

"You read it, please. Tell me what it says."

Eve slit open the envelope, removed the letter. The room was quiet except for Bobby's soft breaths as Eve scanned it. "They give details about the funeral service. . . . They're trying to cope with their shock and grief. . . . They end by saying they hope you and the baby will still come as planned. It says, 'You're our son's wife. Bobby is our grandchild. You'll always have a home with us. We want to take care of both of you.'"

Audrey's heart squeezed in pain. This wasn't the future she and Robert had planned. Her home was supposed to be with him, not his parents.

"You still have time to report to the Army camp in Tidworth, Audrey. I think you should accept their invitation."

"I'm not going to America," she said, shaking her head. "I can't live with strangers. Besides, Robert would still be alive if it weren't for me."

"That's not true. And if you read their letter, you'll see they don't feel that way at all."

"I can't leave home and start all over. Not without Robert. It's impossible."

"You did a lot of things during the war that seemed impossible. This is no different."

Audrey struggled to stay afloat as new wells of grief opened beneath her. "I was raised in a different world than Robert. Did I ever tell you that the year I made my debut into London society, I had an audience with the queen?"

"What good did that ever do you?"

"I'm trying to explain that I know how to function here, in my world."

"And you learned how to function in the Army, didn't you? That life was nothing at all like what you were used to. If you learned to adapt once, you can do it again."

"I can't remake myself all alone. I'm too scared, Eve. I had you to help me during the war."

"Listen, I'll call Tidworth for you. Maybe they'll let you postpone your trip to a later date so you'll have more time to grieve."

"They won't let me come at all if they learn that Robert is gone."

"Then why not go while you have the chance? If you don't like America, you can always come home. You're strong enough to do this, Audrey. Think of all the hard things you faced during the war. You're not a coward."

Audrey shook her head. She stood and carried the baby to the bassinet, too weak and shaky to hold him. He stirred and opened his eyes when she laid him down, so she rocked the basket until he fell back asleep. "I believed I could learn to live in Robert's world as long as he was beside me," she said to Eve. "But I can't do it alone. I would be as lost and helpless as I was in the woods that day we first met. You laughed at the idea of me running away and told me to go home to Wellingford Hall because you recognized how hopelessly out of place I was. This is where I belong, Eve. At Wellingford. I would be just as out of place in America as I was in the woods. Besides, I have my son to think about."

"At least go and meet Robert's parents. Mourn with them at his grave. Then you can decide what to do."

"My mind is made up. My home is here at Wellingford. It's my son's home, too. Robert and I fell in love here. All my memories of him are here, not across the ocean. I'm going to raise Bobby here."

"Audrey, you need to think about this—"

"I don't want to talk about it anymore." She crossed to the desk and scooped up the packet of immigration papers, then tossed them into the rubbish bin. "There! It's done!"

"You're a fool, Audrey. Don't throw away this chance."

"I'll write and tell the Barretts I'm not coming." She opened the drawer with her stationery. "My father will be home next week.

I'll stay here and help him run Wellingford Hall. It's a role I know well. Bobby can grow up here like Alfie and I did."

"Please take more time to think about this. What if you change your mind?"

"I won't. This is who I was before the war. Before Robert. It's who I am without him."

⟨∽◦♥♥◦∽⟩

Eve pulled the thick packet of papers from the US government from the rubbish bin where Audrey had thrown them. Audrey had gone to her bedroom after writing to the Barretts to say she wasn't coming. Her sealed letter lay on the desk, ready to post. Eve peeked at the immigration documents. Audrey was a fool to turn down this opportunity. If Eve had a chance to begin a new life in America, she wouldn't hesitate to go. She sighed and dropped the packet into the bin again and returned to her dusting.

Eve had no idea what the next step in her life would be. With no education and a fatherless baby to support, her future was a bleak dead end, just as her mum's had been years ago. She ran the feather duster over the mantel, then spread a mat in front of the hearth and knelt to clean the fireplace.

Oh, Audrey. If I were you . . .

She shoveled ashes into the bucket. If she were Audrey, she wouldn't be on her knees with sooty hands. She would be on her way to Tidworth, to America, far away from Wellingford Hall and England and the reminders of who she really was—a woman with a child and no future. If only the documents were hers.

Eve swept the hearth and laid new wood in the grate. Harry would need to be fed soon. She would empty the rubbish, gather her bucket, shovel, and mat, change out of her sooty apron, and feed him. She pulled the packet from the bin to add to her ash bucket—then stopped.

What if she went to America in Audrey's place?

Absurd.

Yet the idea tugged at her like a dog with a bone and wouldn't let go. Why not take Audrey's place and start all over in America? Eve sat on the arm of the chair to think it through.

She and Audrey were the same height and weight, the same age. Robert's parents had never met their daughter-in-law. Could they tell from a black-and-white photograph that Eve's hair was a different color? She could easily mimic Audrey's aristocratic manners and speech. She'd lived with her long enough to know everything about her. Their sons, Harry and Bobby, were the same age.

Eve brushed her sooty fingerprints off the packet. Could she get away with it? The more she pondered the idea, the less absurd it seemed. She had masqueraded as one of the gentry on her date at the Savoy with Alfie and had pulled it off.

The documents felt heavy in her hands. It wasn't as if she would be stealing them. Audrey had thrown them away. And while it was true that Eve would be deceiving Robert's parents, she would only need to pretend she was Audrey until she got a new start in America. Once she was on her feet, Eve could make her own way. Who would ever know the difference?

Louis would. If he came to the Barretts' home to visit Audrey and found Eve instead—but no. Louis couldn't give away Eve's secret without destroying his marriage.

Eve took the letter Audrey had written to the Barretts and slipped it in with the other documents. She tucked the packet beneath her arm and gathered up her cleaning supplies. Harry was fussing, so she hurried down the servants' stairs to the basement.

She put the bucket in the scullery, washed her hands, untied her apron, then sat on a stool to nurse him, the packet on her lap beneath his diapered bottom.

Eve would need to read through the materials carefully to make sure she had everything she needed to take Audrey's place. But what a perfect opportunity this would be for her son. How she longed to find a better life for him. If she had to start all over again, why not do it in America? There was nothing for her here, no loved ones to leave behind. Audrey had decided to live the rest of her life at Wellingford Hall as the lady of the manor. The last thing Eve wanted was to be stuck here as her servant. This was no place for her son to grow up.

Harry finished nursing and looked up at her. She would do it. She would go to Tidworth Army Camp as Audrey Barrett. If they believed her, she would sail to America with the other war brides. Eve knew where Audrey kept her identification papers and Bobby's birth certificate. It would be easy to add them to the packet with the other documents. She lifted Harry to her shoulder to burp him and pulled the cover letter from the packet. They had two days to pack their things and report to the camp. Harry deserved a better life. He deserved to grow up in the sunshine, far away from Wellingford's scullery.

"Harry and I are leaving on the train Friday morning," she told Audrey when she brought up her supper tray that evening. "It's time for us to move out and be on our own."

"You're leaving? Why?"

Eve thought of all the answers she could give. How Audrey no longer talked of them being sisters or of them being together no matter what. How Eve was Audrey's servant, a life she didn't want. How neither of them respected the decisions the other one had made. Instead Eve shrugged and said, "Because it's time, Audrey. We both know it."

"Where will you go? What will you do?"

"I'm pursuing a few possibilities. Harry and I will make our way somehow. I don't want to be stuck here in the past. Mum worked hard so I wouldn't have to be a servant all my life, and I'm not going to let her down. I want a better life for Harry."

"Do you have a forwarding address? How will I reach you?"

"I'll write once we're settled. Listen, I'll always be grateful to you for giving Harry and me a place to stay. Thank you for that."

"I . . . I don't know what to say."

"Neither do I."

Eve knew she'd made the right decision when Audrey didn't try to talk her out of it or beg her to stay. But the pain that knowledge caused was like a knife in her heart. They were both dry-eyed as they hugged goodbye at the train station on Friday. They had already shed enough tears for a lifetime.

25

Eve crossed her arms over her chest as she stood with forty other naked, shivering war brides at Tidworth Army Camp, waiting to be examined for venereal diseases and lice. She tried to put on a brave face, telling herself she'd endured worse, but the sound of the other women's embarrassed weeping unnerved her. Audrey certainly would have wept, too. She never would have survived the humiliation. The physical examinations were endless and intrusive—and horribly thorough. The indignity would have crushed Audrey.

"Mrs. Robert Barrett?" It took Eve a moment to realize that the nurse was calling her.

"Sorry," she said as she hurried forward. "I was daydreaming." She needed to pay better attention or they'd flag her for a more thorough hearing test. Eve was still unused to answering to "Audrey" or to calling her son Robbie. She hadn't wanted to call him Bobby—that was what Audrey called her son. Robbie would do.

A long hour later, after being poked and prodded in ways she hoped never to endure again, Eve returned to the dressing room. "That was dreadful! Dreadful!" one of the other brides whimpered. "I can't believe they'd treat us this way!" The others sniffled as they nodded in agreement.

"At least it's over and we're one step closer to getting out of this place," Eve said, trying to cheer them. "Keep thinking of your husband. It will all be worthwhile when you're in his arms again, being smothered by his kisses."

Eve learned on her first day in camp that she'd made a serious mistake in her haste to adopt Audrey's identity. The other brides all kept photographs of their husbands near their bunks and bragged about the handsome American soldiers they'd married. Eve stood out as the exception. The only photograph she had was of Alfie, and he wore a British Army uniform, not an American one. Eve had tried to remedy her error by rifling frantically through her bags, agonizing in front of the other women over misplacing the precious photograph. They eyed her with suspicion. They might also think it odd that she didn't spend hours each evening writing letters to her husband. Eve hadn't even thought to bring stationery and envelopes and had to borrow some from the Red Cross workers. She used it to write to the Barretts, telling them she would soon be on her way.

Eve's regimented life at Tidworth reminded her of the ATS training camp with its spartan bunks, tasteless food, and giggling, squabbling women. When they weren't enduring physical exams, the brides attended classes to prepare them for their new life in America. The lessons were always the same: be adjustable and ready for change. The prospect would have terrified the real Audrey.

As the days passed, Eve did her best not to stand out. She didn't socialize with the other women, including her roommates, adopting Audrey's shy personality—not to mimic her, but so she wouldn't say the wrong thing and be discovered as an impostor. Eve had no idea what would happen if the authorities found out. Would they arrest her? And what would happen to Harry? As her time at Tidworth dragged on with no end in sight, Eve sometimes wondered if she'd made a mistake. She considered walking away from the camp, but she had no place to go and no one to turn to. In the end she stayed, fearing the moment when she would be found out.

But she wasn't found out. Eve passed all the tests, endured the indignities, and the day finally came when her embarkation orders arrived. She and Harry would travel to Southampton to board a ship to America. The ocean voyage would take nine days. Eve stood in line at the telegraph office with the other excited brides who were sending telegrams to their husbands. Eve sent hers to the Barretts, letting them know when her ship would dock in New York City.

The enormous ocean liner loomed above the Southampton wharf, dwarfing Eve and the other brides. It seemed ludicrous that a ship so immense could stay afloat. Smoke billowed from its twin stacks as if the vessel were impatient to set sail. At last it was Eve's turn to board. She felt a moment of heart-pounding panic and regret as she carried Harry up the gangplank. She was leaving her homeland behind. Forever. She had fought so hard to save her country from the Nazis, enduring endless days and long years driving an ambulance, rescuing broken, bleeding survivors. She had lost her mum and Alfie and her friend Iris in the fight, and it suddenly seemed wrong to turn her back on her nation as it struggled to rebuild. Yet Eve continued forward, even as her eyes burned with tears. She had no other place to go.

The crew guided her to the tiny cabin she would share with

another bride from Tidworth. Pamela and her one-year-old daughter were heading to an American state called Montana. "Aren't you coming up on deck to say farewell to England?" Pamela asked when the time came. Eve shook her head. Pamela's parents had come to send her off, but no one stood onshore to wave goodbye to Eve. She waited alone in the cabin with Harry asleep in her arms, the ship's boilers rumbling beneath her feet.

Eve was alone. And yet . . . a smile spread across her face when she realized that she was free. Free from the stigma of her past as a servant. Her lack of education, her affair with a married man, her son's illegitimate birth were all forgotten. She was Audrey Clarkson Barrett, wife of the late Robert Barrett. Her son could grow up feeling proud of the father he would never meet, just as Eve had. The ship's horn sounded a long, low note. Then another. She and Harry would sail toward a new beginning, a promising future.

The ocean voyage proved calm and uneventful—no violent storms, no bouts of seasickness, no delays. Eve kept to herself and didn't mingle with the other brides, worried she would make a mistake and give herself away. The others chatted about their new lives in America, wondering what it would be like, anxious about meeting their in-laws, nervous about seeing their husbands again after so many months apart. Eve shared their fears but for entirely different reasons. Surely Robert's parents had seen a photograph of Audrey. Would they know she was a fraud the moment they saw her? Her biggest fear was for Harry—what would happen to him if she was discovered and arrested?

Eve was so nervous as the ship sailed into New York Harbor that she had to stay belowdecks, her stomach turning itself inside out with vomiting. Harry sensed her fear and became colicky, refusing to nurse. It seemed to take hours for the regular passengers to disembark. The brides who had families meeting them would be next. The Barretts had sent a telegram saying they would be waiting for her. When the time came, she rinsed her mouth and brushed her hair and pulled her hat low to help hide her face. She looked at her reflection in the mirror and saw a pale, frightened woman she didn't recognize. She pinched her cheeks to try to restore some color. It didn't help.

Harry squirmed in her arms, fussing, as Eve waited on deck for Audrey's name to be called. She wore her very best suit and hat, but they weren't the fine quality of Audrey's clothing. Was that another mistake people would spot? Eve wished she had thought to polish her scuffed shoes before leaving Wellingford.

"Mrs. Robert Barrett . . . Robert Clarkson Barrett . . ."

Eve's chest ached from her wildly pounding heart. She felt so weak and dizzy after being sick that she wasn't sure she could make it down the gangplank. A well-dressed couple with Robert's dark hair waited on the dock. This was the final test. If they had Audrey's picture, they would know at once that Eve was an impostor. Her eyes filled with tears as she approached. But then the couple hurried toward her. Mrs. Barrett had tears in her eyes, as well.

"Audrey? . . . Is it really you?" she asked. Eve could only nod. She feared she would be sick again as the Barretts studied her for a long moment. The pier seemed to sway, her legs unaccustomed to dry land.

Then Mr. Barrett gave her shoulder a reassuring squeeze. "Welcome, my dear. Robert told us you were a tiny little thing, and you surely are."

Mrs. Barrett hesitated as if still unsure. Eve shifted Harry to her other hip as he continued to fuss, his cries growing louder. At last, Mrs. Barrett stepped forward. "Will you come to Nana, darling?" she asked, reaching for him. Miraculously, Harry stopped fussing and went into her welcoming arms. "Oh, my darling boy! What a long ordeal you've had!" She kissed his forehead, hugged him, and kissed him again. Harry smiled his charming grin.

"Come, let's get both of you home where you belong," Mr. Barrett said.

Home. The floodgates opened for Eve at the mention of what she longed for the most. She couldn't hold back her tears. Mr. Barrett smiled as he pulled a handkerchief from his breast pocket and handed it to her. "Thank you for coming, Audrey. It means so much to have you and Robert's son with us."

◦≫≫≪≪◦

For Audrey, the days felt as fragile as dry leaves. At times, caring for her son was life-giving, and she bundled him up for walks around Wellingford's spacious grounds. Other days, the slightest brush of a memory caused her composure to crumble into dust, and the hired nurse would take over Bobby's care. Today was one of those days. Audrey sat alone at her desk, rereading Robert's letters, imagining that he was alive and that she would go to him soon. Yet she found comfort here in Wellingford Hall. It was where she and Robert fell in love. Where they first kissed. She could close her eyes and cling to his memory.

Every once in a while, the dry leaves of her life would stir up memories of the war years, and as she relived those experiences, it seemed as though she'd merely read a book about a woman who once drove an ambulance into scenes of unimaginable horror. Audrey was no longer that person. She tried to banish those memories each time they reappeared and struggled to figure out who she was now. Those memories also featured Eve and raised her lingering anger over Eve's desertion. Yet she was glad that Eve was gone. She would accuse Audrey of going through the motions of living without really living at all. And she would be right.

A knock on the door startled Audrey from her reverie. "Rev. Hamlin is here to see you," Robbins said. The fragile leaves stirred, the edges crumbled. The vicar had taught Audrey how to pray during the war, how to find strength in God. He had officiated at her wedding. A lifetime ago.

"Please tell him to come back another day."

Robbins didn't move. "He thought you might say that. He said to tell you he isn't leaving until he has a chance to speak with you."

"Very well. Show him in." She would get it over with.

"Shall I bring tea?" Robbins asked.

"No. He won't be staying long." She stowed Robert's letters inside the desk drawer, steeling herself as she rose to greet him.

"I came to offer my condolences," the vicar said, reaching for her hand. "Your husband was a fine man."

"Thank you." She would say very little and not engage him in conversation. But Rev. Hamlin sat down in one of the chairs by the fireplace as if she had offered it to him. Good manners required her to take the other chair.

"Robbins told me about the tragic circumstances of your husband's death and about the woman who took his life and her own."

"Then there's nothing left to say."

The vicar paused, then leaned forward in his chair. "Audrey . . . why do you suppose your husband got into the car with her?" The kindness in his eyes, the gentleness in his voice, nearly undid her. She couldn't reply. It was a question she had never dared to ask and didn't want to contemplate now. "I didn't come here to cause you more pain," he continued. "My job ever since the war began has been a difficult one as I've tried to defend God and explain the unexplainable. People ask why He allows these tragedies to happen, and I don't have an answer except to say that He knows things that we don't know and sees things we can't possibly see.

I can only urge you to continue forward, like a ship in the fog, perhaps, trusting His love."

A vivid memory came to Audrey—how she'd gripped the wheel of Alfie's boat to steer it through the darkness. She remembered her fear and the dizzying feeling of unreality, as if everything were happening to someone else. It was not unlike what she felt now. "But the ship I'm in has no rudder, Reverend. And the fog never lifts."

He reached for her hand, his fingers calloused and warm. "During the war, we had a tangible enemy, an evil enemy. And thank God, that enemy was defeated. When I comfort those who've lost loved ones, I usually can help them see that their loss had a higher purpose, serving the greater good of combating the Nazis. Do any of us doubt how much more suffering would be unleashed if Hitler had been victorious? Those who died gave their lives as God's soldiers, fighting so the people they loved could be free from that evil. It was the same reason that God allowed His Son to suffer and die an unspeakable death—so the people He loves could be free."

"Robert didn't die in battle."

"Didn't he? Can you explain why he agreed to climb into a car with a woman who obviously hated him?"

Audrey stared down at the vicar's hand, still clasping hers. It was unexplainable. Robert knew Linda was unstable. He should have stayed far away from her. But Audrey also remembered Robert saying, *"I need to see her face-to-face and apologize if I hurt her. I need to ask her to forgive me."*

"It required courage to do what he did," the vicar said. "Courage your husband learned in battle as a soldier."

Robert had compared serving God with serving in the military. *"We can use the lessons we learned while fighting the war to lay aside our own comfort and follow His commands. The fight against evil is far from over."* There were people who needed to be set free. And Linda had been one of them.

"Would Robert have reached out to this woman if God asked him to?" the vicar pressed.

The question angered Audrey. She let go of his hand. "Why would God ask such a thing?"

"Why did you go into dangerous places during the war and risk your life? You drove your ambulance into places where the bombs were still falling."

"I did it to save lives."

"Ah. Then you do understand why your husband did it. And why God would ask him to. Perhaps he hoped to save this woman from a life of bitterness and despair." Rev. Hamlin stood. "I know you didn't really want to see me today, and I imposed myself on you. But I'm a telephone call away whenever you would like to talk."

Audrey walked with him to the door as a courtesy. "Thank you for coming, Vicar."

He turned to her again on the front step. "In these hard times, we have so many questions for God. And I know you're probably at loose ends, wondering where to turn and what comes next. But may I leave you with a question to think about as you sort things through?" She tilted her head in a reluctant nod, not really wanting to hear his question, knowing it likely would be a difficult one. "What might God be asking you to do?" he said.

She didn't reply. She closed the door as if closing it on his question as well.

☙❧

Shortly before Christmas, Audrey's uncle telephoned. "Your aunt and I would like you to join us at our country home for the holidays," he said. "We hate to think of you sitting at Wellingford Hall all alone. Come be with your family."

Audrey bit back an angry reply. When had they ever been a family? There had been no family Christmas celebrations before the war when Mother was alive. As an important member of the House of Lords, her uncle had very little contact with his sister, the black sheep. Audrey had last seen him at her mother's funeral.

"Did you know that I married an American during the war?" she asked. "We have a son. He's six months old."

"You should have contacted us so we could congratulate you."

"Unfortunately, my husband passed away a few months ago."

For a long moment, there was nothing but static on the line. "I'm so sorry, Audrey," he finally said.

"Thank you for the invitation, but I think I'll spend Christmas at Wellingford. I'm still in mourning, you see. I'm sure you'll understand."

"Of course, of course. But I hope you'll contact your aunt and me when you're ready. There's room here for you to stay and also at our London town house. We could introduce you to the people we know. You're our niece, after all."

The people we know. They would be the same people Mother wanted Audrey to meet—boring, unimaginative, cold. Nothing at all like her beloved Robert. She couldn't go back to those people. Not after knowing him.

"Thank you for your kind offer. I'll be in touch when I'm ready." But Audrey couldn't imagine when she ever would be ready.

26

USA, DECEMBER 1946

Like everything else in America, the Christmas celebrations were extravagant. Eve sat in church with the Barretts on her first Christmas Eve, and the sheer weight of the festivities, with twinkling trees, garlands of greenery, and piles of poinsettias, made her feel buried alive. She was back in the ATS training shed in her gas suit, but this time Audrey wasn't here to pull her out. Eve looked up at the beamed ceiling, fighting panic, and recalled the collapsed roof of Guards' Chapel, the buried worshipers. She fought to breathe, shifting her gaze to the side where a stunning stained-glass window across the aisle from the Barrett family pew depicted the Good Shepherd. It was startlingly similar to Granny Maud's picture of the Good Shepherd, now buried in the debris of the Clarksons' town house. Buried along with Eve's faith. She had tried to avoid coming to church, using her six-month-old son as an excuse to stay home. But the Barretts hired a very competent nurse to take care of him. Wealthy families like theirs could hire an army of nannies and nursemaids.

Eve closed her eyes as the choir sang, remembering the waxy

smell of candles in the village church, the holly branches decorating the windowsills. She had sat between Granny Maud and Mum on Christmas Eve, singing "Silent Night" and listening to the story of baby Jesus in the manger. Granny especially loved the shepherds.

"Your daddy and granddaddy were shepherds," she said, year after year. "I like to think that the angels would have appeared to them if Jesus had been born in England." The story intrigued Eve as a child. Jesus was a king, like the king of England, yet He'd been born among common people like her. In a barn, not in Buckingham Palace. "Where else would the Good Shepherd be born but in a stable?" Granny said when Eve asked about it. "Who else should His first visitors be but His fellow shepherds? They wouldn't dare walk into Buckingham Palace, but they would be right at home in a stable."

Eve opened her eyes again. Mrs. Barrett reached for her hand and squeezed it as the pastor spoke of Christmas as a time for families. Eve was aware of the love that had grown between her and Robert's parents in just a few short months. She and Harry filled an empty place in their lives, and they had filled one in hers. They'd enveloped Eve in their love, never questioning who she was, nor had they commented on her son's red hair and blue eyes, so different from Robert's. Audrey had been a fool not to come. The Barretts were the loving parents Audrey had longed for all her life. But Audrey's loss was Eve's gain.

The church lights dimmed. Candlelight flickered as the congregation passed the flame from one person's candle to the next, down the rows of pews. Eve squirmed in her seat, longing for the service to end, the hymns that told of God's love to fall silent. Guilt and shame snaked through her. How dare she come into God's house and pretend to worship? The people around her didn't know she was a fraud and an adulteress, but God knew.

It had been the same at the Christmas party at the Barretts' country club a few evenings ago. Then too, Eve had tried to beg off, knowing she was a fraud, insisting she had nothing to wear. "Clothing and shoes were rationed during the war, Mrs. Barrett, and very hard to come by. That's why everything in my suitcase is so shabby and worn-out." She had worried that the servants would notice the cheap quality of her wardrobe when they washed her laundry and would expose her secret. So far, they hadn't.

"Then we'll simply have to go to New York on a shopping trip," Mrs. Barrett had replied. "Father can tell you how much I adore shopping!" She purchased a full wardrobe for Eve, everything from hats and shoes to knickers and nylons. She took Eve to the hairdresser for a stylish cut. They had manicures together.

The party at the country club terrified her—and Eve wasn't easily frightened. Since adopting Audrey's name, she had become an actress, mimicking Audrey's speech, her ladylike gestures, her manners. It had been one thing to dress up and play Cinderella for one evening at the Savoy with Alfie, another thing to play this role for the rest of her life. She had nothing in common with the other country-club women who talked about their summer homes on the shore, tennis matches, sailing on Long Island Sound. They went on skiing trips to Vail and Switzerland. They'd earned degrees from prestigious women's colleges like Vassar and Radcliffe. They would excuse Eve's shyness as that of a recent widow, newly arrived in America, for now. But sooner or later she would have to adopt their lifestyle.

The Christmas party had exhausted her, and it was only the first of many. The church service drained her as well. She crept into Harry's nursery when she returned home and bent over his crib to kiss him. Only then did the suffocating weight begin to lift. She remembered how Audrey had grabbed her hand in the training shed and led her through the fog and out into the light. Eve missed her friend.

On Christmas Day, Eve sat beside the glittering Christmas tree in the Barretts' formal living room, inhaling the scent of pine and opening the mountain of expensive presents Robert's parents had purchased for her and Harry. The tree would have filled Granny Maud's entire cottage. Eve remembered being grateful for hand-knit mittens at Christmas. An orange. A few sticks of penny candy. America's prosperity astounded her. There were no piles of rubble where homes once stood, no queues for food, no shortages. Soldiers like Robert and Louis had returned home to civilian life as if the war had never happened.

Mrs. Barrett laughed with delight as little Harry—Robbie— watched the electric train that had once been Robert's steam in a circle beneath the tree. Mr. Barrett sat on the floor with Robbie on his lap, manning the controls. Eve had planned to simply get her bearings in America and then move on, find a job, rent a flat, work hard to support her son and herself. But Robert was the Barretts' only child. They asked Eve to call them Mom and Dad. They promised her a good life, and in the three months she'd been here, they'd kept that promise. They would be devastated if Eve moved away with Robbie. Their grief had overwhelmed them until Eve and Robbie arrived, bringing a reason to laugh again. Eve knew she was trapped—but it was a very comfortable trap. She would stay trapped for her son's sake.

The Barretts had driven Eve out to the little tract home that Robert had begun building in a nearby housing development. "It will be finished before Robbie's first birthday in June," they told her. "You can live with us until it's done." She drove Robert's car. She had money in the bank from Robert's life insurance policy.

The Barretts set up a college fund for Robbie. Eve would never have to work another day in her life.

She watched the little train chugging in circles and pushed aside her lingering guilt, determined to enjoy her first Christmas in America.

When the doorbell rang, Mrs. Barrett rose to answer it, since the servants had Christmas Day off. "Someone's here to see you, Audrey," she called. "You and Robbie."

"To see *me*?" Fear made Eve's voice squeak. After going three months without being discovered, she had dared to believe she would get away with the deception. She scooped up Robbie, her stomach twisting as she walked to the door, steeling herself to face uniformed police officers, US government officials, British authorities. Instead, she found a gangly, friendly-looking young man her own age in a plaid wool overcoat. He pulled off a knit stocking cap, and his light-brown hair stood on end from the static. He had warm hazel eyes and such a boyish smile, Eve had to fight the urge to smooth down his hair for him.

"Hi, Audrey? I've been looking forward to meeting you. I'm Tom Vandenberg." He stuck out his hand to shake hers. It took Eve a moment for the name to register.

"Of course! Robert's friend. One of the Famous Four. I'm so glad to meet you."

"Me, too. Bob told me so much about you."

Eve's unease threatened to slide into panic. Surely Robert would have shown his friend pictures of Audrey and talked about her. She longed to run and hide but knew it would be the worst thing to do.

"And here—I brought a Christmas present for your son." Tom handed Eve a lumpy, oversize leather glove with a red bow stuck to it. He must have noticed her puzzled expression because he quickly added, "It's a baseball mitt."

"Thank you. That's very kind of you."

"The glove comes with lessons from me on how to play catch."

He seemed so earnest and genuine that Eve couldn't help smiling. "Robbie is still a little young to throw a ball, Mr. Vandenberg—"

"It's Tom. Please, call me Tom."

"But it's a lovely offer," she said as she took the mitt from him. "Thank you." Robbie reached for it, tugging on the bright-red bow.

"We all promised we'd take care of each other's families after the war if anything happened to one of us. I visit Arnie and his folks whenever I can, help them out if they need it."

This was Eve's chance to ask about Louis, but she needed to take her time. "How is Arnie?"

"Not good. He was the last of us to come home, and he's suffering some sort of shell shock. Barely talks, lives like a recluse."

"Wasn't he studying to be a veterinarian?"

"He could finish on the G.I. Bill, but he won't leave his house. His parents say we should give him time."

"He married a girl he met in Germany, didn't he? I remember Robert saying I wouldn't be the only war bride in town."

"I don't know what happened in Germany, and he won't talk about it. Listen, I can't imagine how hard this must be for you, moving so far from home. But I'd love to get to know you and Bob's son, if you'll let me. When he gets a little older, I can teach him to play all the sports that Bob and I used to play." He reached out to ruffle Robbie's hair. "So Bob had a redhead, huh? Louis is the one we always called Carrot Top."

Eve felt her cheeks grow warm. She wanted to escape his scrutiny. Yet she was Audrey now. She needed to do what Audrey would do. "How is Louis? Does he still live in town? I haven't seen him since we arrived."

"He moved to New Rochelle to open a branch of his father's insurance company. Couldn't stand the small-town life after being abroad. I hardly ever see him. He was devastated when Bob died. We all were."

"Would you like to come in and sit down, Tom?" she finally thought to ask.

"I can't stay. I need to head home. But I also wanted to tell you that you're welcome to come out to the farm whenever you want. I live in the country, just outside of town. Your son might enjoy seeing the animals or exploring the woods. Bob and I spent a lot of time playing in those woods when we were kids."

Eve swallowed a knot of grief, longing to be a girl again, roaming the woods, running barefoot, climbing trees.

"Although maybe you don't like the country," Tom continued when she didn't reply. "Bob said you were related to the king of England."

"The king is a very distant relative," Eve said, laughing. "And even he loves spending time in the country at Windsor Castle."

"Well, our farm isn't a palace, that's for sure, but you're welcome anytime. There's a pond you can skate on, and we have a great toboggan hill behind the barn."

"I would love that, Tom. Thank you." She filed away the information for another day, knowing her soul might need the balm of forests and country hillsides.

"Well, I should be going."

"Yes . . . well . . . thank you for coming, Tom. And for the Christmas present."

"You're welcome. I'll see you around." He gave a salute with his stocking cap and left. Eve closed the door behind him, able to breathe again.

27

The Barretts held the party to celebrate Robbie's fourth birthday at the country club. Eve watched her son running around with thirty other children in expensive party clothes, eating candy and popping balloons, and wondered how the past three and a half years in America could have flown by so fast. There was an enormous birthday cake, clowns doing magic tricks, pony rides in the country club's parking lot. The extravagance overwhelmed Eve, yet Robbie seemed to take it all for granted as if it were his birthright, including the towering pile of birthday presents. Would he grow up shackled to his wealth, like Alfie?

The long afternoon included cocktails and idle chitchat with the other country-club mothers. Eve pretended to be interested in their lives as the children played pin the tail on the donkey, while her heart yearned for the refuge and contentment that only an hour in the woods could provide.

When the party finally ended, she hauled Robbie's carload of birthday presents into her little bungalow, changed into comfortable clothes, and told Robbie to do the same. Then she telephoned Tom Vandenberg. "Hi, Tom. This is Audrey. I was wondering if Robbie and I could come out to the farm for an hour or so."

"Sure. You know you're always welcome."

"I should warn you, though. We just got home from Robbie's birthday party at the club and he's a bit wound up from all the excitement. I need to calm him down so he'll sleep tonight."

Tom laughed. "Well, the farm is the place to do it."

"Thanks, Tom. We'll be there shortly. I'll bring some leftover cake for your reward. There was enough to feed an entire regiment."

Eve's tension from the exhausting day began to release as she left the suburbs and drove into the countryside. She felt free and happy out here, away from the women she had nothing in common with. Memories of her childhood in the village always flooded back as she watched Tom's cows grazing in the pasture or saw his flock of sheep on the hillside. In the years since she first met Tom, he had become a good friend to her and Robbie. She also felt a stirring of affection and attraction toward him, but even though the times when she felt unbearably lonely were too many to count, she resisted the pull. She had loved Alfie and Louis and had lost them both. She wouldn't risk the searing grief love brought. Eve understood, at last, why Mum wouldn't go to the cinema with Williams. Besides, a relationship with Tom would complicate her life. She had committed fraud when she'd assumed Audrey's identity, so a marriage to Tom or anyone else would be illegal under her false name.

Tom waited outside for them. He bent to kiss Eve's cheek as he took the plate of cake she'd brought. "I'll run this inside the house real quick," he said. He was back in a flash. "So did you have a nice party?" he asked as he ruffled Robbie's ginger hair.

"Yeah! You should see all the presents I got!"

"More than any four-year-old could possibly need," Eve added. "How about a walk in the woods?" The stretch of woods lay just beyond the pasture and she instinctively walked toward the trees and the sound of the rushing creek as if pulled by ropes. How she longed to be a carefree girl again, roaming through the trees with one of Granny Maud's sausage rolls and a scone pinned in a napkin. If only she could go back in time to the days before Granny died. Before she went to work at Wellingford Hall. Before the war and the endless days of fear and sorrow and grief. Before Alfie. And Louis. Back to an innocent time when she believed in a Good Shepherd who would never abandon her.

They reached the woods. The lovely sound of birdsong trilled above them. "Hear that, Robbie?" Tom asked. "That's a meadowlark."

"How can you tell?"

"Because every bird sings its own special song. I can teach you some of them, if you'd like."

Eve hurried forward, not waiting to hear Robbie's reply, hoping Tom wouldn't notice her tears. Granny Maud knew all the birds' songs, too, and had been teaching Eve before . . . before she was laid to rest in the graveyard behind the village church and Eve's life changed forever.

She halted beneath a huge tree with branches that nearly touched the ground. "What a perfect climbing tree!"

"It was my favorite when I was a boy. Want to try it, Robbie?"

He drew back, shaking his head. "Uh-uh!"

"Oh, dear. Don't tell me my son is turning into a city boy!" Eve said, laughing. "We can't have that!" She kicked off her shoes and scrambled up the trunk, halting on a branch above them. "This brings back so many memories," she said, laughing again. "Oh, how I've missed the woods! Come on up, Robbie."

Tom lifted him up to the first branch, helping him until Eve could reach down to pull him up beside her. But she could tell he was scared, so she let Tom lift him down. She sat on the branch, legs dangling, the bark rough against her palms. "I would be content to live in a tree if there was a way to do it," she said with a sigh.

"You surprised me, Audrey," Tom said when she'd climbed down again.

"Oh? Why's that?"

"Well, the way Bob described you, I pictured a dignified princess who lived in a castle. Where did you learn to climb trees?"

"Um . . . My friend Eve Dawson taught me." She looked away so he wouldn't see she was lying.

"I heard all about Eve, too."

"Really? What did you hear?"

"That she was funny and brave and full of life. Whatever happened to her?"

"We lost touch after the war."

"Well, she did a good job teaching you to climb. You scrambled up that tree like a monkey."

Eve met his gaze, and the love and longing she saw in Tom's eyes startled her. Her heart lurched. She could easily fall in love with Tom if she allowed herself. He was her closest friend. She imagined being held in his arms, kissing him, and her heart skipped faster. Maybe she already was in love with him. Eve quickly looked away, dismissing the thought. Impossible. The Barretts would never approve.

But Mum would. Granny Maud, too. They would have liked Tom Vandenberg.

Eve continued walking, following the creek through the woods. The rushing water was like music to her soul. Her sighs of contentment blended with the sigh of the branches swishing in the wind, the rustle of leaves and twigs beneath her feet. Much too soon, Robbie slowed down. "You're not tired already, are you?" she asked.

"My tummy hurts."

"I'm not surprised after all the cake and ice cream you ate."

"Can we go home?"

I am home, she wanted to say.

"Want me to carry you, buddy?" Tom asked. Robbie nodded, and Tom swung him up onto his shoulders as if he weighed nothing at all. Eve had never known her father, but he must have been a lot like Tom, a hardworking man who loved the land and his animals, a man with a warm smile for everyone. She knew the ache of growing up without a father and regretted that her son would know it, too.

"Right, then. I guess we'd better head home," Eve said when they reached the farmyard. Tom settled Robbie into the backseat. "Thanks, Tom," she said after a quick embrace. She loved the scent of woods and fresh air on his clothing but didn't dare to linger in his arms.

"Anytime."

She drove away, sorry she had to leave. The Barretts had so enfolded Eve into their lives that she forgot, at times, that they weren't her real family. But today she felt the uncomfortable tug between the woman she truly was and the woman she had become. Between the woman who belonged in the woods and the one who threw elaborate birthday parties at the country club. Eve wiped away tears as she drove, wishing for Robbie's sake, for her own sake, that she had never chosen to become Audrey Barrett.

WELLINGFORD HALL

Tildy baked a birthday cake for Bobby when he turned four. Mrs. Smith stuck candles on top of it and the servants gathered around to sing "Happy Birthday to You." Audrey remembered her own birthday parties on Wellingford's lawn with white tablecloths and silver serving dishes and children she didn't know. She had stood off to the side and watched them play, too shy to join them. But Alfie would always come and take her hand and pull her into the festivities.

"Make a wish, Bobby," Audrey told him. "Then blow out the candles." He did as he was told. Audrey wondered what he wished for. She had given up on wishes the day Robert died.

When they'd all eaten their fill, Audrey asked Tildy to put a piece of cake on a plate for her father, and she carried it to him in his study. "Father?" she said, knocking on his door. "I brought you a piece of cake. It's Bobby's birthday today." He didn't reply. She slowly opened the door and went in, steeling herself. He had returned to Wellingford Hall shortly after Eve disappeared four years ago, and had become increasingly reclusive ever since, holing up in his study, day after day, year after year until it had become a hoarder's lair. He seldom left the room, eating here, sleeping here, and refusing to allow the servants inside to clean. Audrey skirted around mounds of trash and piles of newspapers and approached his desk, where he sat staring at an empty Scotch bottle. "I thought you might like some cake, Father. Tildy made it for Bobby's birthday."

"I'm selling the manor house," he said without looking at her.

"Excuse me?"

"Pack your things and get out. Tell the servants they're through working here. I'm selling Wellingford Hall and moving back to the north country where I belong." He slurred his words. He was drunk.

"You don't really mean that, Father—"

He cut her off with a shout. "It's done! I've already signed with an estate agent! I never want to see this cursed place again!" His words knocked the wind from her. She needed to sit down, but rubbish covered every chair except the one he sat on.

"What about your grandson? Wellingford Hall is his inheritance. You can't sell his family home."

"What grandson?" he said with a growl. "I don't have a grandson."

A well of pity opened in Audrey's heart. Losing Mother and then Alfie had been too much for him. His grief and long confinement in this room had caused his mind to slip. She tried to speak slowly, to help him understand. "Yes, you do, Father. My son, Bobby, is your heir. Robert Clarkson Barrett, remember?"

He turned to look at her, eyes glittering. "I know who you mean, Audrey. I haven't lost my mind. But that boy is *not* my heir."

Audrey stared at him, certain he was merely confused. "Of course he is. Bobby is my son. I'm your daughter—"

"No, you're not!" His shout roared through the room. "You're not my daughter!"

His words slammed into Audrey as if he had knocked her against a wall. Father wore a sick smile on his face as he stared at her.

"Didn't your mother, the great Lady Rosamunde, ever tell you the truth?" he asked. "You aren't mine, Audrey. I never did learn who sired you, but it wasn't me. You're the product of one of her many *dalliances*. An unfortunate *accident*. She probably didn't know who your real father was, either."

Audrey wanted to run from the room to escape his words, but she couldn't move, galvanized by his hatred and her utter shock. All she could think was *No wonder you never loved me.*

"I'm done with all of this," Father said, gesturing to the ravaged room. "I've lived my entire life for nothing. Nothing! I'm going to sell this monstrosity and be done with it."

Desperation dropped Audrey to her knees. "Please don't do this to us! What about me? What about my son?"

"Go find a rich, gullible fool to live off like your mother did."

Audrey couldn't believe he would be so cruel. "You wouldn't really leave us destitute, would you?"

His expression softened, but only for a moment. "Your mother had a trust fund from her grandfather. I have no idea how much is left in it, but maybe there's a quid or two."

Audrey rose to her feet on trembling legs. She no longer pitied this wreck of a man. She hated him. He was leaving her and her son homeless and alone. Where would they go? What would they do? She ran upstairs to the room that was no longer her room, struggling to comprehend that her father wasn't her father. The home she loved wasn't her home. The shock of it nearly paralyzed her. And the shame. Audrey longed to dissolve into tears and sob her heart out, the way she had as a child before Eve comforted her with strawberries. The way she'd fallen apart after Robert died. Eve said she had to go on living for her son's sake, and she'd been right. Audrey couldn't break down now, either.

She wished she knew what had become of Eve. Eve had always given her courage when she'd needed it—and she needed it now. But she had no idea where she was. She hadn't written to Audrey as she'd promised. None of the servants had heard from her, either. Why had Audrey ever allowed her best friend to walk away? Why hadn't she begged Eve to stay? Audrey had been so disappointed in Eve for having an illegitimate baby, when all along, Audrey was an illegitimate child herself.

She couldn't dwell on that right now. She had to come up with a plan. If Eve could struggle through her own pain and shock after the V-1 rocket attack in order to save Audrey's life, then she would set aside her own anguish and outrage in order to provide for her son. Father had mentioned Mother's trust fund, so she would begin there. She would contact her uncle in London.

Audrey composed herself, waiting for her hands to stop trembling, her weak knees to strengthen. Then she hurried downstairs to the sitting room and riffled through her desk for her address book. How long had it been since her uncle last telephoned? Audrey couldn't recall. He had long grown tired of inviting her to London and hearing her refusals. She had become as much of a recluse as her father.

She found the telephone number and went into the front hall to make the call. "Hello, this is Audrey Clarkson, your niece," she said when her aunt came on the line. "There's something I need to discuss with Uncle Roger, and I wondered if it would be convenient for me to drive up to London to see him this weekend."

"Let me check our calendar, dear . . ."

Audrey twisted the telephone cord around her finger. "It's rather urgent," she added.

"Right, then. Why don't you come on Friday afternoon and join us for dinner? Sylvia will be here with her family, but I'm sure we can make room for you, too." Audrey wrote down directions to the town house, barely remembering it from years ago. She would leave Bobby with the nurse for the weekend and drive up to London alone. She wondered if her uncle knew that Alfred Clarkson wasn't her father. Should she tell him? Might he know who her real father was? She closed her eyes as she hung up the phone, wishing she could awaken from this nightmare.

Audrey remembered her uncle's London town house as if she'd dreamt about it a long time ago. From the outside, the five-story home that had belonged to their family for several generations seemed to have survived the war unscathed. She remembered it as being more opulent than her own home, with a centuries-old coat of arms in the foyer and gold-framed oil paintings of her ancestors. But once inside, Audrey found that the splendor she remembered from childhood had faded, as if the war had sanded all the gilt from the edges of this once-splendid house. It occurred to her that her uncle might have reached out to her after the war because he needed her father's money.

The housekeeper met Audrey at the door and showed her to one of the bedrooms. "The missus said for you to come down for drinks at seven. Dinner is at eight."

"Is one still expected to dress for dinner?" she asked.

"Yes, of course."

Audrey remembered the ritual from before the war. Mother and Father always changed into formal attire for dinner. Audrey thought that the war had done away with such formalities but had added a gown to her bag just in case. She was glad she had. She brushed her hair, slipped into her dress, and made her way down to the parlor shortly after seven.

"Audrey! So good to see you!" her uncle said. "You look splendid! Let me fix you a drink."

She normally didn't drink, wary of following in her mother's footsteps, but she accepted it, hoping it might steady her nerves. She had come prepared to grovel and plead as she asked her uncle to help her find a place to live and a way to support herself and her son, ready to return to her place among the aristocracy. But first she needed to make polite conversation with him and her aunt, who were nearly strangers to her, and then with her cousin Sylvia and her husband after they joined them downstairs. Audrey dreaded making small talk and felt as awkward now as she had as a young girl. Perhaps even more so, knowing she would be forced to beg. She took a sip of her drink, then set it aside, despising the taste.

By the time the family assembled, drinks in hand, Audrey's

stomach had twisted into a tight knot. She was about to ask her uncle if she could speak to him in private before dinner to end the suspense of waiting, when her cousin's young son and daughter joined the gathering, interrupting them. The son was perhaps eight years old, the daughter a year or two younger. *Like Alfie and me.* They had come downstairs with their governess to see their parents for a few minutes before going to bed. Audrey's heart squeezed when she saw the daughter nervously biting her lip, the son standing stiffly at attention. Their parents might have been strangers, greeting them for the first time. Audrey remembered standing before her parents this way, desperate for their approval and love. And never receiving it.

She held her breath, hoping her uncle's family would be different from hers, hoping for signs of warmth and affection for the children's sakes. Yet the icy ritual played out just as it had for her and Alfie. This was how the gentry lived and raised their children. One must control one's emotions. One mustn't cry or carry on. *"Oh, for pity's sake, Audrey."*

As she witnessed the frigid scene, Audrey suddenly caught a glimpse of her own mother. She would have been raised this way, too, with parents who were cold and aloof. Parents who disdained displays of emotion. Might Mother have longed for warmth and affection as a child, just as Audrey had—and been denied? This might explain why Mother treated Audrey the way she had. How could her mother show warmth and tenderness if she had never experienced them herself?

Nor had she received love from Father. Their marriage had been a mutually beneficial arrangement, lacking love. Mother had never known the joy that Audrey had discovered with Robert, loving her husband with complete abandon, opening her heart and soul to him, and being fully loved in return. Had Mother been so desperate to be loved that she had turned to other men? As shameful as the circumstances of Audrey's conception had been, Audrey felt a stab of pity for her mother.

Her cousin's children were bidding the adults good night. The girl bussed her grandmother's cheek, then nodded to her mother. None of the adults set down their drinks or shifted from their languid poses to envelop the children in a hug. The governess led them away. Did they long for the warmth of their parents' arms as much as Audrey had?

She turned away to hide her tears, pretending to look for something on the bar cart. She tried to imagine Robert and herself sitting here while their son, Bobby, stood rigidly before them, waiting for a gesture of approval and love. The image made Audrey shudder. Robert wouldn't want this legacy for his son. He wouldn't want Bobby to grow up the way she and Alfie had. And Audrey knew with all her heart that she didn't want it for her son, either. She had come to London determined to reenter life among the gentry, as her mother would have wished. But as she observed her uncle's family, she knew she needed to find some other way to support her son besides returning to this. But where could she go? How would she and Bobby live?

The family proceeded into the dining room for dinner, then politely discussed unimportant things while they ate. Audrey's mind raced, searching for a way out as if she were trapped in the dark ATS training shed again, the room slowly filling with gas. The question the vicar had asked four years ago sprang to mind, unbidden. *What might God be asking you to do?* It was a much bigger question than where she would live or how she would survive. It meant finding a greater purpose in life than pleasing other people. It was what Robert would have wanted for her, as well.

"You said you had something you wanted to discuss?" Audrey's uncle asked after dinner. He led her into his stately library while the others retired to the sitting room for brandy.

Audrey drew a steadying breath and got right to the point. "Father is selling Wellingford Hall."

"My goodness. Why?"

Audrey debated whether or not to tell him the truth and decided not to. If her uncle didn't already know that Alfred Clarkson wasn't her real father, she wouldn't tarnish Mother's memory by telling him. Some secrets were better left hidden. "Father is moving up north. But my son and I won't be going with him."

"Do you plan to resettle here in London?"

"That seems to be my best option."

"Your aunt and I will be happy to introduce you to the right social circles. I believe you'll do very well here once you find your place."

Audrey could only nod, fighting tears as she remembered how bleak and pointless her life had seemed before the war. Before Robert.

"The first step will be to hire an estate agent and get you settled in a flat. Did your father say what your annual allowance will be for living expenses?"

"Father won't be providing anything."

"My dear! If you two have had a row, I urge you to reconcile as swiftly as possible. It costs a great deal to live in London these days."

"I'm afraid a reconciliation isn't possible. But Father did mention that Mother had a trust fund. I was hoping you might know something about it."

"Our family's banker will know. But I doubt if there's much left. Rosamunde did enjoy the finer things, you know."

386 · IF I WERE YOU

Audrey swallowed the last of her pride. "Might you be able to help us get on our feet?"

He sighed and looked away. "I wish I were in a position to help, but I'm not. However, I will be happy to speak with your father on your behalf. Surely he can—"

"No. Please don't." Audrey's cheeks burned with shame. "Just let me know about the trust fund."

"Of course. I'll look into it."

"Thank you, Uncle Roger." She rose, longing to flee to her room, yet good manners required her to return to the sitting room and visit with the others.

"I have one further thought," her uncle said before Audrey reached the door. "In the event that the trust is depleted, as I'm guessing it is, might your husband's American family offer some support?"

"Perhaps." The thought had occurred to Audrey before she'd come to London, but she had quickly dismissed it. She had refused the Barretts' offer after Robert died, and they hadn't contacted her since. How dare she ask them for help now?

As she drove home to Wellingford the following day, Audrey had time to consider her dwindling options. And to pray. She hadn't prayed in a while. *"What might God be asking you to do?"* She still had no idea, but the visit with her uncle had convinced her that she didn't want to return to a cold, loveless life with the gentry. She would use whatever funds remained in the trust to live in London on her own. After all, Eve had once taught her to cook and run a household without servants.

Uncle Roger telephoned a few days later. "I'm afraid I have bad news, Audrey. Barely five hundred pounds remain in the trust account—not nearly enough to provide interest for a monthly allowance. I'm so sorry."

Audrey couldn't speak, couldn't think.

"Are you still there?" her uncle asked when she didn't reply.

"Yes, I'm here."

"Are you certain you don't want me to speak with your father?"

"No. Thank you, but no." She and Bobby would be disgraced if all of London society learned the truth about her birth. "I will contact my husband's family in America." She thanked him again and rang off.

It had been difficult enough to ask Uncle Roger for help, but how did one go about asking American strangers for support? Not by mail, certainly. She would seem grasping and conniving if she contacted them after all this time simply to ask for money. What if she used the five hundred pounds to go to America and ask them in person? If they met Bobby, surely they would want to help, wouldn't they?

Audrey sat on the bench in the front hall, unmoving, for so long that Robbins approached and asked if she was feeling all right. "Yes, I'm fine. Thank you." He and the other servants needed someplace to go, too, and had asked her for references. Father had turned all of their lives upside down. Going to America was Audrey's only option. "Will you kindly fetch my steamer trunk from the storage room, Robbins? My husband's family in America have never met their grandson, and I believe Bobby is old enough now to learn more about his father."

"How long do you plan to stay, Miss Audrey?"

"I'm not sure . . ."

A shiver of fear washed through Audrey as she tucked her son into bed that night. They were going to America, alone. She had spent the afternoon looking at travel timetables and ticket costs and deciding what to pack, what to leave behind. Desperation fueled her courage. She had no idea what to expect in America, or what sort of welcome she would receive, but she would try to give her son the life Robert wanted him to have.

No matter what her future might be, Audrey would make certain that her son knew he was loved, every single day of his life.

28

Eve unfolded two webbed lawn chairs for herself and Audrey, and they sat together in the bungalow's back garden. "This grass needs to be cut again," Eve mumbled—as if cutting it would transform the barren space. "I wish George was here to help me."

"Wellingford's gardener?"

"He was a genius with hedge clippers. He could turn this place into a paradise. He set a standard I can never live up to."

A cricket chirped nearby. Fireflies blinked in the bushes—a mating ritual, Tom had told her. A lawn sprinkler whirred in a neighbor's garden. A dog barked. "Is it always this hot here?" Audrey asked, breaking the silence.

"In the summertime, yes. It could get even hotter next month." Eve didn't want to talk about the weather. The boys were asleep, and she and Audrey needed to have it out with each other. Neither of them seemed to know where to begin. Ever since breakfast with Tom and his parents, Eve's mind had raced with feverish plans and outrageous schemes for solving this crisis. Clearly Audrey wasn't leaving. She had no place to go. Everything Eve and her son had benefited from these past few years—the house, the car, the income, the grandparents—belonged to Audrey.

Eve knew she couldn't face the people she'd deceived once they learned the truth. That left her with only one option: she had to disappear. She would rather run away and start all over again in a different city than confess the truth and face the people she'd grown to love. She would have to create a new life, just as she'd been forced to do in the past. And she could think of only one person who might help her. She inhaled the sweet, grassy air, then let out her breath.

"Listen, Audrey . . . I think I know how to fix this 'mess,' as you called it. But I'm going to need a little more time. I promise I'll go away and give everything back to you, but first I have to find a job and a place to live and—"

"I would never turn you out with no place to go, Eve. There's no need for you to vanish in the middle of the night, is there?"

"You said yourself that what I've done is monstrous—lying to everyone and stealing your name and your money. A lot of people will agree with you. I could never show my face in this town again. I certainly can't count on help from the people I've deceived."

"Maybe if we explain—"

"No. They'll see the same thing you see—an immoral woman with a fatherless son who lied and committed fraud and took advantage of them for the past four years."

"Eve—"

"Just listen." She swatted at a mosquito. "I think I know someone who'll help me, but I'll need to drive to a different town."

"Who?"

Eve didn't want Audrey to know. "Will you stay here tomorrow and watch Robbie for me until I get back? And if anyone calls or comes to the house, please don't tell them who you are. I just need a little more time to get settled someplace new."

"If that's what you want, Eve. But—"

"Thanks. That is what I want."

Eve fixed her hair and applied her makeup very carefully the next day, then dressed in a red-and-white polka-dot sundress and a string of pearls that her mother-in-law had bought for her. Eve loved shopping with Mrs. Barrett, who lavished her and Robbie with everything they could possibly want. "I've always wished for a daughter to take on shopping trips," Mrs. Barrett said the day they'd bought the dress—and matching shoes and hat and purse, of course. Today would be the last day Eve would wear these clothes. They belonged to Audrey, the real daughter-in-law.

Eve kissed her son goodbye and promised to buy a half gallon of chocolate ice cream on the way home. She used the map in the glove compartment of her car to find the city, thirty miles away, where Louis lived. She would tell him about their son, Robbie. *Harry. His real name is Harry, after my father.* She would show Louis his picture, ask him to help her find a typist's job and a place to live and someone to watch Robbie during the day while she worked. She wouldn't ask for money, just for help to disappear.

The knot in Eve's stomach twisted tighter as she drove. When she reached Louis's town, she stopped at a telephone box and checked the advertising section in the directory for the Dubois family's insurance company. An older gentleman walking his dog gave her directions to the street where the office building was located. Eve found it without any trouble, a prosperous-looking business in an affluent area of town. The sight of Louis's name painted on the glass window in black-and-gold letters made her heart hammer painfully. She sat in the sweltering car for several minutes, unable to move, her insides writhing. If she sat here much longer, her clothes would be drenched with sweat. *Get ahold of yourself, Eve. This is for your son. Louis will want to help his son.*

She walked to the door on wobbling legs. An attractive young receptionist greeted her inside, guarding Louis's office from behind an enormous desk with a typewriter and a telephone. Eve could easily do that girl's job or one like it—answering the telephone, typing letters. The girl smiled prettily. "Good morning. May I help you?"

Eve battled to control her shaking voice. "Is it possible to see Mr. Dubois for a few minutes? It won't take long."

"May I tell him what it's about?"

Eve's heart hadn't hammered this hard since the endless nights of the London Blitz. "I knew him when he was stationed in England during the war. My . . . um . . . my husband and I were friends of his. I happened to be in town today, so I thought . . . well, I just wanted to say hello. Should I have made an appointment?"

"No, no. Mr. Dubois is with a client, but he shouldn't be much longer." The girl checked her appointment book. "He has a few minutes before lunch. May I tell him your name?"

She would have to lie. Louis would run straight out the back door if he knew Eve was here. "Yes. Mrs. Robert Barrett." The name rolled easily from her tongue.

"You're welcome to wait here, Mrs. Barrett, or there's a nice little café next door."

"Thank you. I'll wait here."

"Would you like a cup of coffee?"

"No thank you." The thought of it made her writhing stomach burn. She couldn't stand American coffee, but she rarely requested tea because no one in America knew how to brew a decent pot of it. Tea steadied her nerves rather than leaving them jangled like tangled lengths of barbed wire the way coffee did. As for walking to the café, Eve's heart was racing so fast she wasn't sure she could walk anywhere.

She chided herself for behaving like a frightened rabbit. She'd faced bombs and infernos and much, much worse, so surely she could face her child's father, the man she'd once loved. It seemed like a lifetime ago.

Watching the receptionist at work helped calm her nerves. Eve remembered her days as a typist, sitting at her desk for hours and hours until her back and shoulders ached. When she first arrived in America, she'd planned to work to support herself and Robbie. But after meeting the country-club wives, she quickly realized that the Barretts would never allow their daughter-in-law to work, especially as a typist.

At last, a door opened and an older gentleman came out. The receptionist pressed a button on her intercom. "Mr. Dubois, you have a visitor who would like to say hello. Mrs. Robert Barrett, from England."

Louis was at the door a moment later, a broad smile on his face, his eyes alight with anticipation. Then he saw Eve and the blood drained from his face as if she'd slit one of his arteries. "Eve? What . . . ?"

She rose and hurried toward him to prevent him from saying more. "Hello, Louis. I was in town and thought I would stop by and say hello." Her voice shook like an old woman's. She thought she'd been prepared to see him, but he took her breath away in his dark tailored suit and tie, his ginger hair parted and neatly combed. His smile still gleamed like an advertisement for tooth powder. Eve felt as badly shaken as he looked. Guilt and longing waged war as she stared at him. She remembered their times together. His warmth and gentle strength. His love.

It had been a mistake to come.

Eve still loved him. And it was wrong to love him. She would never forgive herself for what she'd done. And God certainly couldn't forgive her, either. That's why she and her son were being punished. She fought to hold back her tears. She wouldn't cry. She wouldn't.

Louis recovered before she did. "What a surprise! Um . . . let's talk in my office." He held the door until she entered, then closed it behind them. For a moment, they simply stared at each other. Then he reached for her and pulled her close. How long had it been since she'd felt his embrace? Any man's embrace? She was back in Louis's arms again, but it wouldn't last—couldn't last. The battle between guilt and longing raged like the fires in the East End. Did he sense the battle, too? For Eve, guilt would always win.

He released her a moment later and walked behind his desk to sit down as if hiding behind a fortress. Thank goodness he hadn't kissed her. She would have come undone if he had, just as she had the first time he'd kissed her on that terrible, wonderful night after the V-1 nearly killed her and Audrey. He gestured to a chair in front of his desk. "Have a seat, Eve. I . . . um . . . I thought my receptionist said you were Audrey Barrett. I . . . You surprised me. I mean . . . this is a shock!"

"I'm sorry. I was afraid you would bolt out the back door if I gave my real name." She clung to the back of the chair for support but didn't sit in it, fearing her knees would never allow her to stand again if she did.

"No, of course I wouldn't bolt. You're the one who left that day. You said it was over between us."

"It was the right decision. The only decision."

He looked unconvinced. "It's wonderful to see you, Eve."

"You haven't changed a bit." It was a silly thing to say after nearly five years, but she couldn't string her thoughts and words together into coherent sentences.

It was enough to see him one more time. Now she needed to leave. Asking for his help was a terrible idea. They were still drawn to each other with a power that neither of them had been able to control. She didn't dare become entangled with Louis again. They would hurt too many people. Eve couldn't tell him why she had come. She would have to find another way out of her dilemma.

"Did you come to America to visit Audrey?" Louis asked. "I heard she and her son moved here a few years ago. I've been meaning to get over there to see her, but . . . the truth is, I was afraid that seeing her would remind me of you."

Eve nodded and struggled to shake off her confusion. She was Audrey. But Louis didn't know that. She cleared her throat and tried to corral her thoughts. "Louis, I can't stay more than a minute or two. I didn't come here to interrupt your life. I just wanted to see you again and to say that . . . that I hope you and your wife are very happy. Your daughter must be getting big."

"Karen's eight years old already. And we have another daughter now." He turned a framed picture around on his desk to show two ginger-haired girls holding a lamb. Eve barely noticed his daughters. The sight of the lamb stunned her—an unwelcome reminder of the Good Shepherd. The Shepherd who had abandoned her. Or was she the one at fault? Had she wandered away from Him? The photograph of Louis's daughters made the answer painfully clear.

"Are you raising sheep now, Louis?" she asked with a nervous laugh.

"That picture was taken last Easter. The lamb belonged to the photographer. Although the girls begged Jean to bring it home." A long silence fell at the mention of Jean's name. Then they both spoke at the same time.

"I should—"

"Eve, listen—"

"You go first," she said.

"Eve, I'm so sorry for everything that happened . . . I never meant to hurt you—"

"Please don't apologize. We both made a terrible mistake."

"It didn't feel like a mistake."

She looked down at the floor, not at him. It was more than a "mistake." They had broken one of God's commandments. For the first time, she saw herself the way God must see her. No wonder she was being punished. *"When you sin against the Lord,"* Granny Maud used to say, *"you may be sure that your sin will find you out."*

"Those were terrible years, Louis. But I wanted you to know in case anything ever happened to me, that we—" She stopped. Should she tell Louis he had a son? He would be so proud of Robbie.

Eve raised her head to look at the framed picture of his family again, then turned the photograph around to face Louis. She couldn't do it. She had ruined her own life—she wouldn't ruin his. Or his family's. "We helped each other through a very dark time. I'm glad we were friends, even if . . ."

"I love you, Eve."

"Please don't say that. I can't be in your life, Louis. I just wanted to see you again and thank you for helping me through one of the hardest times in my life. I hope and pray that you and Jean are happy."

"I never told her about us. I still think about you nearly every day, and sometimes the guilt is more than I can stand. After Bob died, I needed to talk to somebody about what happened, so I told my friend Tom Vandenberg about you."

Eve closed her eyes for a moment. How could she ever face

Tom again after he learned who she was? He had been such a good friend to her and Robbie. Her best friend.

"Tom advised me not to confess to Jean," Louis continued. "He said I should never tell her or anyone else."

"I agree with him, Louis. Please promise me one thing." Eve paused as if waiting for him to say, *"Cross my heart and hope to die"* the way she and Audrey used to do. "Promise me you'll take Tom's advice and never tell Jean about what happened during the war. If you confess, you'll free yourself from the guilt, but then the knowledge will weigh on Jean's heart for the rest of her life. She'll always wonder if she can trust you and if you love her. Don't do that to her. Promise?"

"I promise," Louis whispered.

"Let your guilt be your penance. And don't ever, ever cheat on her again." Eve let go of the chair she'd been clinging to and took a step backward toward the door. "I have to go."

"No, Eve! Don't walk away!" He started to rise, but she held up both hands.

"Don't. Please don't hold me again, Louis. Just let me go." She turned, battling to control tears of shame and regret as she hurried outside to her car.

Now what? She pressed her forehead against the steering wheel as her tears flowed. *What am I going to do now?*

She would be alone again, without a home—like she was after Granny Maud died, like she was after Mum died. If this was her punishment for turning away from God, Eve didn't think she could bear it.

29

Eve couldn't go back to the house and face Audrey. Not yet. Not until she figured out where to go, how to live. Turning to Louis for help had been a last resort, but as she drove home after seeing him, steering blindly, she knew it would be a mistake to involve him. That left her without a plan. She'd always been strong, able to think on her feet and adjust to adversity. Her new life in America seemed firmly under control—until Audrey arrived.

As she neared the woods west of Tom's farm, Eve pulled to the side of the road. She needed the forest, the solace of deep silence. She turned off the engine and opened the door, then realized she was still wearing her expensive polka-dot sundress and high-heeled pumps. How could she walk in the woods in such a fancy outfit? A better question might be, what was she doing in these clothes to begin with? They weren't hers. She was an actress playing a part—the role of Audrey Barrett.

Had she really been happy in that role these past three and a half years? In all honesty, no. She had not. She and Robbie had been safe and well cared for, but there had been an underlying loneliness and emptiness that no amount of fancy clothes or parties at the country club could ever fill. If she gave Audrey her life back, maybe she could find a more satisfying one. But what about Robbie? The only life he'd ever known would be ripped away, along with all the people he loved, replaced by a life in a tiny flat, barely scraping by. Happy or not, Eve would gladly continue living a lie for his sake.

But now she no longer could.

Eve kicked off her shoes, unfastened her nylons, and rolled them off. She wiggled out of her crinoline, took off her pearls, then climbed out of the car and entered the woods. She seldom walked barefoot anymore, and the rough forest floor hurt her feet. Eve ignored the pain as she moved deeper into the woods, the pain from the choices she'd made outweighing her discomfort. In the distance, a creek laughed and burbled, drawing her. The canopy of trees reminded her of the woods back home, and she remembered the joy she used to feel as she'd played there. At the edge of the woods was the church she attended with Granny Maud and Mum and George, the church where she had felt so loved and cared for—until God had abandoned her.

Or had He?

Maybe Eve had used God's abandonment as a handy excuse to go her own way. If she was honest, she had to admit that she had turned her back on God, allowing bitterness and grief to lead her, wandering, in the wrong direction, away from Him. Into Louis's arms. Into a life of lies. Now she was lost, and she had no one to blame but herself. Her own choices. Her own willfulness.

She had drawn such comfort as a child from the picture of the Good Shepherd that had hung in Granny's cottage and from the stories she'd learned about His love and care for her. Granny said

He would search for His lost sheep the way Daddy used to do when one of his sheep foolishly wandered away. He would never leave her lost and alone.

Eve stopped walking. She stood still to listen. "God, where are You?" she whispered. The silence told her that He was gone. It was too late. She sank down on the ground, not caring about her dress, and buried her face in her hands. "God, I'm sorry," she wept. "I'm so, so sorry!"

Sorry for committing adultery with Louis. Sorry for stealing another woman's husband, a little girl's father. She had done wrong, and she couldn't use the war as an excuse. She was sorry for stealing Audrey's identity, her home, her family. It didn't matter that Audrey had thrown them away. What Eve did was wrong. Her lies would cause pain to good, undeserving people like the Barretts and Tom Vandenberg and his family. Worse, Eve had dragged her innocent son into this mess. He would be hurt the most by her sins. Little Harry had already lost his name, and now he would lose his home, his grandparents, his very identity as Robbie Barrett. Would he ever forgive her? Eve wouldn't blame him if he couldn't.

That was the destructive power of sin and lies—they harmed the innocent along with the guilty. Hitler's lies had dragged the entire world into six long years of hell. Eve would face humiliation and shame when her sins were exposed, and rightly so. She hadn't been able to get away from God after all. He'd known the truth about her all along.

"I'm so sorry, God!" she sobbed. "So very, very sorry!"

Eve didn't deserve His forgiveness. She didn't deserve anyone's forgiveness. She deserved anger and condemnation and shame. The life she'd built had collapsed, burying her, leaving no way out, no one to dig her free from the rubble. She sobbed with hopelessness. Granny Maud would be so disappointed in her. If only her stories about the Good Shepherd could be true, the Shepherd who would take her punishment for the mess she'd made so she could be forgiven. If only He would find her, His lost sheep, and forgive her. Eve covered her face and wept and wept.

After a very long time, a strange sound caught Eve's attention. She lifted her head and listened. The wind sighed through the tree branches. Birds called to each other. The creek rushed and gurgled. She heard it again—the sound of a baby crying. No, not a baby. The plaintive cry of a lamb.

A lamb? It couldn't be.

The underbrush rustled as an animal moved among the trees. She heard a pitiful bleat. Eve stood. She saw it then—a small woolly lamb surrounded by forest. Dwarfed by it. She limped toward the animal on bruised feet, then sank to the ground again as she gathered the lost lamb in her arms. It licked her hand, her face with its warm, rough tongue. Eve closed her eyes, sobbing against the lamb's nubby fur. Could it really be true? Would God really search for her and forgive her for everything she'd done?

She waited, barely breathing.

Footsteps rustled through the woods. She heard Tom's voice, calling to his lamb.

Joy overwhelmed her, flooding through her. Everything Granny said was true. "Over here!" Eve called out. "We're over here!"

The Good Shepherd had come to fetch His lost sheep and bring her home.

⁂

"When's my mommy coming home?" Robbie asked.

"Soon, I think." Audrey hoped he wouldn't start crying. Eve had been gone all morning, and the truth was, Audrey didn't know when she would be back. "Do you have any more books? I'll read you and Bobby another story while we wait."

Robbie slid off the sofa and started toward his bedroom, then halted at the sound of a car pulling into the driveway. "Mommy!" He rushed to the front door and ran outside. Audrey stood and peered out the window, hoping Eve had returned with a solution to their dilemma. But the car was a sleek black one with whitewall tires and what looked like shark fins in the rear. Two women stepped out, a blonde driver and her raven-haired passenger. They were Audrey's age, dressed as if posing for photos for a fashion magazine. Audrey drew away from the window, hoping they hadn't spotted her. Eve had said not to talk to anyone. But Robbie stood on the front steps, waiting for them.

"Hi, Robbie. Is your mommy home?" the blonde asked.

"No, but her friend's here." He led them through the front door. Audrey had no choice but to greet them.

"Hello, you must be Audrey's guest from England," the blonde said, extending her gloved hand. "I'm Phyllis West."

"Doris Anderson," the other one said, offering her hand as well.

"Yes. Hello." Audrey didn't give her name, unwilling to lie. "She isn't here, I'm afraid. She's off on an errand." The women made their way past her into the living room, their eyes roving as if cataloging the contents. Audrey remembered doing the same thing whenever she and Mother called on someone in London, as if an individual's worth could be appraised by her possessions.

"Audrey's mother-in-law told us she had a visitor from England," Phyllis said. "And that your son is sick?"

"He had roseola. He's nearly recovered." Audrey cleared a nervous lump from her throat. "I'm not sure when E—" She'd nearly said *Eve*. "Um . . . when she will be back. I'm sorry."

"We don't mind waiting." They sat down in the living room

and pulled off their white gloves. Their visit didn't seem to have a purpose. Audrey had the unsettling feeling that they were simply nosy and had come to snoop.

"Would . . . would you care for a cup of tea?"

"A cup of *tea*?" Phyllis asked. The women laughed, a brittle, tinkling sound like breaking glass. The girls in boarding school had giggled that way, especially when planning something mean.

"No thank you!" Doris said dramatically. "But I'll take some coffee if you have it."

"Sorry, but I don't really know where things are yet. I've only been here a short time, you see. But I believe there's some iced tea." She hurried into the kitchen to escape their scrutiny, with Bobby clinging to her skirt. Now they reminded Audrey of her classmates at finishing school—barging in with their air of entitlement, sitting down with feline languidness, as sleek as pedigreed cats. Audrey heard them whispering while she poured iced tea into two glasses. She couldn't get the ice cubes out of the metal tray and had to serve it without ice.

"Do you play tennis?" Phyllis asked when Audrey returned with the tea.

"I . . . I once did. I haven't since before the war." She sat down and pulled Bobby onto her lap.

"That's Audrey's excuse, too," Phyllis said. "She keeps turning us down."

Audrey had never known Eve to play tennis and couldn't imagine that she could. She'd been a scullery maid, a typist, an ambulance driver. Where and when would she have learned to play tennis?

"We came to convince her to join our league at the club. We're not leaving until she agrees. We play every Tuesday and Thursday and we desperately need a reserve player."

Doris pulled out a packet of cigarettes and fitted one into an ivory holder.

Like Mother's. The sight of it shook Audrey. She wanted these women to leave.

"We told her she could take a few lessons from the club's pro if she needs to brush up," Doris said after lighting the cigarette with a silver lighter.

"Maybe you could play with us while you're here," Phyllis said.

"You're an aristocrat, too, aren't you?" Doris asked, exhaling a puff of smoke.

"She must be. Listen to how she talks! So refined, *my dear!*"

A trickle of sweat ran down Audrey's back. These women intimidated her. Worse, they infuriated her, presuming things about her that they didn't know. She decided to take control and change the subject. "What else do you do for fun here in America besides play tennis?"

"Go shopping, of course," Phyllis said.

"In New York City, not here in town," Doris added. She was looking around for an ashtray. Audrey stood and fetched a saucer from the kitchen. Nearly five years in the Army, yet neither she nor Eve had ever smoked. "Thanks, dear," Doris said. "All the good stores are there—Lord & Taylor, Saks, Bergdorf Goodman. You and Audrey should join us for lunch next week and we'll shop together."

Audrey could think of nothing she would hate more. Besides, she didn't have any money. "Do either of you work outside the home?" she asked. Her question was met with laughter.

"Why would we want to do that?"

She recalled the vicar's question *"What might God be asking you to do?"* and didn't think the answer would be *Play tennis and shop in New York City.* She disliked these women and had a hard time imagining Eve as their friend, especially the vivacious, free-spirited

Eve Dawson she'd once known. If Audrey resumed her rightful place as the Barretts' daughter-in-law, would she have to befriend Phyllis and Doris and be part of the country-club life? She would hate it as much as Robert had.

"Do you know if Audrey remembered to register Robbie for sailing lessons?" Doris asked. "The class fills up quickly, you know."

"I have no idea. . . . Isn't Robbie a bit young to sail?"

"Not at all. Our children live on sailboats in the summertime, almost from the time they can walk."

Audrey longed to tell them the story of how she and Eve had sailed into a war zone on rough seas in the middle of the night. She wanted to be that woman again.

The ladies finished their iced tea. Eve still wasn't back. They decided not to waste any more time waiting. "Tell Audrey to call me," Phyllis said as she waved goodbye.

"And let us know if you can play tennis on Thursday," Doris added.

Audrey closed the door behind them and leaned against it in relief, glad to be rid of them.

"Where did my mommy go?" Robbie asked. Audrey had no idea.

"She'll be here soon. Let's read another story." But before Audrey had time to sit down and open a book, the doorbell rang. Phyllis and Doris were back.

"I need to use your telephone," Phyllis said. "My car has a flat tire."

Audrey stifled a groan. She didn't want to be stuck in the house for another hour with these women, waiting for a mechanic. She looked past them at the car. "Is it a puncture? A slow leak?"

"How in the world would I know? That's why I need to call a mechanic."

"Let me have a look." Audrey slipped past them and went out to the driveway, the two boys trailing behind. The front tire was definitely flat. "It shouldn't be hard to change," Audrey said after looking it over. "Have you a spare tire?"

"Probably. But you . . . you certainly can't expect me to change it myself."

"I can change it for you." Audrey savored the look of astonishment on Phyllis's face.

"You're joking." Doris snorted.

"No, I'm not. I changed lorry tires all the time during the war. So did Princess Elizabeth, the king of England's daughter. Set the hand brake for me, please. Then open the boot."

"The brake and the . . . what?" Phyllis asked. She opened the car door, somewhat reluctantly, Audrey thought, and set the brake.

"Now the boot." Audrey walked around to the back of the car and pointed. "I need to see if you have a jack and a spare tire."

Phyllis stepped to the rear on her pointy heels and opened it. "Wouldn't it be easier to just call a repair truck?"

Audrey didn't reply as she pulled out the jack and lug wrench. "It's a bit different from the lorry jacks I'm used to, but I believe I can figure it out." She hauled out the spare tire with a grunt and set it on the ground. Audrey hadn't changed a tire in five years, but she remembered her training. "It's best to remove the hubcap and crack the lug nuts before jacking up the car," she said as she worked. "Otherwise, the tire simply spins around, making them impossible to unscrew." Two of the nuts were screwed on so tightly she had to jump on the wrench to loosen them. "Ha! Got them!" she said in triumph. The look of surprise and admiration on her son's face as he watched her nearly brought tears to her eyes.

Audrey assembled the jack and set it beneath the bumper. The car slowly rose as she pumped the handle up and down. The women watched Audrey as if observing a new species of animal. She enjoyed shocking them. Doris and Phyllis would certainly rescind their shopping invitation after this. The offer to join the tennis league, too. But Eve would have loved it—the old Eve, that was.

Audrey pulled off the filthy tire, rolled it to the boot, and hoisted it inside, wishing she had on her ATS coveralls. Dirt now covered her hands and the front of her dress. After a few more minutes of work, Audrey had the spare tire in place, the lug nuts tightened, and the wheel back on the ground. Her sergeant major would give her high marks for speed and efficiency.

"Right, then. That should get you home," she said as she stowed the jack and closed the boot.

The women hurried to get into the car as if eager to escape from this madwoman. Audrey bit her lip to hide a smile. Eve would have been rolling with laughter by now.

Eve's friendship had meant so much to Audrey through the years as she'd shown what true courage was. Eve had saved her life. But perhaps Eve's most courageous act had been leaving home at the age of twelve to become a scullery maid, without bitterness, without looking back.

"Tell Audrey we'll call her later," Phyllis said before driving off.

Audrey turned to find her son hopping with excitement. "You did it, Mummy! You fixed their car!"

"Yes . . . I surely did."

"Your hands are very dirty, though."

Audrey held them out, surprised to see that such filthy things belonged to her. They were the hands of the competent, capable woman she had been during the war. The woman she wanted to be again. "Yes. They're quite lovely, aren't they?" She laughed and waved them at Bobby as if threatening to rub dirt on him.

He darted away, shrieking with delight at this new game. Robbie joined them, and the three of them ran around the yard in circles, laughing with glee.

Audrey knew what she needed to do. She would let Eve continue to be Mrs. Robert Barrett with her country-club friends and their tennis games and sailing lessons. Robert didn't want this life for himself or his son, and neither did Audrey. In fact, Robert would be disappointed in her if she took the easy way out instead of moving forward on her own. She thought of Alfie and how their father's wealth had poisoned him, becoming more important to him than lasting love. Audrey would find a way to support herself and Bobby and teach him to value the right things. She would teach him to give, not take.

A ripple of excitement coursed through Audrey. She would tell Eve what she had decided the moment she returned.

⁂

Eve sat in the woods with the lamb on her lap as Tom hurried toward her. "Audrey? What in the world . . . ?" She must have looked a mess with her tear-streaked face and rumpled clothes. But Eve couldn't stop smiling.

"Are you looking for your lost lamb?" she asked, stroking its head.

"Yes, but . . . are you all right? What are you doing here? Where are your shoes?"

"It's a long story," she said, wiping her tears. "Do you have time to hear it? I need to ask your advice. I'm in a bit of a mess."

"Sure." He sank down on the ground facing her. "I could tell you were worried about something when you came over the other day. I hope your friend didn't bring bad news from home."

"To be honest, she dropped a bombshell into my life." Eve

drew a steadying breath. "You've been a good friend to Robbie and me . . . which may not be true when you hear what I have to tell you."

"You can trust me, Audrey."

"I've made a mess of things, and I don't know what to do. Please promise you won't hate me when I tell you."

"I promise."

"Cross your heart and hope to die?"

Tom smiled and drew an X over his heart. "Cross my heart and hope to die."

"I'm trapped in a web of lies, Tom. I'm not really Audrey Barrett. I'm—"

"Eve Dawson."

She went cold, as if a chilling wind had blown through the woods. "Did someone tell you?"

"No. I figured it out all by myself."

"How . . . ? When . . . ?"

"I've been suspicious for some time, but I think I knew for sure on Robbie's birthday when I watched you climb that tree down by the creek."

She looked away, afraid to face him. And Tom was only the first of many people to learn the truth.

"There were a few other clues I picked up on," he continued. "Like your freckles—Louis said Eve had beautiful freckles. But even if I'd guessed right, I figured you had your reasons for saying you were Audrey, and those reasons were none of my business."

Eve felt relieved—and yet terrified. "I'm tired of all the lies, Tom, but I don't know how to fix them. I never dreamed that Audrey would show up here in America. She's the woman who was at my house the other day, in case you haven't guessed. She came to visit the Barretts while I was using their pool—the long-lost

410 · IF I WERE YOU

daughter-in-law and grandson. Thankfully, Mrs. Barrett wasn't home."

"Audrey didn't know you'd taken her place?"

"No. She decided to stay in England after Robert died. I didn't steal her life, Tom; she threw it away. I fished the papers from the rubbish bin and took her identity because I had no family, no place to go, and no way to support my son. Now she's here."

He was quiet for a moment before saying, "May I ask you a question? And you don't have to answer it if you don't want to."

Eve shrugged. "Sure, go ahead." Her life and the lies she'd told were already laid bare before this kind, sweet man.

"Is Louis Dubois Robbie's father?"

"I suppose that's obvious, too?"

"Only because I know Louis so well."

Eve lowered her head again, unable to face him. She was sorry for ever starting this conversation. Yet the truth was the only path to forgiveness.

"Louis and I had a long talk after the war ended," Tom continued. "He said he needed to confess something, so he told me about you. How he'd fallen in love with you without ever intending to. How there was no hope of ever being with you because of Jean and the baby. He was riddled with guilt for betraying Jean, and he asked me if he should come clean and confess everything to her."

"And you told him not to."

"I told him he should confess to God but not to Jean. God would forgive him, but Jean might never get over his betrayal. I don't think it's right to unburden your own heart by laying the load on someone else's. Some secrets are better left untold."

Eve nodded. She'd given Louis the same advice. "You can't imagine how hard it is to live with the guilt of something like this," she said.

"Does Louis know he has a son?" Tom asked.

She shook her head. "The truth would ruin his life and destroy his family. I can't do that to him. I've already ruined my own life—except it isn't completely ruined because Robbie is the best thing that ever happened to me."

"He's a great kid. You're a wonderful mother."

"But I'm so ashamed," she said, her tears starting again. "It's bad enough that everyone will know that I lied about who I am, but even worse that you know I committed—" *Adultery.* She couldn't say the word. She wiped her tears and lifted her head again. "Louis and I made a terrible mistake. We never meant for it to happen."

"We've all done things we're ashamed of, Eve. Every last one of us."

"But my sins are piled a mile high! And now Audrey is here with Robert's son, and my sins will all be exposed. The Barretts are going to hate me for lying to them. They love Robbie and they think he's their grandson. And they've been so good to us. But it's all been a lie! My house and my car belong to Audrey. The life insurance and trust fund are hers. I know the right thing to do is to leave town, but where can I go? How will Robbie and I live? I have no one! Nothing!"

"Hey . . . hey . . . don't cry," he said, pulling her into his arms. The lamb squirmed and bleated, pinned between them.

"I'm sorry, Tom. I'm so very, very sorry. Your mother is such a saint. She'll be horrified to learn what kind of person I really am. And you've done so much for Robbie and me because you thought we were Robert's wife and son. I don't know how you and your family and everyone else will ever forgive me. I wouldn't blame any of you for walking away from me."

"None of us is in a position to throw stones."

"You haven't done anything this bad, I'm sure!"

"I'll tell you the same thing I told Louis. God will forgive you if you ask Him to. And once Jesus takes away your guilt, you can start all over again. Your past is forgiven and forgotten by God." He released her and handed her his handkerchief. "You want my advice?" he asked.

"Yes," she replied, sniffling. "Please."

"I think you should tell everyone the truth, just like you told me. The people who know you and love you may be shocked and surprised, but they won't stop loving you and Robbie. That includes me and my parents and the Barretts."

"Are you sure about that?"

"Yeah. I am. Jesus said we have to forgive others if we want Him to forgive us. Besides, you're part of our lives now. We know the funny, charming, wonderful woman you are, and it doesn't matter what your real name is."

Eve wasn't convinced. People hated being deceived, hated liars. "I don't know where Robbie and I will go. There's nothing for me to return to in England."

"Well, I'm selfish enough to hope you'll stay here. But I suppose the answer depends on Audrey."

Eve's future, Robbie's future, rested in Audrey's hands.

"From what Bob and Louis told me, I always thought you and Audrey were as close as sisters. How did that change?"

"We were close when we were children. Then we drifted apart . . . Then the war drew us together again." Eve paused, remembering the endless years of war and how they had shaped the two of them, binding them close. She remembered her terror when the V-1 rocket exploded and she thought Audrey would die. "The truth is, I don't know what happened to us. We came to a fork in the road and we chose different directions. Our friendship has survived a lot, but I don't think it will survive this." She rested her hand on Tom's arm as she looked up at him. "Please, Tom. Please don't tell anyone else the truth until I decide what I'm going to do."

"It's your story, Audrey—or I should say Eve? It's not mine to tell." He stood and offered Eve a hand to help her up. "Let's get both of you home," he said. He lifted the lamb and put it over his shoulders, the way the Good Shepherd in Granny Maud's picture did. The message was as vivid to Eve as if God had spoken it aloud. He had forgiven her. And now she needed to ask Audrey for forgiveness.

"How did you get here?" Tom asked. "Where's your car? And your shoes?"

"I parked on the road, back through the woods . . . some-where . . ." She glanced around, not sure which direction she had come. She hadn't followed a path.

"It might be easier to walk back the way I came, and I'll drive you to your car. Can you manage in bare feet? Or should I carry you instead of Cloudy?"

Eve laughed. "I can manage."

They took their time, with Eve watching where she put her feet. She was limping, her feet scratched and sore, by the time they reached the farmyard.

"Give me a minute to lock Cloudy in the barn," Tom said. "She'll think I'm punishing her but it's for her own good, to keep her safe."

The lamb protested, bleating loudly. Might the Good Shepherd also be acting for Eve's own good?

"Climb into my truck," Tom said when he returned. "I'll duck in the house and get the keys." He was carrying a small basket of strawberries when he came out. "My mother picked these this morning. She wants you and Robbie to have them." Eve gripped the basket in both hands, tears blurring the road as they drove. They found her car a short distance away.

"I know you have a lot to think about," Tom said before she got out. "But I just want to say . . . I'm glad you're not Audrey Barrett, lady aristocrat and the Barretts' daughter-in-law. It means I might stand a chance with you." He leaned close and kissed her cheek. Tom's words rested gently on Eve's bruised heart as she drove home.

She arrived to find Audrey chasing their sons around the front yard, her hands and the front of her dress black with filth. "Audrey? What's going on?"

"Mummy changed the flat tire on a great big car!" Bobby announced.

"Mrs. West's car," Robbie added.

"She did what?"

Audrey laughed, panting to catch her breath. "You should see your face! You look so shocked."

"I am shocked."

Tears filled Audrey's eyes. "We need to talk, Eve."

"Yes, Audrey. We do."

30

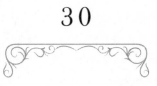

"Have you been changing tires, too?" Audrey asked. "You looked beautifully groomed when you left here this morning, and now . . ." Eve was disheveled, barefoot. She carried her nylons, red shoes, and crinoline in one hand, the string of pearls and a basket of strawberries in the other. Her pretty red-and-white polka-dot dress was rumpled and stained, her eyes red as if she'd been weeping.

"I guess I chose the wrong clothes for a walk in the woods," she said with a half smile.

"So I see. Good thing your friends Phyllis and Doris didn't see you this way. They paid a visit to talk you into joining their tennis league."

"Oh no," Eve groaned.

"When they were ready to leave, their front tire was flat—so I changed it. They were appalled. From the looks on their faces, I might have stripped naked and danced in the street."

"You really changed a flat tire for them?"

"I did. And I'm quite proud of myself, too."

Eve released a long sigh. "Listen, I've been doing a lot of thinking, Audrey—"

"So have I," she interrupted. "And before you say anything else, you need to know that I want you to keep my name."

"What?"

"No one ever needs to know the truth. You can be Audrey Barrett and live in this house and keep your country-club membership and all the rest. I don't want any of it." Saying the words out loud brought Audrey enormous relief. And enormous fear. The summer sun felt hot in the shadeless yard.

"Are you serious?"

"Very serious."

"Why would you do that?"

"For selfish reasons, really. Robert didn't want this life and neither do I. The weight of people's expectations is too heavy here. The war freed me from that burden and I don't ever want to carry it again."

"That's very generous of you, Audrey, but as it happens, I don't want to be you anymore. I'm going to tell everyone the truth."

"Why?"

"Because it's wrong to keep living a lie. I want to be myself and make my own decisions and run barefoot through the woods whenever I feel like it, and maybe . . . just maybe, fall in love again."

"Then let's both be ourselves," Audrey said. "The women we became during the war. We were brave and unselfish and determined—and we were best friends. I don't know what happened to those women, but we need to find them again."

"You're right. Listen, this is too big to talk about out here," Eve said, linking arms with Audrey. "Let's change our clothes and wash up. There's someplace I need to take you before you make any more decisions."

Audrey's heart plummeted when Eve drove the car through the

gates of a cemetery a short time later. Insects buzzed and droned in the summer heat. Sweat pasted Audrey's skin to the car's upholstery. She didn't want to move.

"Mommy, can I go see the angel statues?" Robbie asked.

"Yes, you may," Eve replied. She got out of the car and opened the rear door for the boys.

Robbie started across the grass, then turned to Bobby. "Wanna see them, too? Come on." Audrey was surprised when Bobby followed him. She pried herself from the car.

"I've noticed your son has an American accent," she told Eve.

"It's dreadful, isn't it?" Eve linked arms with her again. "Are you ready for this?" Audrey could only nod, her tears already starting. Eve halted beside a dark granite marker with Robert's name engraved on it. Audrey fell to her knees. Her tears flowed the moment her forehead touched the gravestone. The words of Robert's favorite poem echoed through her heart:

I love thee with the breath,
Smiles, tears, of all my life; and, if God choose,
I shall but love thee better after death.

Eve sat on the grass beside her, rubbing her back as Audrey wept. When she finally lifted her head and wiped her eyes, she saw that Eve was crying, too. She handed a basket of strawberries to Audrey. "Here. I think we need these."

Audrey managed a smile as she ate one. "Robert and I had so many plans for our life together."

"And I'm guessing it wasn't the life I've been living in your place."

"No. He didn't want our son to grow up the way he did, pressured into joining the country club and the family's law firm."

"What did Robert hope for *you*, Audrey?" she asked softly.

She exhaled. "That I would learn to be myself, not bowing to anyone's pressure. . . . I wanted to become a nurse after the war. Robert said we could find a nursing school here where I could study. He encouraged me to . . ." She couldn't finish.

"You can still pursue that plan. You have a house and a car and enough money to live on and go to nursing school. Dream big, Audrey."

The boys came running back before she could reply. "What's wrong, Mummy?" Bobby asked when he saw Audrey's tears.

She pulled him close, holding him tightly for a moment. "Remember the picture of your father that I showed you? This is where he's buried. I'm crying because I miss him. But only his body is here. Your father is in heaven with the Savior he loved."

"Is he an angel?"

"No, but he's with the angels." She handed him a strawberry. "Here. These are the best medicine for tears."

Robbie took one, too. "There's a statue of a soldier over there," he told Bobby. "Wanna see it?" Bobby nodded and they took off running again.

"You must come here a lot," Audrey said.

"With Robert's mother, yes." They were silent for a moment as the peace of the quiet cemetery stole over them. "Audrey? Will you please forgive me for stealing your identity?"

Audrey nodded as she took Eve's hand. "The greater sin was mine. You're here because of my mistakes. Forgive me for letting you walk away. For judging you harshly because of Louis and Harry. I was cold and critical—like my mother. I had Wellingford Hall but you had nothing. Forgive me for not offering to stick together until we both figured out what came next."

"Oh, Audrey . . ." They held each other for a long moment. Then they each smiled and ate another strawberry.

The boys came hurtling back, panting as they flopped onto the grass. Audrey brushed her son's sweaty hair from his forehead. "When they were babies, I remember wishing they could grow up to be friends. Like we were . . . like their fathers were."

"Maybe they can," Eve murmured. She passed the strawberries to their sons. "Here, let's finish these."

The car was sweltering when they climbed back inside. Everyone rolled down their windows. "How is your courage holding out?" Eve asked.

"Pretty well. It's funny, but changing that tire this morning gave me strength I'd forgotten I had."

"Good. Because our next stop is going to be difficult for both of us."

"Where are we going?"

"To see Mrs. Barrett. I need to confess what I've done and ask her to forgive me. Then I'll introduce her to her real daughter-in-law and grandson."

"Oh, Eve . . . I—I don't know . . ."

"She's a wonderful woman, Audrey. She raised Robert to be the man he became, didn't she? I've often thought she's the mother you deserved to have."

"But look what I'm wearing! I'm a mess—"

"Audrey, stop. She won't judge you. She'll love you because her son loved you."

Audrey couldn't imagine it would be that way. Fear of facing the Barretts, fear that they blamed her for Robert's death had kept her from coming to America four years ago.

Robbie bolted through the door and straight into Mrs. Barrett's arms when they arrived. "Nana! I missed you!" Mrs. Barrett knelt to hug him tightly, and Audrey saw the warm, loving mother she'd yearned for all her life.

"Sorry to arrive without any warning," Eve said. "Do you have time to talk? I want you to meet my friend."

"Yes, of course, dear. Come in." Mrs. Barrett led them into the living room and invited them to sit. It was a cold, uncomfortable place, an imitation of a grand manor house like Wellingford Hall with three separate seating areas in the vast room. It didn't seem to fit the warm, smiling woman who'd greeted them. Audrey couldn't take her gaze off Robert's mother. Her thick, wavy hair resembled his, but with gray threads woven through it. She had Robert's dark eyes, his gentle smile. "Would you like something cold to drink?" she asked.

"No, please don't fuss," Eve said. "I just need to say what I've come to tell you." She drew a deep breath and let it out in a rush.

This must be so difficult for her, Audrey thought.

"I've come to beg you to forgive me, Mom. I've done a terrible, unforgivable thing. . . . I'm not really Robert's wife, Audrey. She is."

Mrs. Barrett stared at Audrey, stunned. She suddenly looked older than she had a moment ago. Audrey's pulse sped up, afraid for Eve.

"And Robbie isn't Robert's son. He is." Eve gestured to Bobby.

"I—I don't understand . . ." Mrs. Barrett had been standing, but she sank down on the edge of the nearest chair as if her legs wouldn't hold her.

"I know what I did was horrible," Eve said, "and that I don't deserve your forgiveness, and I'm so very, very sorry!"

"But . . . but why would you do such a thing?"

"I was desperate. I had no home, no family, no way to support myself and my son. I know that doesn't excuse all my lies, but at the time, I didn't know what else to do."

Mrs. Barrett turned to Audrey. "And you agreed to this?" she asked.

"No!" Eve said before she could reply. "Audrey had no idea what I'd done. We were best friends during the war, and when she decided not to come to America after Robert died, I stole her immigration papers and came in her place. It was a terrible, terrible thing to do, and I'm so sorry for deceiving you. But please don't blame Audrey. She didn't know anything about it until she arrived in America a few days ago."

Audrey saw the pain and hurt in Mrs. Barrett's expression and feared her reaction would be unkind. She and Eve both seemed shattered. "I'm at fault, too, Mrs. Barrett," Audrey quickly said. "Eve was my best friend and I should have helped her. I shouldn't have left her with no other choice."

"I . . . I don't know what to say . . ."

"You've been so good to Robbie and me," Eve said. "And I'm so sorry for what I've done. I never intended to hurt you or take advantage of your kindness and generosity. I just . . . I just wanted a home."

The children were watching the drama and didn't seem to understand what was happening. Eve's son moved to nestle close to Mrs. Barrett and took her hand. "Don't be sad, Nana. Are you sad?"

She bent to kiss the top of his red head. "I'm not sad, darling. Just . . . surprised." She pulled Robbie close for a hug, then faced Bobby, who stood a few feet away near Audrey's chair. Tears filled Mrs. Barrett's eyes. "He looks just like Robert did at this age. May I give you a hug, too, darling?" He hesitated for a long moment, and Mrs. Barrett smiled. "Robert was the same way. He always needed to think things through before he tried anything new."

Audrey's tears flowed when her son finally moved toward his grandmother and allowed her to hold him and kiss his forehead. Family. They would be part of a loving family, something Audrey had wished for all her life. She remembered the frigid scene at her uncle's house and knew she had made the right decision.

"Are you going to be his nana, too?" Robbie asked Mrs. Barrett.

"Yes, sweet boy. I'm both of your nanas." She pulled a handkerchief from her pocket and wiped her eyes.

Eve knelt beside her. "Can you ever forgive me for lying to you?" she asked.

Mrs. Barrett stroked Robbie's head. "This has come as quite a shock, of course. But in a way . . . You know, I suspected you weren't Audrey the first time I saw you and this redheaded boy of yours. You didn't resemble the photograph of Audrey that Robert had shown us. But then I took Robbie into my arms, and from that moment, I didn't care who you were. My husband and I were grieving, and you brought new life into our home. And hope. You and Robbie filled the hole in my heart and helped me heal." She kissed Robbie's hair again. "I'm . . . I'm shocked and . . . and disappointed in you. And I feel like such a fool for allowing myself to be deceived."

"I'm so sorry," Eve murmured.

"I'm . . . I'm going to need some time . . ." She wiped her eyes again. "And yet, when all is said and done, you and Robbie are part of my life now, whether you're my real daughter-in-law or not."

Eve closed her eyes, and Audrey saw her relief. Then she opened them again. "What about Dad—Mr. Barrett? Will he—?"

"He'll be shocked, of course. I don't know how he'll react. But deep down, he loves you, too, dear. And Robbie is the best thing that ever happened to him."

Eve went into Mrs. Barrett's arms, murmuring, "Thank you . . . thank you."

When they'd parted again, Audrey knew what she needed to do. "Mrs. Barrett, I need to ask you to forgive me, too. It was selfish of me not to come four years ago. You'd lost your only child, and Bobby and I were all you had. But I—I was afraid you would blame me for his death. If he had married Linda instead of me . . ."

"I never felt that way. Every mother wants her child to be happy, and I could tell from the way Robert talked about you that he loved you very much. His relationship with Linda had always been tumultuous. I didn't want Robert to go with her that night. I—I wish . . ." She couldn't finish.

"I know why he went with her, Mrs. Barrett. Before he left London, Robert told me he needed to see Linda face-to-face and apologize for hurting her. He wanted to ask her to forgive him."

"That sounds like Robert," she replied.

"Yes. We can be very proud of him. He taught me not to question God's ways. But to trust Him."

Mrs. Barrett closed her eyes, nodding as if deep in thought. "And now look," she said when she opened them again. "It seems I've been doubly blessed, with two grandsons."

"Why is everybody crying?" Robbie asked.

"These are tears of joy, honey, not sadness. Come, let's sit out on the patio and get to know each other better."

"With Popsicles?" Robbie asked, hopping up and down.

"Yes, sweet boy. With Popsicles for everyone!"

31

"Mrs. Barrett is a lovely woman," Audrey said when they were in the car again. Eve could only nod, still too emotional to speak. "That took a lot of courage, Eve. You're still the bravest woman I know."

"Thanks." She exhaled, then said, "You won't need courage for this last visit, but I will." Her heart lay heavily in her chest just thinking about it.

"Where are we going?"

"Out to the farm. I want you to meet Robert's friend Tom Vandenberg. Remember the Famous Four?"

"Yes, of course."

"He's one of them. He's been like a father to Robbie and a good friend to me. Probably my best friend. I told Tom this morning who I really am—although he said he'd already guessed. Now I need to tell his mother."

"Are you close to her, too?"

"Yes. She reminds me of Granny Maud. And she's become a

second granny to Robbie." Eve could only hope that she would be as gracious and accepting as Mrs. Barrett had been.

"Shall I wait in the car while you go inside?" Audrey asked when they parked behind the farmhouse.

"Absolutely not. The Vandenbergs are part of your new family, too. You'll love them, Audrey. And they're going to love you and Bobby. . . . That's Tom, coming out of the barn." Robbie leaped from the car and dashed across the driveway to him, shouting for Bobby to come with him and see the lamb.

"Another tall, good-looking American," Audrey said with a smile. "Is there something between you two?"

"Maybe . . . It would have been impossible when I was pretending to be you."

"But now?"

"I don't know." Eve felt her face growing warm. "We'll see." She asked Tom to show the boys around the farm while she and Audrey went inside to talk with his mother. He nodded. He would know why she had come.

Mrs. Vandenberg was boiling jars for strawberry jam when she welcomed them into the well-worn farmhouse kitchen. "This is my friend who recently arrived from England," Eve told her.

"Welcome, my dear," Mrs. Vandenberg said. If she thought it was odd that Eve didn't give Audrey's name, she was polite enough not to say anything about it. "How did you like my fresh strawberries?" she asked. "They taste so good when they're right off the vine, don't they?"

"They were wonderful. We gobbled them down," Eve replied.

Mrs. Vandenberg offered them iced tea and biscuits—what she called cookies—but Eve wanted to get this over with.

"I have something I need to confess, and I wanted you to hear the truth from me before . . . well, before all the gossip starts because I . . . I admire you so much, and . . ." Eve's throat closed and she couldn't finish.

Mrs. Vandenberg sat down at the table beside Eve and took her hand. "What is it, Audrey, dear? I hope you know you can tell me anything."

Eve swallowed, pulling herself together. "Yes . . . well . . . for starters—my name isn't really Audrey. It's Eve. Eve Dawson." It felt surprisingly good to say it after all this time. "This is the real Audrey Barrett. I've been pretending to be her because I had no home and no family and no way to support my son. Audrey is my best friend and she had decided to stay in England after Robert died—until now. She had no idea I was here, pretending to be her."

Mrs. Vandenberg squeezed Eve's hand, and when Eve dared to look up at her, she saw kindness in Mrs. Vandenberg's eyes. "How tragic that there was no one you could turn to for help when you needed it."

"I'm so sorry for lying to you and Tom and everyone else—and not just because my lies are going to be exposed, but because I know that what I've done is very wrong. Can you ever forgive me for lying to you?"

"Of course, dear one. You and Robbie have been a blessing in our lives, no matter what your names are."

Eve felt a measure of relief, but the photograph of Louis's two daughters still scorched her soul. There was more she needed to confess. "I—I've done other terrible things . . . I was never married to Robbie's father. He had a wife and daughter." She lowered her head to the table, resting it on her arms, unable to face anyone. "I've asked Jesus to forgive me, but . . . but I don't blame Him for punishing me now. I deserve it."

The kitchen was quiet except for the water bubbling in the pot on the stove. Mrs. Vandenberg gently rubbed Eve's back and allowed her to cry. Then she said, "Eve, dear, I want you to look at me." She waited until Eve lifted her head. "If you have confessed your sins and laid them at Jesus' feet and asked for forgiveness, then it is done. Finished. You are a new woman in Christ. The old is gone. It's as if you've swapped places with Jesus, and God sees His righteousness whenever He looks at you. You get to start all over again, and you don't need to feel ashamed anymore."

"How can it be that simple?" she said, wiping her eyes. "I've made such a mess of my life—and Robbie's."

"Well, our sins have consequences, and you will still have to sort through them all and make as many things right as you can."

"I'll help you, Eve," Audrey said. "We'll figure things out together, like we always have in the past. You won't be alone ever again. And neither will I."

"And I'm here for you, too," Mrs. Vandenberg added. "But, Eve, listen, now. Sometimes the hardest part of forgiveness is forgiving yourself—and truly believing in Christ's forgiveness. There will be days when you'll be tempted to doubt that you are a new person, days when you'll be very hard on yourself. Especially as you face the painful consequences of your mistakes. And other people's disapproval. But there is a Scripture verse I hope you'll memorize that says, 'If any man be in Christ, he is a new creature: old things are passed away; behold, all things are become new.' You are loved and forgiven, dear one."

They spent another hour with Mrs. Vandenberg, who prayed for Eve and Audrey and both of their sons. When Eve walked out into the waning sunshine of a beautiful summer day, she felt as if she could fly. She introduced Audrey to Tom, then rounded up the boys—who were both reluctant to leave the farm—and piled everyone into the car. For Eve, the day had been long and event-filled, beginning with her visit with Louis and ending with the

428 · IF I WERE YOU

relief of knowing that her life of lies and playacting was over. She was forgiven. She could be herself again.

"Do you ever talk about the war?" Audrey asked as Eve drove toward home. "What we did, what we experienced?"

"No. And the funny thing is, no one ever asks me about it. They have the attitude here in America that the war is over and done with, and we'd all be better off to forget about it."

"That isn't right—for us or for the soldiers who fought in it. We need to talk about it. It changed us. We're different people than we were before the war, and if we simply go back to being the girls we used to be, we're not being true to ourselves."

"During that last year of the war I felt so numb, so deadened by everything," Eve said, remembering. "I longed to feel alive again. That's why . . . well, that's when I got involved with Louis. I'm not justifying it, but that's what the war did to me. I lost my faith. I blamed God for the evil in the world instead of seeing that evil is inside us. I envied your life, Audrey. You had money, an education, a beautiful home, servants . . . If I had been raised in a family like yours, maybe Alfie would have married me."

"That's funny," Audrey replied with a little laugh. "I envied *your* life. You had so many friends. Everyone loved you. You were so free, so happy. And I longed for a mother like yours. I'll always be sorry that Mother's selfishness caused your mother's death."

Eve didn't want to hold on to her resentment toward Lady Rosamunde any longer. As Tom had said, if she wanted God to forgive her, she needed to forgive others—the same way that Mrs. Barrett and Mrs. Vandenberg and Tom had forgiven her. "My mum chose to stay with yours, Audrey. I think it was for the same reasons that Robert got into the car with Linda. It was her way of showing God's love. I'm proud of Mum."

They came down the hill into town, nearing home, but Eve

didn't want to return to the tiny, claustrophobic house just yet. She wanted to enjoy the blue sky and late-afternoon sun for a little while longer, the cool breezes that blew through the car's open windows. She turned at the first intersection and headed out of town again. "We're going on a road trip," she announced. "Get the map out of the glove box, Audrey, and let's see where this road takes us." Audrey raised her eyebrows as if asking if Eve was sure. "Find us a route. You were always better with maps than I was." Audrey pulled it out and unfolded it on her lap, her finger tracing the blue coastline as she searched for their town. "I loved driving, didn't you, Audrey?"

"Most of the time. I have to admit, it was a great feeling to be behind the wheel, heading someplace new."

"I've loved driving since the first day Williams let me try it."

"If I recall, my first driving lesson was under very different circumstances."

"That's right!" Eve said with a laugh. "I made you drive home from Dover, with Army roadblocks and no signposts or head-lamps. But you did great once you got the hang of it. Want to drive now? I'll pull over. This is your car, after all."

"Not on your life! They drive on the wrong side of the road over here. I'll need a bit of practice before I'm ready to give it a go."

"Remember driving in the blackout? We would study the map to see all the possible routes, but once we started off, we could only see what was right in front of us."

"It's a bit like life, don't you think? We make plans, but we really can only see a little way ahead. The thing was, we had a pur-pose back then. A goal to accomplish. Ever since the war ended, I've been fooled into thinking that life was like a voyage on an ocean liner, and the seas should always be smooth. Whenever a storm hit, I wanted to hunker down and wait until it blew over and everything was calm again. Wellingford Hall became my refuge. But ships have destinations, Eve. They're going somewhere, and storms are part of the journey. I haven't had a purpose since the war ended."

"I know what you mean. We fought the war and helped save England. We accomplished something big, and now . . ."

"Let's find a new purpose, Eve!"

The notion excited Eve. Something had been missing in her life for the past four years, in spite of how comfortable it had been. "Right, then! We're off!" She pressed down on the accelerator and the car sped up.

"Where are we going, Mommy?" Robbie asked.

"We're off to find the future. You boys keep an eye out for it, okay?"

"What does it look like?" Bobby asked.

Audrey laughed and leaned toward Eve. "He thinks we're talking about an animal he can spot like a cow or a sheep. . . . I don't know what it looks like, Bobby," she called back to him. "We'll have to wait and see."

Eve grinned. "But I'm sure we'll know it when we find it!"

Prologue

THE NETHERLANDS, MAY 1945

Every sound in the coal-black night seemed magnified as Lena lay awake in bed, waiting. She heard the quiet rustlings of the shadow people as they crept through the darkness downstairs in her farmhouse. The creak of the barn door and whisper of hay as they moved through her barn on this moonless night. The shadow people were also waiting. Did they hate it as much as she did?

The war had taught Lena DeVries to do many things. Hard, impossible things. She had learned to be courageous, propelled by adrenaline and faith. She'd even learned to face death, gripping the Savior's hand. But waiting was the hardest lesson of all. Every minute seemed like an hour. Every hour stretched endlessly. The sun stood still in the sky during the day then took its time dawning after each endless night—a night like this one. Sometimes she would hold her breath without realizing it. Other times, she would find herself hoping against all reason that her husband, Pieter, was alive and would come home and she could hold him in her arms. Or hoping that her daughter Ans and son Wim were still alive and would return. She knew that if one of them walked through

432

her door, her joy would swallow up the long months of waiting. If they ever did return.

The past seven days had been the longest week in all of Lena's forty-five years. Tonight, her imagination partnered with fear, squeezing her heart dry, extinguishing hope. She released her breath with a sigh and rolled over in bed, whispering a silent prayer for Pieter and Ans and Wim. And for all the shadow people who waited in the darkness with her.

Sleep was impossible. She hadn't slept soundly since the Nazis invaded five years ago. She rose from her bed, careful not to awaken her daughters Maaike and Bep, asleep in the bed beside her where Pieter should be. Lena kept her girls close to her side these days. She pulled a sweater over her nightgown and felt her way downstairs, familiar with every narrow step on the steep, angled stairs. She halted at the bottom. A shadow moved around her kitchen as if searching for something. Her heart leaped. "Pieter?" she whispered.

The shadow turned. It was Wolf, her contact in the Dutch Resistance. She didn't know his real name. It was safer that way. "Did I wake you?" he whispered. "I'm sorry. I was looking for a pencil. I wanted to leave you a note."

"Do you have news of my husband?"

"No. I'm sorry. But I do have good news. Allied troops are in Holland. Canadian tanks have liberated some of the towns. Here's the latest newspaper." He pulled the flimsy underground newssheet from his pocket and handed it to Lena. She glanced at it, then instinctively rolled it up so it would fit inside her bicycle frame. She would hide it there from the Nazis and deliver it to her friends in the village.

"But the Allies haven't come this far yet?" she asked.

"Soon. I came to tell you and the others that it won't be long. Maybe even tomorrow."

Three more shadows slipped into the kitchen as Lena and Wolf talked. They left their hiding places only at night and had to disappear before dawn. How they must long to feel the sun on their faces again.

"This isn't another false alarm like last fall, is it?" one of the shadows whispered. Lena remembered "Mad Tuesday," when rumors of liberation had swept the country. There had been panic among the Nazis and rejoicing among the Dutch people. Many Nazi occupiers and their collaborators had fled east. When it proved to be a false alarm, they returned. Hope withered.

"This time it's true," Wolf said. "I saw the Canadian tanks myself." Lena closed her eyes for a moment. Would the waiting truly be over?

"How will we know when it's safe to come out?" another shadow asked.

"They'll ring the church bells in town. . . . I have to go," Wolf said, backing toward the door. "I need to tell the others."

"Wait," Lena said. "Are you hungry? Have you eaten?" Wolf was shadow-thin. The deep hollows on the planes of his face made him appear skeletal in the darkness. Thousands of people who were trapped in the cities were dying of starvation every day. Cities like Leiden, where Lena's daughter Ans had lived.

Wolf shook his head. "You already have so many mouths to feed."

"Then one more won't make a difference." She opened the warming oven above the stove and pulled out a baked potato, wrapped in a cloth to keep it warm. "Here." She pushed it into his hands. "I only wish I had more to offer you." The potato was small and shriveled, one of the last ones from her depleted root cellar. "Thank you for coming, Wolf. I'll spread the news." He had given Lena hope. And hope would make waiting harder still.

She sat down at the kitchen table with the shadow people after Wolf left, talking about the war and reading the underground newspaper to them while they each ate a potato and a little boiled cabbage. She knew only their false names—Max and his wife, Ina—and that they were Jewish. Max forged false ID cards for the Resistance during the night, down in Lena's root cellar.

When it was light enough to see, Lena helped the family crawl back into their hiding place behind the piano in her front room. Pieter had boarded up a closet on the other side of the wall as if it had never been there, then built a secret door leading into it through the lower panel of their upright piano. The bass keys no longer worked, but the rest of the piano keys did. Few people knew about the secret place, including Lena's two younger daughters, or that this Jewish couple had lived there for more than a year.

Lena put the rest of the baked potatoes and a half loaf of bread she'd been saving in a basket, and carried it through the door that led from the kitchen into the barn. She never knew how many shadows were hiding in her barn, or how long they would stay. More were hidden at the very top of the old windmill that pumped water for their fields. The Resistance would position the windmill blades to signal when it was safe for the shadow people to hide on her farm. Again, it was better for Lena not to know too much. She simply cooked whatever food she had and took it to them, asking the Lord to multiply it like the loaves and fishes.

Six men of various ages crept out of their hiding places in the barn as Lena sang a verse of the hymn that served as a signal. She read Wolf's newspaper to them as they ate. Four of the shadows were in their late teens—her son Wim's age. The other two looked like ordinary husbands and fathers. They were *onderduikers*, men who'd been forced to "dive under" to avoid being sent to German slave-labor camps. Some might be railroad workers who'd been ordered by the exiled Dutch government to go on strike to hinder the Nazis. The slender young man with wire-rimmed glasses and ebony hair was undoubtedly Jewish.

"What's the first thing you want to do once the Allies arrive and Holland is free?" she asked them.

"Go home," was their unanimous reply. The shadow men talked about the other things they missed as they finished their bread and potatoes, and about the food they hungered for.

"I heard that the Allies are giving out cigarettes," one of them said. "I'd give anything for a smoke."

At dawn, one of the shadow men offered to milk Lena's cow for her. "I grew up on a farm in Friesland," he said. "Milking her reminds me of home." He stroked the cow's shoulder as if greeting an old friend before straddling the milking stool. "Shall I let her out to graze when I'm finished?" he asked.

"No, she has to stay inside the barn again today. Three cows were killed in a neighboring village by a stray Nazi rocket. And with the Allies moving closer, there's always the danger of falling shrapnel from aerial battles overhead."

"Someone might steal your cow for food, too," another shadow said.

"Yes, there is that."

Lena gave her daughters some of the milk to drink with their breakfast. They looked thin and shadowlike, too. Wim and Ans had been plump and rosy-cheeked when they were their age. Before the war. When life was gentle and good. When food was plentiful. "I think we'll take the rest of the milk into town this morning," she told the girls, "and see what we can trade it for."

Little Elizabeth, whom they'd nicknamed Bep, bounced with excitement at the prospect of a trip into the village. She was four years old, and full of life and energy. "May I wear a bow in my hair?" she asked.

"Yes, why not? You'll look so pretty." Lena brushed Bep's long, dark hair after breakfast and tied a bright bow in it. It fell naturally into thick curls. "Do you want one, too?" she asked Maaike.

She shook her head. At eleven years old she was no longer interested in girlish bows. Lena braided Maaike's straw-blonde hair—the same color as her own—into a thick braid that fell nearly to her waist.

When it was time to go, Lena fetched her broken-down bicycle from the barn. The rubber tires were long gone, replaced with clunky wooden wheels that Pieter had made. In peacetime her bicycle would be considered a piece of junk—and it was—but at least the Nazis wouldn't confiscate it. She lifted little Bep onto the handlebars, and Maaike climbed onto the board Pieter had attached to the rear fender. Lena tied the two containers of milk to her body, hidden beneath her sweater and apron, and set off on the three-mile trip into the village.

The pastures between her farm and the town looked tired and pale this morning, like an invalid who'd lain in bed too long. More fenceposts were missing, and several more trees had disappeared, chopped down for fuel this past winter. They were calling that long, endless season the "Hunger Winter." With the railroad workers on strike, food had become so scarce in the cities that hundreds of starving people had staggered out to Lena's farm every week from Leiden or even Den Hague to beg for food. Her little nation would have much rebuilding to do once the war finally ended. But Lena suspected that the hardest task would be repairing the discord and mistrust among neighbors and even families. For the past five years, no one had known whom they could trust or who might sell their secrets to the Nazis to feed their starving children.

She and Pieter had known, when they'd hidden Jews and *onder-duikers*, that if they were discovered, they would be arrested and imprisoned.

Lena was nearly to town when she heard the glorious cacophony of church bells ringing in the distance. She slowed to a halt as joy leaped in her heart. "Listen, girls! Do you hear the bells?"

"But it isn't Sunday, Mama," Bep said.

"I know. It means the Netherlands is free! We're free!" Her breath caught in her throat. She was saying the words but could barely comprehend that they were true.

"Does that mean the soldiers will go away?" Maaike asked.

"Yes, they will be gone for good. The Netherlands will be free again!" She couldn't imagine it. Lena wondered if Maaike even remembered a time when Nazi soldiers and their roaring motorcycles weren't a common sight. She had been six years old when they'd invaded the Netherlands. Little Bep was too young to remember freedom at all.

Lena picked up her pace as she pedaled the last mile into town. The village square and the street in front of her father's church were packed with rejoicing people as if it were Easter Sunday. The church bells clamored so loudly they could probably be heard all the way out to her farm. Lena's friends and the neighbors she had known all her life were laughing and embracing each other, their faces streaming with tears of joy. Her cousin Truus pushed through the crowd and hugged Lena tightly, the milk cans clanking as the women rocked in place. "Isn't it wonderful, Lena? We're free! The Nazis are gone at last!"

"And look at all these people who must have been hidden," Lena said when Truus released her again. Crowded among the people she knew were strangers Lena had never seen before. Their milk-white skin and frail bodies told her they were shadow people.

"I had no idea so many of them were hiding right here in the village!"

"And do you notice who isn't here?" her cousin asked. "The filthy collaborators have all fled."

"What a relief." Lena wondered if they would face justice for what they'd done. They had much to atone for.

Lena had known these villagers all her life, had worshipped beside them in church every Sunday, and she knew that the war had brought tragedy into every life, every home. Now they were cheering and hugging each other, and asking, "Is it really over? Are they finally gone?" One of the elders from her father's church burst into song, and everyone joined in singing the words to the psalm: "'O God, our help in ages past, our hope for years to come; our shelter from the stormy blast, and our eternal home.'" Lena gripped Bep's hand and wiped tears as she sang. If only Lena's husband and father were here to see this. She needed to hurry home and tell her own shadow people the good news. Max and Ina could come out from behind the piano. The *onderduikers* could go home to their families. Maybe Pieter and Ans and Wim were on their way home right now.

She traded the milk for some cheese and a loaf of bread from the bakery. "You can carry these for me on the way home," she told her daughters. "There's no need to hide them anymore." Joy and hope warmed her like spring sunshine as she pedaled. The fields looked greener now than they had on the way into town. "You can come out! It's safe!" she called as she parked her bicycle in the barn. "The Netherlands is free!"

"You're sure?" a voice called.

"Very sure! Quick! Run over to the windmill and tell the others." Lena's daughters hovered close to her as shadows emerged from every corner of the barn. Maaike and Bep would have no idea who these men were. Lena laughed and motioned for them to follow her through the passageway to the kitchen, then into the front room. She bent down and rapped on the lower panel on the piano. "It's safe to come out! The Netherlands is liberated! We're free!" The girls watched in astonishment as the panel opened and Max and Ina emerged as if in a daze. Lena flung the front door wide for them and said, "Look! It's a glorious day! You can go outside at last!" They moved as if in a dream as they joined the other shadow people outside in the barnyard. Like the villagers, they gazed around in wonder, laughing and rejoicing. Ina dropped to her knees, her face hidden in her hands as she wept. Across the field, several men stood on the windmill's upper deck, cheering and lifting their faces to the sun. She waved to them from her front door.

"Who are all these people, Mama?" Maaike asked. She stood in the doorway beside Lena. "What are they doing here?"

"They were hiding from the Nazis. Papa said they could stay here with us, where it's safe. But they don't need to hide anymore." She looked around for Bep and saw her crouching down to peek beneath the piano.

"Look, Maaike!" Bep said. "There's a little room inside the piano, with blankets and a bookshelf and everything! Come and see!"

As Maaike went over to take a peek, Lena spotted the studio photograph of her family on top of the piano. She lifted it down to study her loved ones' faces. The photo had been taken in 1939 during a trip to Leiden, a year before the Nazi invasion, before any of them ever imagined they would be engulfed in a war. Her oldest daughter, Ans, had been eighteen—so beautiful with her pale-blonde hair and slender frame. Her bold smile and confident stance revealed her strong will. Wim stood beside his sister, already as tall as she was, his fair hair bleached nearly white by the sun. He'd been a curious eleven-year-old boy before the invasion, who loved to swim in the canals and tease his sisters. The war had forced Wim to become a man before his time. Five-year-old Maaike nestled on Lena's lap in the picture, her little surprise baby, born when Lena was thirty-four. Lena had convinced her father to pose with them for the family portrait too. He stood behind Wim and Ans, looking every inch the stern pastor. Or maybe he had simply been grieving the loss of Lena's mother, who had died a few months earlier. Pieter, the love of Lena's life, stood behind her with his hands resting on the back of her chair—his strong, calloused, sun-browned hands. Would she ever take those hands in hers again? Out of the six people in the photograph, only Lena and Maaike were left.

Jesus had told His followers, "Anyone who loves his father or mother more than Me is not worthy of Me; anyone who loves his son or daughter more than Me is not worthy of Me; and anyone who does not take his cross and follow Me is not worthy of Me." It was a hard, hard truth, put to the test by the fires of war.

Lena felt a tug on her skirt. Little Bep looked up at her with a worried expression. She was Lena's child by love if not by blood, and had come to them two years after the invasion. "Is Papa going to come home now?" she asked.

"And Wim and Ans, too?" Maaike added.

Lena didn't reply. She didn't know. A tendril of fear sprouted and curled through her, and she knew if she allowed it to grow, it would strangle her faith. She used to believe that the enemy of faith was doubt, but she'd learned during the war that faith's destroyer was fear. *"Let your fear drive you into the arms of God,"* her father had said.

"Well, we will hope and pray that they do come home," Lena replied.

"I miss Opa," Maaike said. She had pulled the photograph down to her level to look at it, pointing to her grandfather. Lena stroked her daughter's fair hair and thick braid.

"I miss him, too."

"Are you crying, Mama?" Bep asked. Lena quickly brushed away her tears.

"Sometimes we cry because we're happy."

"I'm happy, too." Bep wrapped her thin arms around Lena's legs and hugged her tightly. This child was so dear to Lena's heart. She couldn't love Bep more if she had come from her own womb.

But she hadn't.

And now, with the liberation, the truth would also come out of hiding, like the shadow people. Lena needed to prepare Bep for it. And to prepare herself. She needed to start now, before her courage failed. She set the photograph back in its place. "How would you girls like to help me dig for buried treasure?" she asked.

"Real treasure? Like in the book we read?" Maaike asked. Lena had read *Treasure Island* out loud to the girls to help pass the time after the village school was closed.

"Yes, but it isn't pirate treasure. Come with me." She fetched shovels and a pitchfork from the barn and carried them into the vegetable garden behind the kitchen. Lena had watched Pieter bury the cache late one night, digging the hole beside the corner fencepost so they could find it again. She went to the spot and shoved the pitchfork into the ground to loosen the soil. After a few turns of the spade, she heard the clunk of metal against metal.

"Here it is! Help me dig!" The girls bent down beside her, using their hands and a garden trowel to uncover two buried sacks.

Bep wiggled with excitement. "What is it, Mama? What's inside them?"

She tugged on the larger canvas sack and heaved it out of the hole, the metal rattling inside. "These are all of our pots and things made of copper and brass. The soldiers wanted to take them, so your papa buried them out here." She untied the bag and let the girls peek inside at the various buckets and pots and a brass tray, the copper tarnished a dull green color. Then she pulled out the smaller sack and brushed away the dirt. Inside was a wooden box.

"What's in the box, Mama?" Bep asked.

Lena looked at her daughter's beautiful face and dark eyes, and her heart squeezed. It had been hard for Lena to lie to Bep these past three years, but telling her the truth was going to be harder still—harder than Lena had ever imagined it would be on the day when Ans had first placed the little girl in her arms.

"You know that you came to live with us when you were a baby . . . ," Lena began. She brushed Bep's hair from her face, smoothing it back. She still wore the bow in it. "We've talked about what the word *adopted* means, remember?"

Bep nodded. "I had another mama before I came to live with you. And another papa."

"That's right. Well, they asked me to keep this box for you. They loved you very, very much. Every bit as much as Papa and I love you." Lena's throat tightened.

"But they weren't able to take care of me anymore," Bep said, repeating the story she'd been told. It was the first lie that would need to be replaced with the truth. Lena swallowed, remembering the grisly stories from the underground newspapers that revealed the horrifying truth about the Nazi atrocities. The truth about where the trains traveling east from Westerbork had carried Holland's Jews. Lena didn't know if Bep's parents had been among them.

"Let's take this into the house and wash our hands, and then we'll look inside the box together." Lena used their precious sliver of soap to scrub the dirt from Bep's hands, wondering how to explain to this child the evil that had forced her to hide and lie and pretend. How could Lena explain that while there was a chance her parents might be coming soon to take her home, there was also a chance that they might never come back? The nature of this war and the Nazi occupation had meant living a life of countless lies and deceptions. It meant asking few questions, accepting few answers, knowing it was better to know very little in case you were arrested and tortured. Should she shield Bep from the truth a little longer before telling her why her identity had to be buried inside this box for the past three years? How could Lena explain to this four-year-old why the Nazis had wanted to kill her when Lena didn't understand it herself?

But little Bep needed to be ready, whether her family came back or whether they didn't. She would need to mourn if they were dead, just as Lena would mourn if her loved ones in the portrait never returned. Mourning couldn't begin until she faced the truth. And her life couldn't move forward until she mourned. Lena glanced up at the photograph again. Even after she'd mourned, she would never leave these precious ones behind. They would always be part of her, carried in her heart as she moved forward from the place of grief.

With Maaike beside her on the sofa and little Bep on her lap, Lena opened the wooden box. Inside was a photograph album and a pair of silver candlesticks, tarnished black. "Your mama and papa gave you these pictures so you would remember who they are, and who you are." There was also a letter Bep's mother had written to Lena on ivory stationery. Lena remembered reading it on the night Bep came to her, three years ago, before Pieter buried it along with the box. She unfolded it and silently read it again:

Dear Mrs. DeVries,

In giving you my daughter, I'm giving you part of my heart. For however long this war lasts, you'll be the one who will watch her grow and teach her to skip and run and sing. You'll brush her hair in the morning, and hug her good night, and dry her tears. I pray that you will love her as if she is your own, and that she'll know comfort and security in your arms. If God wills it, we will meet one day, and I will be able to thank you for protecting my little girl. If He wills otherwise, I ask that you tell her about her father and me, Avraham and Miriam Leopold, through these photographs. Tell her that her Hebrew name is Elisheva, and that it means "God's promise." Tell her how much we loved her. And how very hard it was to let her go.

Lena refolded the letter, knowing how this mother must ache to hold her daughter in her arms. How many months had it been, now, since Lena had seen her own daughter Ans and son Wim? Lena understood the pain of loving a child so deeply and having to let her go. Ans and Wim had left Lena in a different way and for different reasons, but releasing a loved one to God's care, not knowing what that child's future would be, was an impossible choice for any mother to face.

"What are these?" Maaike asked, fingering the tarnished candlesticks.

"They're silver candlesticks. They'll be beautiful once we polish them." Lena set them and the metal box aside and opened the photograph album. The first three pictures were loose, not glued to the page. She read the writing on the back, translating the German. "This is your mother, Miriam Leopold, and your father, Avraham Leopold. Look, here they are holding you when you were a tiny baby."

Bep studied the pictures for a moment before reaching to turn the page.

"These are your grandparents," Lena continued, reading the captions. "Your grandfather was a professor at the university, see?" She pointed to a photograph of a distinguished-looking man in academic regalia. "This is your mother's home in Cologne, Germany." It was a mansion, three stories tall with stately pillars in front, shaded by tall trees. "This is your mama when she was a little girl. She looks like you, don't you think? Look, here she is on a holiday with her parents at Lake Konstanz."

Bep seemed overwhelmed by it all as they paged through photographs of aunts and uncles and cousins. She hadn't grasped the full meaning of the album yet. Between two of the pages, Lena found a sealed letter that Miriam had written to Bep. Lena set it aside, deciding to wait until Bep had more time to get to know the strangers in these photographs.

As they leafed through the album, Miriam slowly grew up and became a young woman, a solemn beauty with a shy smile and shining dark hair like Bep's. In many of the pictures, she was holding a violin. By the time they reached the last page, Miriam was a slender young adult, seated at a dining table, surrounded by her parents and aunts and uncles and cousins. The table was spread with a white tablecloth, flowers, platters of food, and crystal glass-ware. "Look what's in this picture . . . ," Lena, said, pointing. In the center of the table, with flames gleaming brightly, were the silver candlesticks.

Tears filled Lena's eyes at these glimpses of Miriam Leopold's life. The album painted a picture of a gracious, genteel life, a lov-ing family. But they were pictures of a world that had vanished in a whirlwind of flames and hatred.

A Note from the Author

I hope you enjoyed meeting Audrey and Eve and experiencing a bit of life in England during World War II. *If I Were You* began as a simple story about a British war bride and an American soldier. I have always been intrigued by my friend Janet Sharp's parents, now deceased, who met during the war much like Audrey and Robert did. Janet's mother, a lovely, tea-drinking English lady, was serving as an air-raid warden in Enfield when she met her handsome American pilot. They moved to Illinois after the war and had two children. A sweet, romantic story.

But as I dove into the research, I discovered how greatly the two World Wars altered everyday life in England, putting an end to the divide between the upper classes and their servants. Being a huge fan of the TV series *Downton Abbey*, I knew I wanted to take my story in that direction. Audrey and Eve (and their mothers) quickly sprang to life. Then all the rest—their friendship, their rivalry, their loves and losses—fell beautifully into place as these two women searched to redefine who they really were.

One of my favorite parts of writing novels is the research. For this book, my husband and I wandered around London so I could put myself in my characters' shoes. We enjoyed traveling on the Underground, but I don't think I would like sleeping there night after night. We visited the Imperial War Museum and sat inside a tiny Anderson shelter during a simulated bombing, and I sympathized with Eve's claustrophobia. I developed a deep admiration for the women of Britain who served in so many different capacities in order to save their nation, everything from laboring on farms and operating complicated radar systems to driving ambulances into scenes of utter devastation the way Audrey and Eve did. I'm sure that many of them found resources of strength and courage that they didn't know they possessed.

Aside from the attacks on Pearl Harbor and on 9/11, we don't really know what it's like to have our homeland here in America bombed and threatened with invasion. As I read accounts of what the people in Britain endured and the courage they displayed in refusing to surrender, I kept asking myself what I would have done. Would my faith have proven strong enough, or might it have faltered? None of us will really know until our faith is tested. But if and when it is, we will have a marvelous opportunity to see and experience God's faithfulness.

I know that different readers will see different things in this novel and take away different lessons. But if you learn only one thing, my prayer is that you will begin to believe that God has a unique plan and purpose for your life. And that like Eve and Audrey, you will journey with our loving God to discover what it is. "For we are God's workmanship, created in Christ Jesus to do good works, which God prepared in advance for us to do" (Ephesians 2:10).

Blessings!
Lynn

Acknowledgments

Writers are always pictured as lonely souls, sitting in our cloistered offices for hours and hours, laboring to bring our stories to life. This can be an accurate picture of my own process at times, except for the "lonely" part. I have discovered over the years that I experience more joy in the creation of each book when I partner with other creative people to bring my vision to fulfillment. I want to stop and thank some of those partners now.

My husband, Ken, is always my first reader, plowing through my half-finished chapters and unresolved plot ideas and listening to me ramble on and on about what might or might not happen. He is also quick to tell me how my male characters would *really* think and what they would *really* do. My longtime friends and fellow writers Jane Rubietta and Cleo Lampos are also vitally important to me in the brainstorming and development process. We have been meeting and critiquing each other's writing for more than twenty-five years, since before any of us was ever published, and I'm quite certain that I couldn't write a book without them.

My nonwriting friends Ed and Cathy Pruim and Paul and Jacki Kleinheksel are also irreplaceable and essential to my writing process. They allow me to air my frustrations, they pray with me, and they offer me spiritual insights and down-to-earth advice whenever

I need it. I'm so grateful to them for keeping me grounded—and for getting me out of my office to have fun!

Christine Bierma is my assistant who is so much more than my assistant! She brought me into the twenty-first century with web pages and blogs and social media and all of that other technology that I still don't understand. And she doesn't even laugh at me (much) when I struggle to use it. She is a partner to me in every way, and I would not want to write or launch a book without her and her online business, Launch Right.

My team at Tyndale House are my newest partners and have guided and shaped this book into a finished product. Stephanie Broene has been alongside me from the beginning stages and throughout the rewriting, cover design, and marketing processes. I so appreciate her insight and partnership. My editor, Kathy Olson, has patiently guided me through a new way of doing edits, and has made it (almost) fun and painless. She also made this a better book.

Last, but absolutely not least, is my amazing agent, Natasha Kern. The publishing world is changing so quickly and so dramatically that my writing career would be lost at sea without her knowledge and expertise. But more than that, Natasha offered valuable input into this story and gave me encouragement and advice when I needed it most.

Thank you, and God's richest blessings to each of you. *If I Were You* would not be the same book without you.

Discussion Questions

1. Belonging, home, and family are recurring themes in *If I Were You*. How do Eve and Audrey each experience these things throughout the book? How does their desire to belong and to have a home and a family motivate the decisions each young woman makes?

2. Which of the characters did you more easily identify with, Eve or Audrey? Why?

3. How do Eve and Audrey respond differently to adversity? To love? Give examples from the story. What accounts for their differences? Is it nature, nurture, or a combination of both?

4. The author uses Eve and Audrey to contrast the different classes in Britain prior to World War II. Describe the different lifestyles and expectations the girls and their families have. How does each girl grow and change as a result of their friendship?

5. Part of what Eve and Audrey learn is that the roles expected of them by society and their families don't necessarily reflect what God wants for them. What purpose might God have for your life that could differ from the expectations of society or family? What relationships has He placed in your life that have helped you—or could help you—to discover His plans for you?

6. The author also contrasts the way the war affected Britain with the way it affected America. Eve notes in 1946 that "America's prosperity astounded her. There were no piles of rubble where homes once stood, no queues for food, no shortages. Soldiers like Robert and Louis had returned home to civilian life as if the war had never happened." She tells Audrey that no one ever asks her about life during the war, that Americans seem to have the attitude that "the war is over and done with, and we'd all be better off to forget about it." In what ways is it helpful to be able to share about traumatic experiences we've had? Why is it hard for us to want to hear about the challenges others have faced? Think about times you've been on either side of this situation—how have you responded?

7. Eve blames Audrey's mother for the death of her own mother. Do you think Eve's reaction to her mother's death is fair? How does she eventually come to terms with it?

8. While urging Audrey to pay attention to her evolving feelings for Robert, Eve tells her, "The war has erased the rules and traditions we grew up with." What does she mean? Can you think of any examples from contemporary culture that are parallel to this? Have those changes been good or detrimental?

9. Eve is adamant about not having intimate relations with Alfie without the security of marriage, despite his pressure and her fears for his safety. What has changed by the time she meets Louis? Why does she make a different choice with him?

10. When Audrey visits her uncle in London in 1950, she debates whether to tell him the truth about her parentage. She decides not to, concluding that some secrets are better

left hidden. Do you agree? How would you have handled the news Audrey had just received from her father?

11. Why does Audrey decide not to go to America when she first has the chance? What changes her mind later? Have you ever had second thoughts about a major life decision? Is it ever too late to change your path?

12. Were you surprised by Tom's advice to Louis to not tell his wife about his affair with Eve during the war? How is this different from Audrey's situation regarding her parents—or is it? Would the advice be different today from what it was in the mid-twentieth century?

13. What did you think of Eve's decision not to tell Louis about their child when she meets him again? Would you have done anything differently if you were in her situation?

14. Near the end of the book, Eve seems to believe that her circumstances are God's punishment for past actions—for her affair with Louis, for turning away from God. Have you or someone you care about ever felt that way? How can we know that God does not punish us for our sins once we have repented and accepted His forgiveness? If He's not punishing us, why do we still have to live with the consequences of our wrong choices?

15. Mrs. Vandenberg tells Eve, "There will be days when you'll be tempted to doubt that you are a new person, days when you'll be very hard on yourself. Especially as you face the painful consequences of your mistakes." Have you ever found it difficult to accept God's forgiveness? What has helped you?

About the Author

Lynn Austin has sold more than one and a half million copies of her books worldwide. A former teacher who now writes and speaks full-time, she has won eight Christy Awards for her historical fiction and was one of the first inductees into the Christy Award Hall of Fame. One of her novels, *Hidden Places*, was made into a Hallmark Channel Original Movie. Lynn and her husband have three grown children and make their home in western Michigan. Visit her online at lynnaustin.org.

CONNECT WITH LYNN ONLINE

at LynnAustin.org

OR FOLLOW HER ON:

f facebook.com/LynnAustinBooks

🐦 @LynnNAustin

g Lynn Austin

CP1586